For Charlotte and Ben.

Library of Congress Control Number: 2015957762

ISBN 978-0-545-77088-0 (hardcover)
ISBN 978-0-545-77089-7 (paperback)

10 9 8 7 6 5 4 3 2 1   16 17 18 19 20

Printed in China 62
First edition, August 2016
Edited by Adam Rau
Book design by Phil Falco
Creative Director: David Saylor

The KING of KAZOO

by NORM FEUTI

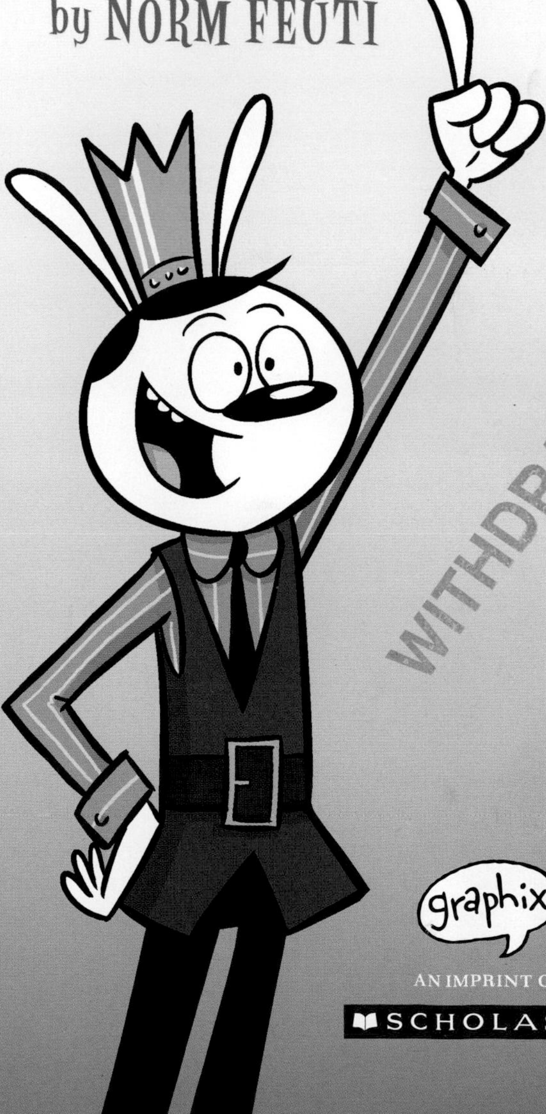

graphix

AN IMPRINT OF

SCHOLASTIC

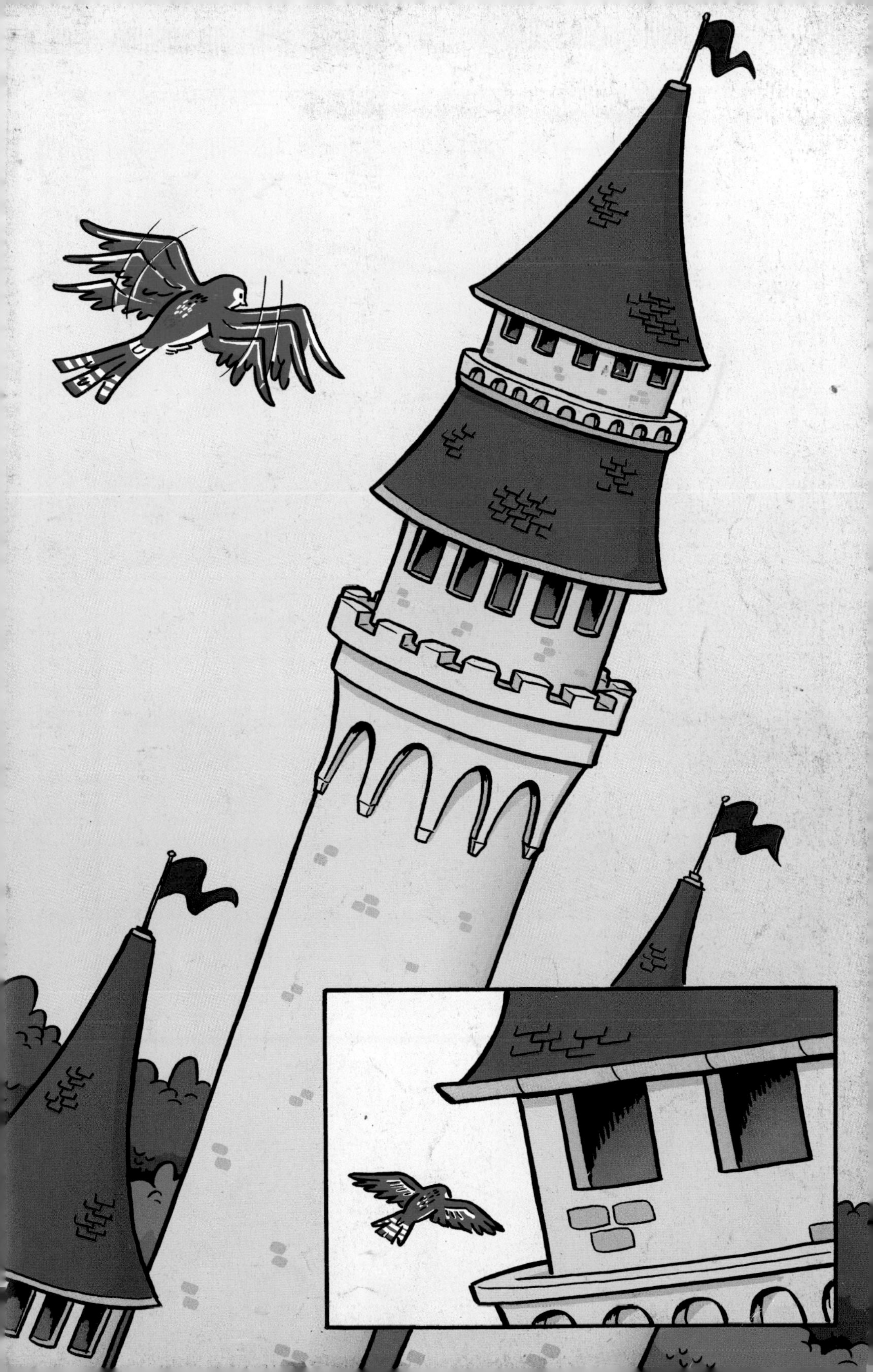

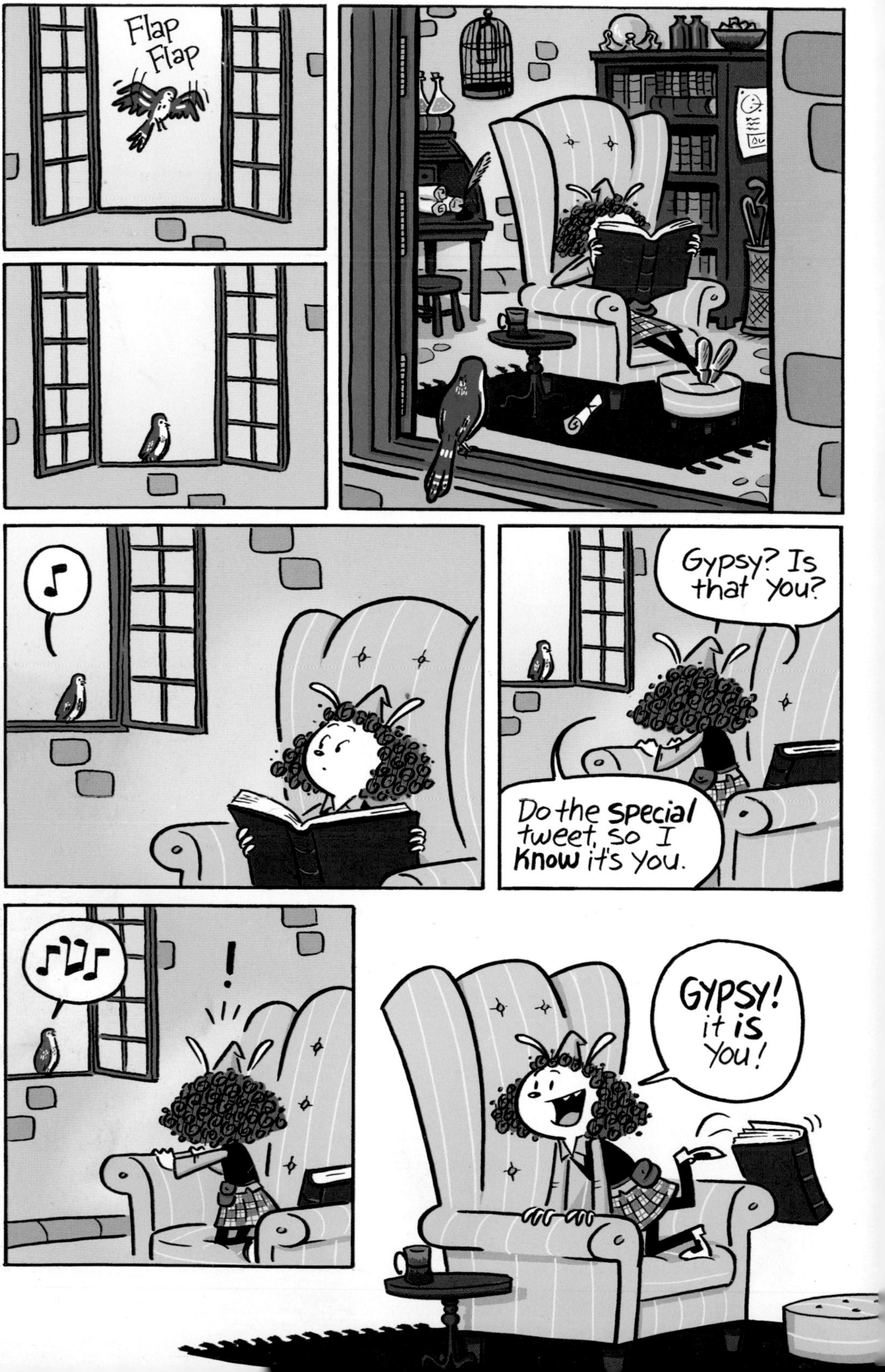
Flap
Flap
♪
Gypsy? Is that you?
Do the special tweet, so I know it's you.
♪♫♪
!
GYPSY! it is you!

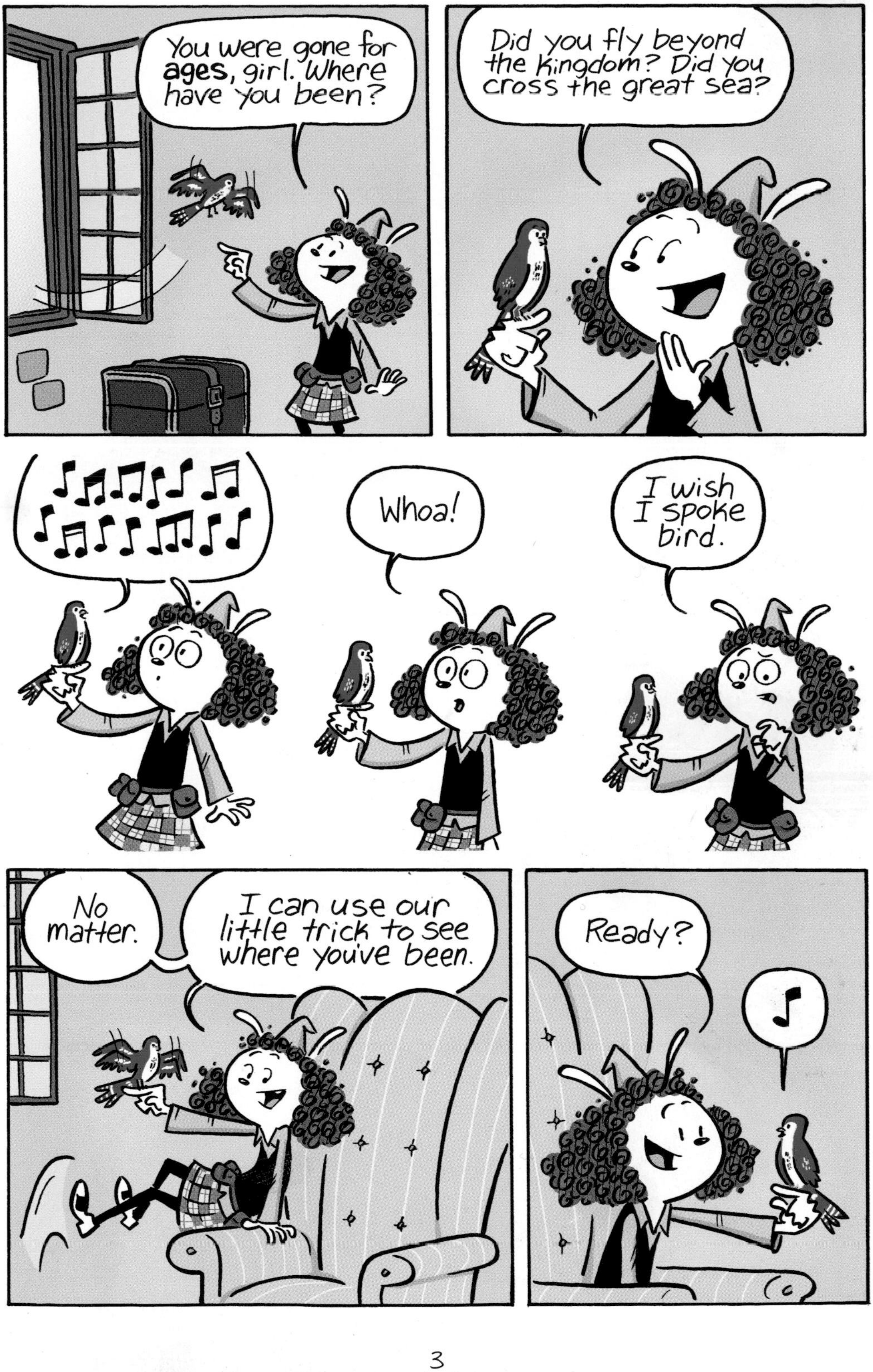
You were gone for **ages**, girl. Where have you been?
Did you fly beyond the Kingdom? Did you cross the great sea?
Whoa!
I wish I spoke bird.
No matter.
I can use our little trick to see where you've been.
Ready?

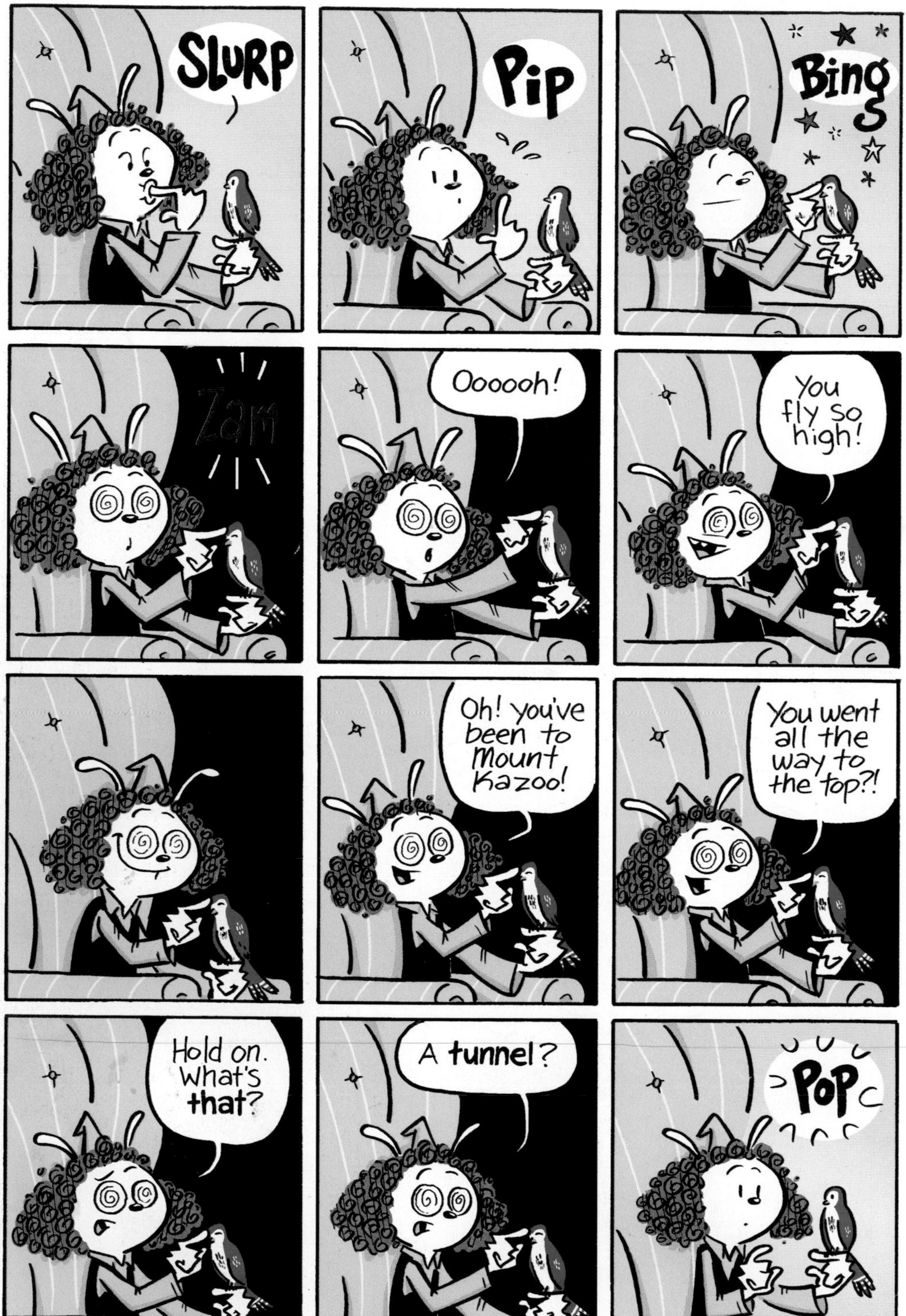
SLURP
Pip
Bing
Zam
Oooooh!
You fly so high!
Oh! you've been to Mount Kazoo!
You went all the way to the top?!
Hold on. What's that?
A tunnel?
POP

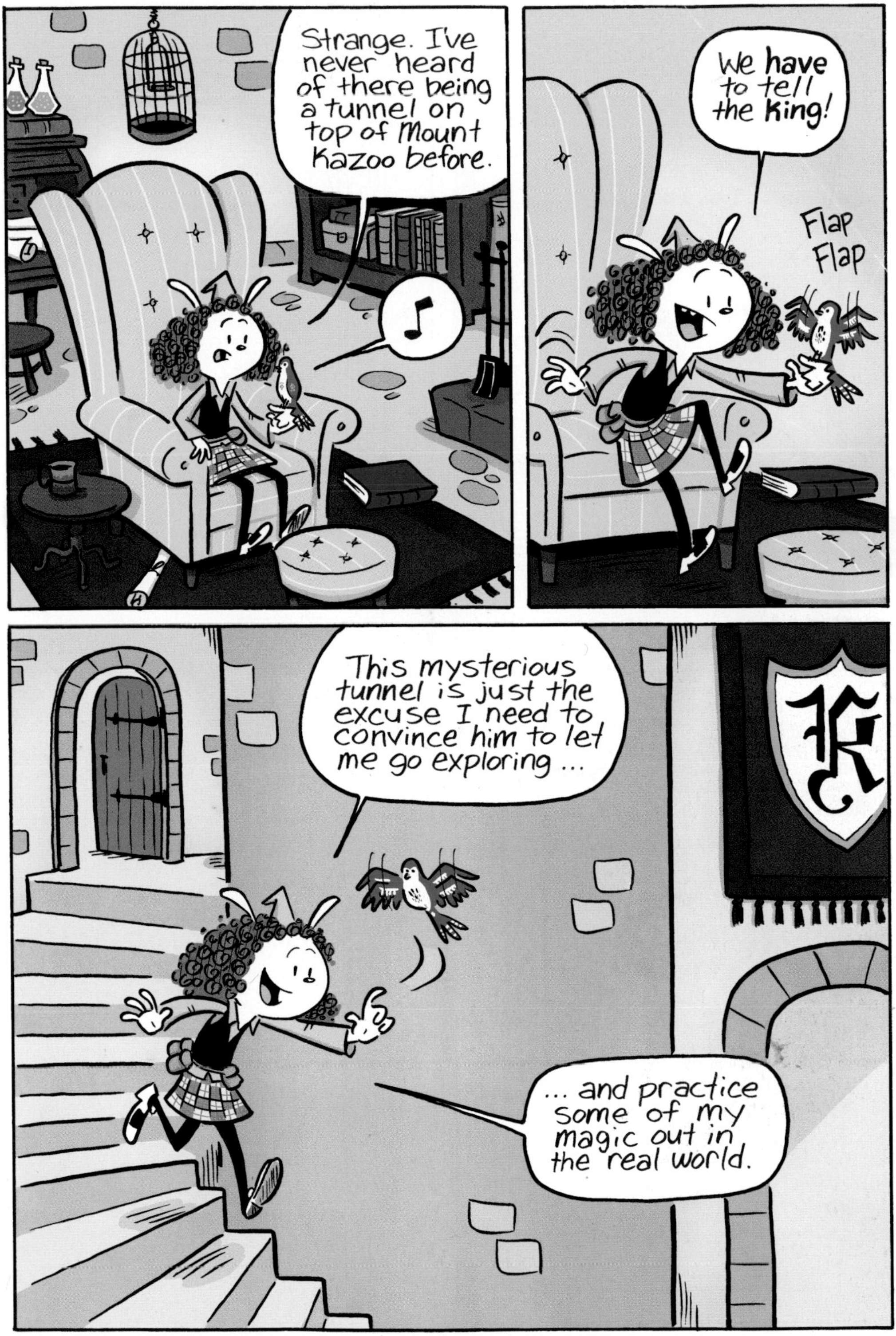
Strange. I've never heard of there being a tunnel on top of Mount Kazoo before.
We have to tell the King!
Flap Flap
This mysterious tunnel is just the excuse I need to convince him to let me go exploring ...
... and practice some of my magic out in the real world.

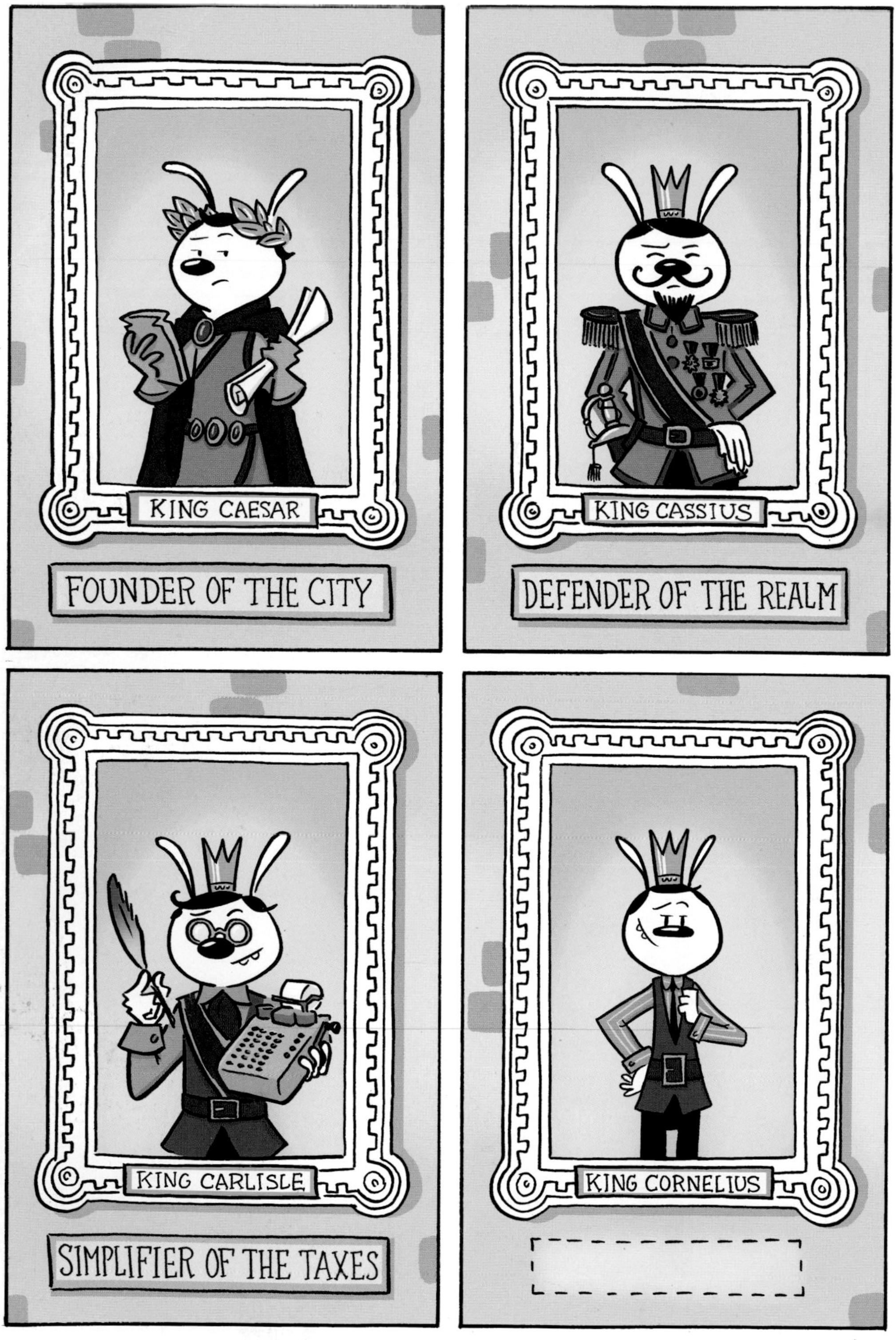
KING CAESAR
FOUNDER OF THE CITY
KING CASSIUS
DEFENDER OF THE REALM
KING CARLISLE
SIMPLIFIER OF THE TAXES
KING CORNELIUS

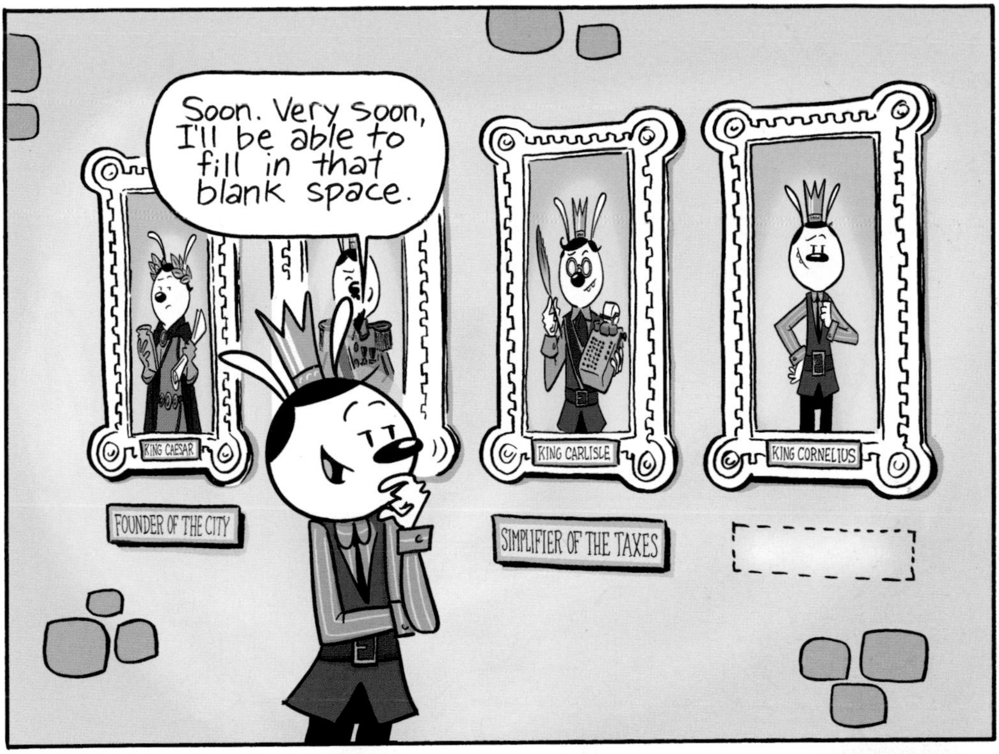
Soon. Very soon, I'll be able to fill in that blank space.
KING CAESAR
KING CARLISLE
KING CORNELIUS
FOUNDER OF THE CITY
SIMPLIFIER OF THE TAXES

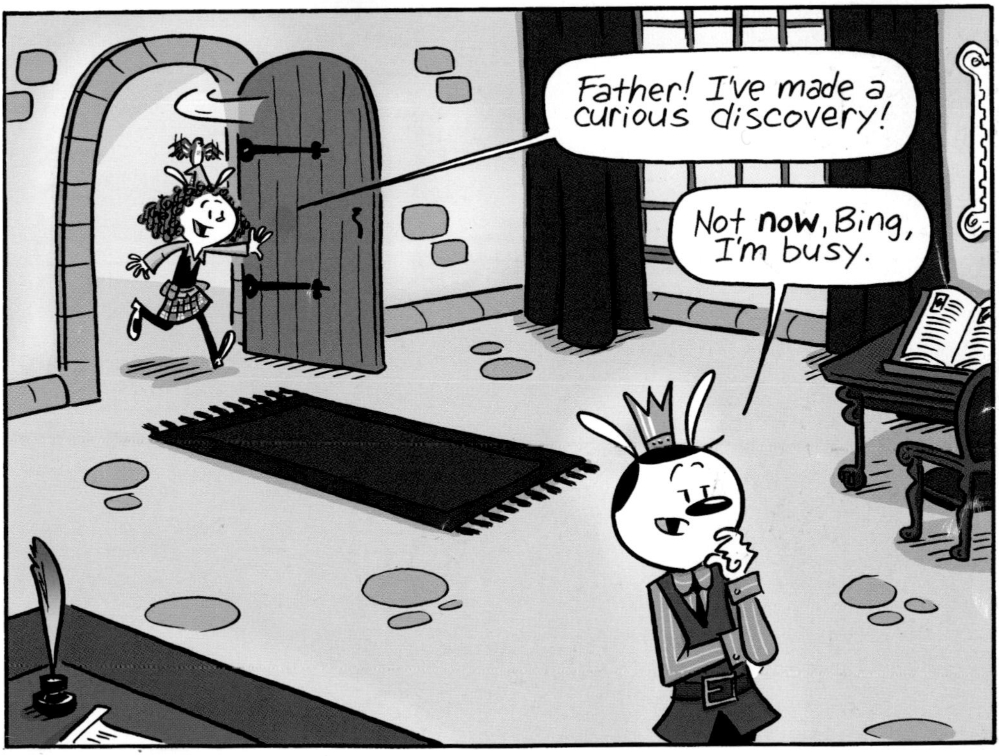
Father! I've made a curious discovery!
Not **now**, Bing, I'm busy.

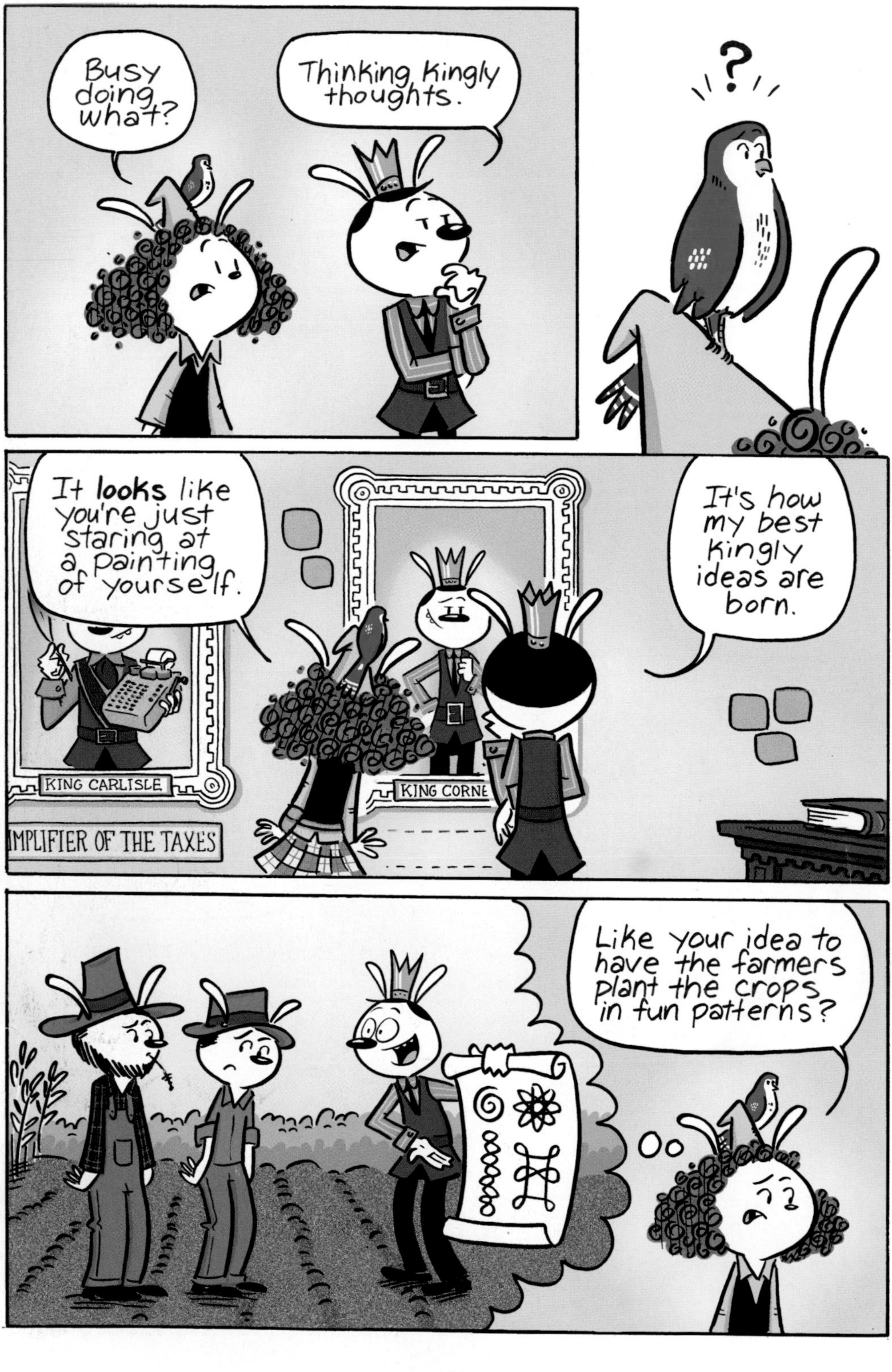
Busy doing what?
Thinking kingly thoughts.
?
It **looks** like you're just staring at a painting of yourself.
KING CARLISLE
IMPLIFIER OF THE TAXES
KING CORNE
It's how my best kingly ideas are born.
Like your idea to have the farmers plant the crops in fun patterns?

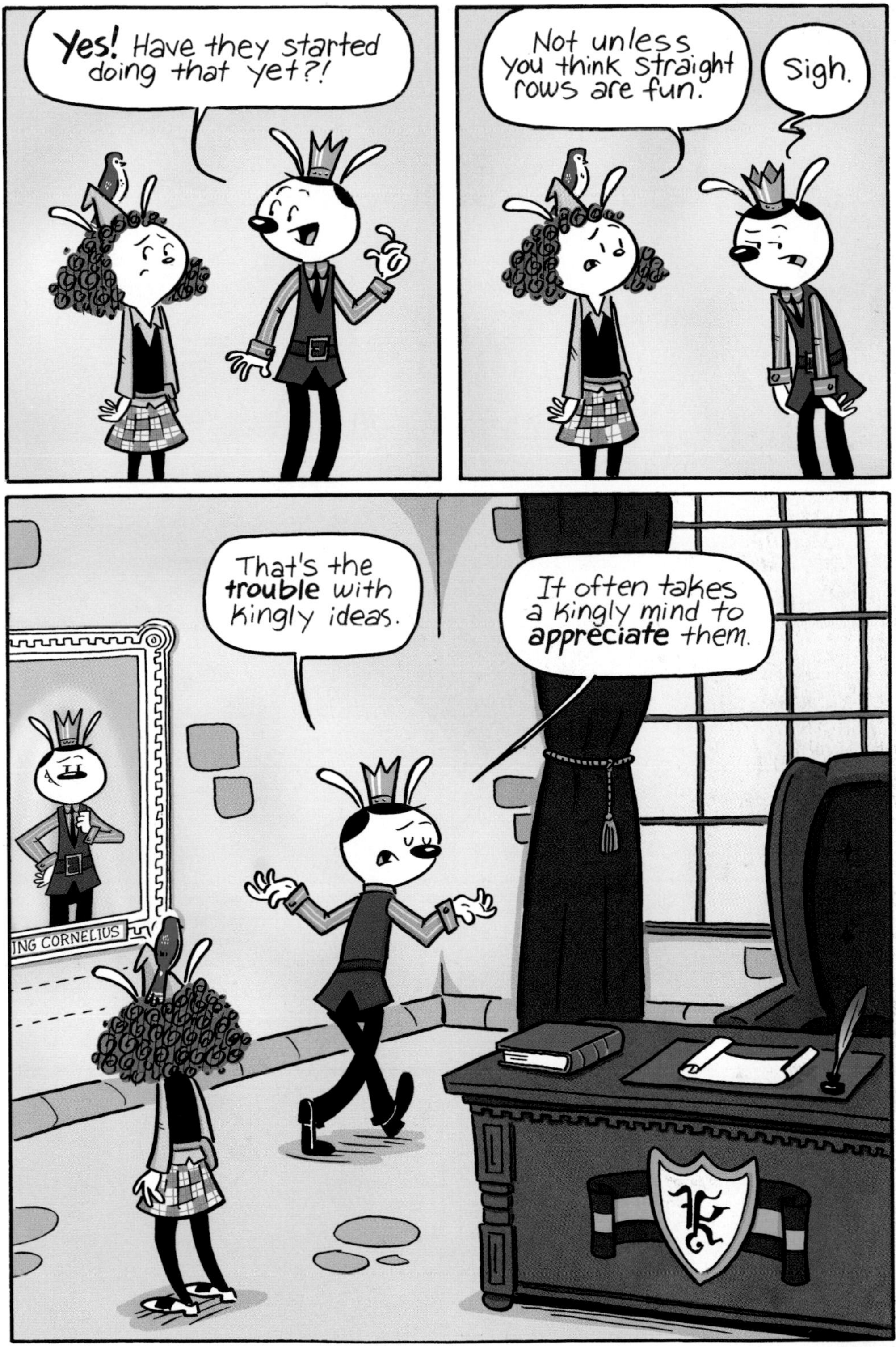
Yes! Have they started doing that yet?!
Not unless you think straight rows are fun.
Sigh.
That's the **trouble** with kingly ideas.
It often takes a kingly mind to **appreciate** them.
UNG CORNELIUS

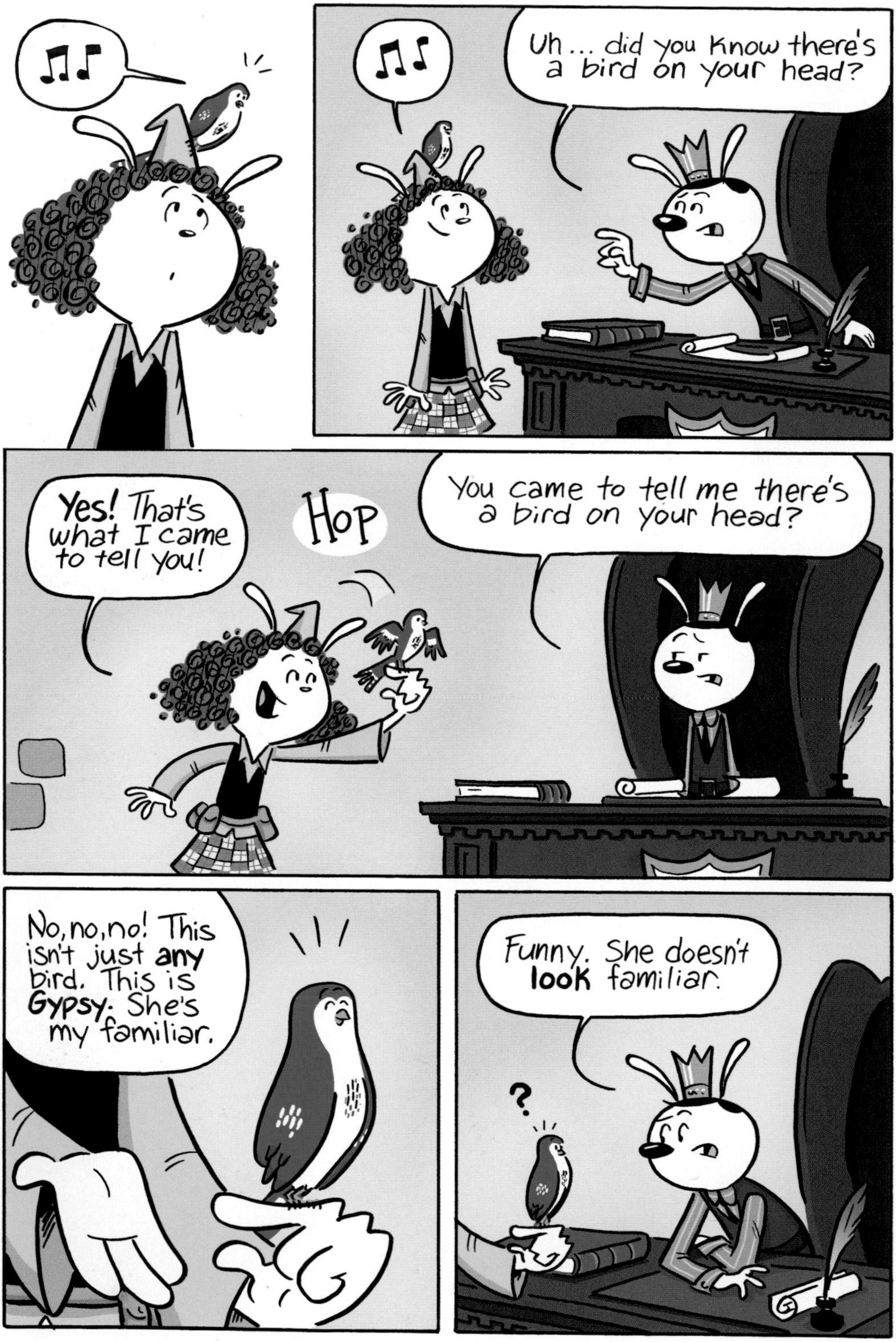
♫♪
♫♪
Uh... did you know there's a bird on your head?
Yes! That's what I came to tell you!
HOP
You came to tell me there's a bird on your head?
No, no, no! This isn't just any bird. This is Gypsy. She's my familiar.
?
Funny. She doesn't look familiar.

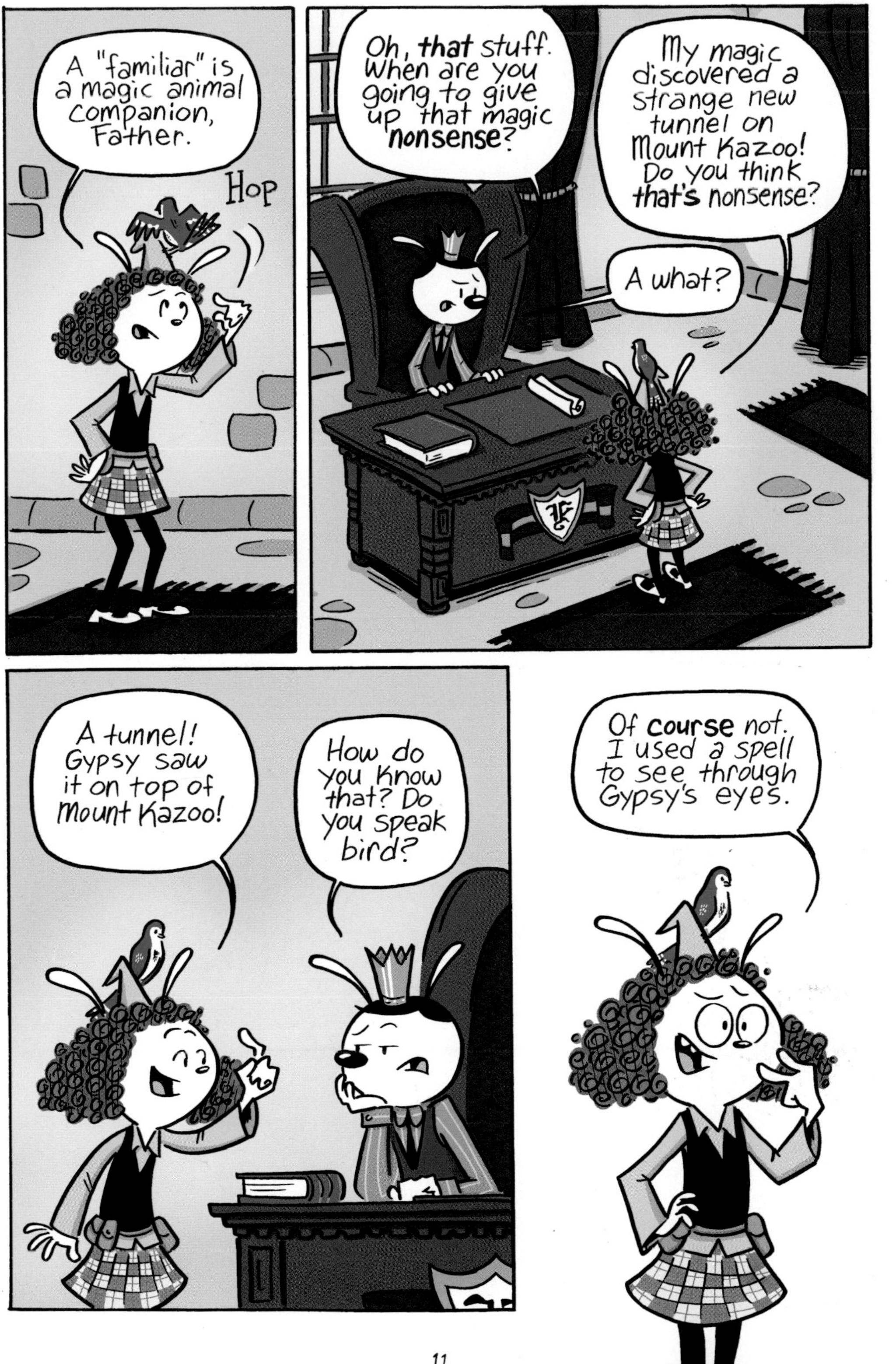
A "familiar" is a magic animal companion, Father.
HOP
Oh, **that** stuff. When are you going to give up that magic **nonsense**?
My magic discovered a strange new tunnel on Mount Kazoo! Do you think **that's** nonsense?
A what?
A tunnel! Gypsy saw it on top of Mount Kazoo!
How do you know that? Do you speak bird?
Of **course** not. I used a spell to see through Gypsy's eyes.

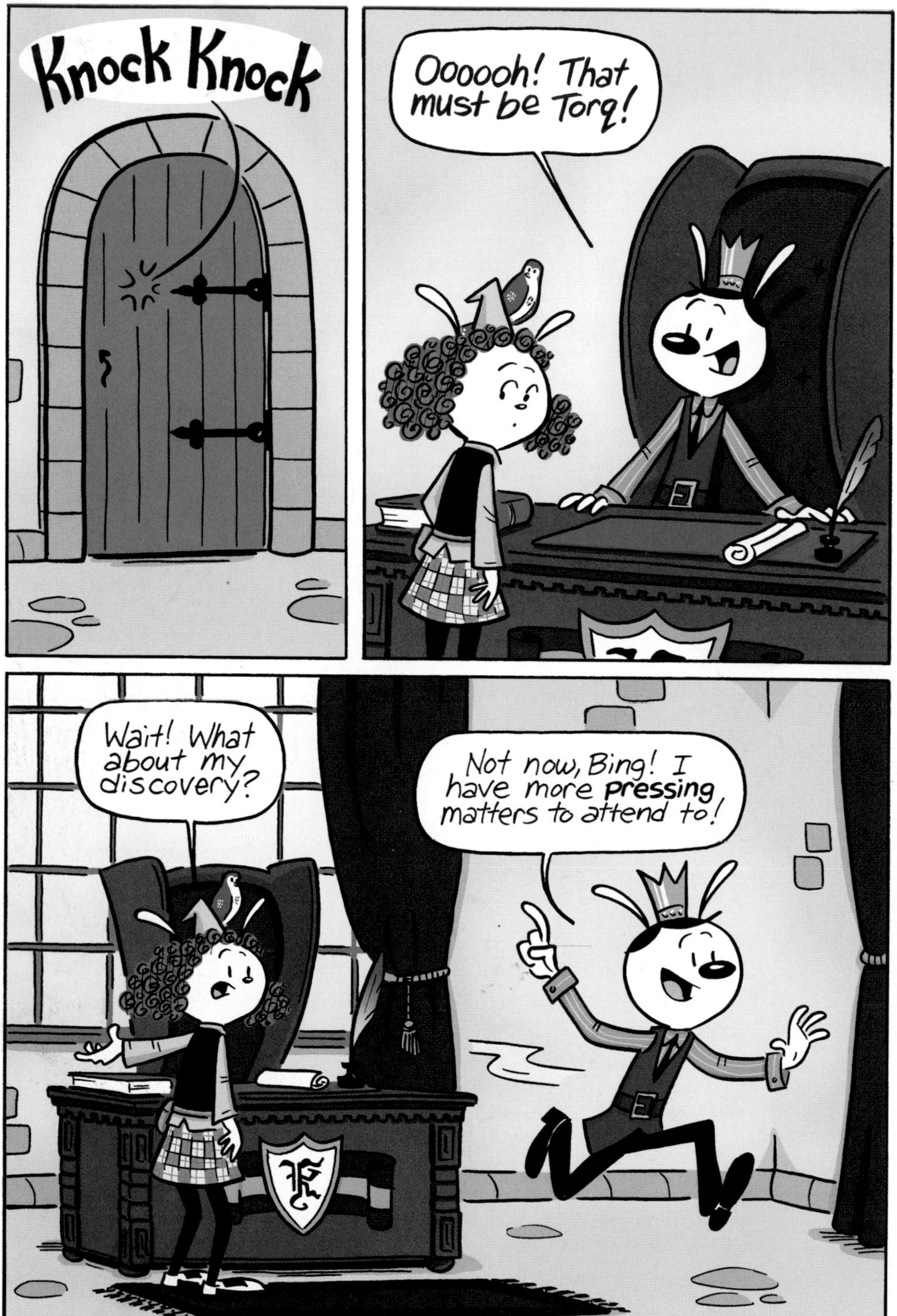
Knock Knock
Oooooh! That must be Torq!
Wait! What about my discovery?
Not now, Bing! I have more **pressing** matters to attend to!

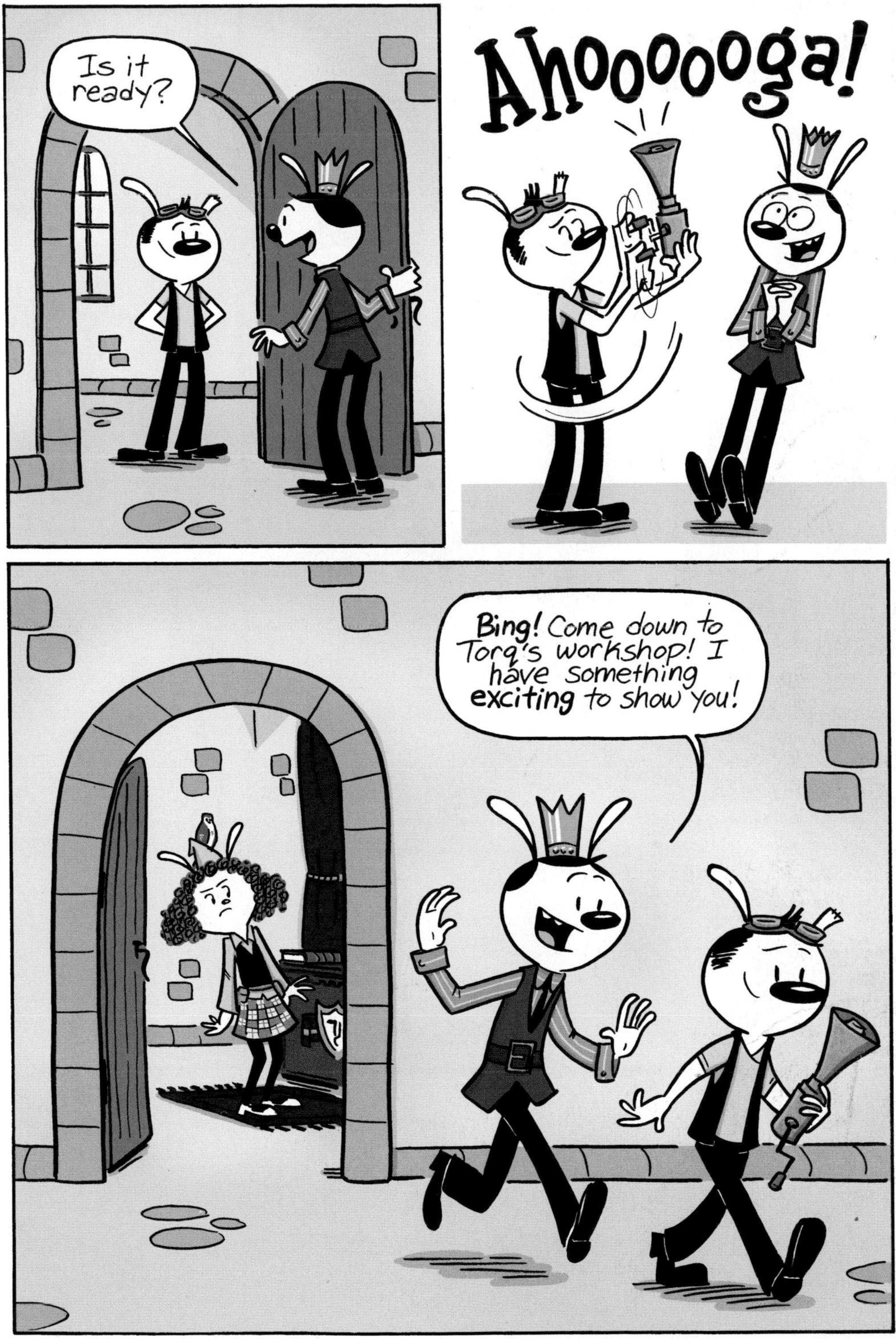
Is it ready?
Ahooooga!
Bing! Come down to Torq's workshop! I have something exciting to show you!

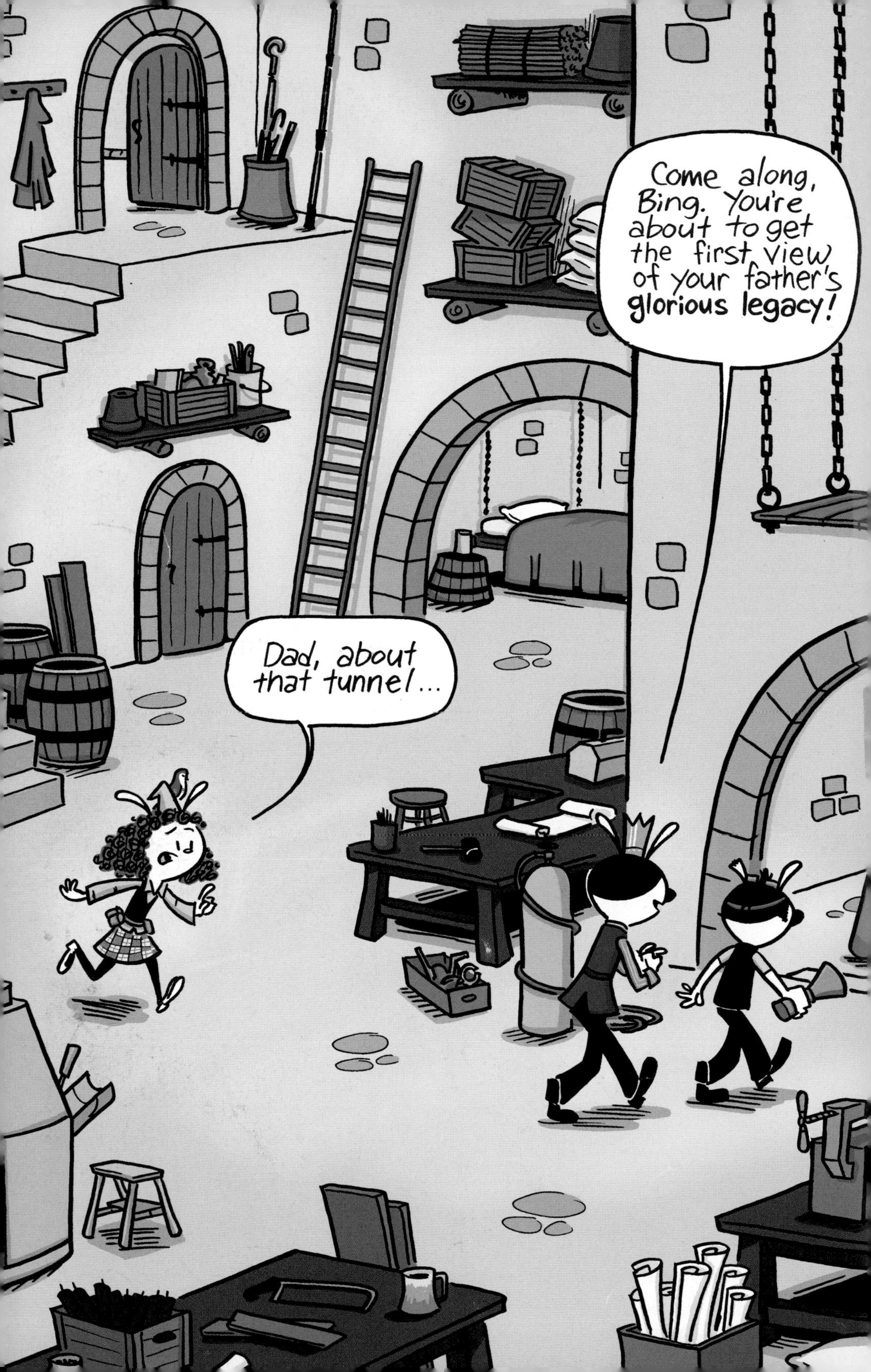
Come along, Bing. You're about to get the first view of your father's **glorious legacy**!
Dad, about that tunnel...

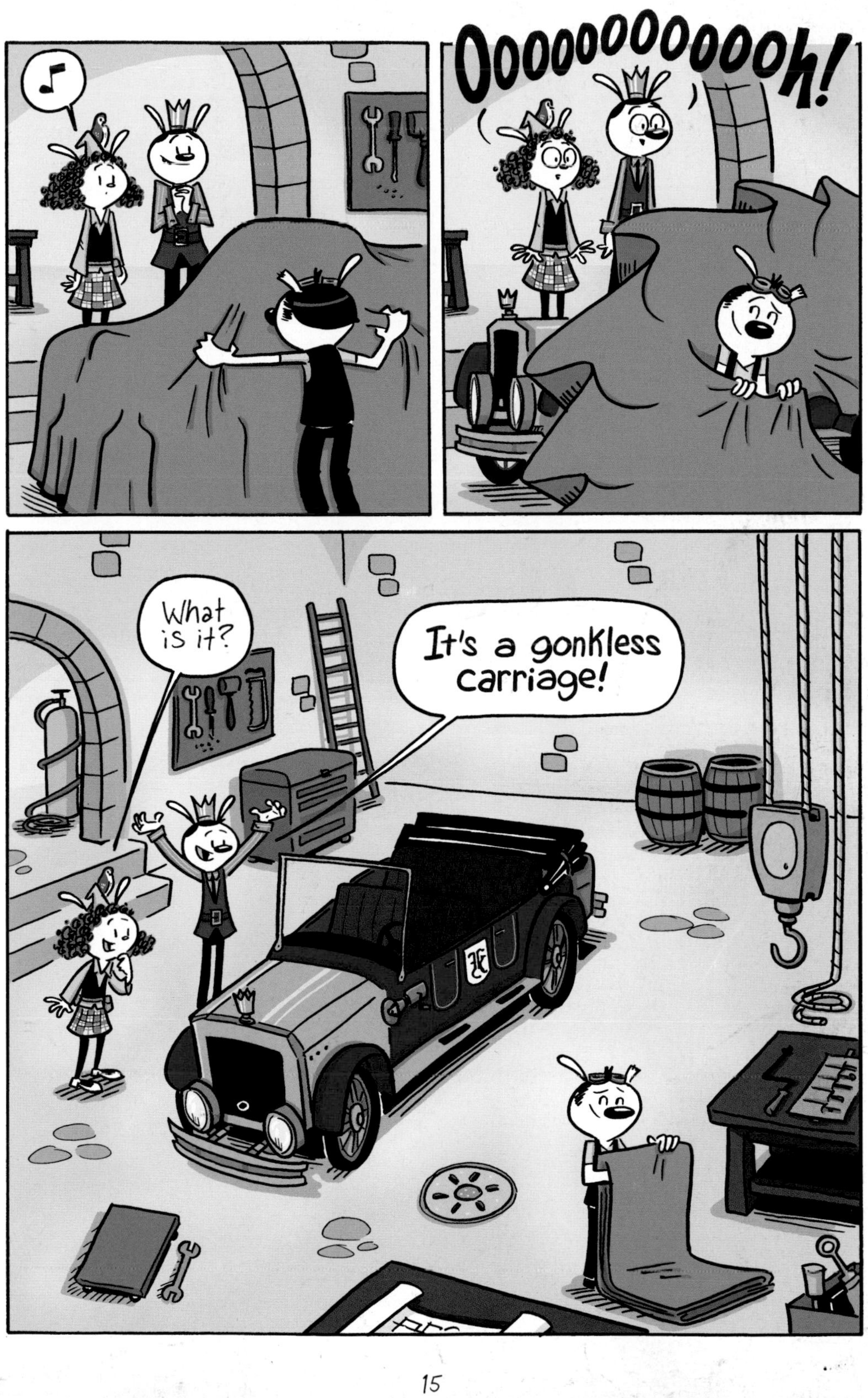
Oooooooooooh!
What is it?
It's a gonkless carriage!

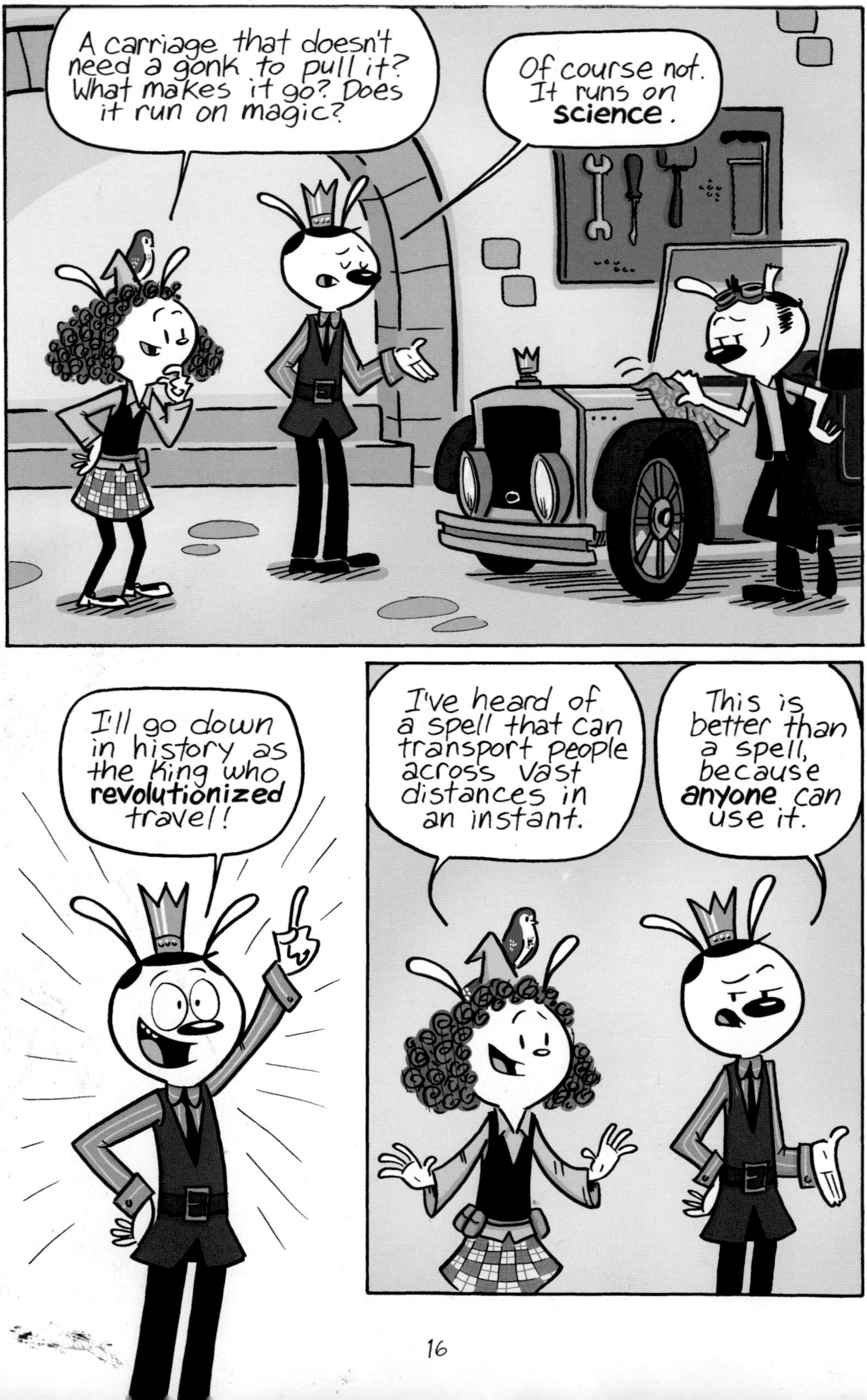
A carriage that doesn't need a gonk to pull it? What makes it go? Does it run on magic?
Of course not. It runs on **science**.
I'll go down in history as the King who **revolutionized** travel!
I've heard of a spell that can transport people across vast distances in an instant.
This is better than a spell, because **anyone** can use it.

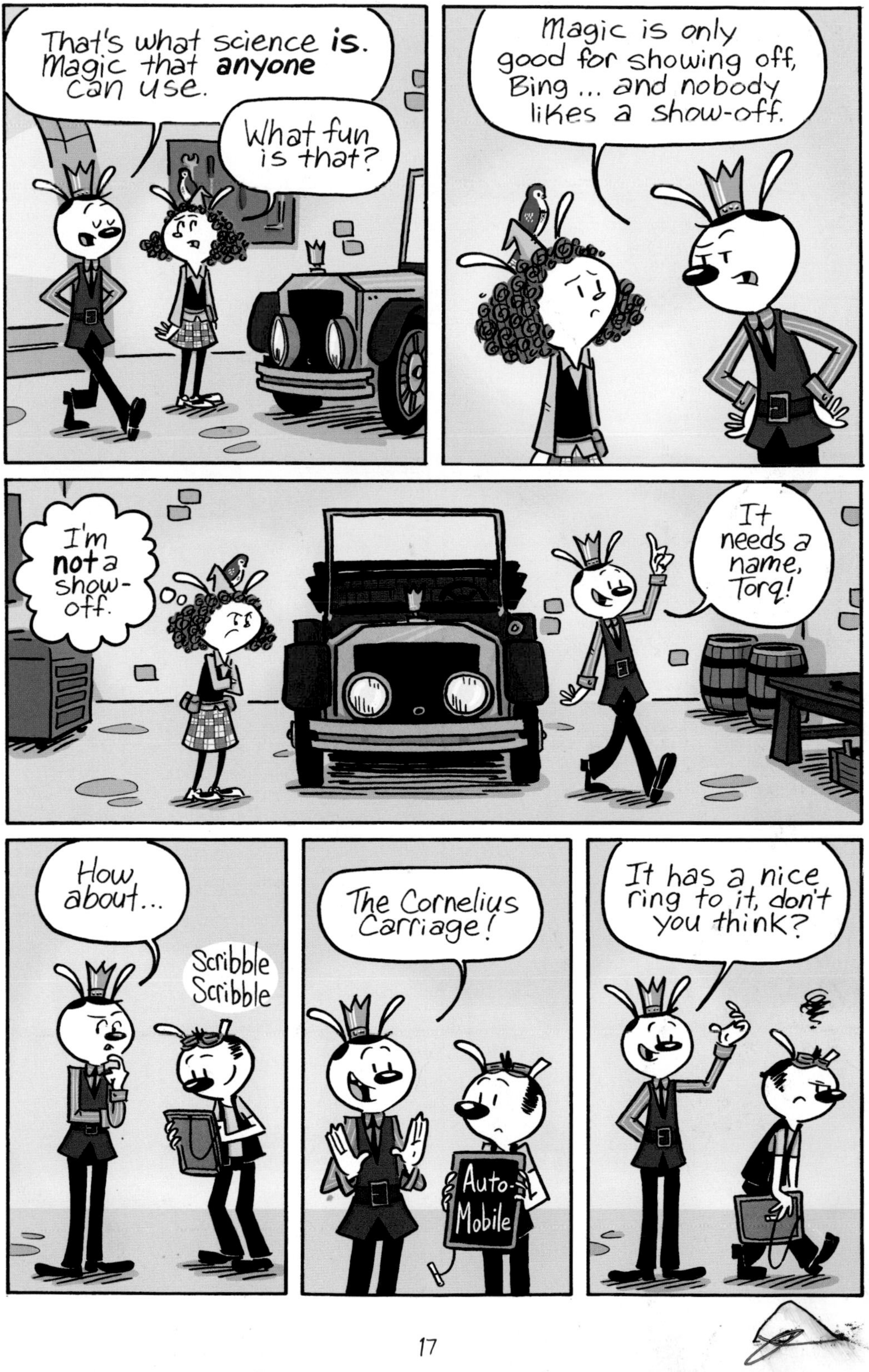
That's what science **is**. Magic that **anyone** can use.
What fun is that?
Magic is only good for showing off, Bing ... and nobody likes a show-off.
I'm **not** a show-off.
It needs a name, Torq!
How about...
Scribble Scribble
The Cornelius Carriage!
Auto-Mobile
It has a nice ring to it, don't you think?

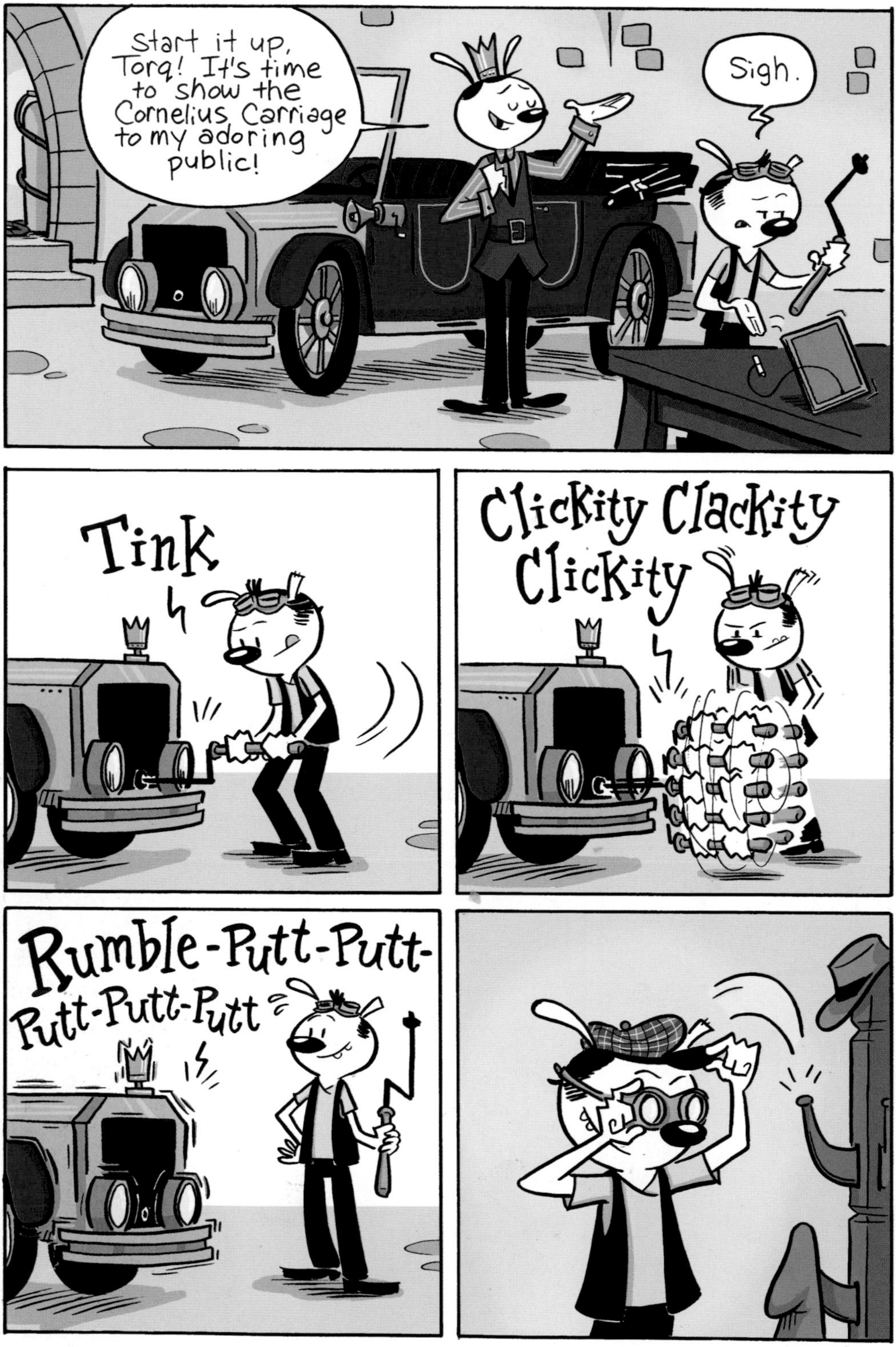
Start it up, Torq! It's time to show the Cornelius Carriage to my adoring public!
Sigh.
Tink
Clickity Clackity Clickity
Rumble-Putt-Putt-Putt-Putt-Putt

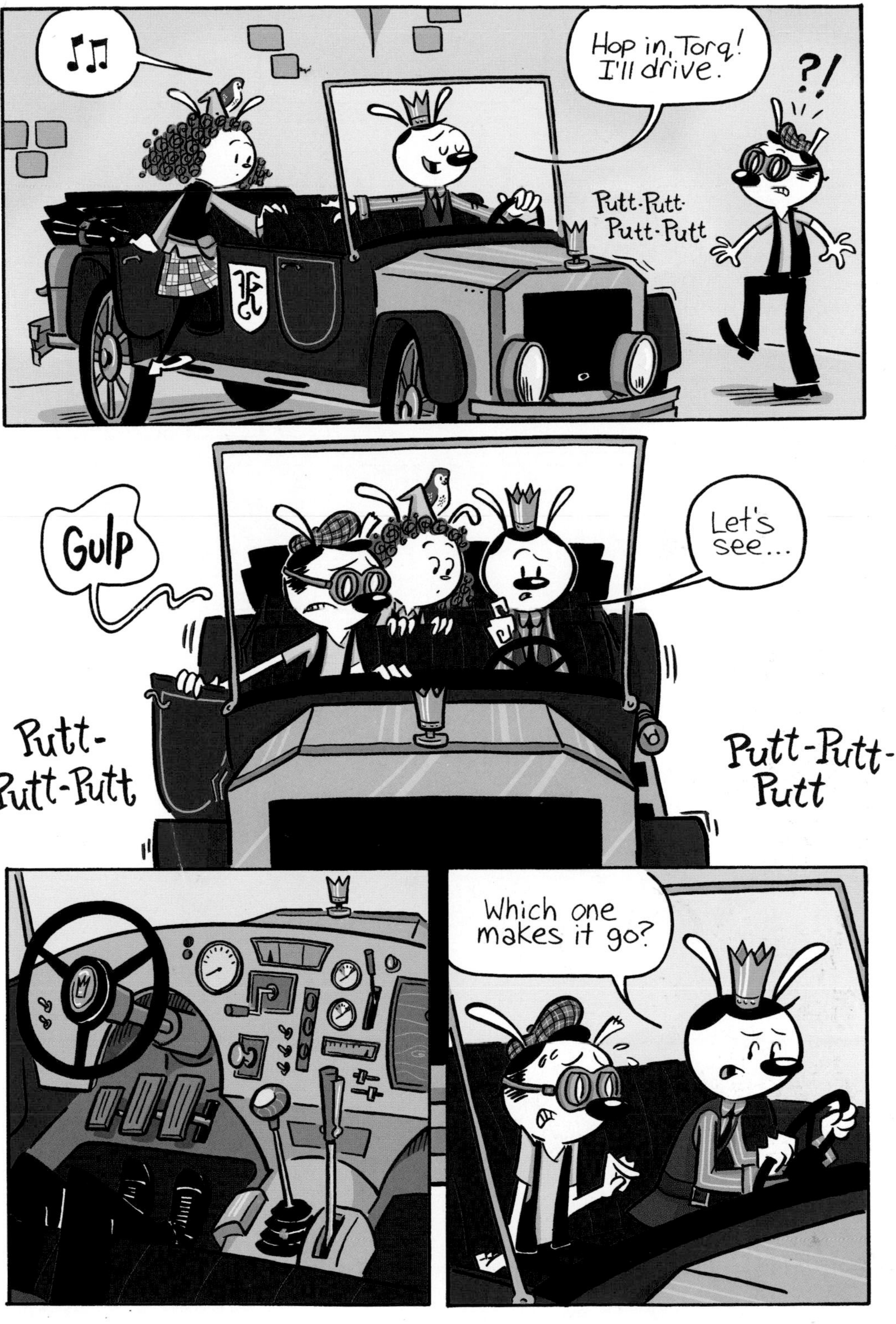
♫
Hop in, Torq! I'll drive.
?!
Putt-Putt-Putt-Putt
Gulp
Let's see...
Putt-Putt-Putt
Putt-Putt-Putt
Which one makes it go?

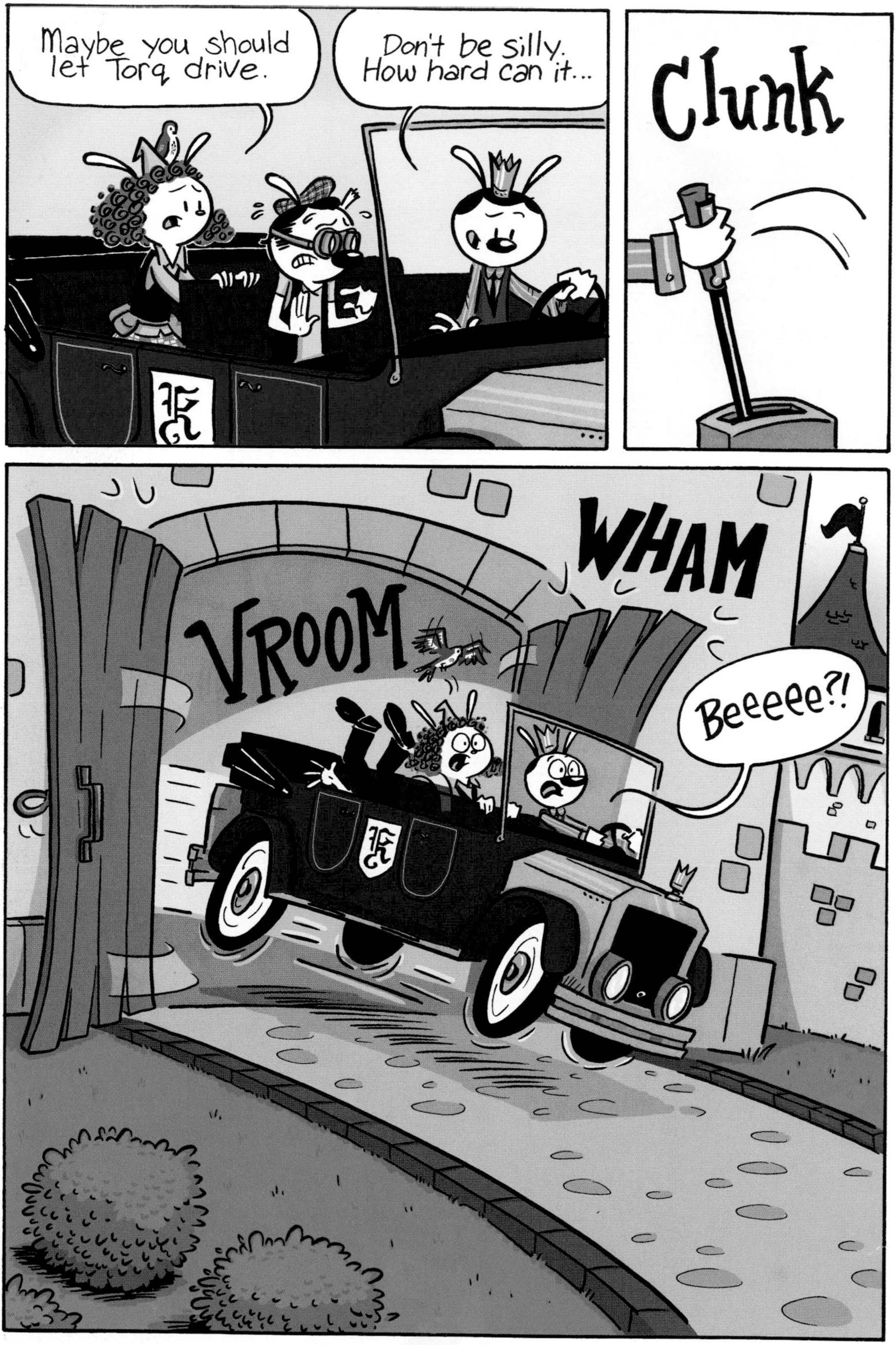
Maybe you should let Torq drive.
Don't be silly. How hard can it...
Clunk
VROOM
WHAM
Beeeee?!

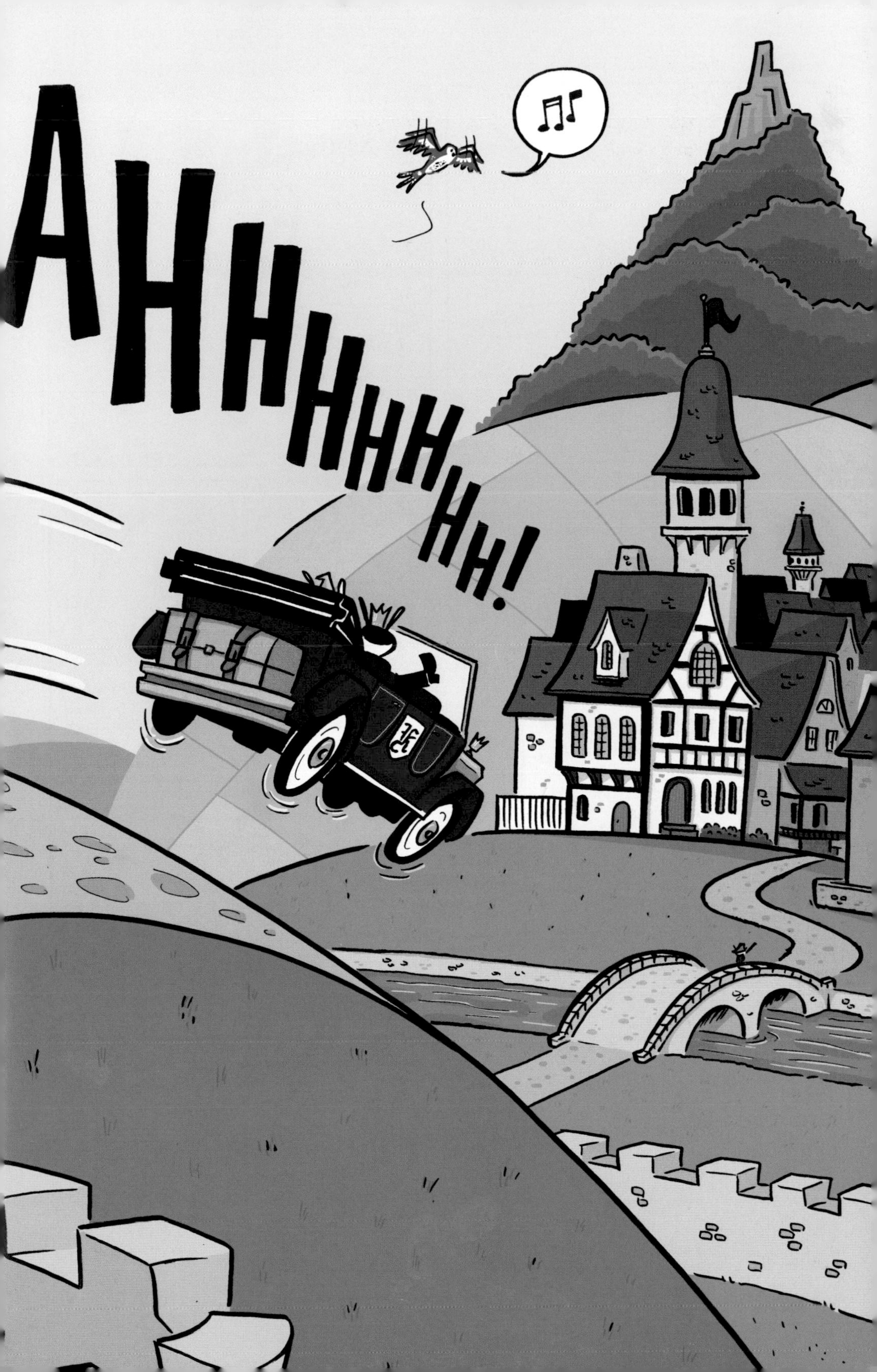
AHHHHHHHHH!

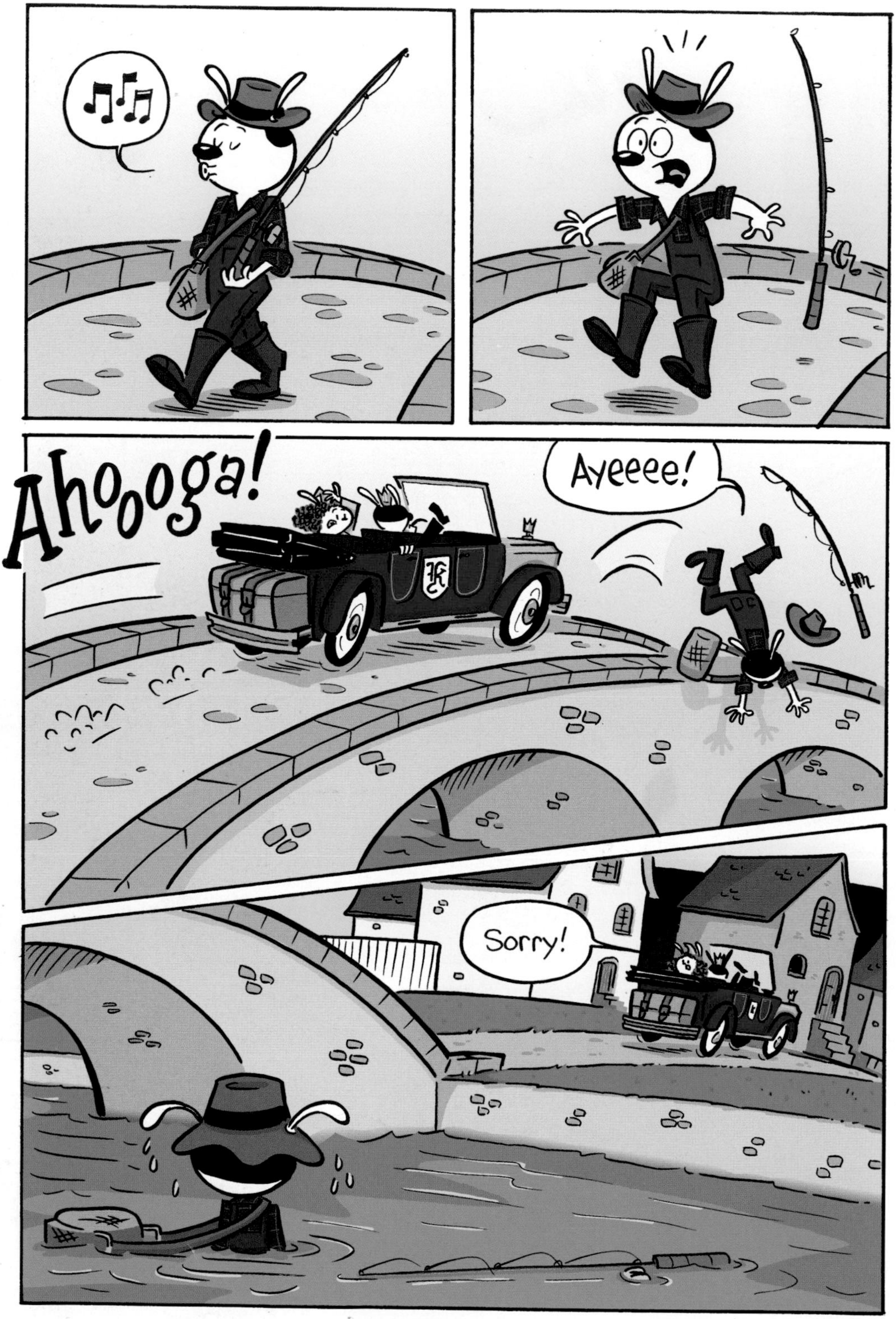
Ahoooga!
Ayeeee!
Sorry!

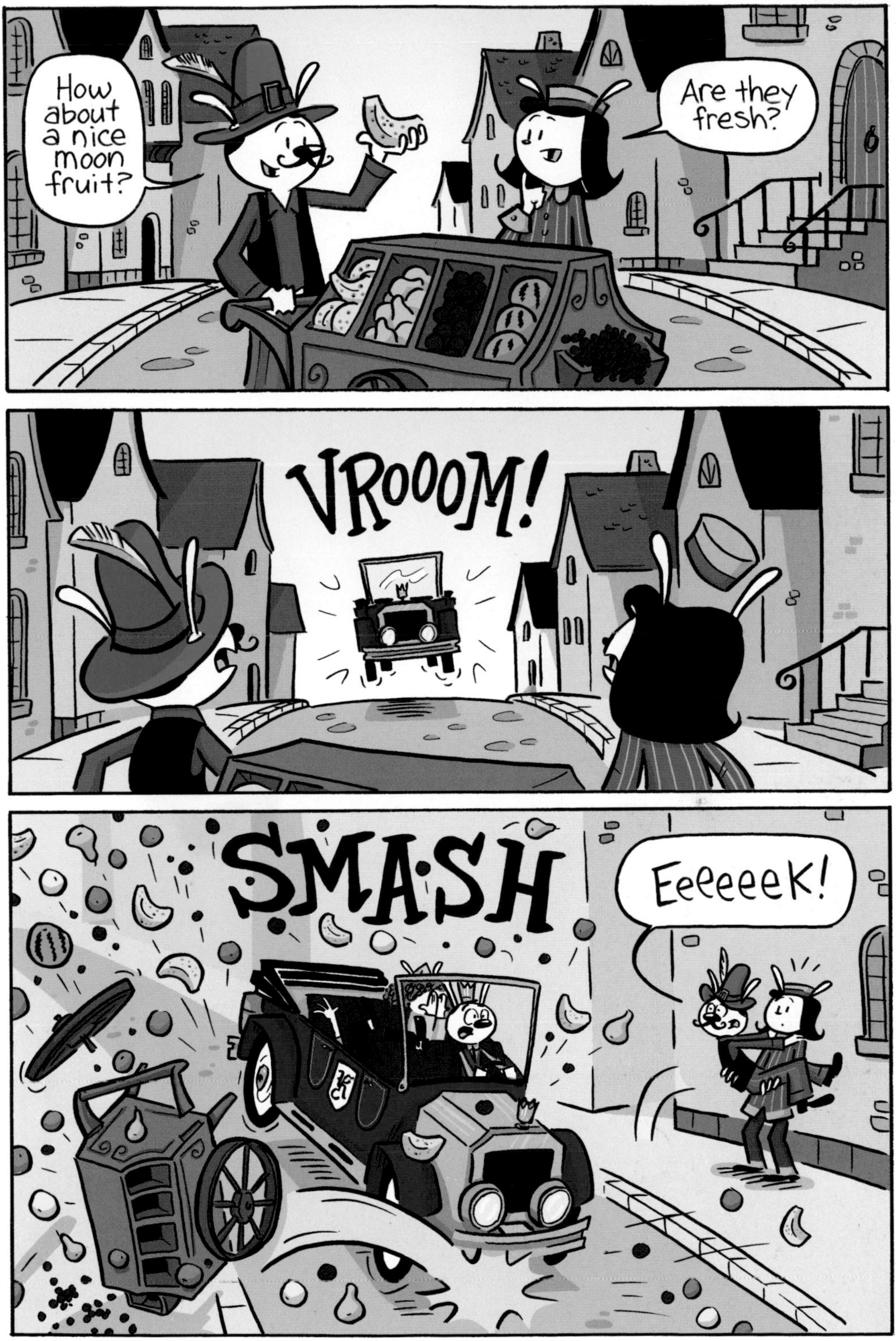
How about a nice moon fruit?
Are they fresh?
VROOOM!
SMASH
Eeeeeek!

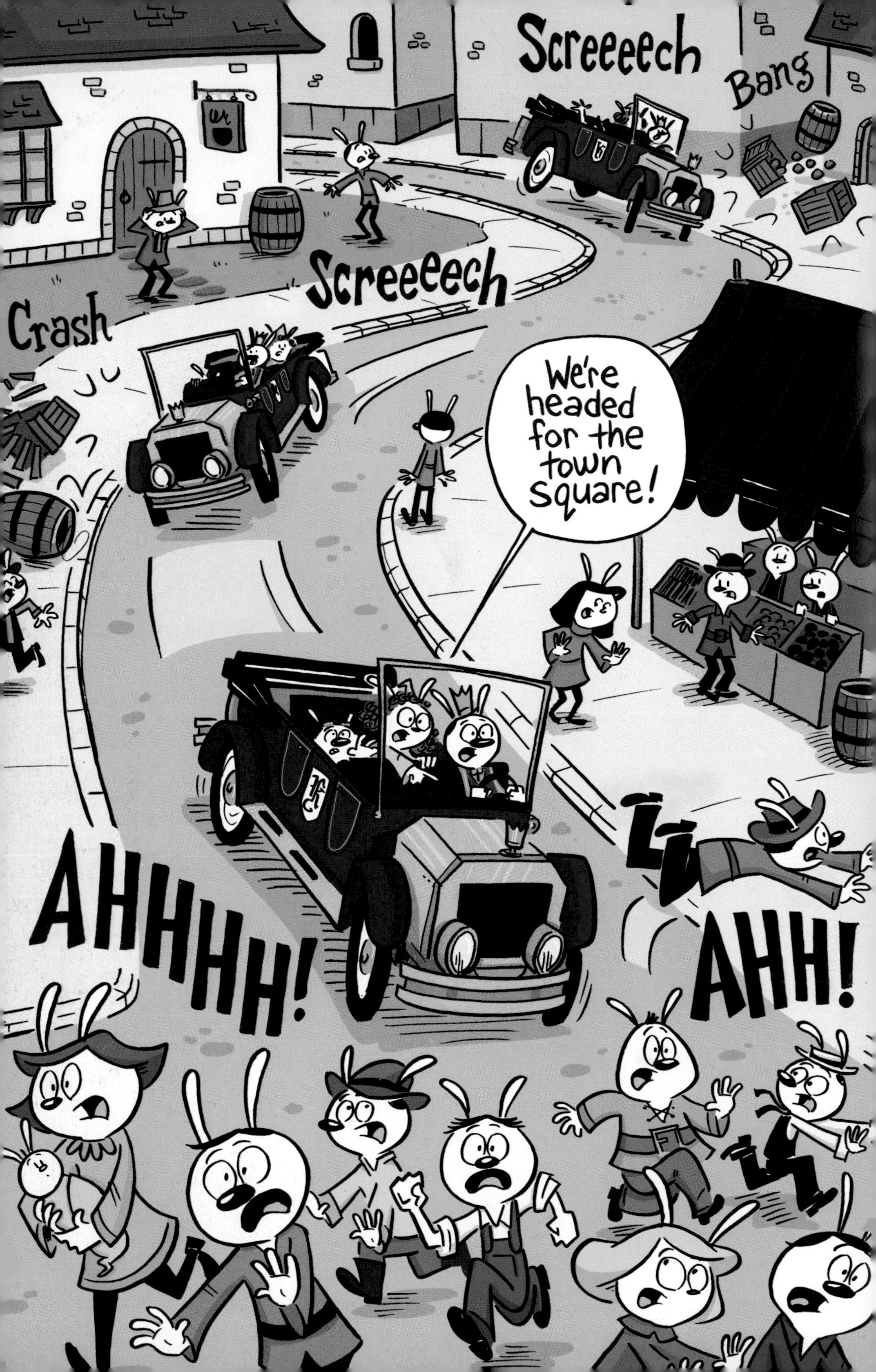
Screeeech
Bang
Crash
Screeeech
We're headed for the town square!
AHHHHH!
AHH!

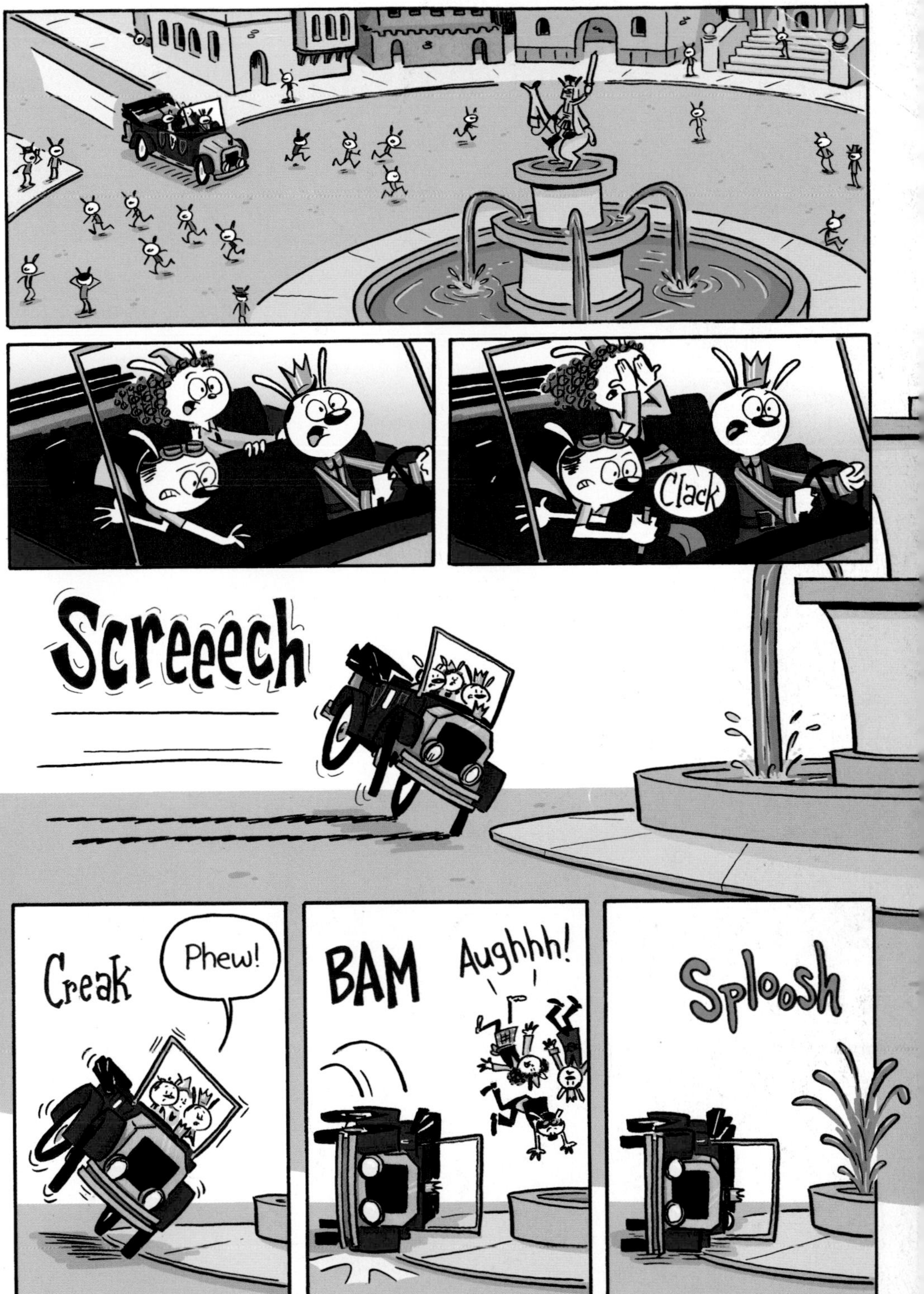
Clack
Screeech
Creak
Phew!
BAM
Aughhh!
Sploosh

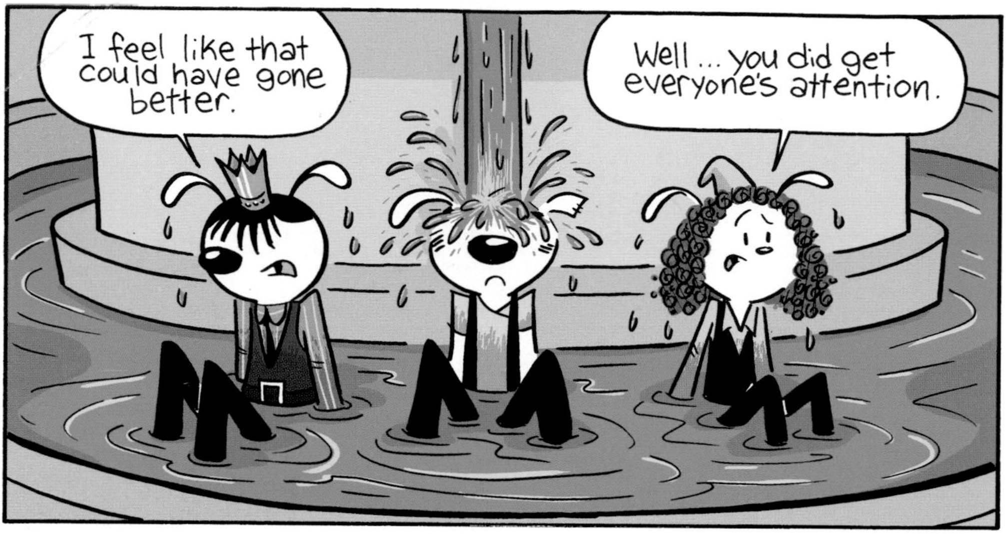
I feel like that could have gone better.
Well ... you did get everyone's attention.

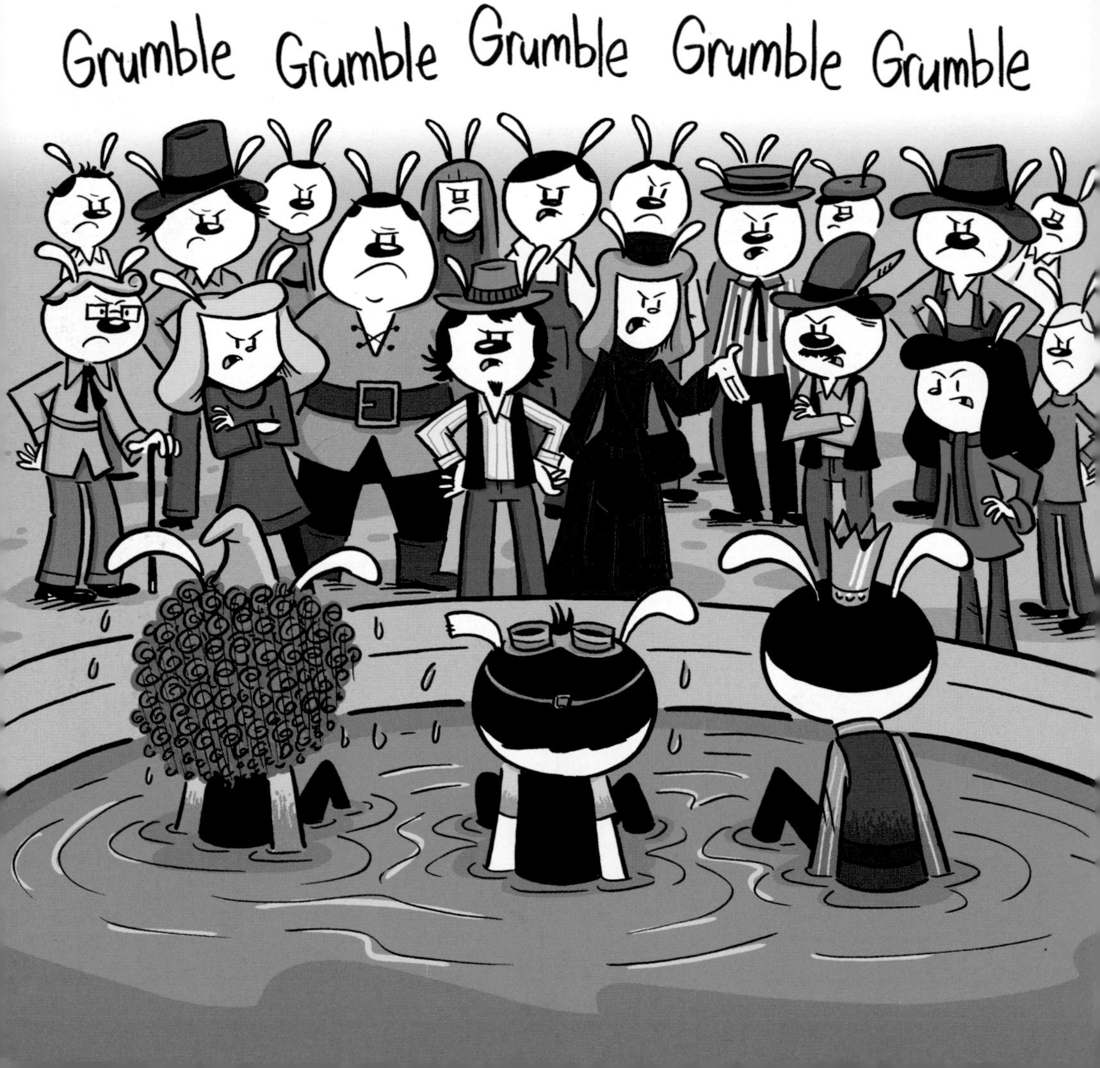
Grumble Grumble Grumble Grumble Grumble

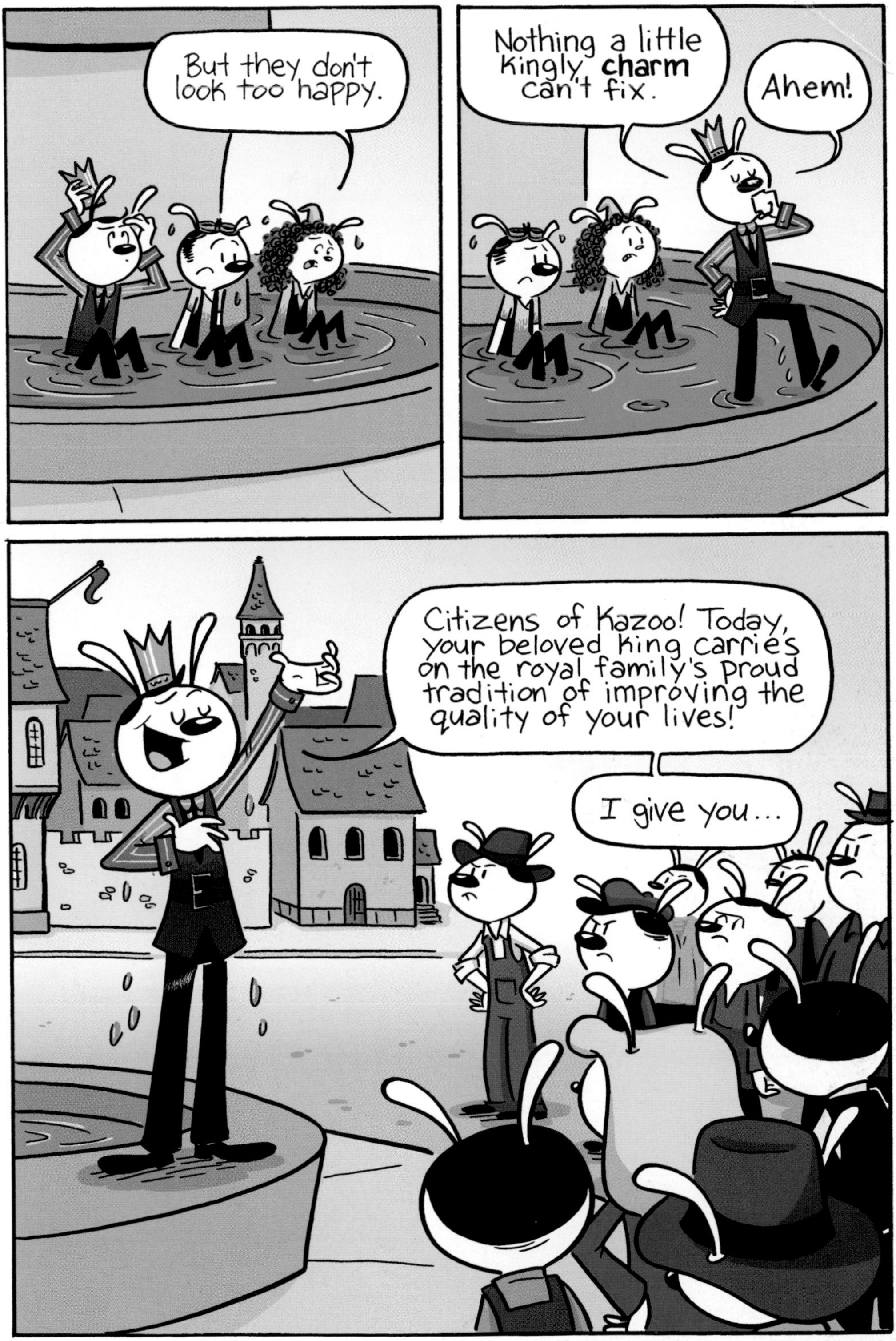

But they don't look too happy.
Nothing a little Kingly **charm** can't fix.
Ahem!
Citizens of Kazoo! Today, your beloved king carries on the royal family's proud tradition of improving the quality of your lives!
I give you...

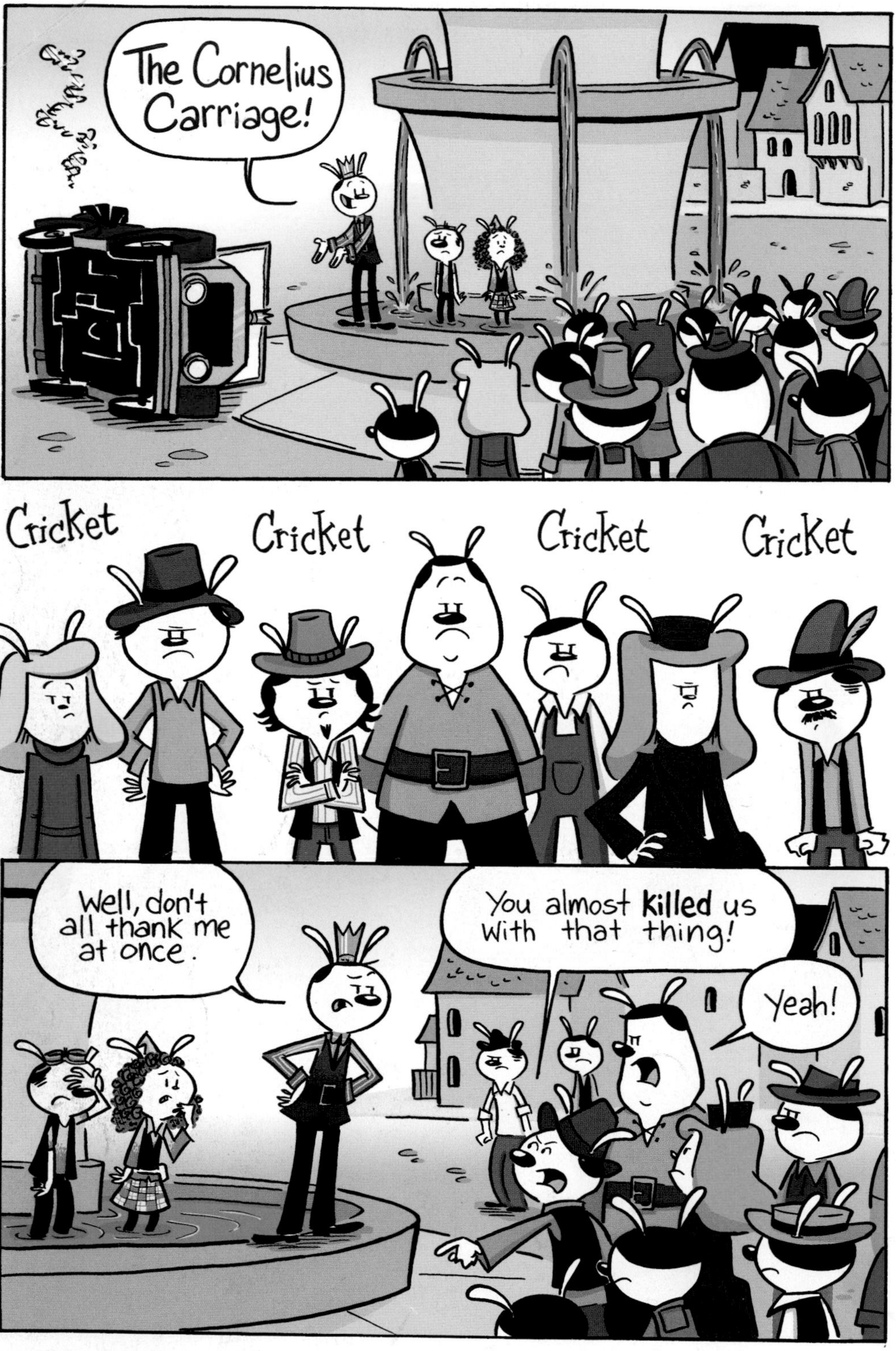
The Cornelius Carriage!
Cricket
Cricket
Cricket
Cricket
Well, don't all thank me at once.
You almost **killed** us with that thing!
Yeah!

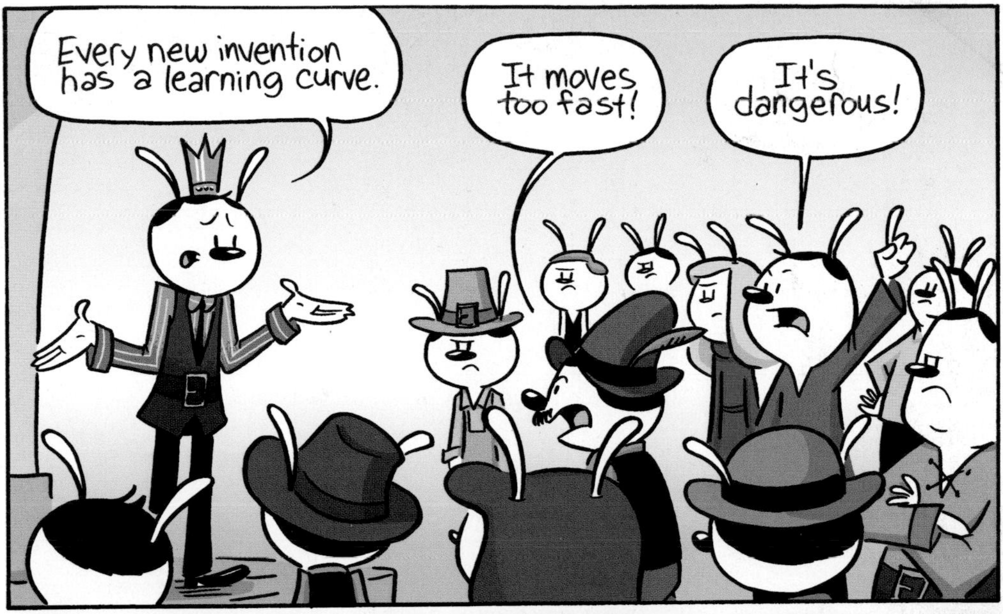
Every new invention has a learning curve.
It moves too fast!
It's dangerous!

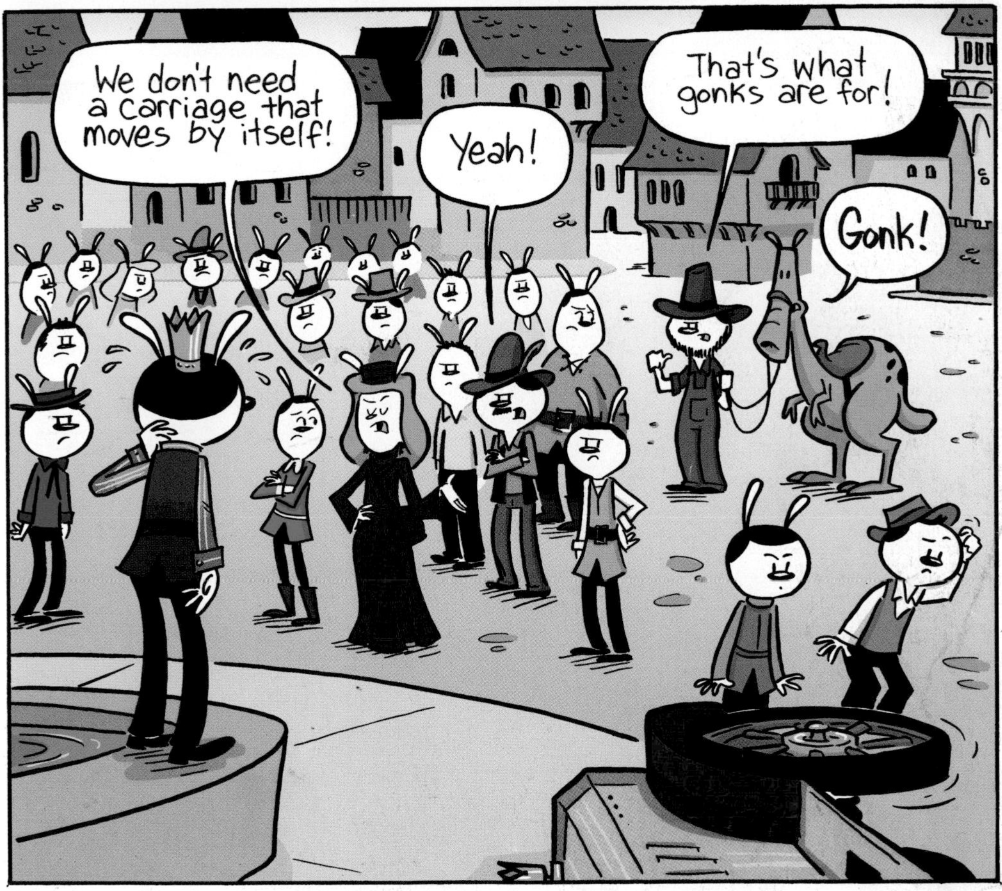
We don't need a carriage that moves by itself!
Yeah!
That's what gonks are for!
Gonk!

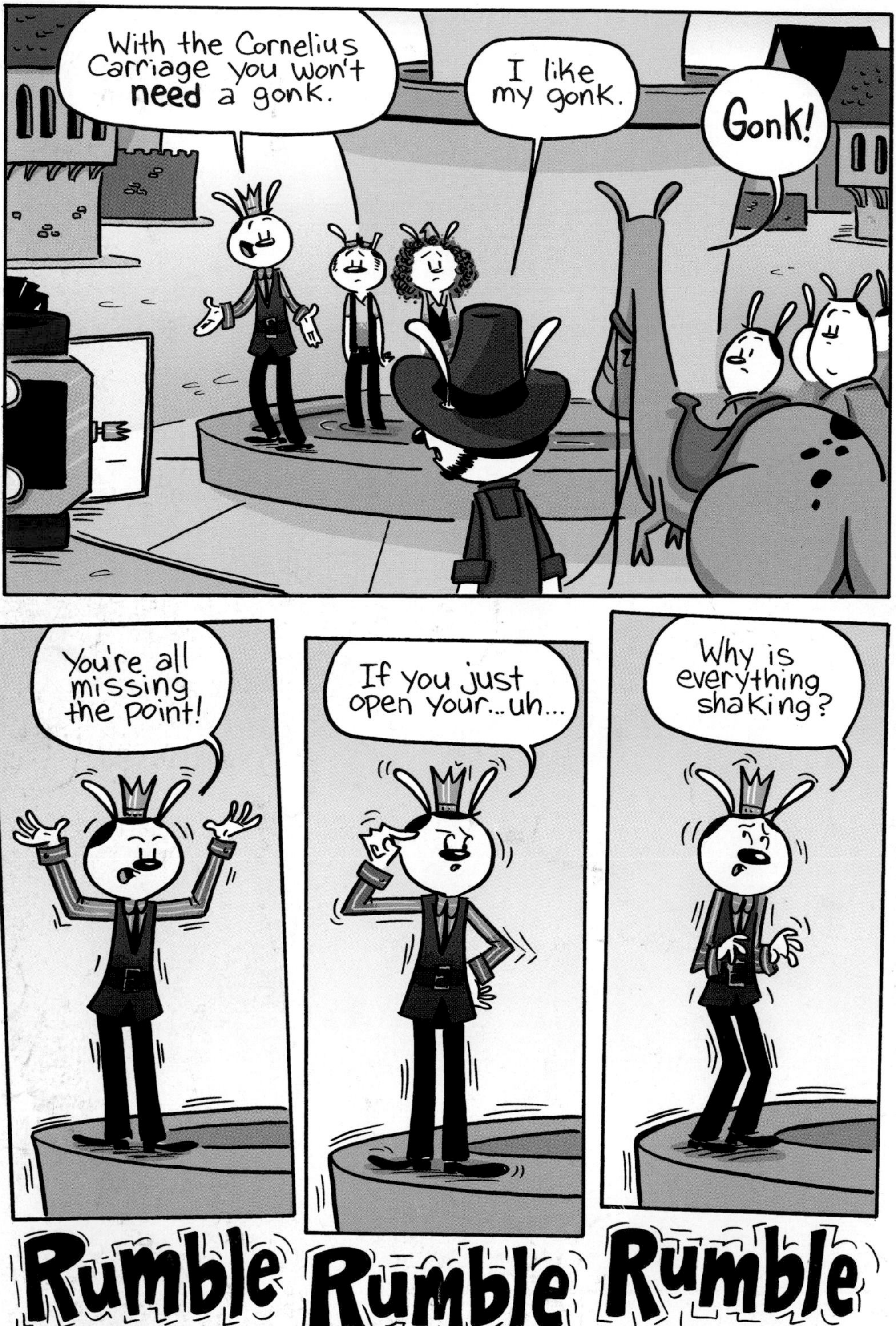
With the Cornelius Carriage you won't **need** a gonk.
I like my gonk.
Gonk!
You're all missing the point!
If you just open your...uh...
Why is everything shaking?
Rumble Rumble Rumble

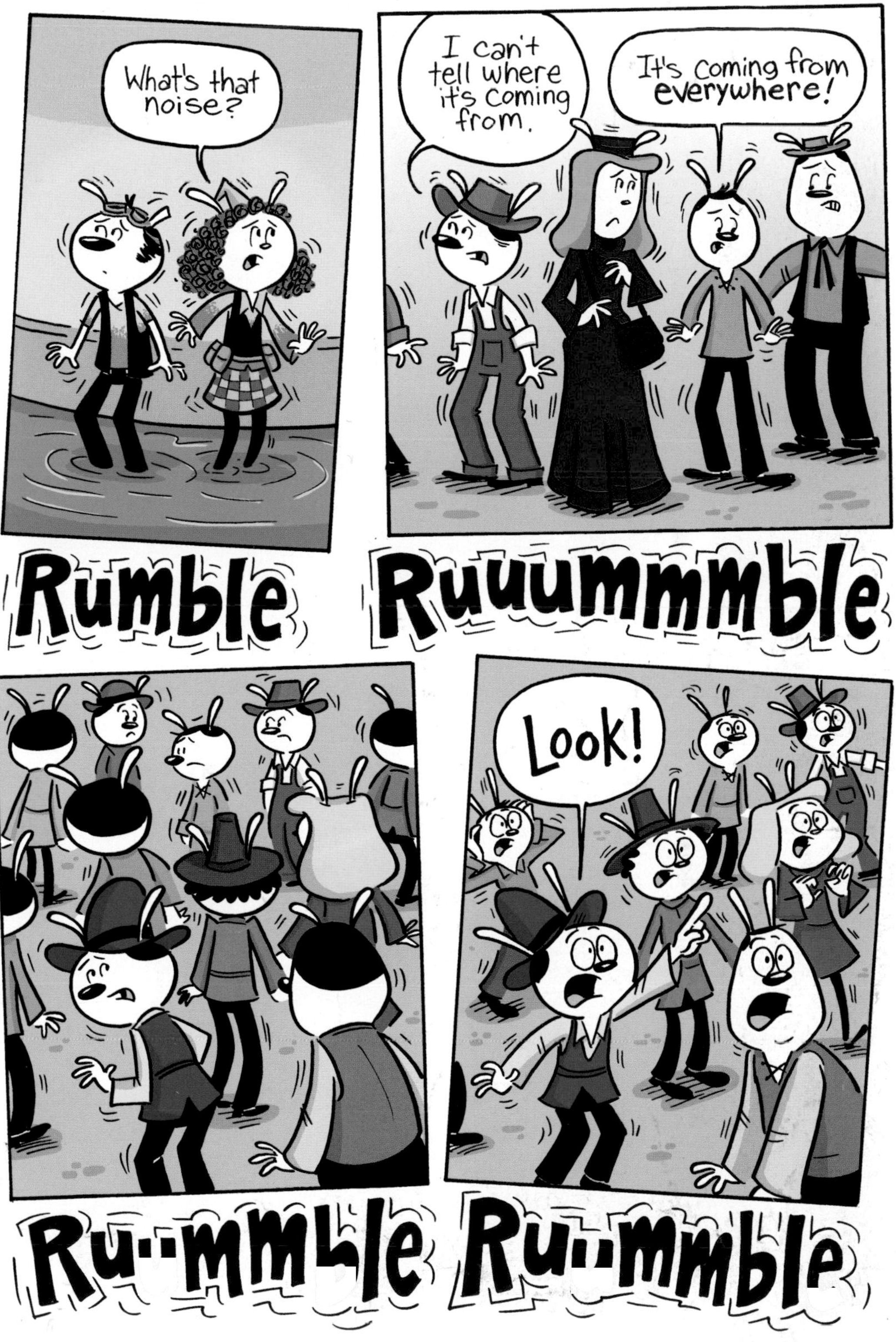
What's that noise?
I can't tell where it's coming from.
It's coming from everywhere!
Rumble
Ruuummmble
Look!
Ru··mmble
Ru··mmble

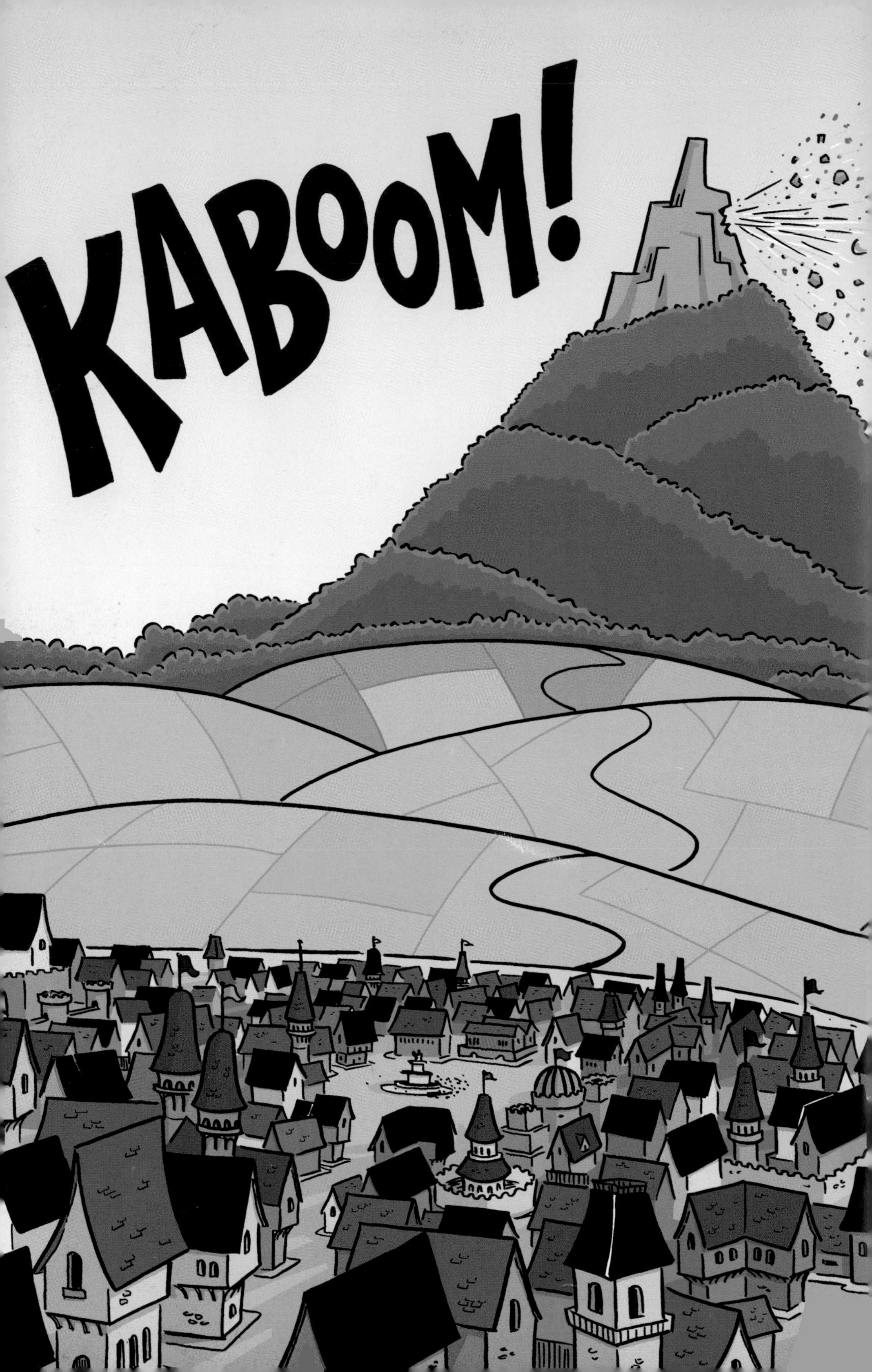
KABOOM!

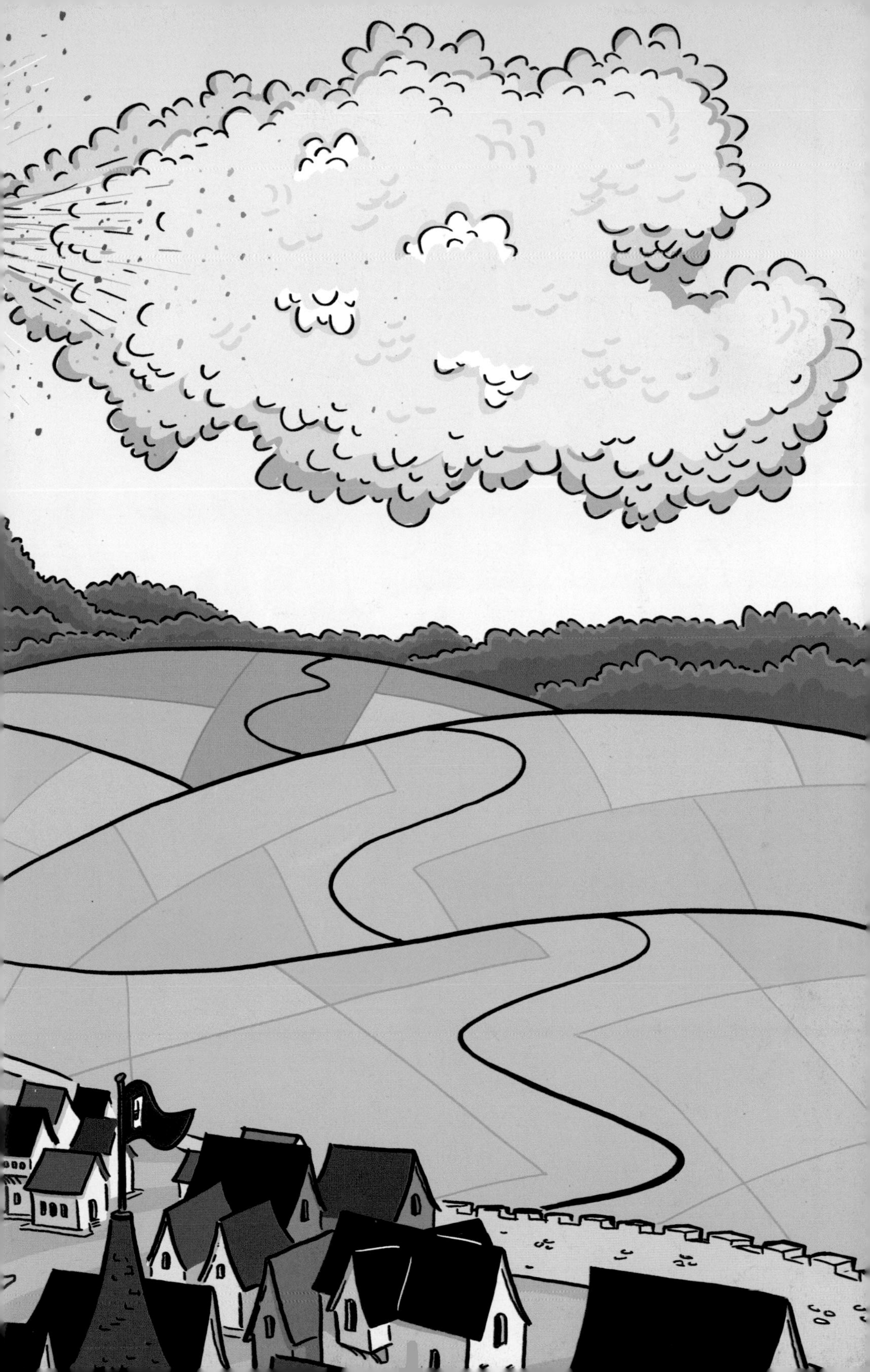

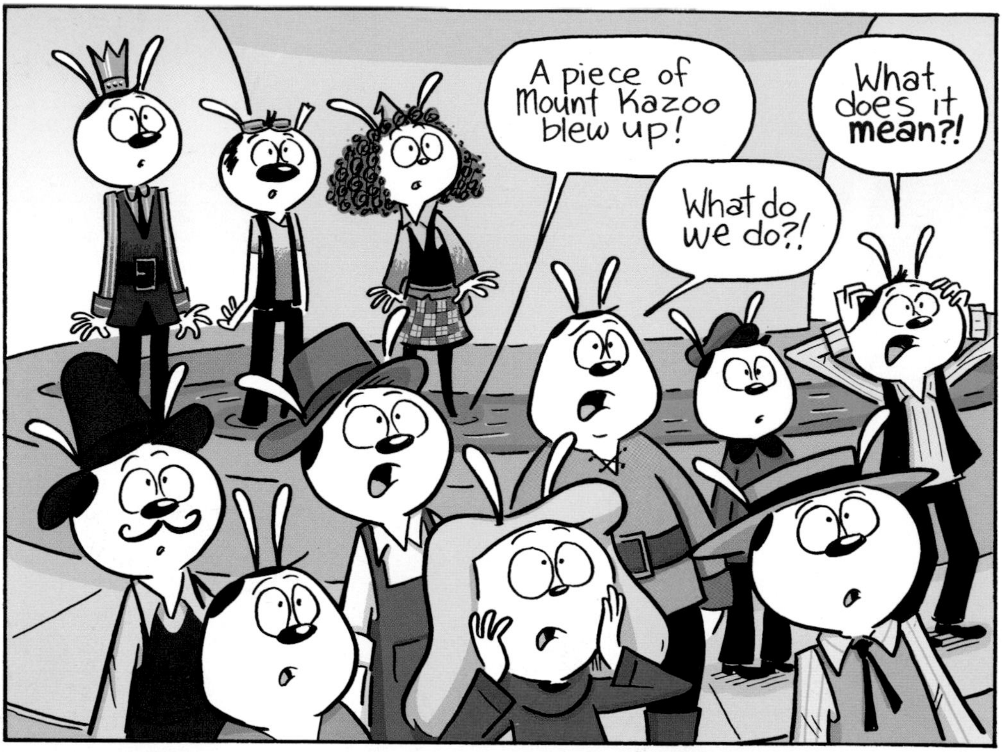
A piece of Mount Kazoo blew up!
What do we do?!
What does it mean?!

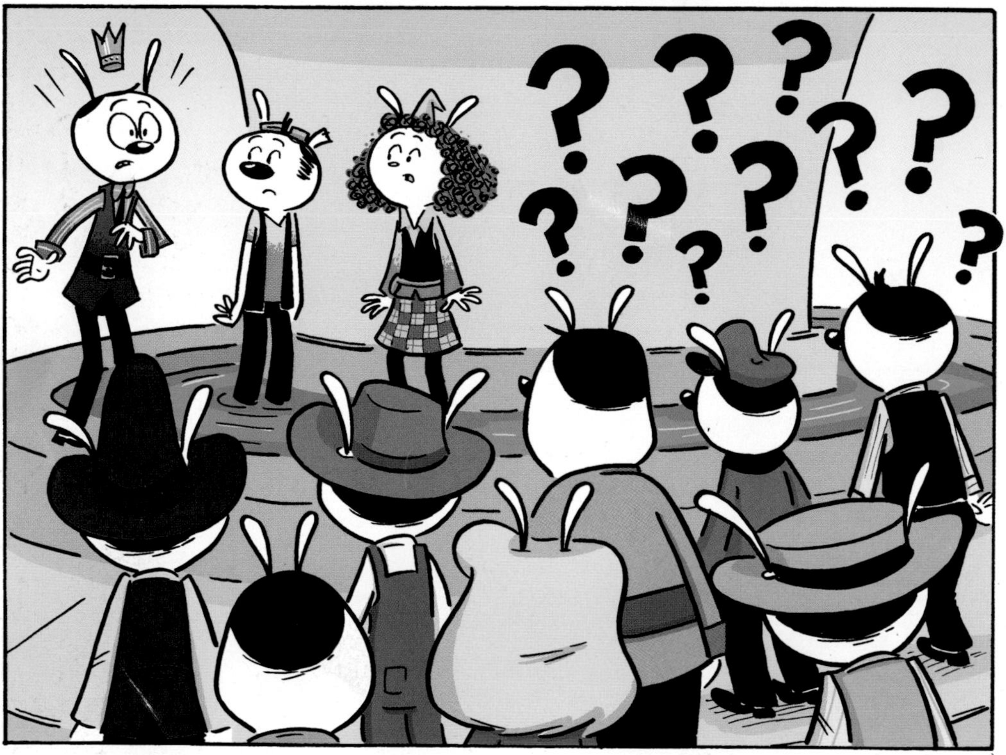
? ? ? ? ? ? ? ? ? ?

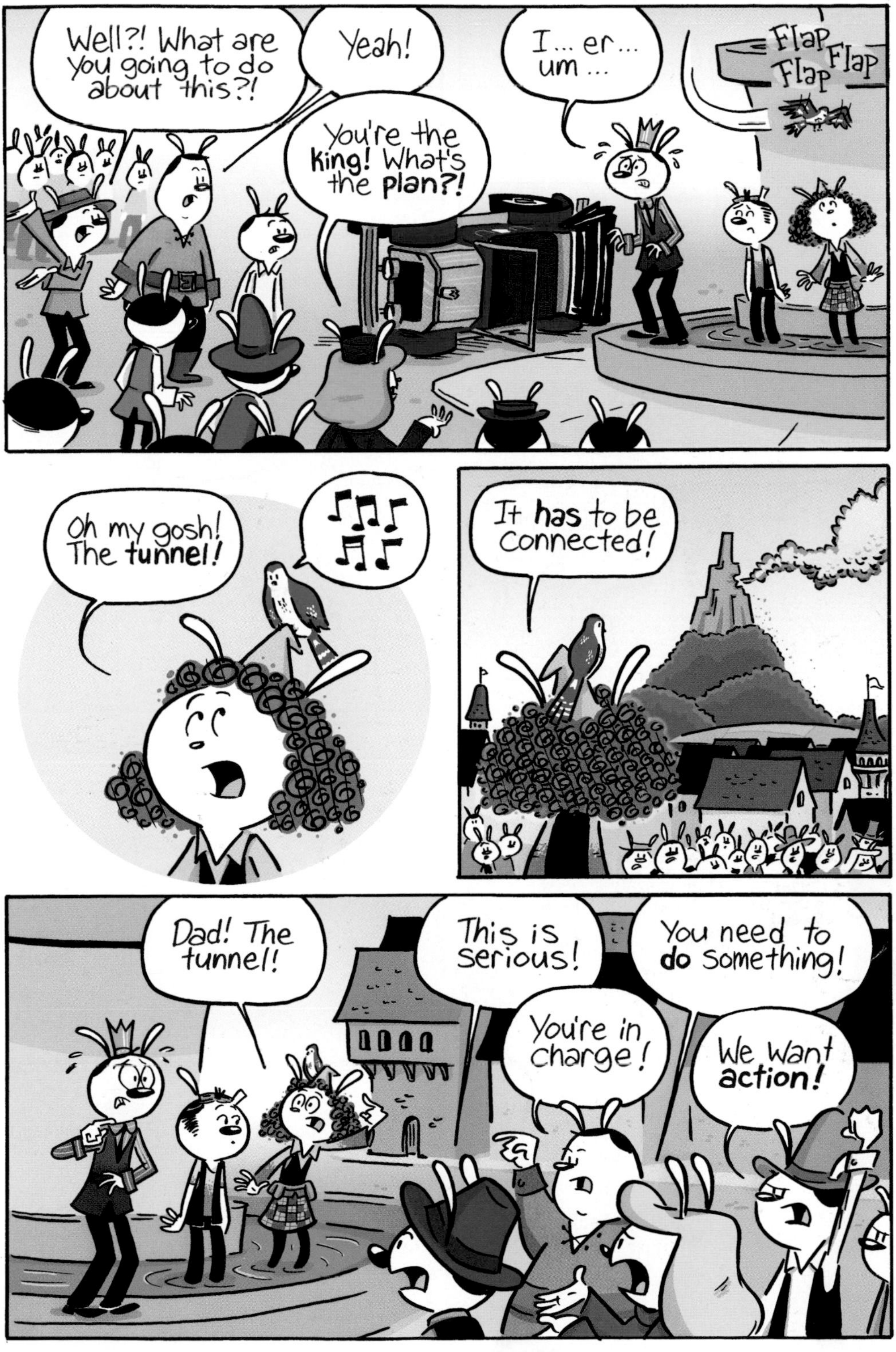
Well?! What are you going to do about this?!
Yeah!
You're the **king!** What's the **plan?!**
I... er... um...
Flap Flap Flap
Oh my gosh! The **tunnel!**
♫♫♫ ♫♫
It **has** to be connected!
Dad! The tunnel!
This is serious!
You need to **do** something!
You're in charge!
We want **action!**

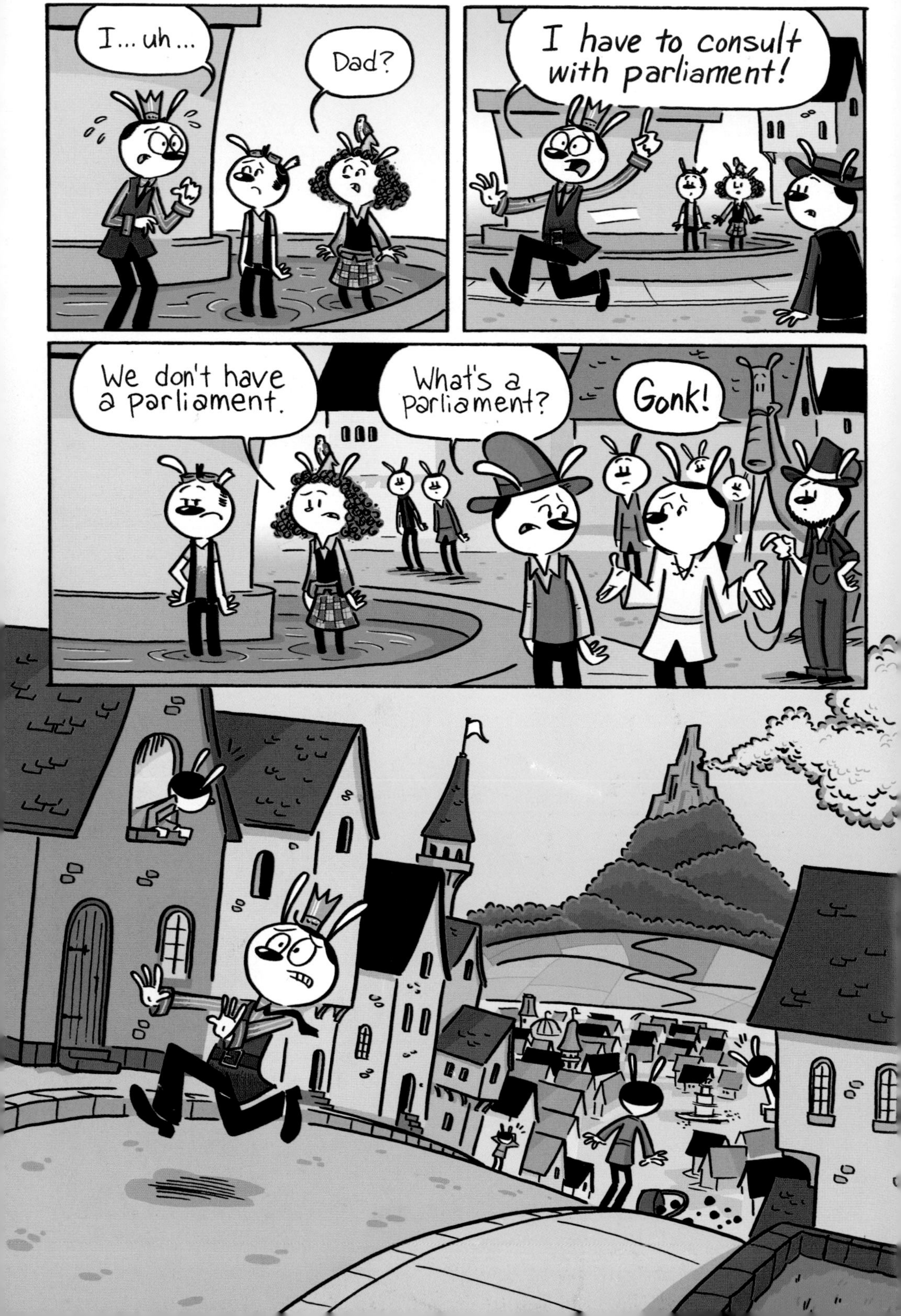
I... uh...
Dad?
I have to consult with parliament!
We don't have a parliament.
What's a parliament?
Gonk!

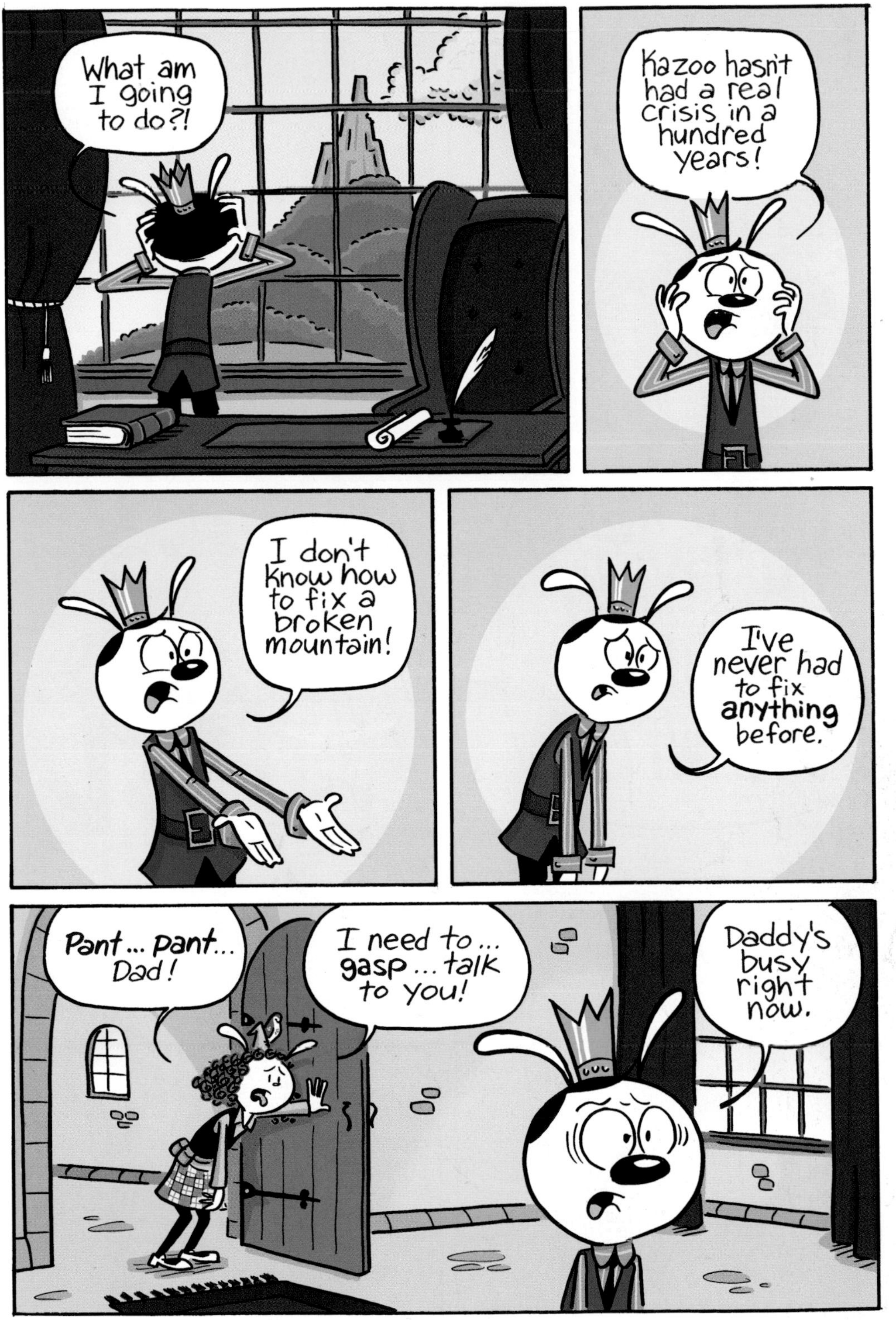
What am I going to do?!
Kazoo hasn't had a real crisis in a hundred years!
I don't know how to fix a broken mountain!
I've never had to fix **anything** before.
Pant... **pant**... Dad!
I need to... **gasp**... talk to you!
Daddy's busy right now.

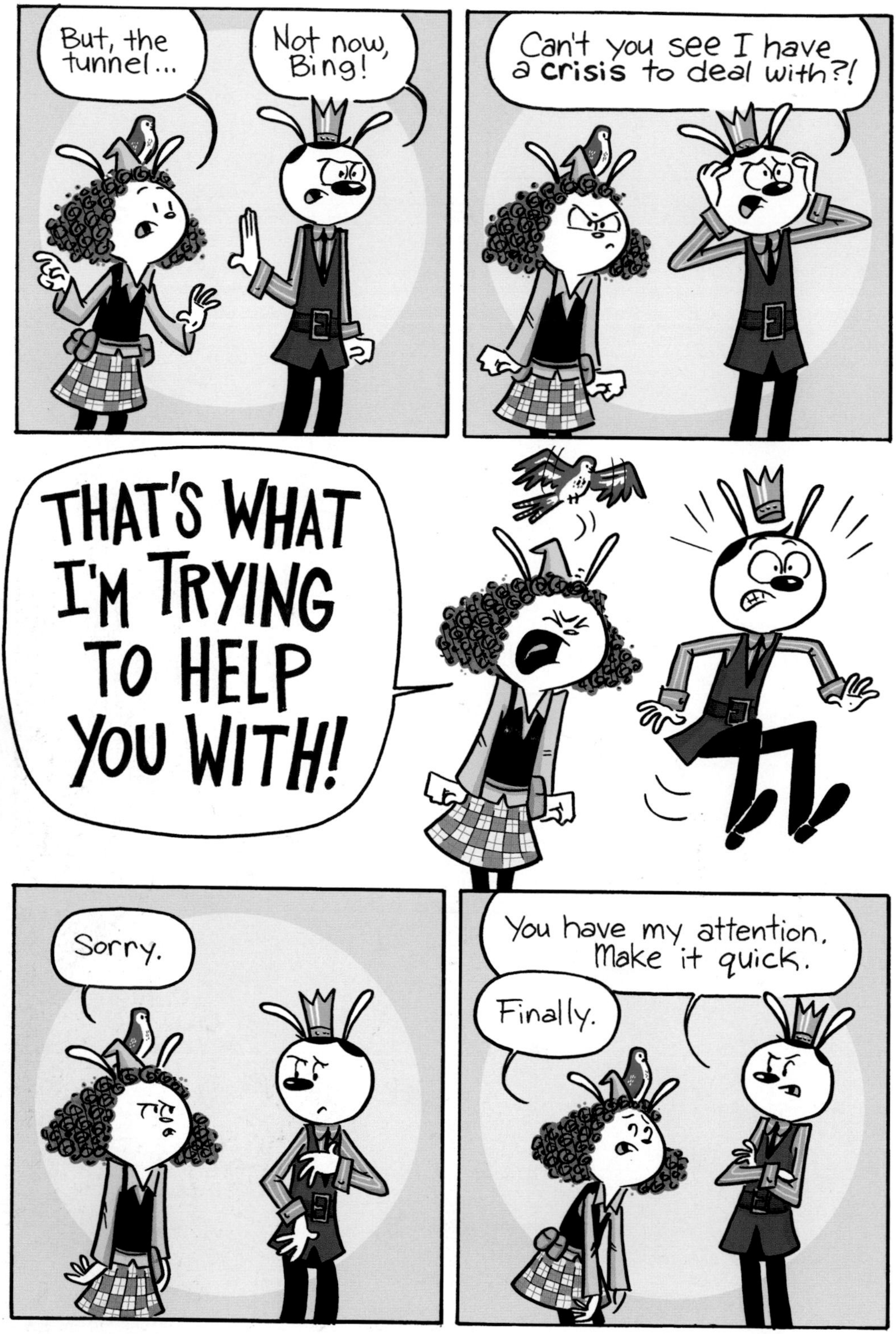
But, the tunnel...
Not now, Bing!
Can't you see I have a **crisis** to deal with?!
THAT'S WHAT I'M TRYING TO HELP YOU WITH!
Sorry.
You have my attention. Make it quick.
Finally.

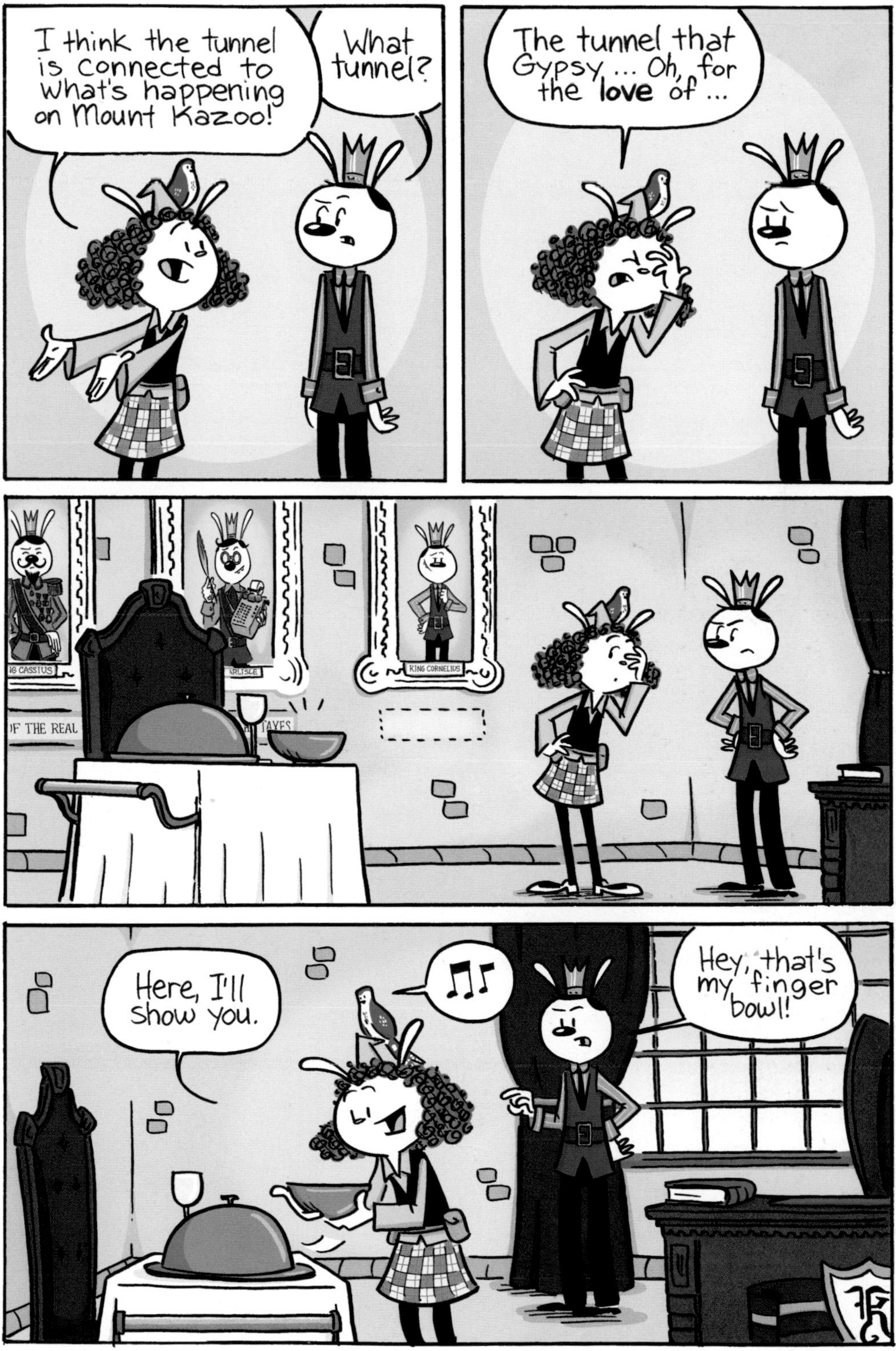
I think the tunnel is connected to what's happening on Mount Kazoo!
What tunnel?
The tunnel that Gypsy ... Oh, for the **love** of ...
KING CORNELIUS
Here, I'll show you.
Hey, that's my finger bowl!

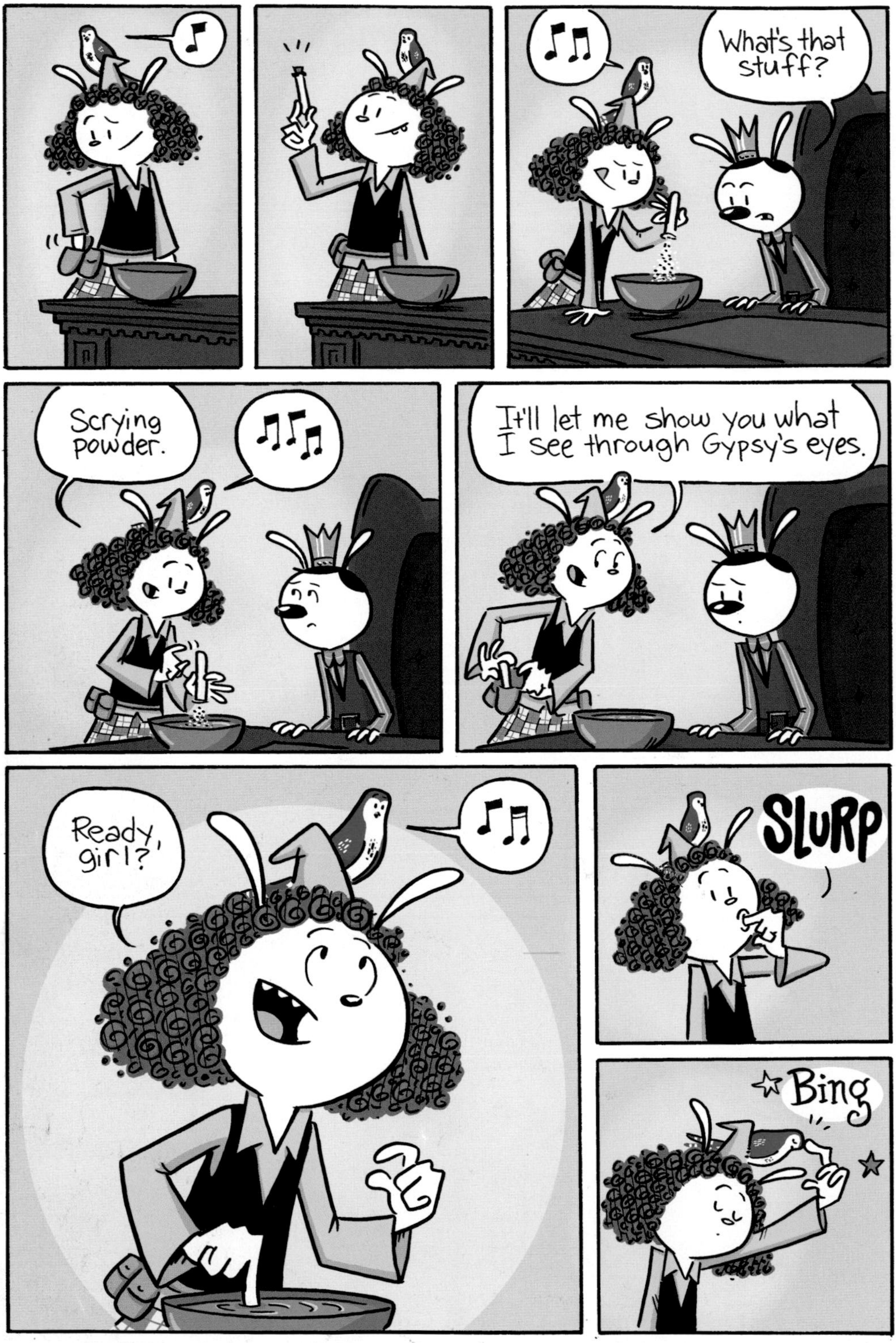
What's that stuff?
Scrying powder.
It'll let me show you what I see through Gypsy's eyes.
Ready, girl?
SLURP
Bing

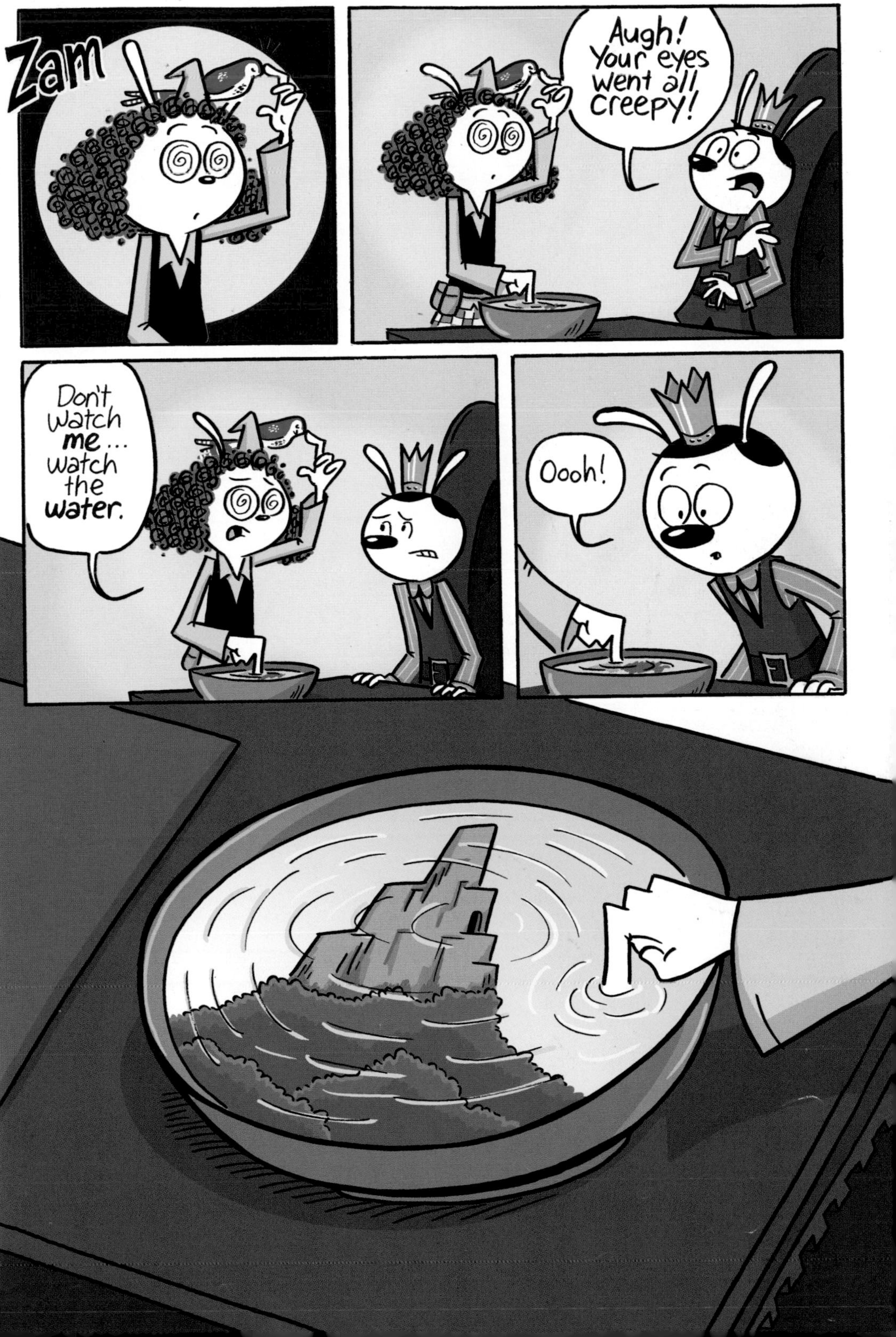
Zam
Augh! Your eyes went all creepy!
Don't watch **me**... watch the **water**.
Oooh!

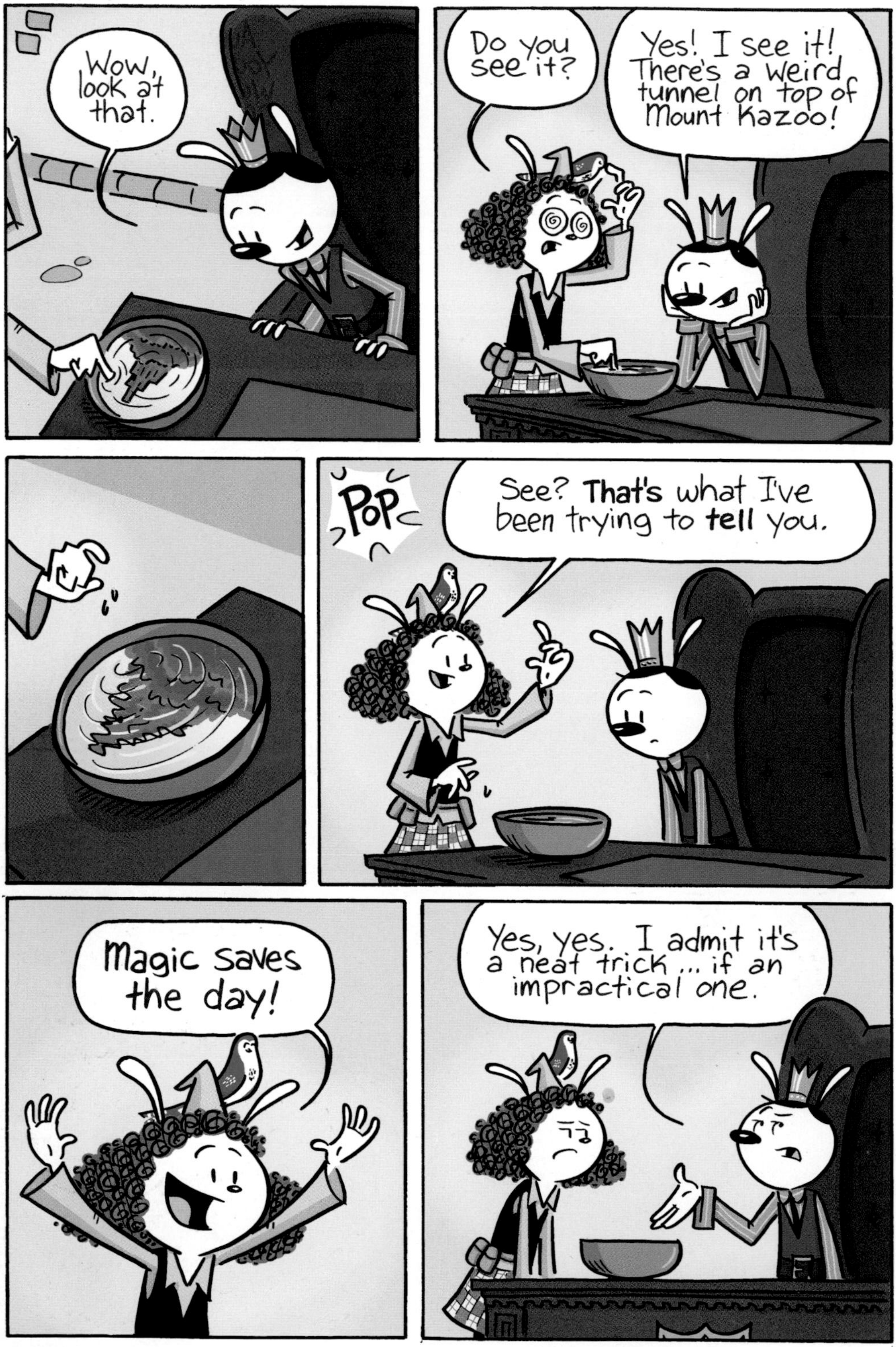
Wow, look at that.
Do you see it?
Yes! I see it! There's a weird tunnel on top of Mount Kazoo!
POP
See? **That's** what I've been trying to **tell** you.
Magic saves the day!
Yes, yes. I admit it's a neat trick ... if an impractical one.

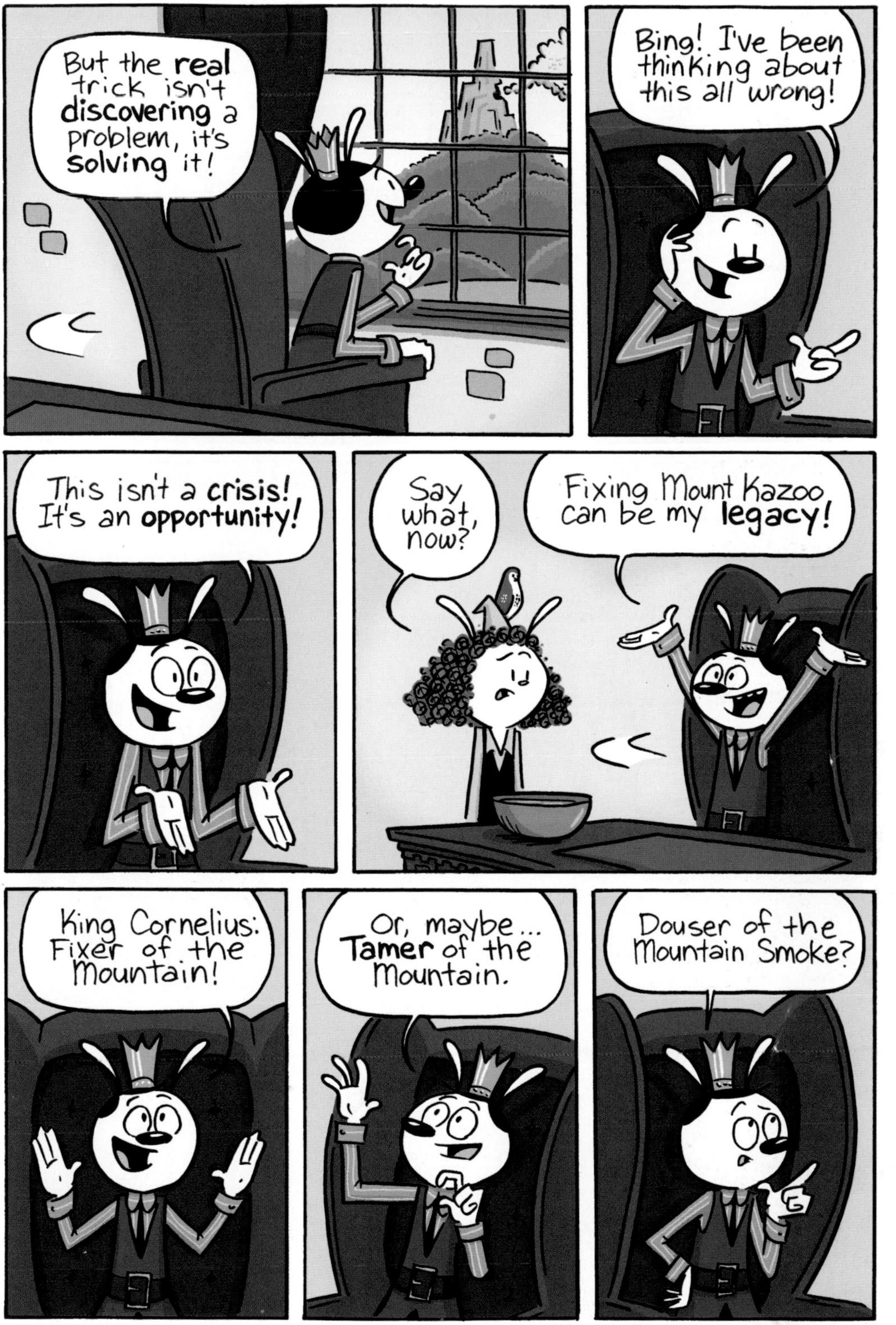
But the **real** trick isn't **discovering** a problem, it's **solving** it!
Bing! I've been thinking about this all wrong!
This isn't a **crisis**! It's an **opportunity**!
Say what, now?
Fixing Mount Kazoo can be my **legacy**!
King Cornelius: Fixer of the Mountain!
Or, maybe... **Tamer** of the Mountain.
Douser of the Mountain Smoke?

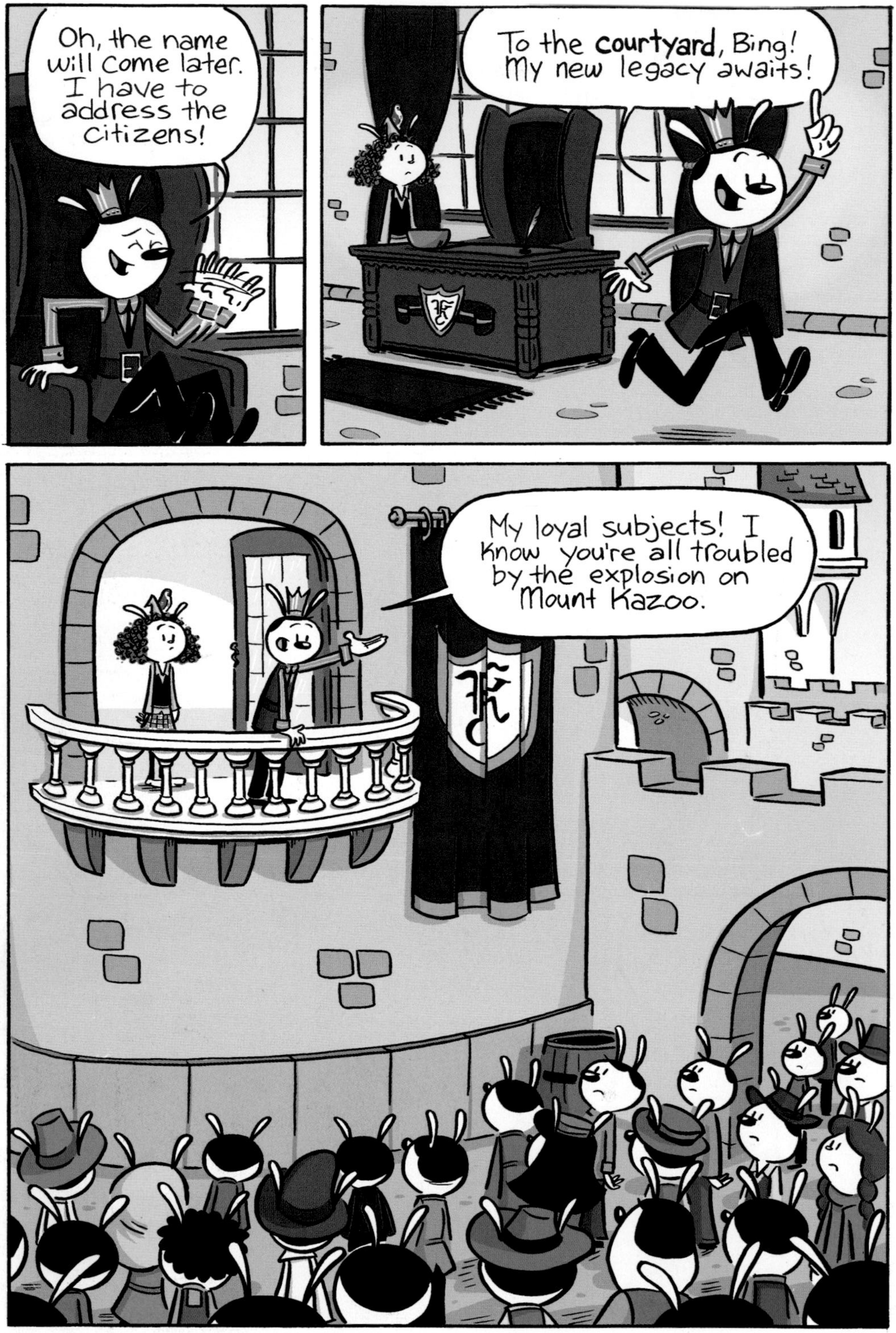
Oh, the name will come later. I have to address the citizens!
To the **courtyard**, Bing! My new legacy awaits!
My loyal subjects! I know you're all troubled by the explosion on Mount Kazoo.

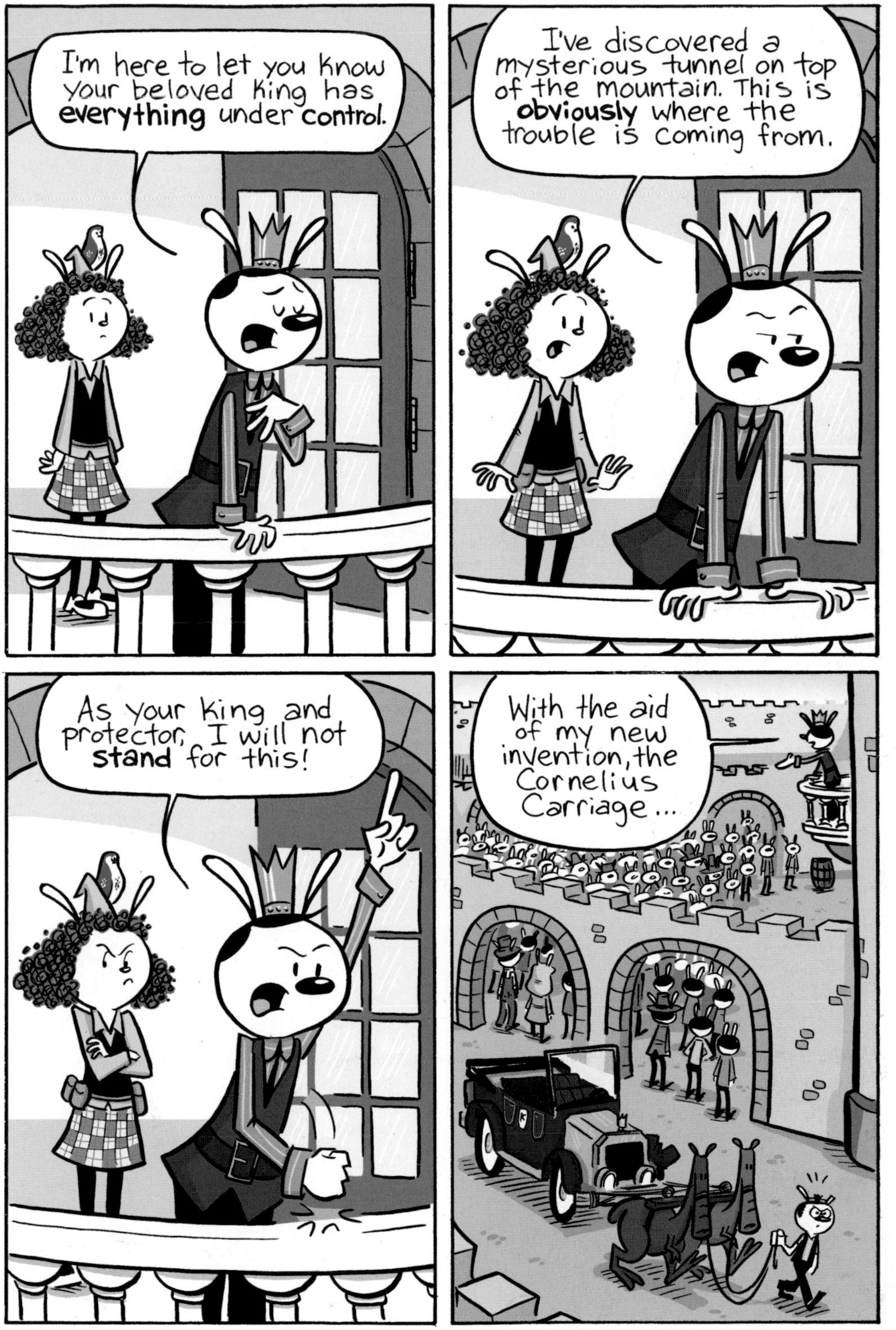
I'm here to let you know your beloved king has **everything** under **control**.
I've discovered a mysterious tunnel on top of the mountain. This is **obviously** where the trouble is coming from.
As your king and protector, I will not **stand** for this!
With the aid of my new invention, the Cornelius Carriage...

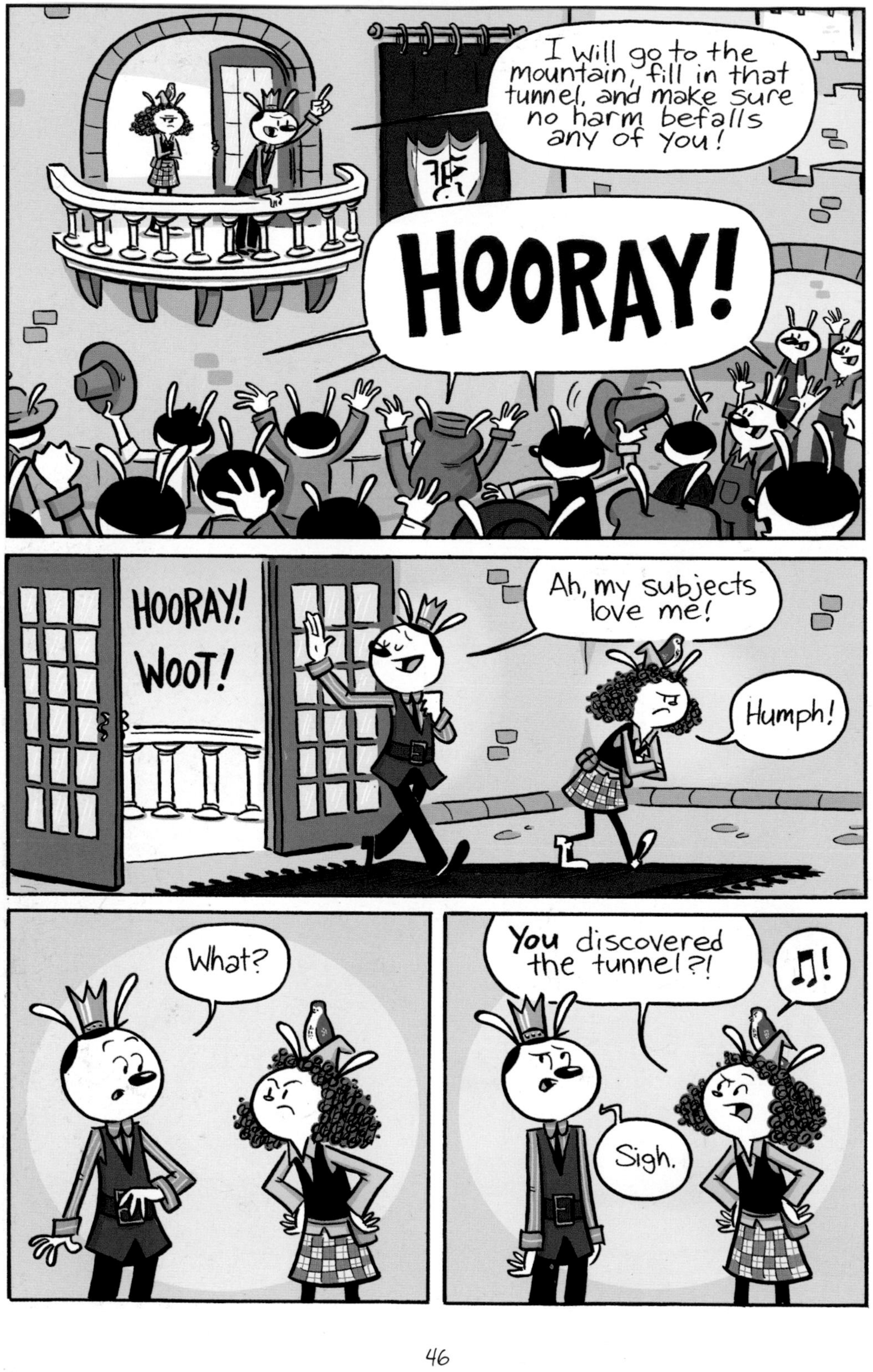
I will go to the mountain, fill in that tunnel, and make sure no harm befalls any of you!
HOORAY!
HOORAY!
WOOT!
Ah, my subjects love me!
Humph!
What?
You discovered the tunnel?!
!
Sigh.

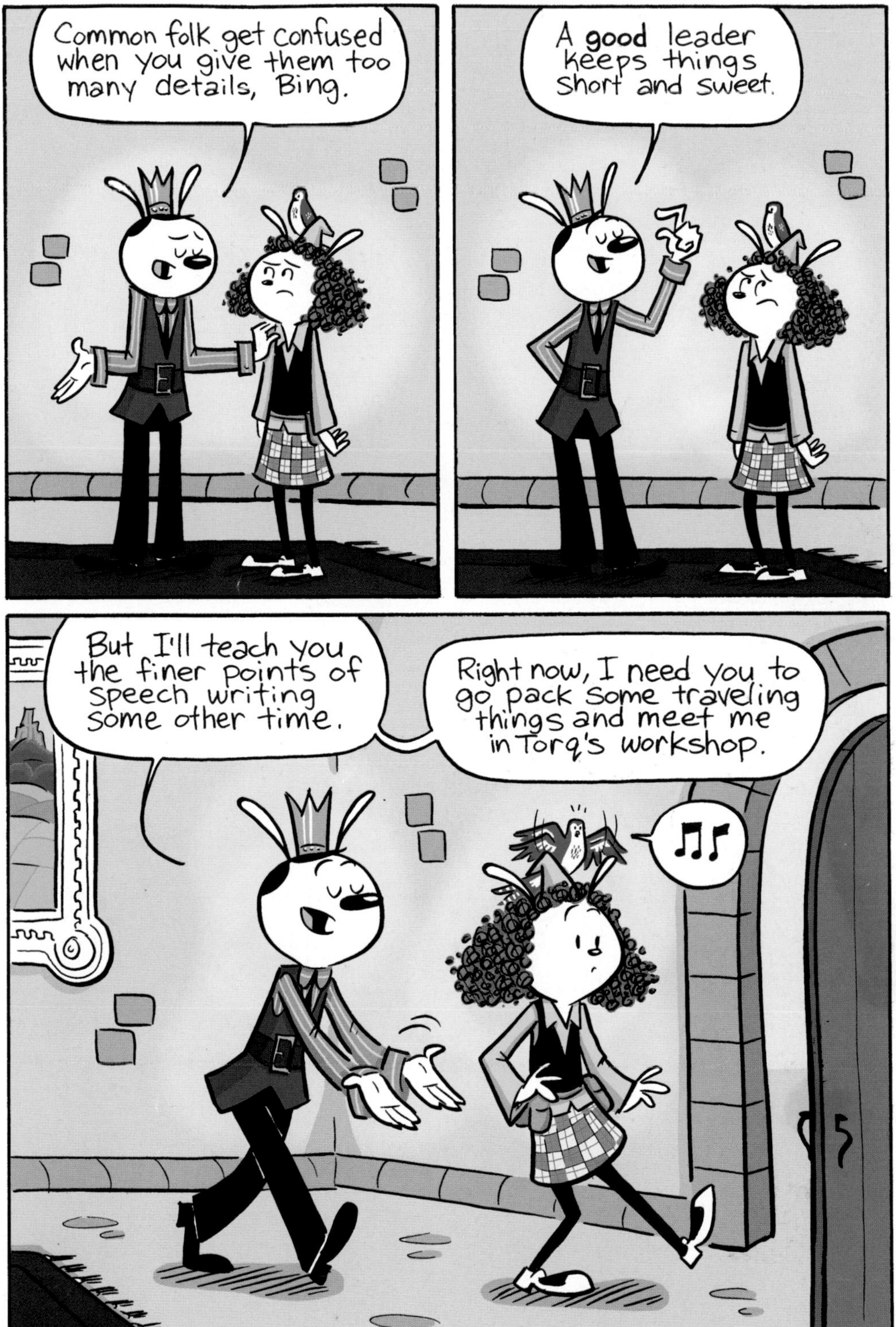
Common folk get confused when you give them too many details, Bing.
A **good** leader keeps things short and sweet.
But I'll teach you the finer points of speech writing some other time.
Right now, I need you to go pack some traveling things and meet me in Torq's workshop.

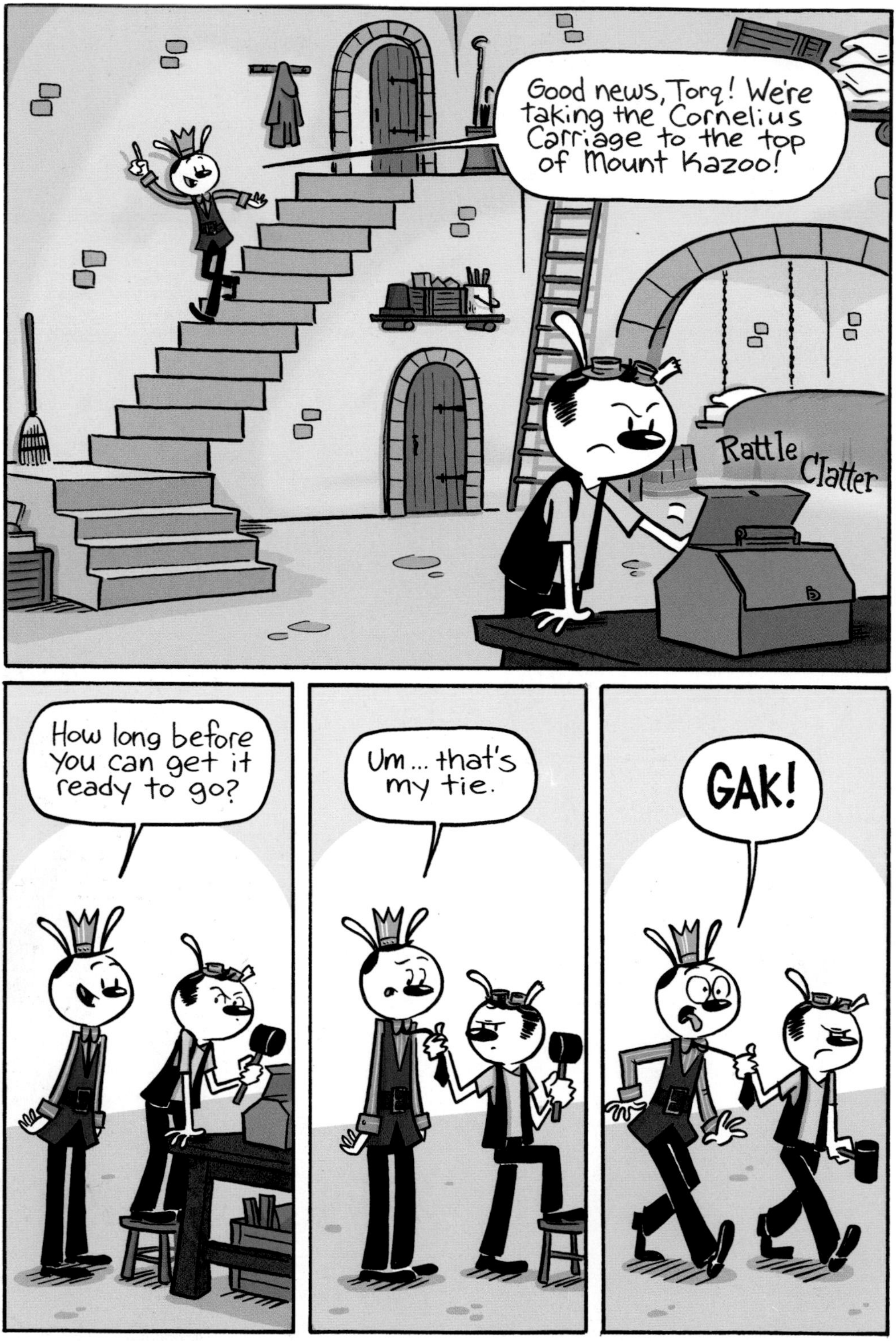
Good news, Torq! We're taking the Cornelius Carriage to the top of Mount Kazoo!
Rattle
Clatter
How long before you can get it ready to go?
Um... that's my tie.
GAK!

Okay! I'm coming! Sheesh! You don't have to manhandle me!

Ah, yes... I see. That **is** a nasty dent.

You really should have made that part stronger.

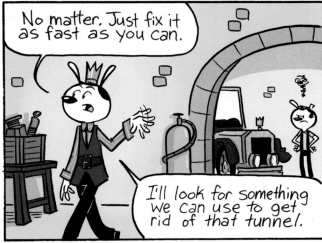

No matter. Just fix it as fast as you can.

I'll look for something we can use to get rid of that tunnel.

Let's see now...

Hey! Exactly what we need!

DYNAMITE

DYNAMITE

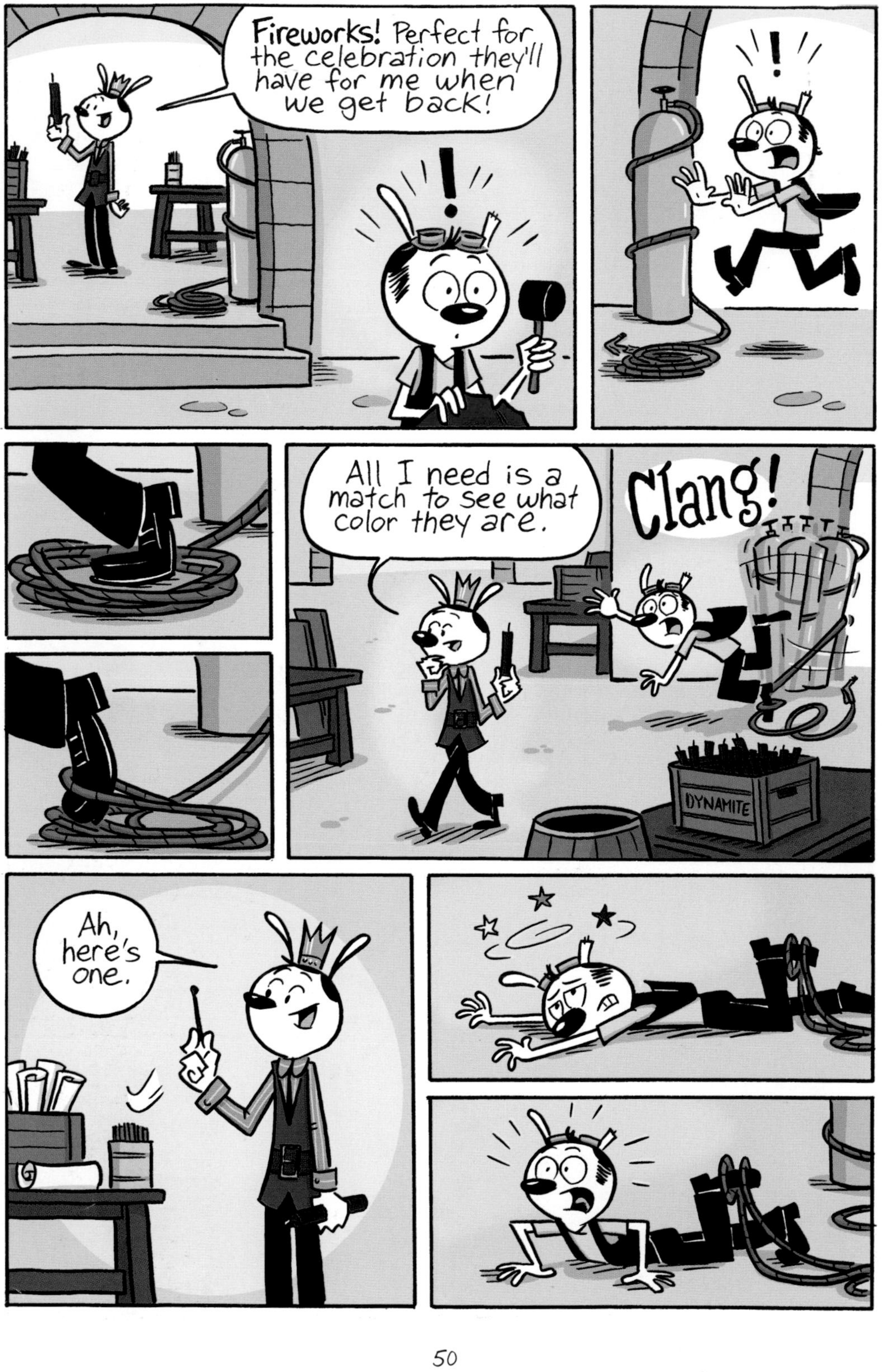
Fireworks! Perfect for the celebration they'll have for me when we get back!
!
!
All I need is a match to see what color they are.
Clang!
DYNAMITE
Ah, here's one.

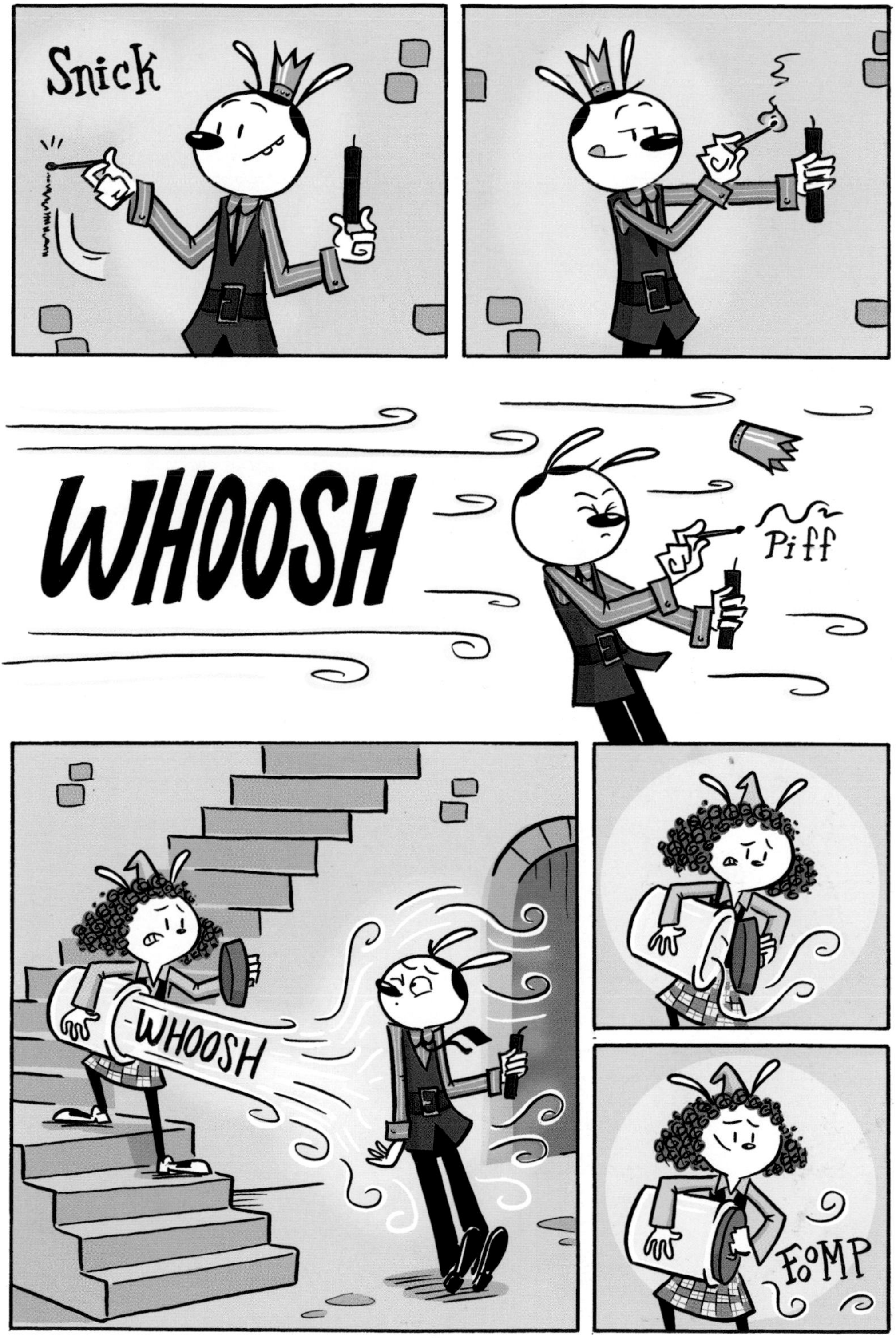
Snick
WHOOSH
Piff
WHOOSH
FOOMP

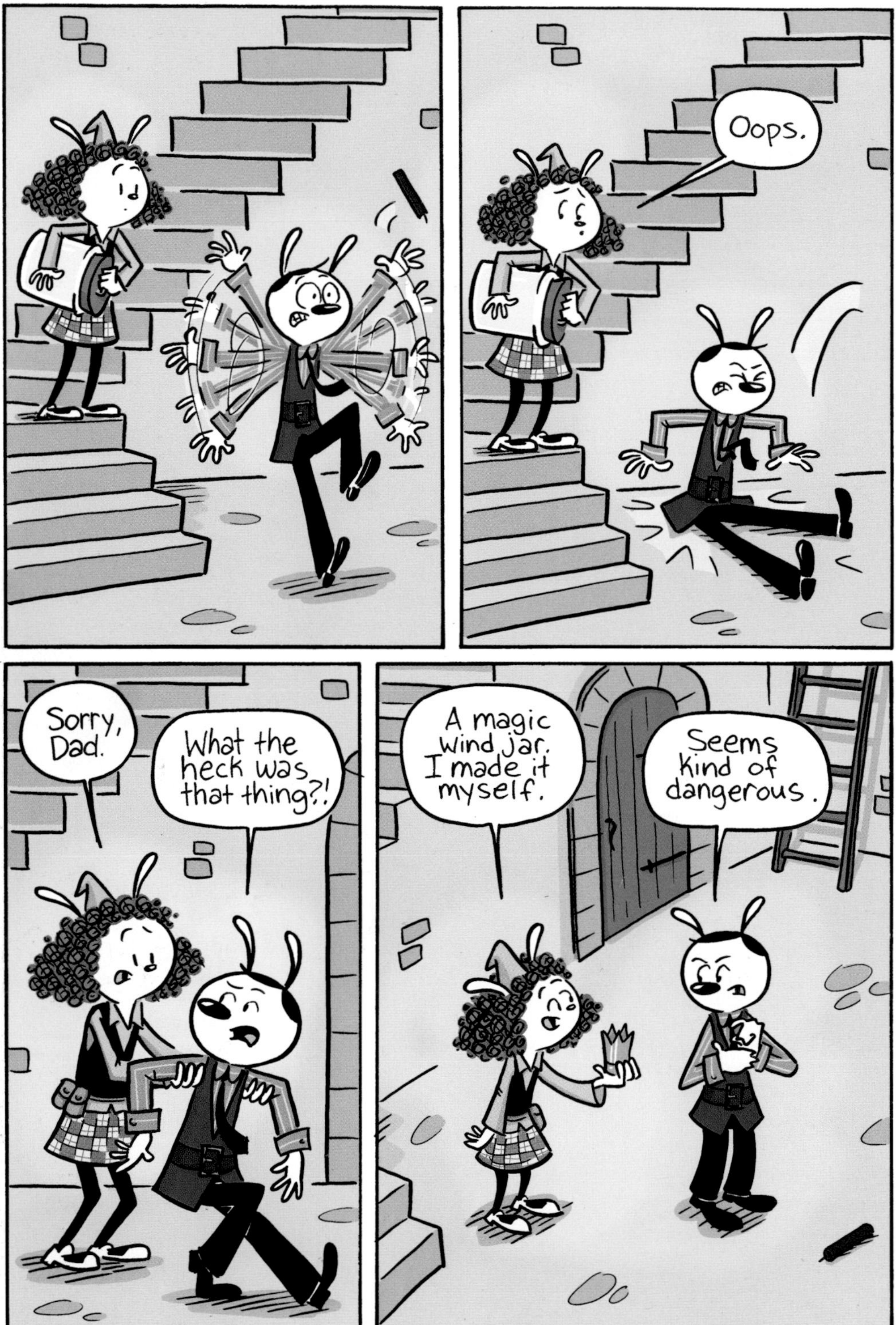
Oops.
Sorry, Dad.
What the heck was that thing?!
A magic wind jar. I made it myself.
Seems kind of dangerous.

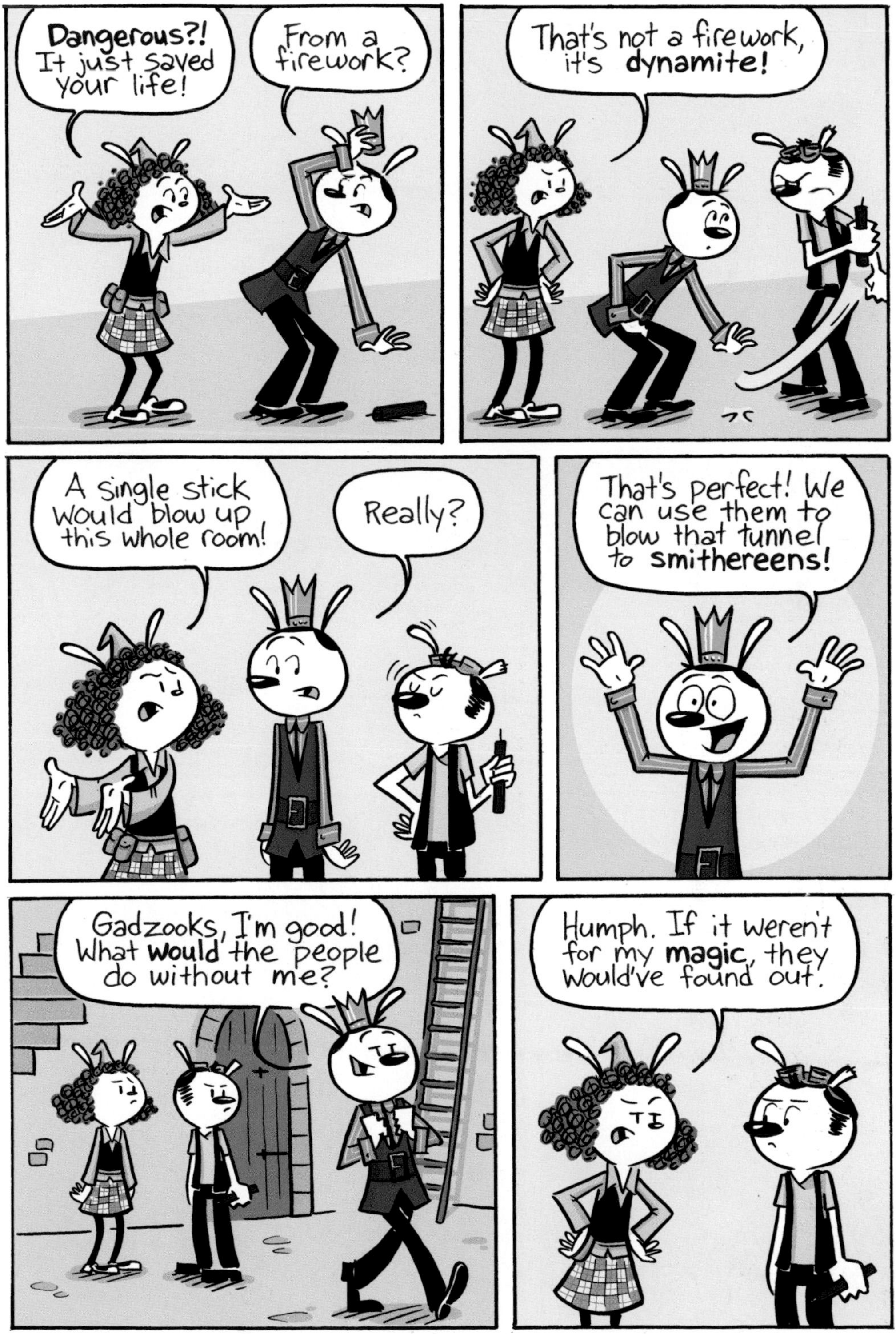

Dangerous?! It just saved your life!
From a firework?
That's not a firework, it's dynamite!
A single stick would blow up this whole room!
Really?
That's perfect! We can use them to blow that tunnel to smithereens!
Gadzooks, I'm good! What would the people do without me?
Humph. If it weren't for my magic, they would've found out.

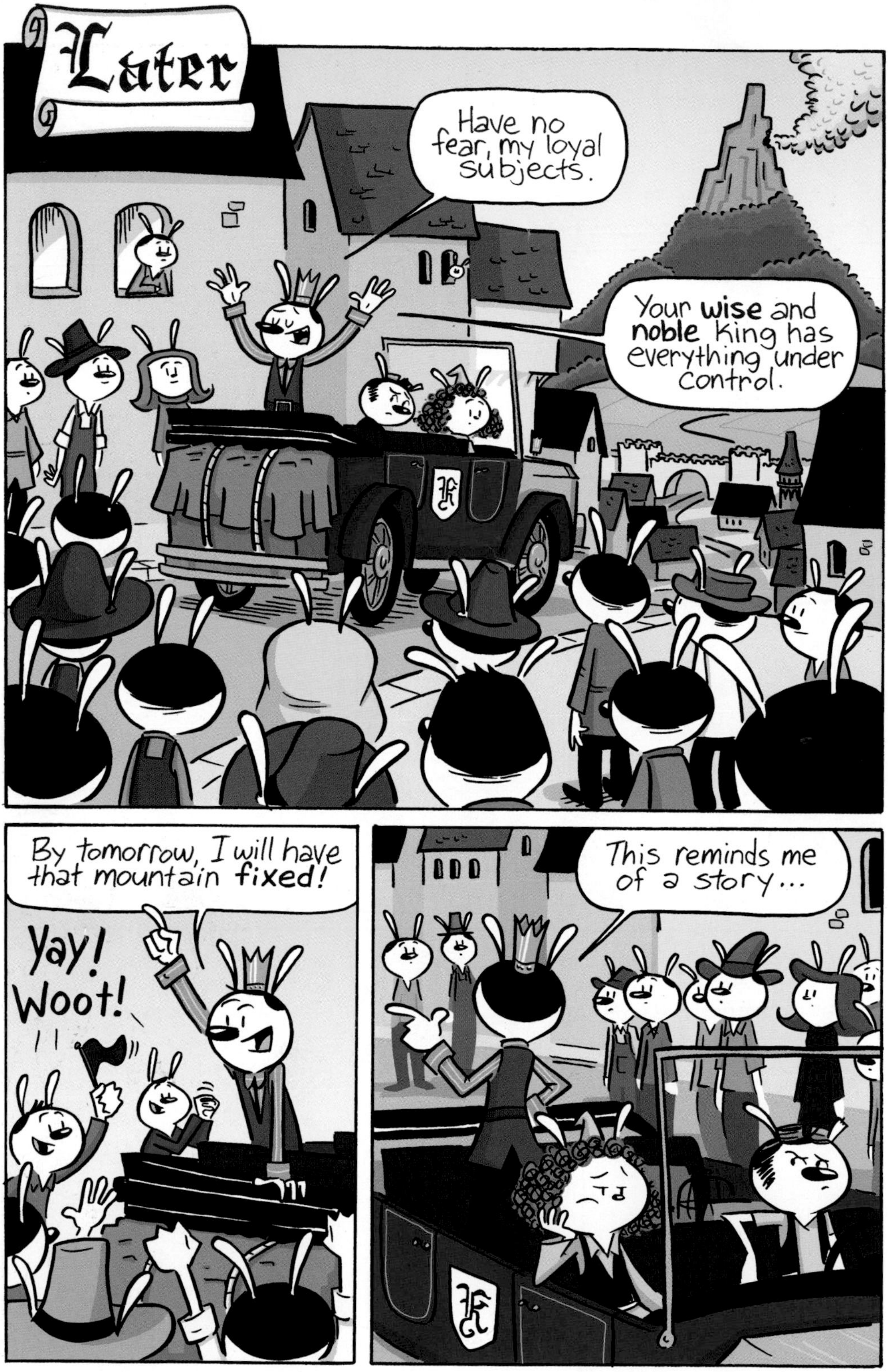
Later
Have no fear, my loyal subjects.
Your **wise** and **noble** King has everything under control.
By tomorrow, I will have that mountain **fixed**!
Yay!
Woot!
This reminds me of a story...

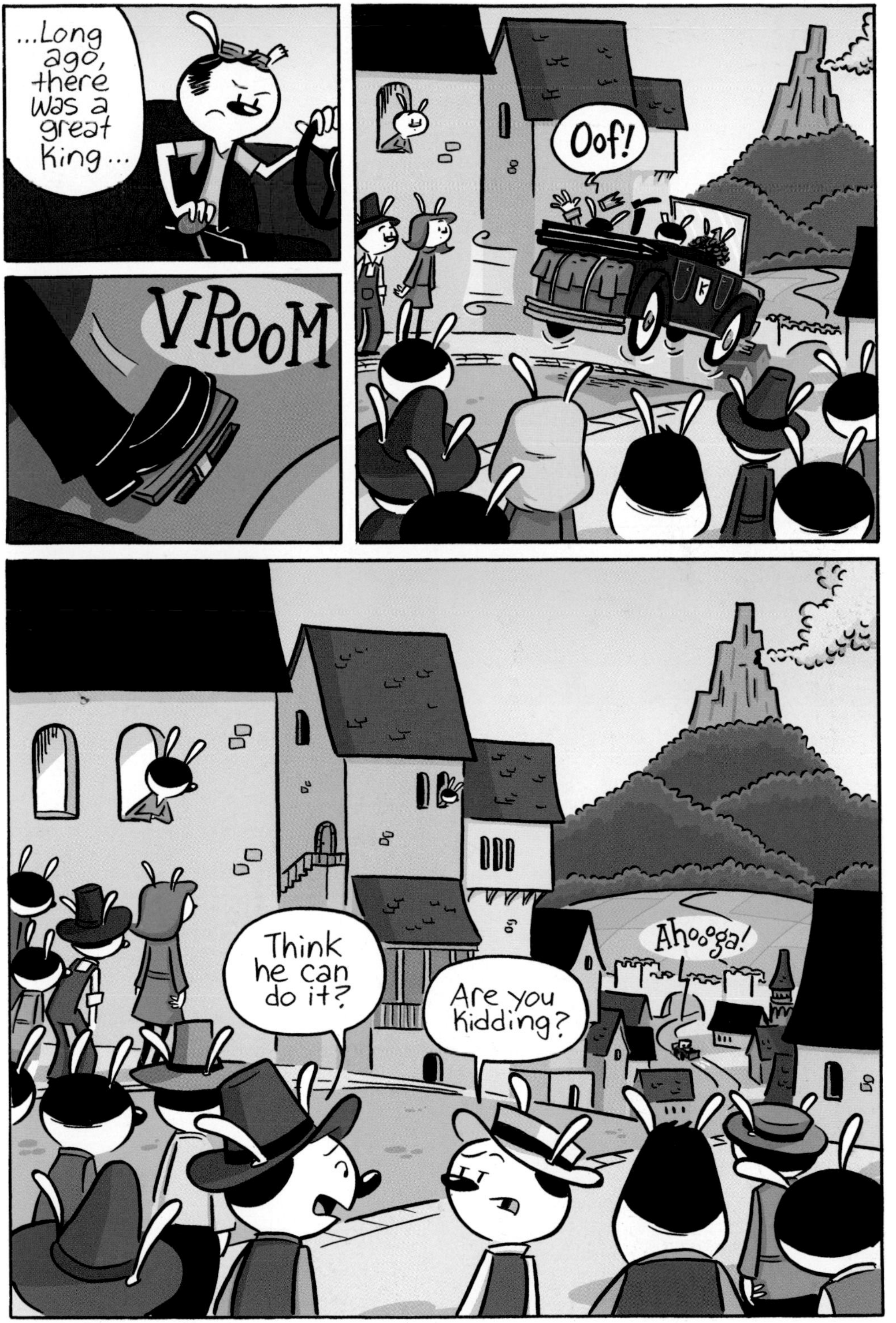
...Long ago, there was a great King...
VROOM
Oof!
Think he can do it?
Are you kidding?
Ahooga!

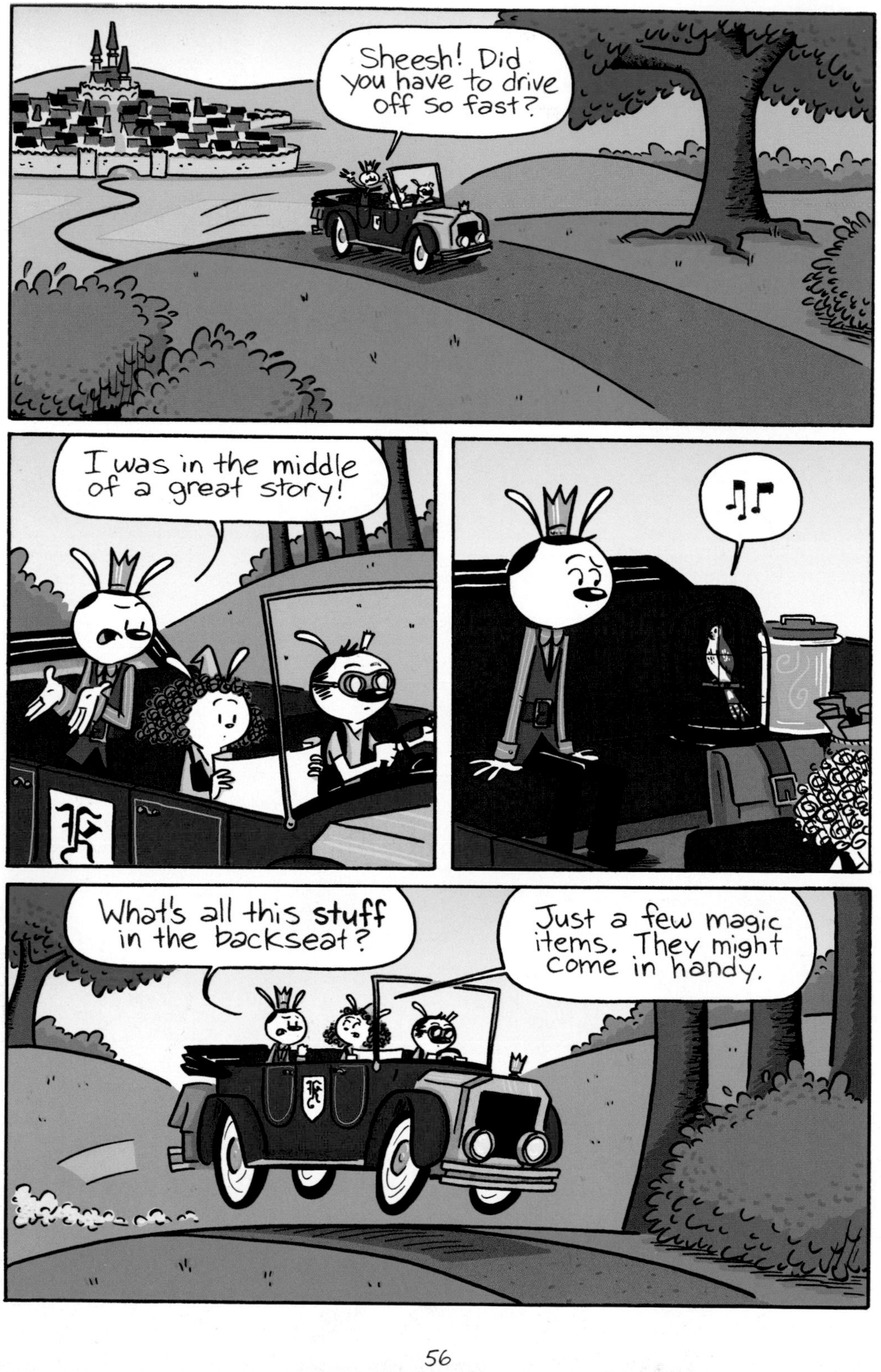
Sheesh! Did you have to drive off so fast?
I was in the middle of a great story!
♫♪
What's all this **stuff** in the backseat?
Just a few magic items. They might come in handy.

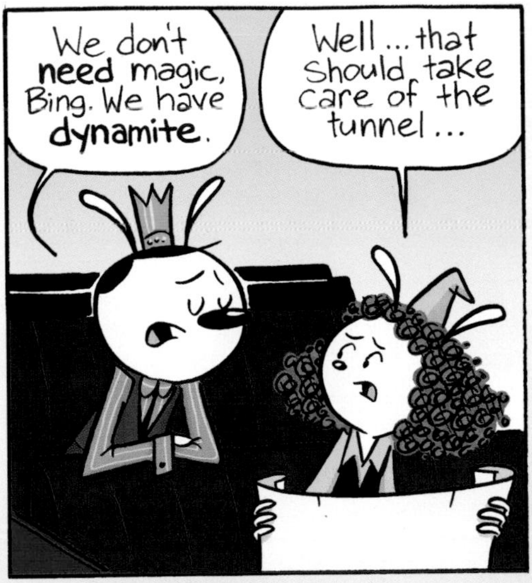
We don't **need** magic, Bing. We have **dynamite**.
Well ... that should take care of the tunnel ...

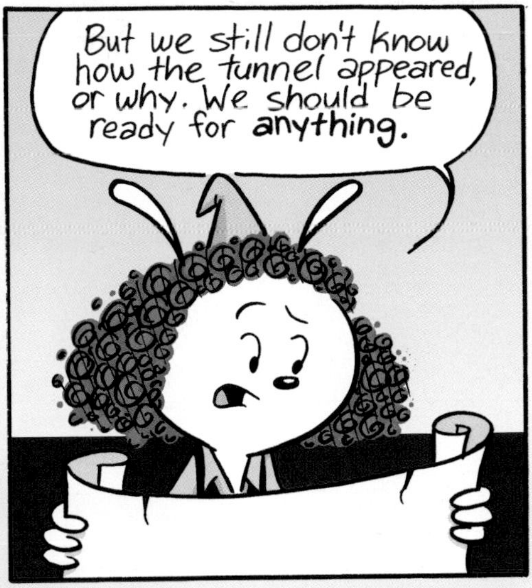
But we still don't know how the tunnel appeared, or why. We should be ready for **anything**.

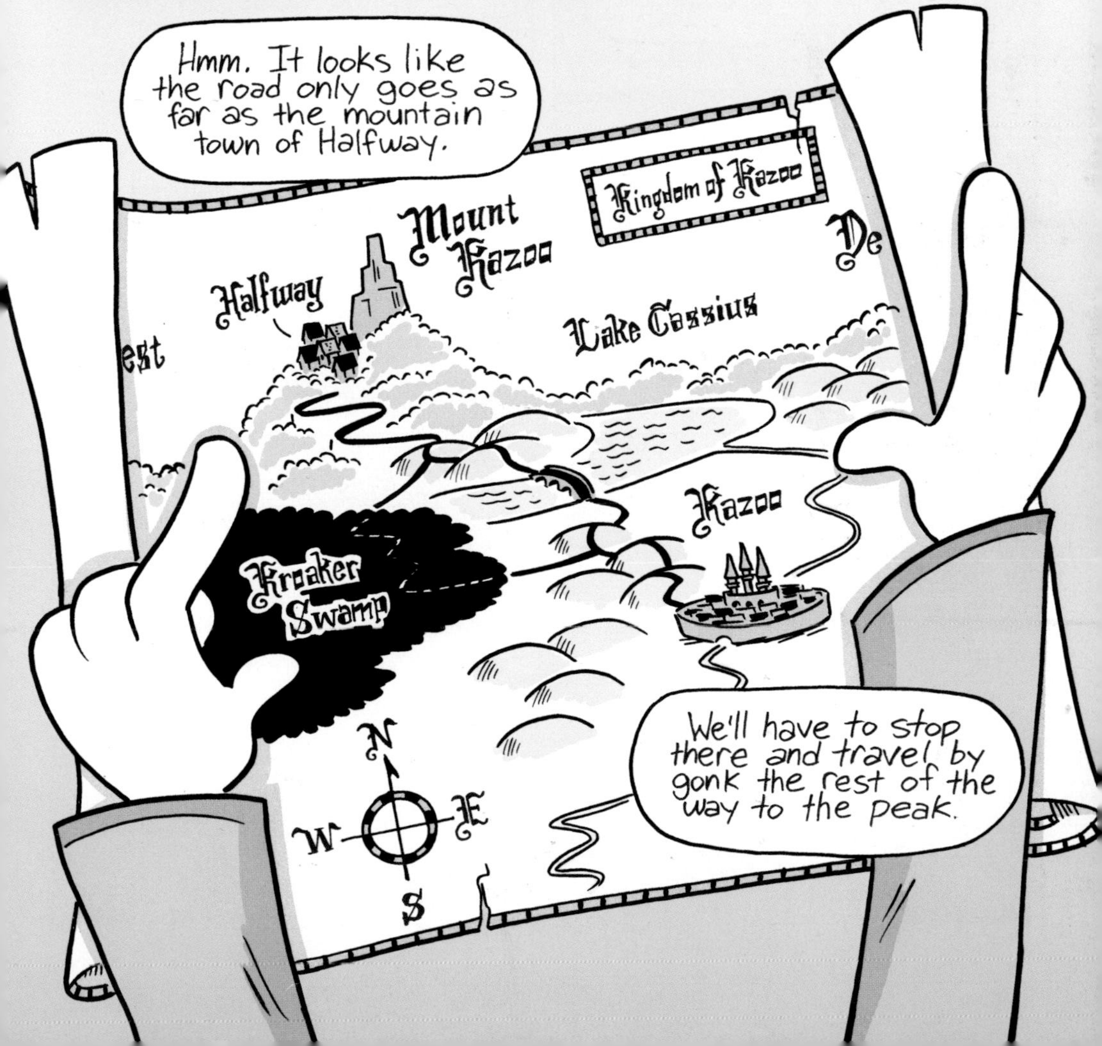
Hmm. It looks like the road only goes as far as the mountain town of Halfway.
Kingdom of Kazoo
Mount Kazoo
De
Halfway
Lake Cassius
est
Kazoo
Kroaker Swamp
N
W
E
S
We'll have to stop there and travel by gonk the rest of the way to the peak.

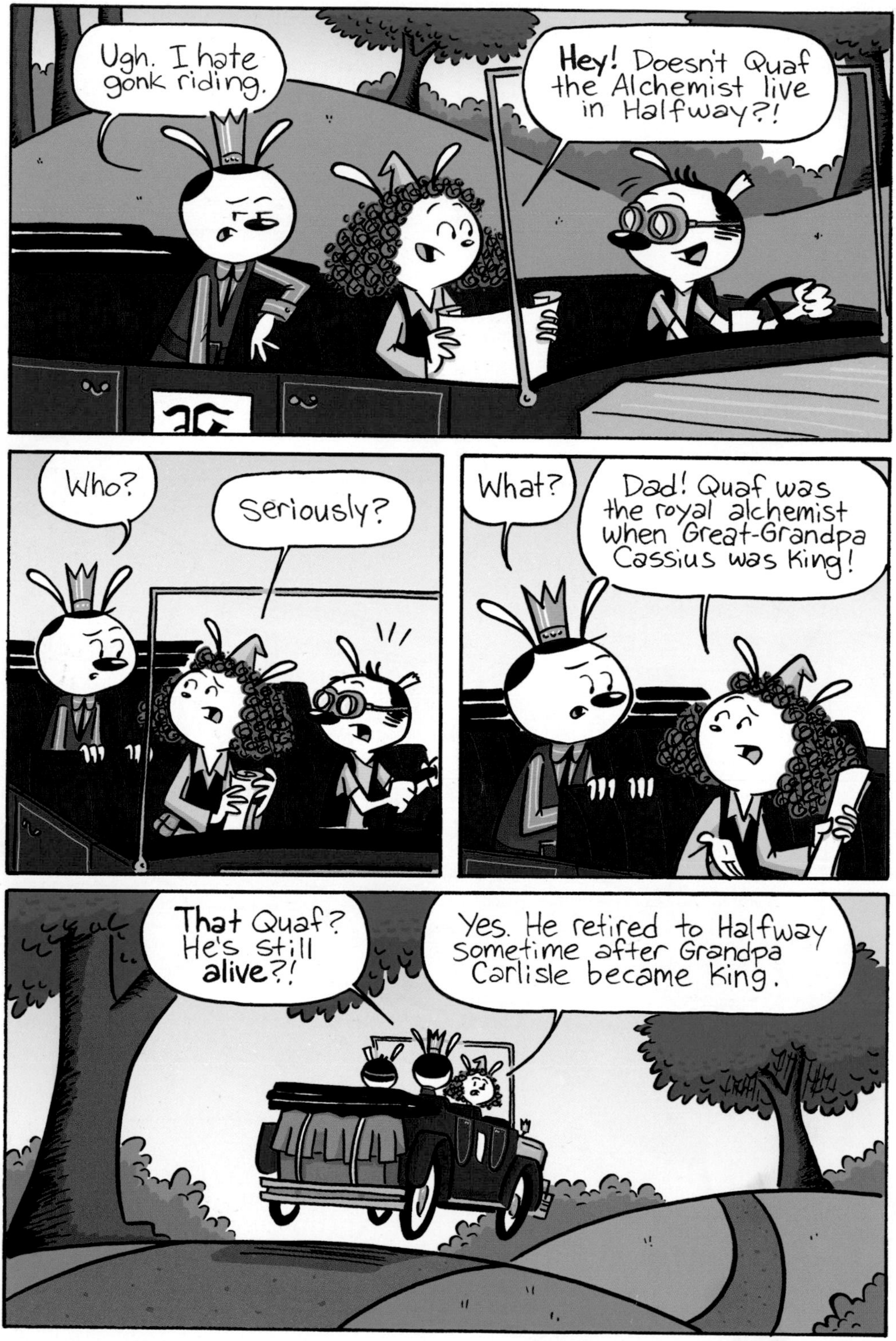

Ugh. I hate gonk riding.
Hey! Doesn't Quaf the Alchemist live in Halfway?!
Who?
Seriously?
What?
Dad! Quaf was the royal alchemist when Great-Grandpa Cassius was King!
That Quaf? He's still alive?!
Yes. He retired to Halfway sometime after Grandpa Carlisle became King.

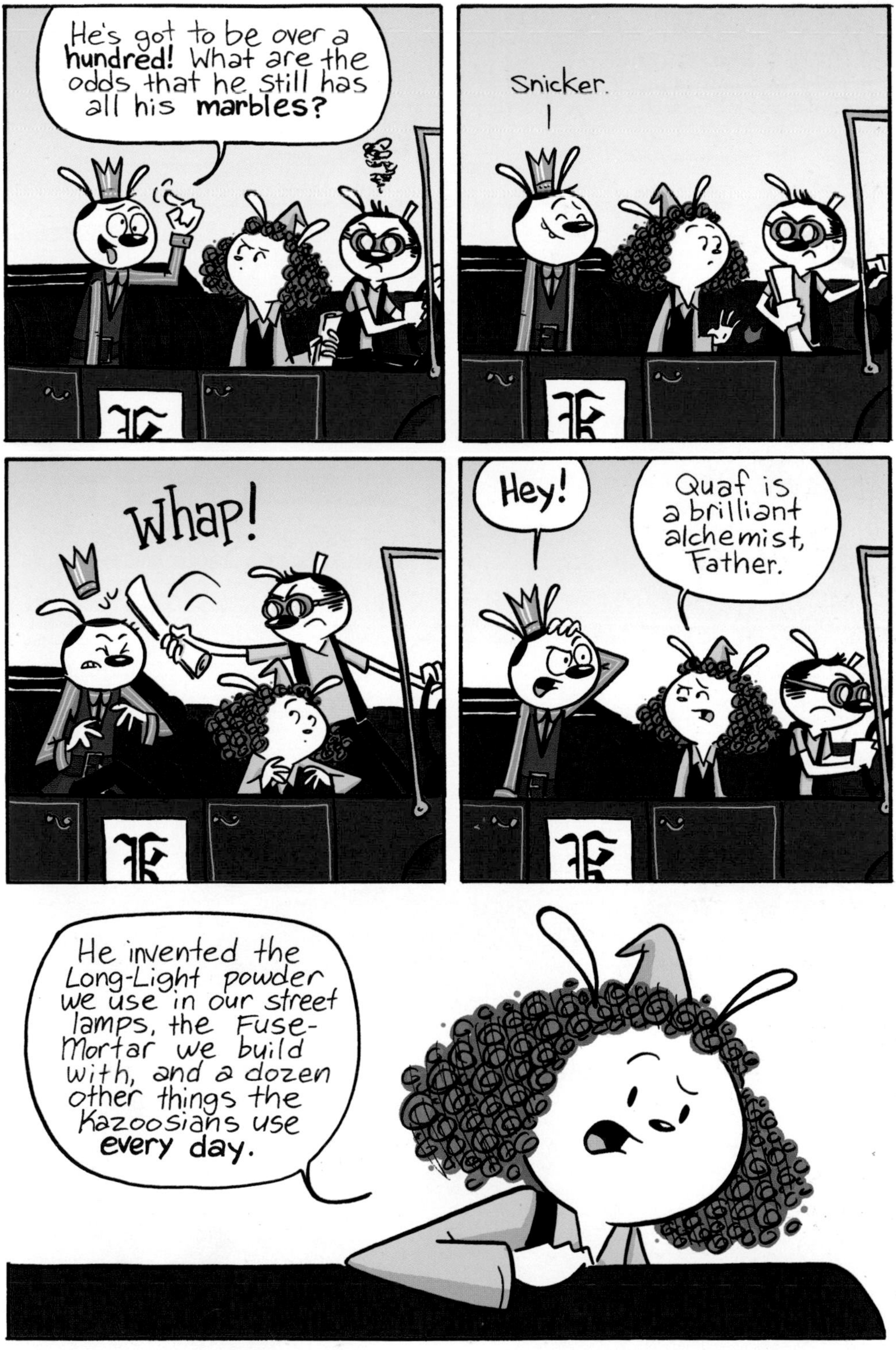
He's got to be over a **hundred!** What are the odds that he still has all his **marbles?**
Snicker.
Whap!
Hey!
Quaf is a brilliant alchemist, Father.
He invented the Long-Light powder we use in our street lamps, the Fuse-Mortar we build with, and a dozen other things the Kazoosians use **every day**.

He's a master of magic **and** science-- a true genius. He deserves our respect.

Yes, yes, fine. I guess, it can't hurt to **talk** to him.

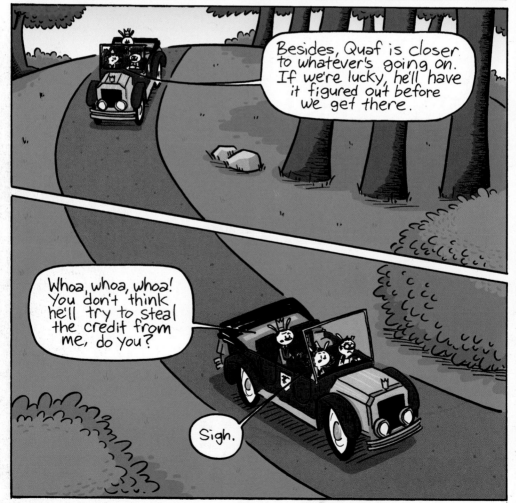

Besides, Quaf is closer to whatever's going on. If we're lucky, he'll have it figured out before we get there.

Whoa, whoa, whoa! You don't think he'll try to steal the credit from me, do you?

Sigh.

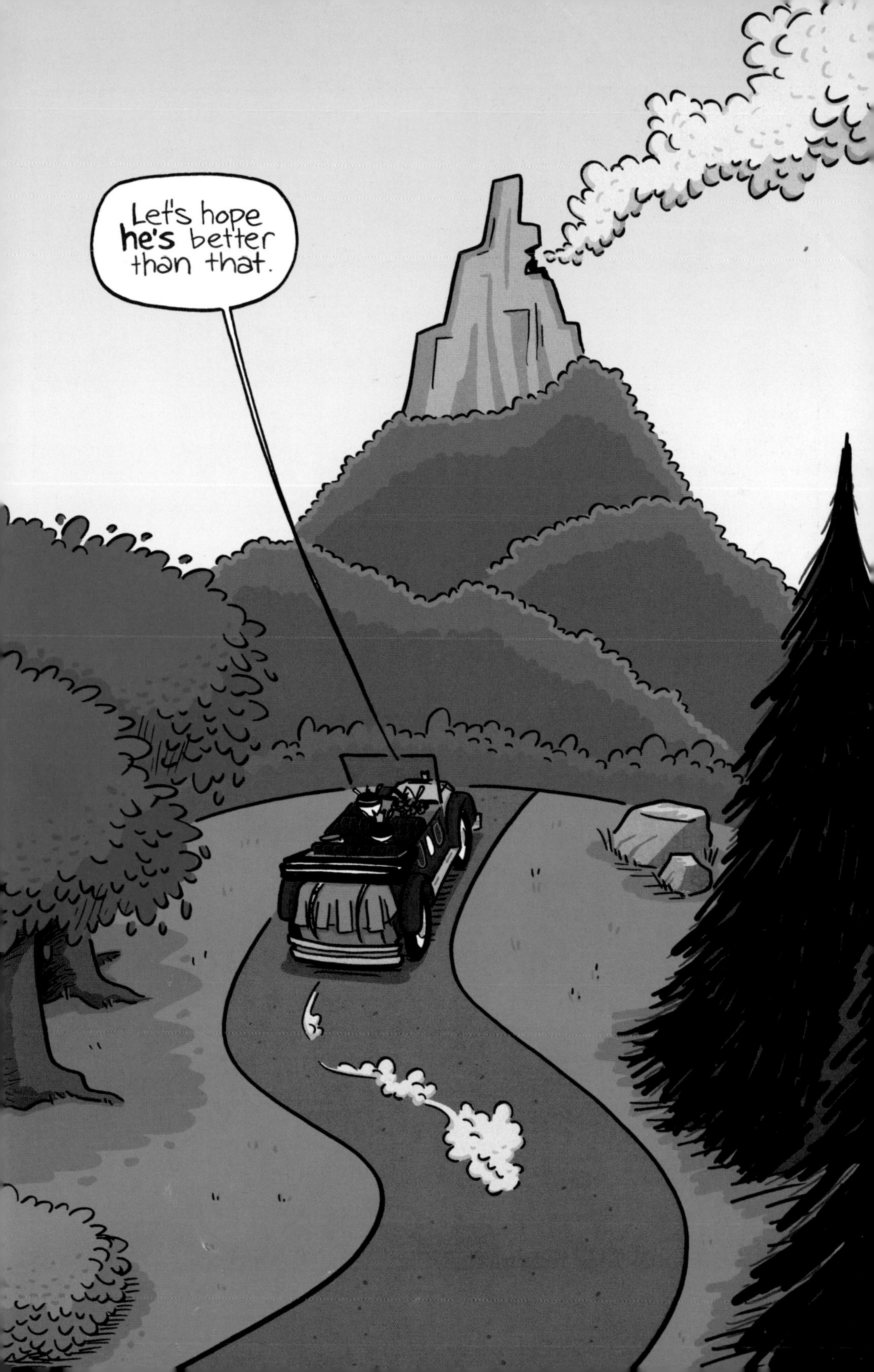
Let's hope **he's** better than that.

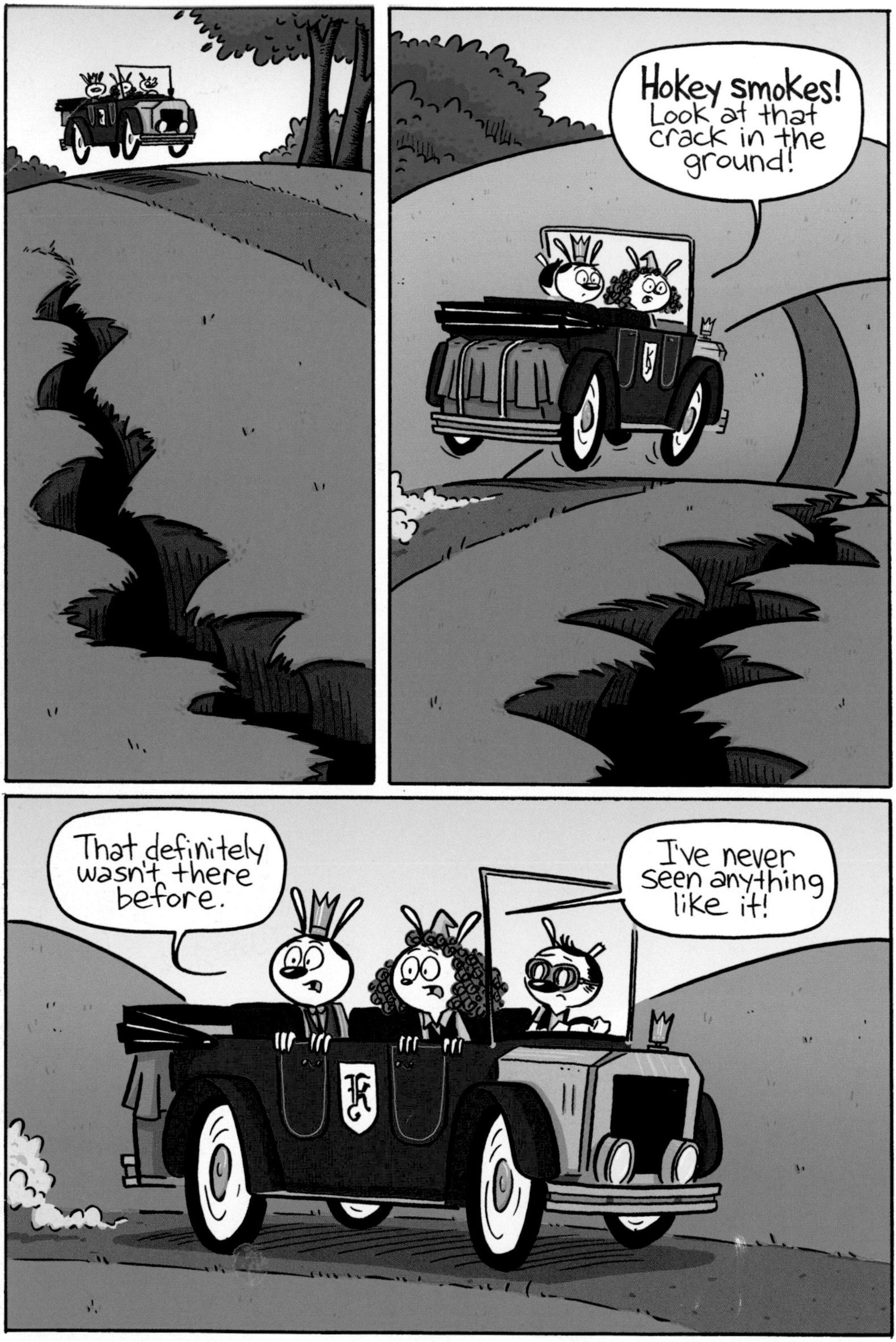
Hokey smokes! Look at that crack in the ground!
That definitely wasn't there before.
I've never seen anything like it!

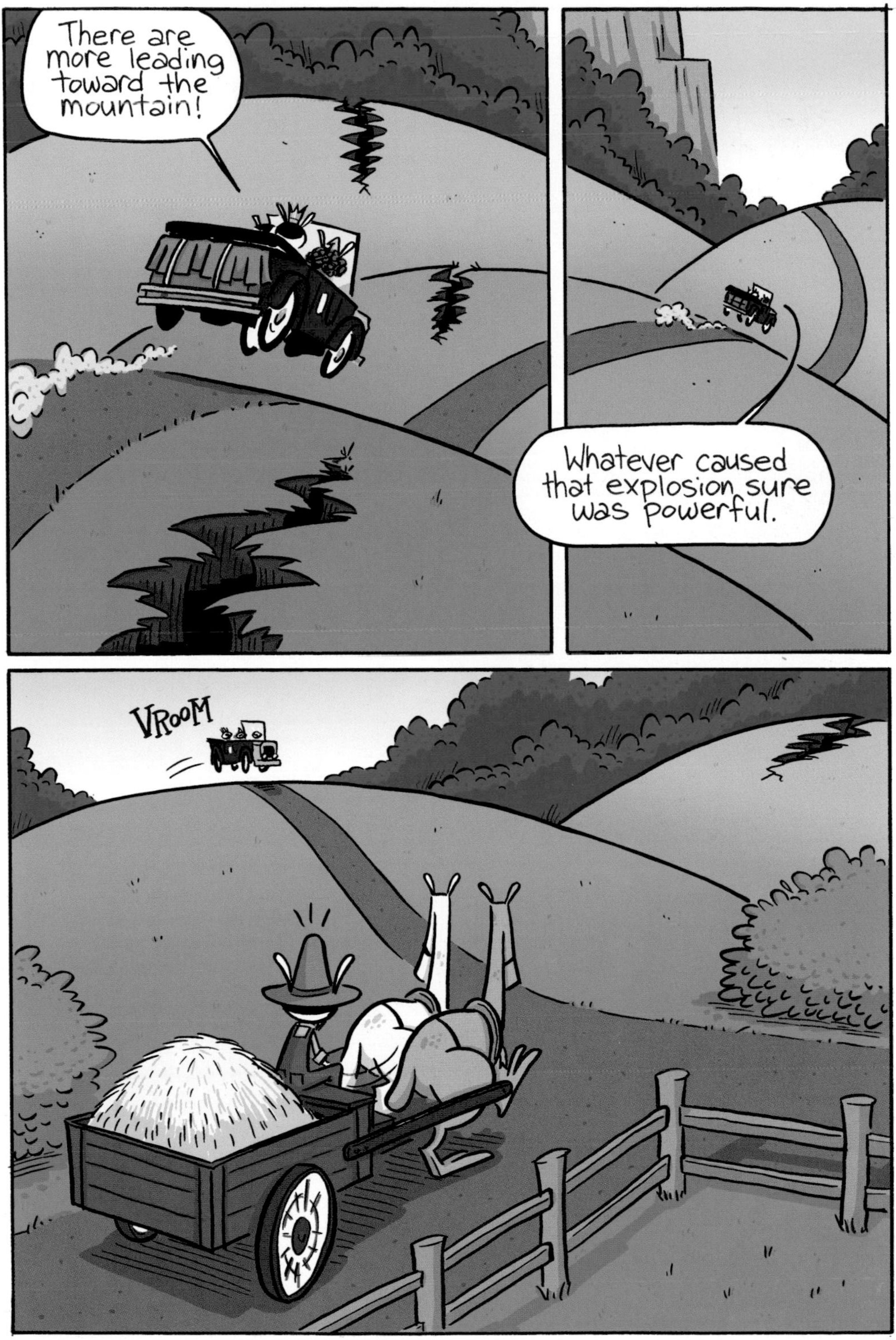
There are more leading toward the mountain!
Whatever caused that explosion sure was powerful.
VROOM

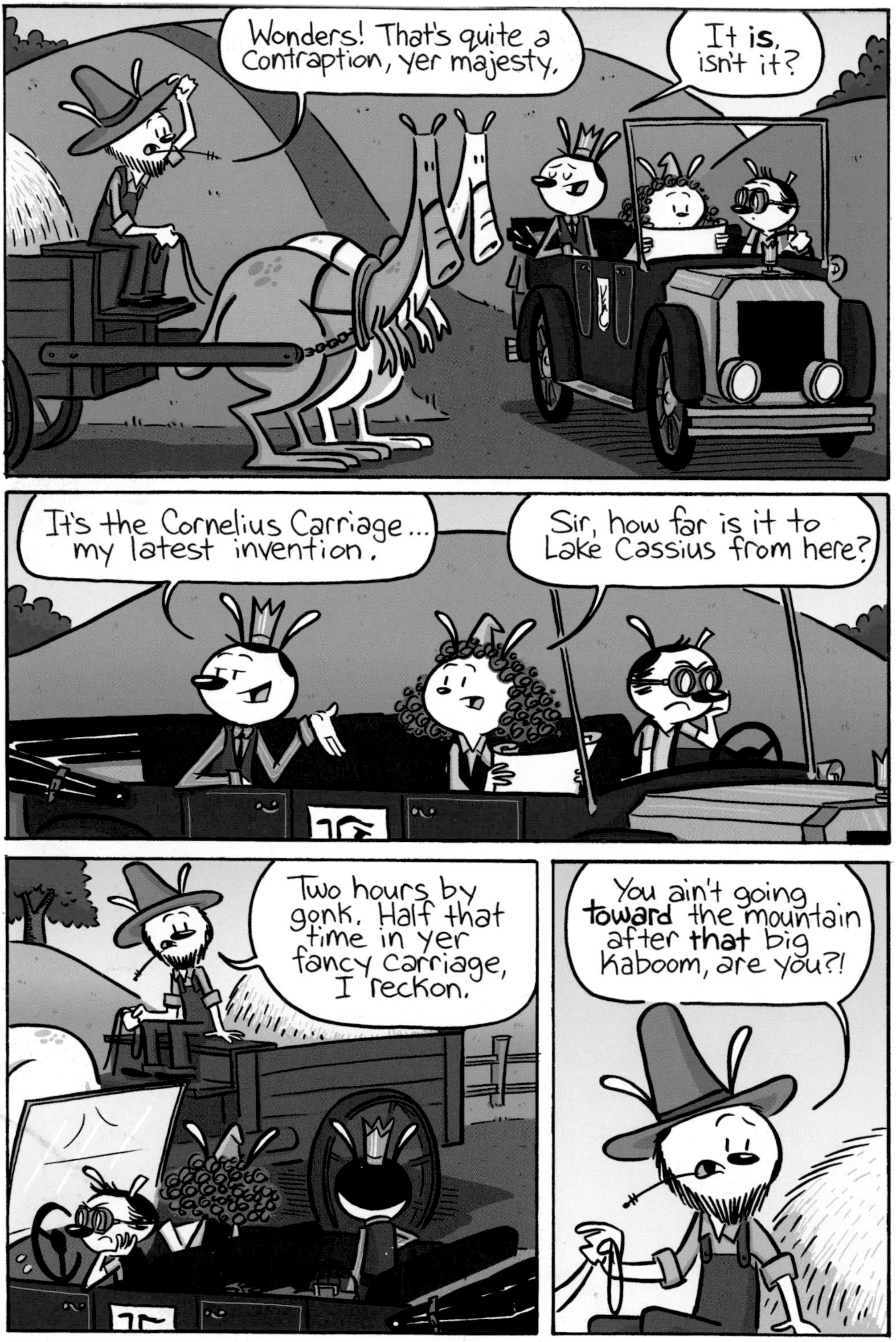
Wonders! That's quite a Contraption, yer majesty.
It **is**, isn't it?
It's the Cornelius Carriage... my latest invention.
Sir, how far is it to Lake Cassius from here?
Two hours by gonk. Half that time in yer fancy carriage, I reckon.
You ain't going **toward** the mountain after **that** big Kaboom, are you?!

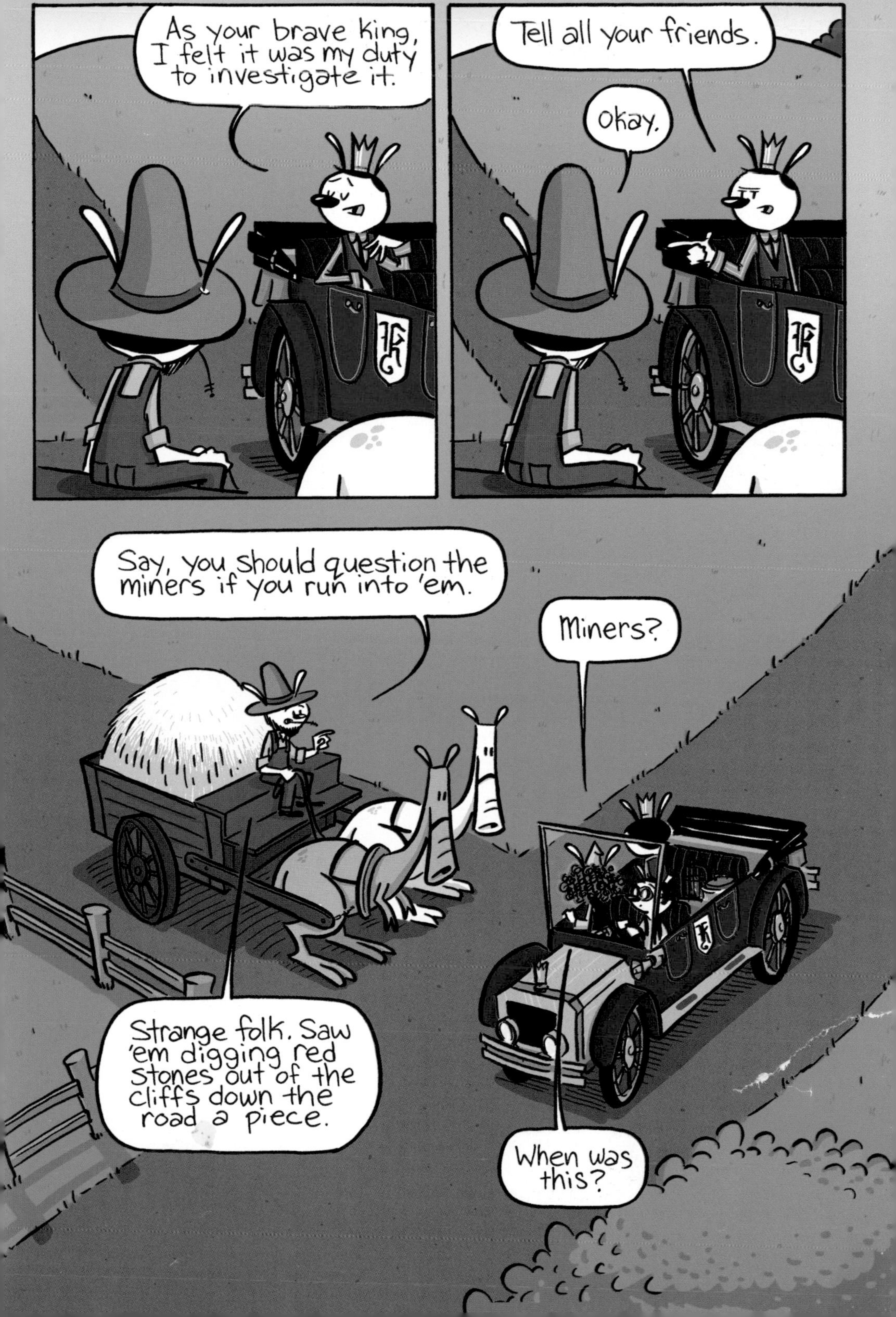
As your brave King, I felt it was my duty to investigate it.
Tell all your friends.
Okay.
Say, you should question the miners if you run into 'em.
Miners?
Strange folk. Saw 'em digging red stones out of the cliffs down the road a piece.
When was this?

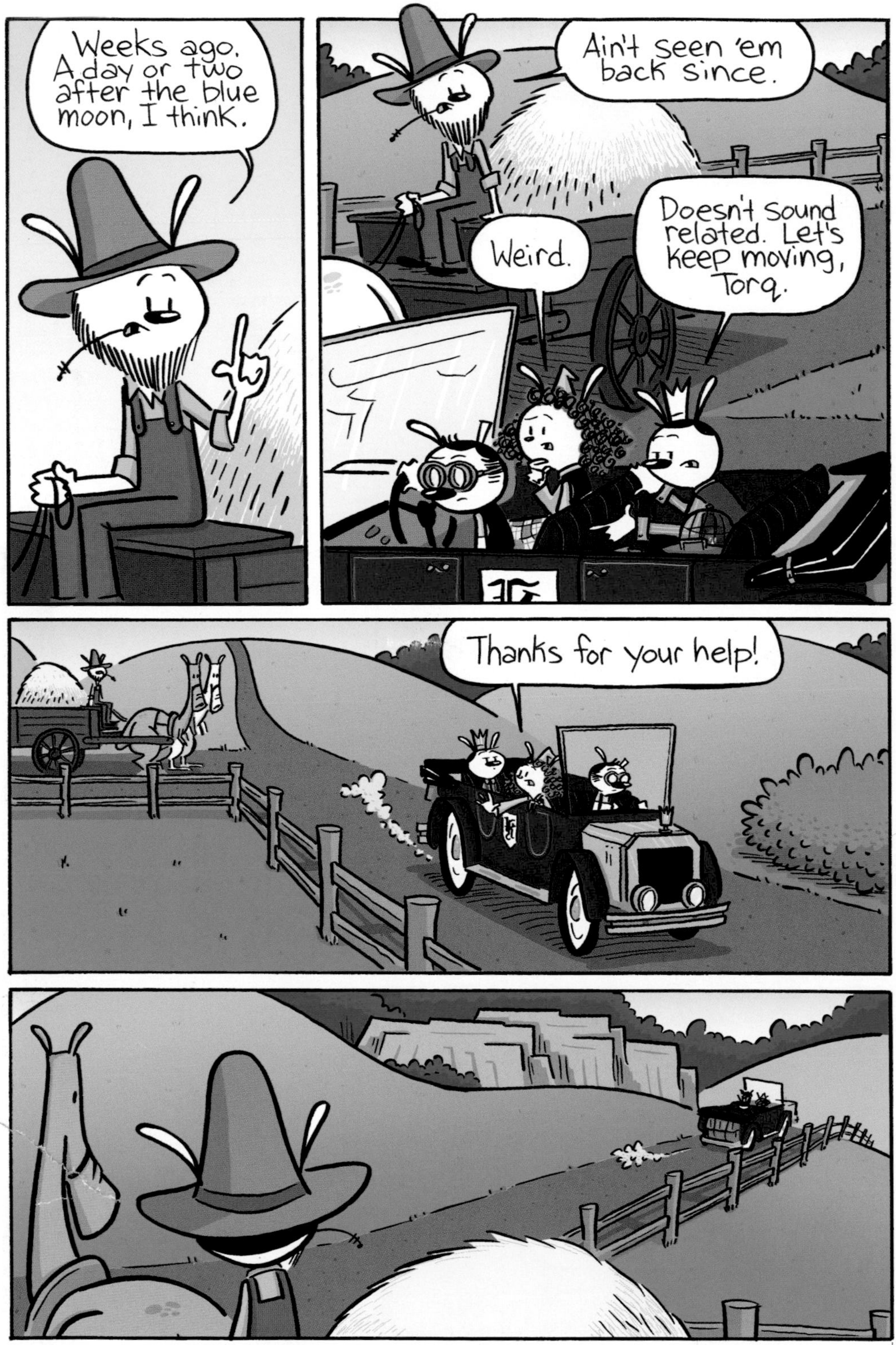
Weeks ago. A day or two after the blue moon, I think.
Ain't seen 'em back since.
Weird.
Doesn't sound related. Let's keep moving, Torq.
Thanks for your help!

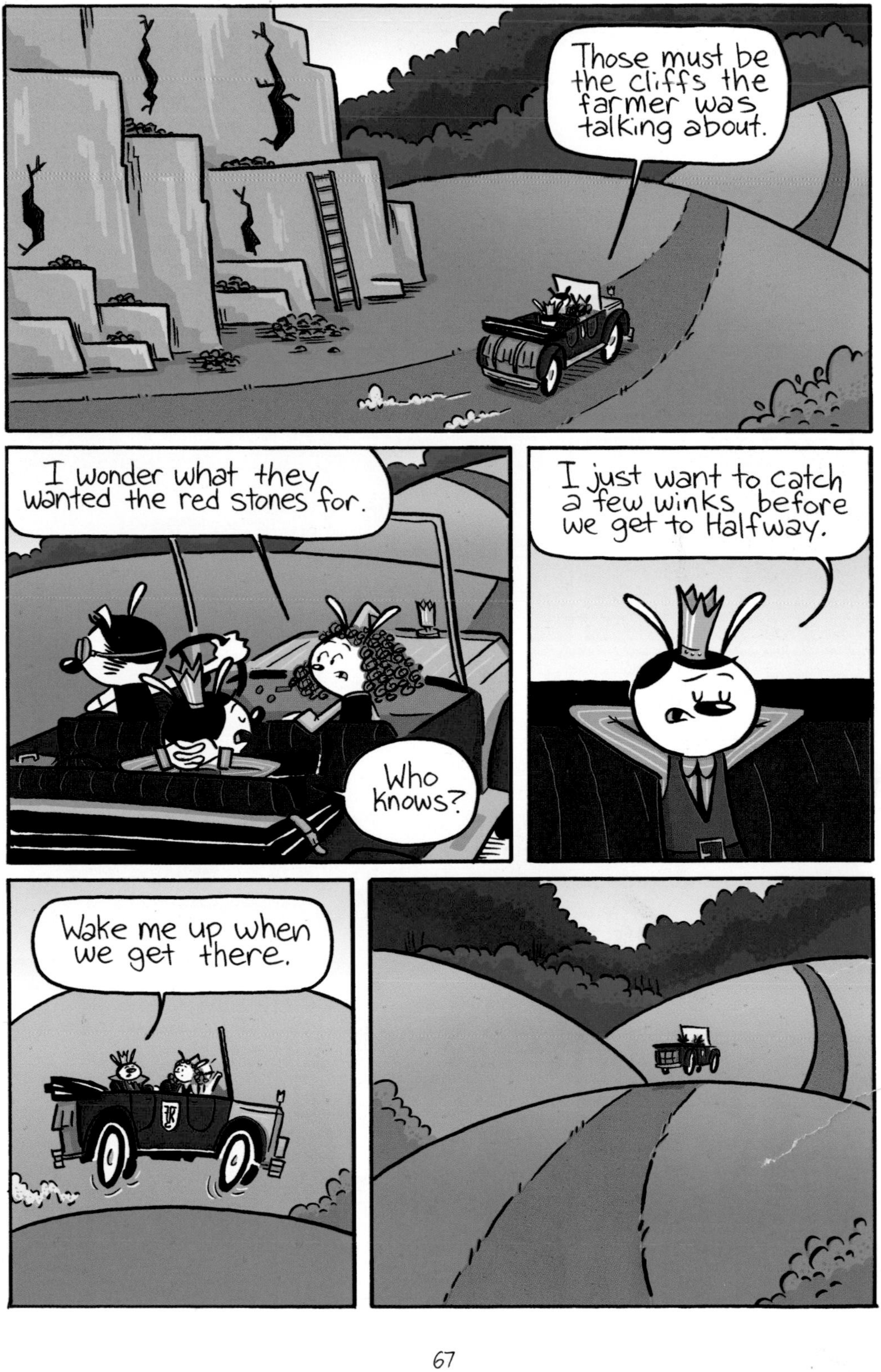
Those must be the cliffs the farmer was talking about.
I wonder what they wanted the red stones for.
Who knows?
I just want to catch a few winks before we get to Halfway.
Wake me up when we get there.

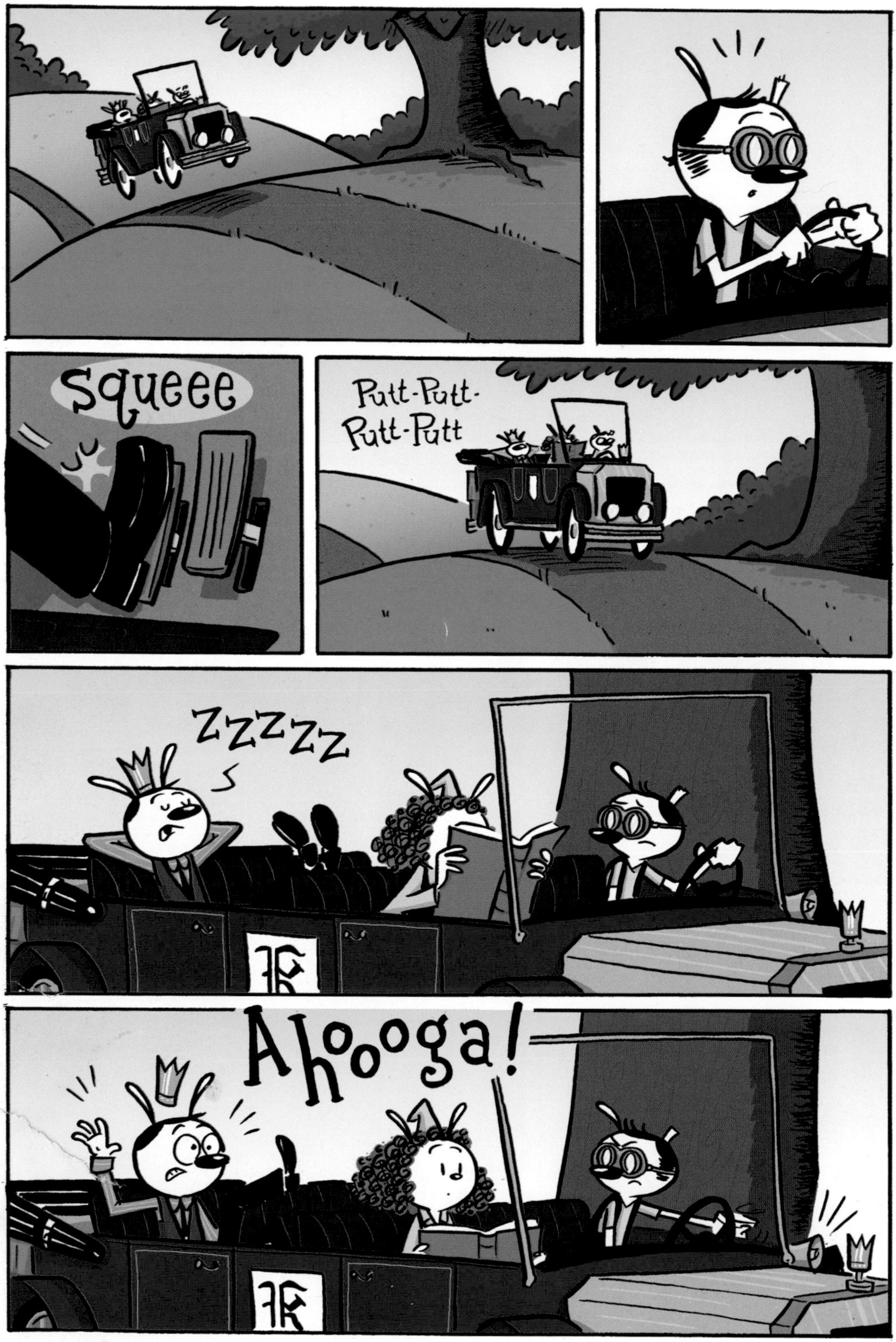
Squeee
Putt-Putt-
Putt-Putt
ZZZZZ
Ahoooga!

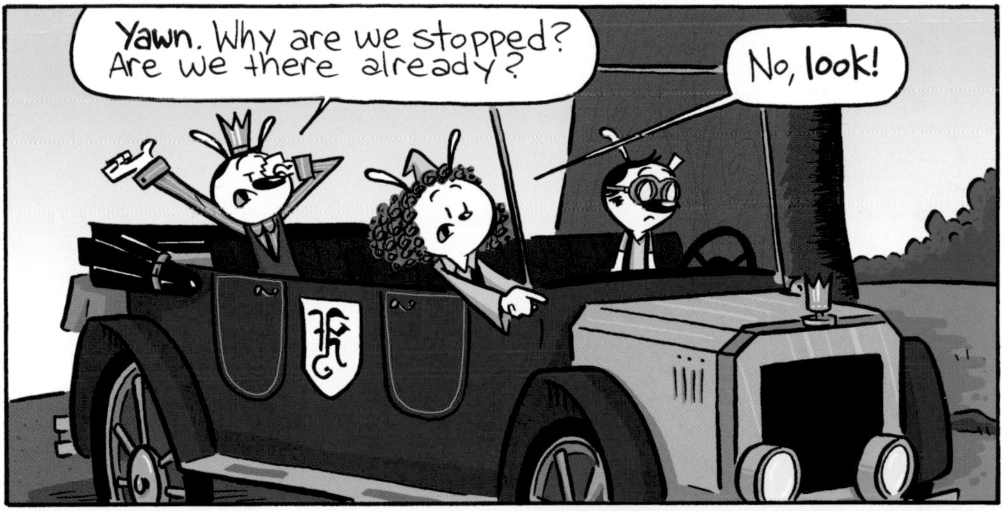
Yawn. Why are we stopped? Are we there already?
No, look!

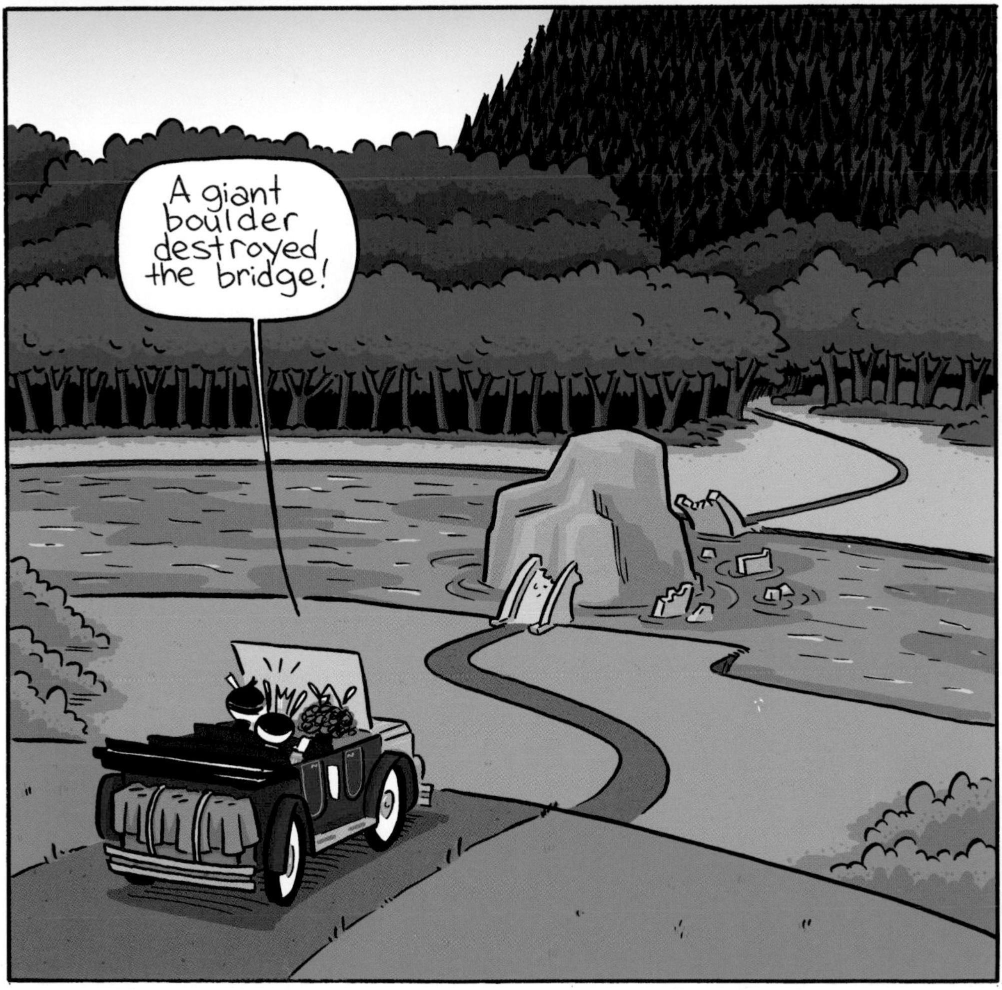
A giant boulder destroyed the bridge!

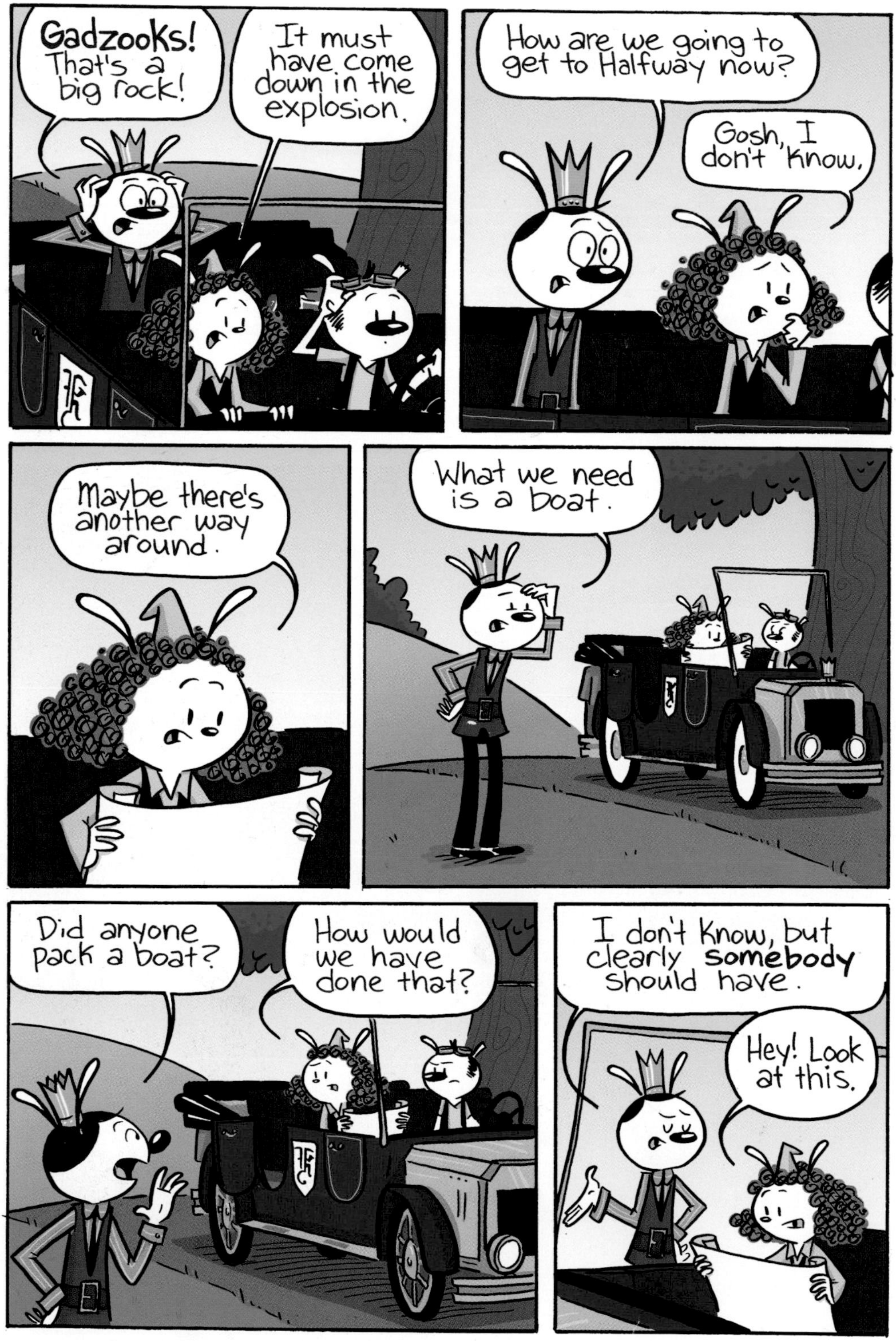
Gadzooks! That's a big rock!
It must have come down in the explosion.
How are we going to get to Halfway now?
Gosh, I don't know.
Maybe there's another way around.
What we need is a boat.
Did anyone pack a boat?
How would we have done that?
I don't know, but clearly **somebody** should have.
Hey! Look at this.

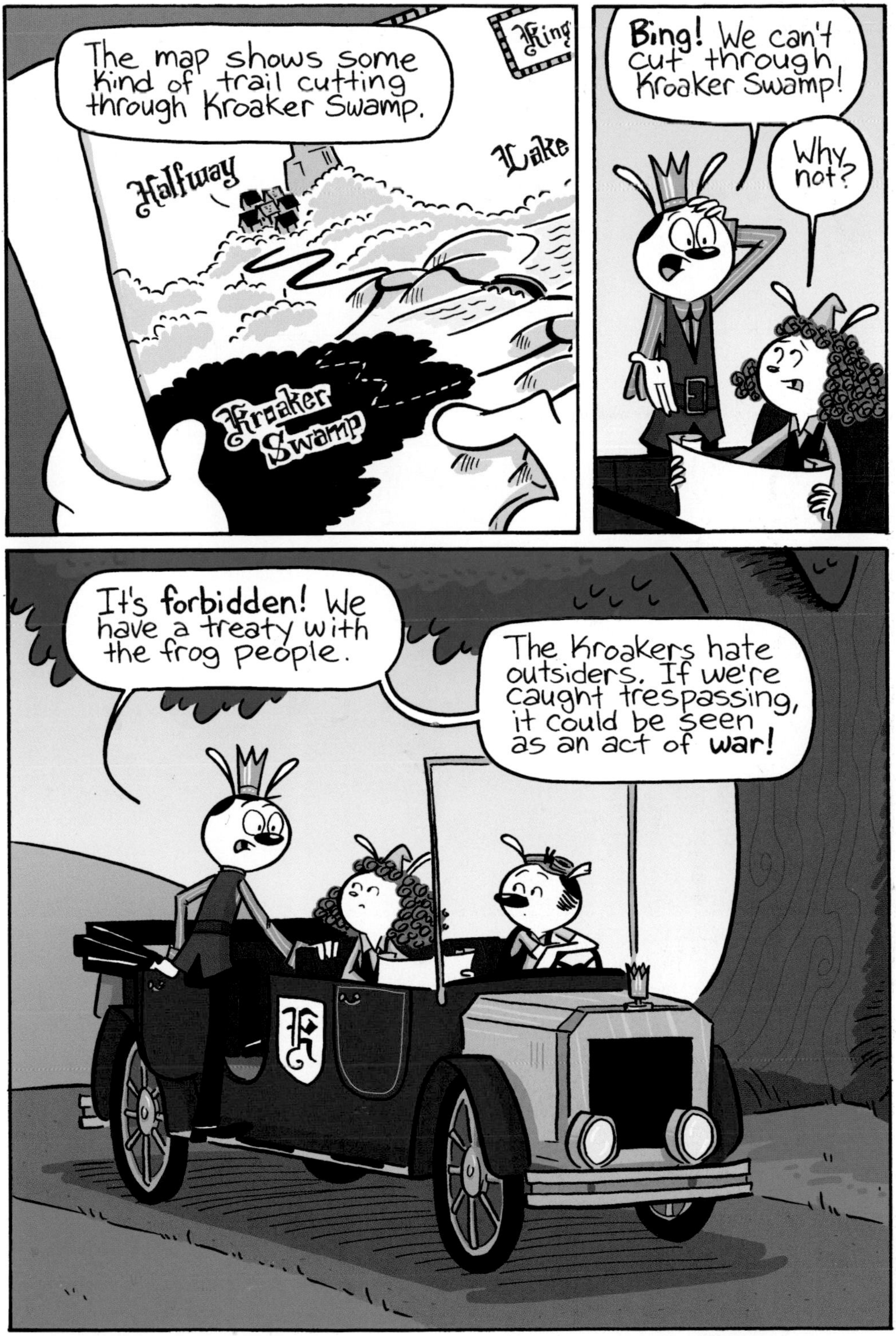
King
The map shows some kind of trail cutting through Kroaker Swamp.
Lake
Halfway
Kroaker Swamp
Bing! We can't cut through Kroaker Swamp!
Why not?
It's **forbidden!** We have a treaty with the frog people.
The Kroakers hate outsiders. If we're caught trespassing, it could be seen as an act of **war!**

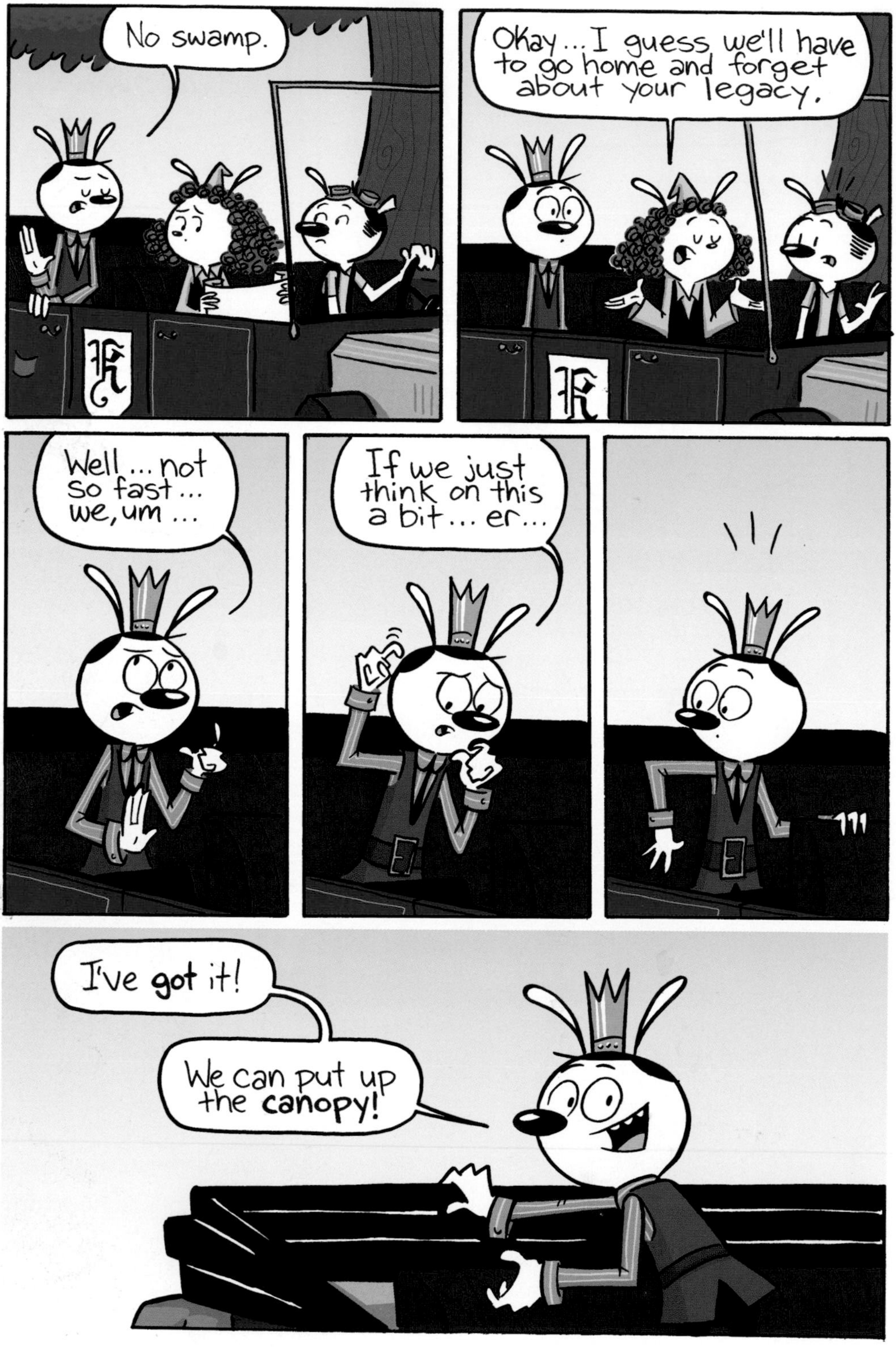
No swamp.
Okay... I guess we'll have to go home and forget about your legacy.
Well... not so fast... we, um...
If we just think on this a bit... er...
I've **got** it!
We can put up the **canopy**!

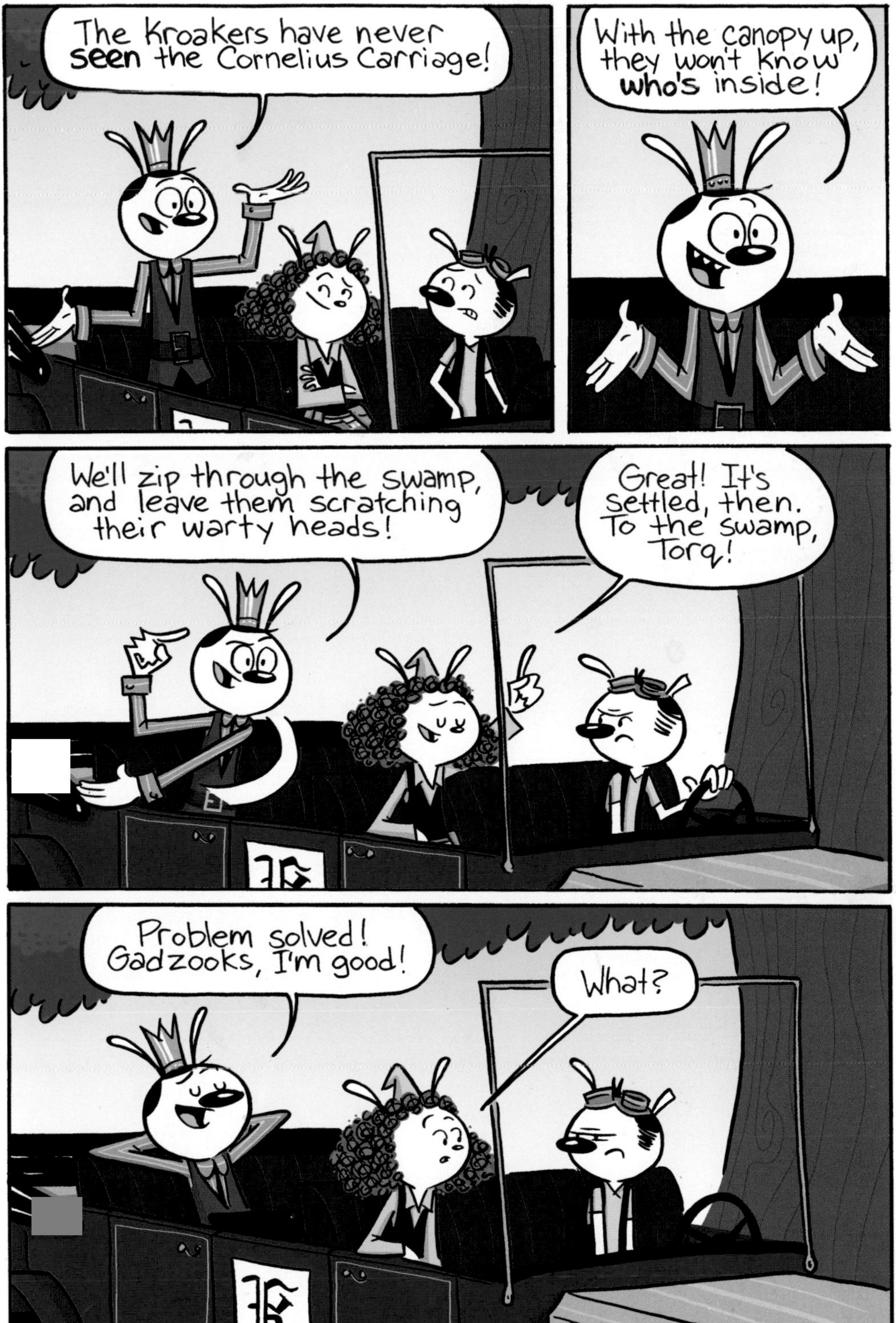
The Kroakers have never **seen** the Cornelius Carriage!
With the canopy up, they won't know **who's** inside!
We'll zip through the swamp, and leave them scratching their warty heads!
Great! It's settled, then. To the swamp, Torq!
Problem solved! Gadzooks, I'm good!
What?

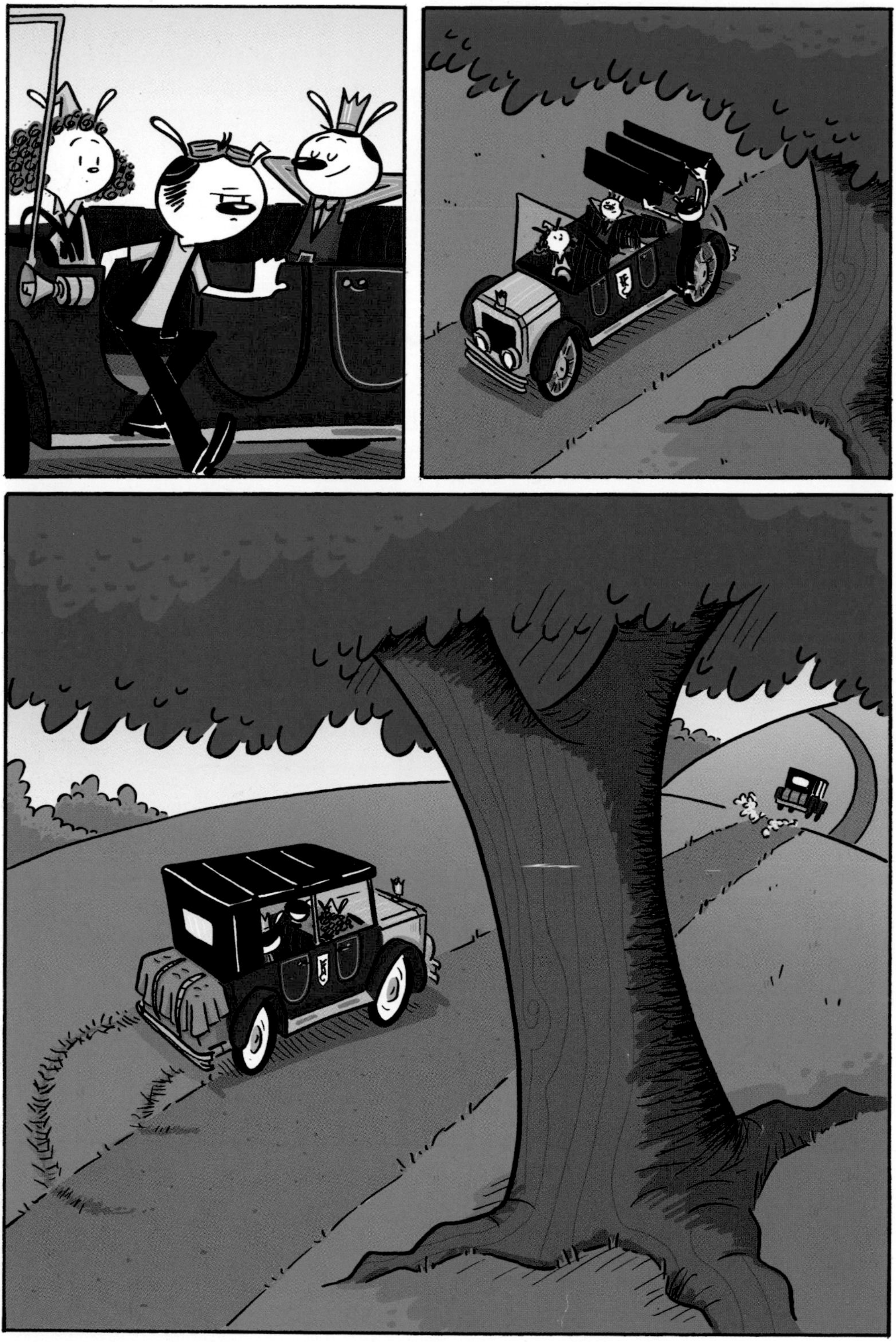

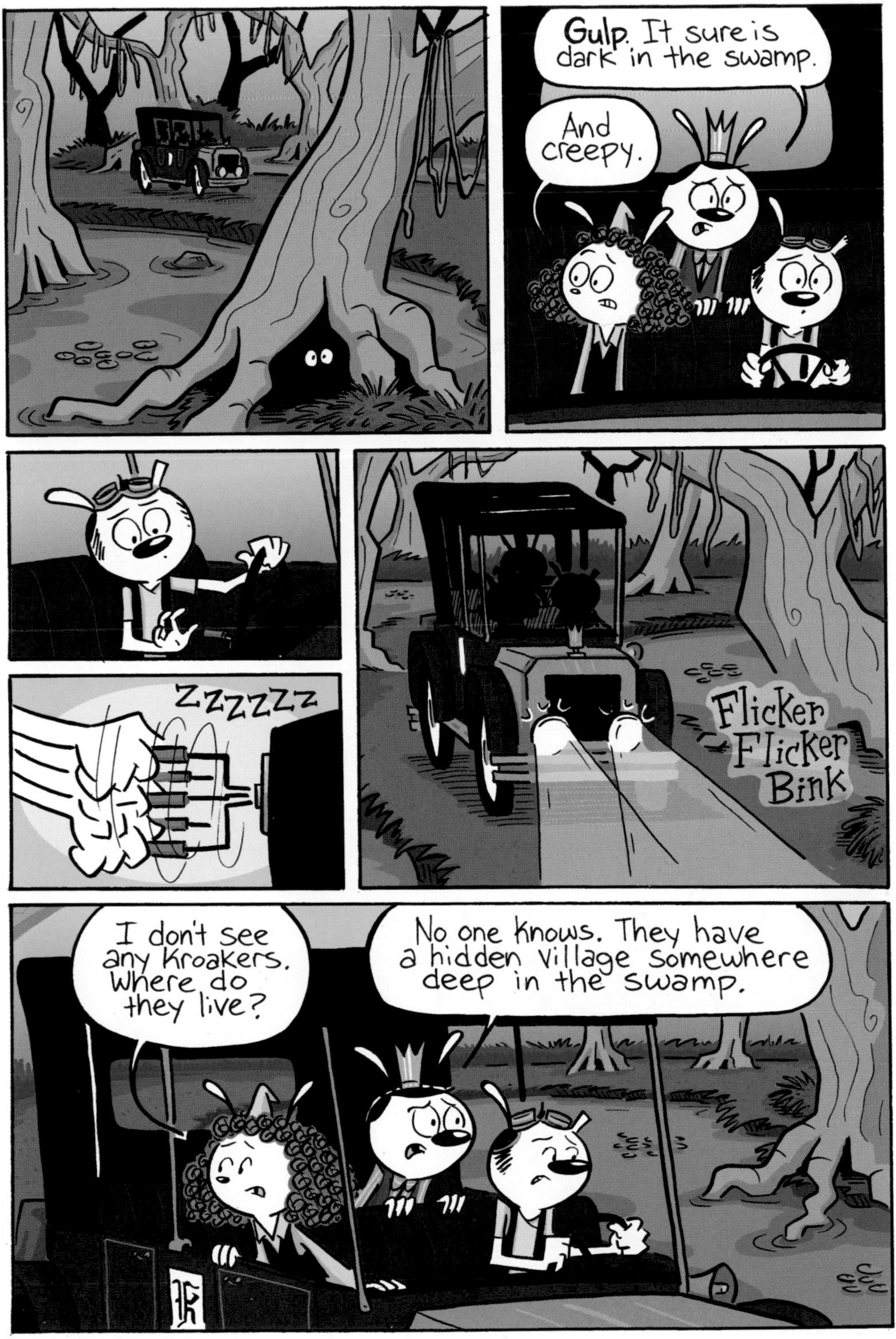
Gulp. It sure is dark in the swamp.
And creepy.
ZZZZZZ
Flicker Flicker Bink
I don't see any Kroakers. Where do they live?
No one knows. They have a hidden village somewhere deep in the swamp.

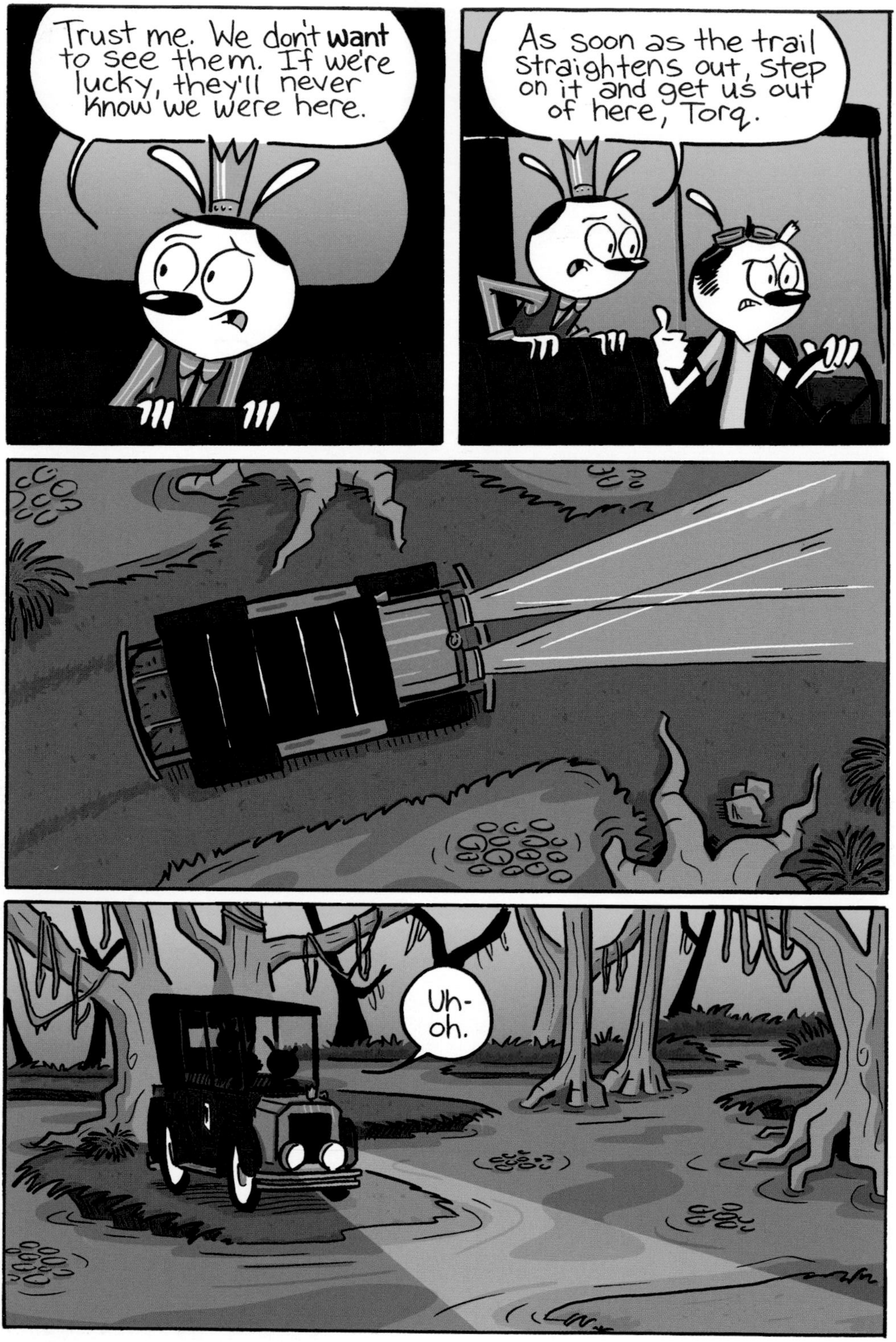
Trust me. We don't **want** to see them. If we're lucky, they'll never know we were here.
As soon as the trail straightens out, step on it and get us out of here, Torq.
Uh-oh.

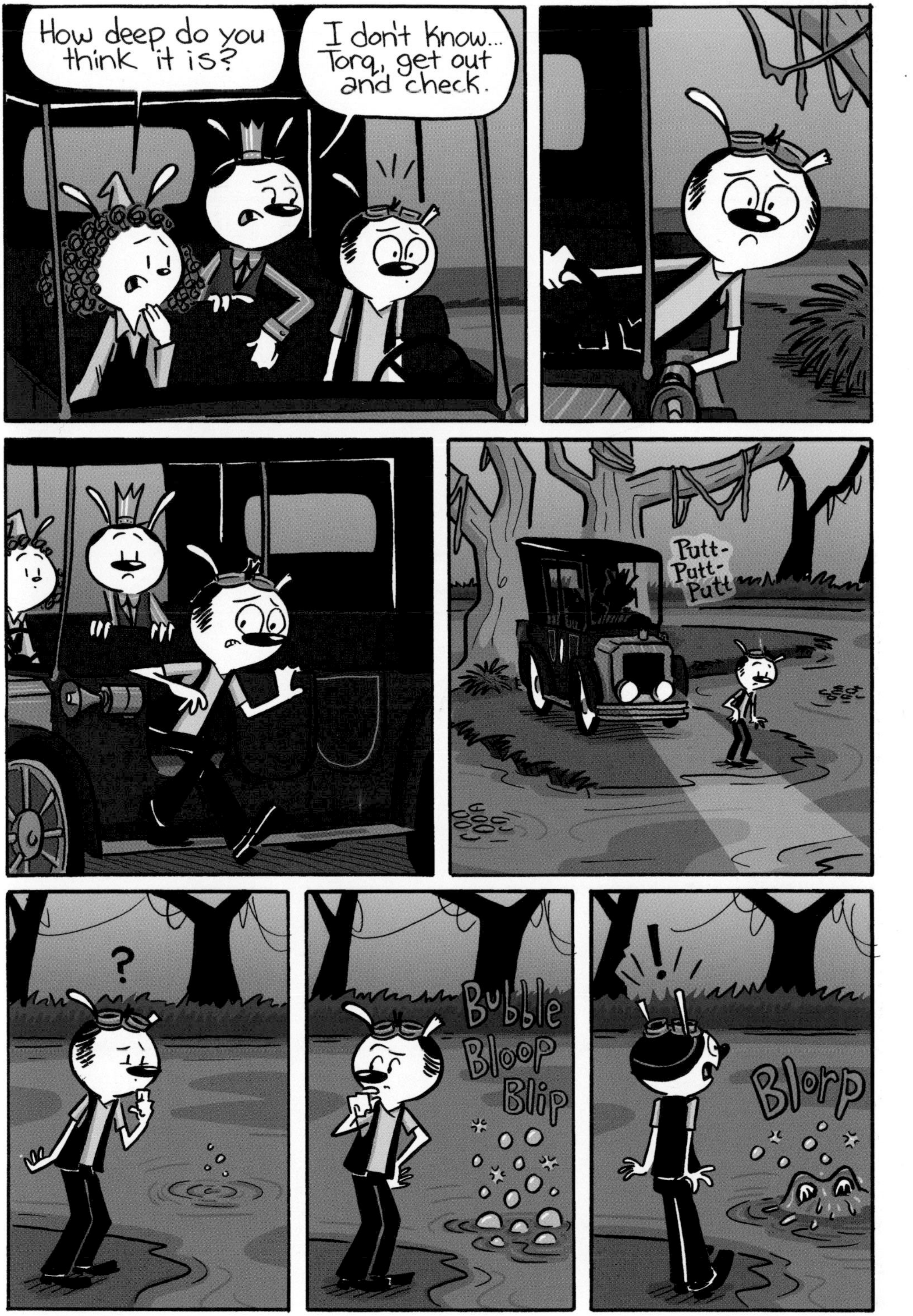
How deep do you think it is?
I don't know... Torq, get out and check.
Putt-Putt-Putt
?
Bubble
Bloop
Blip
!
Blorp

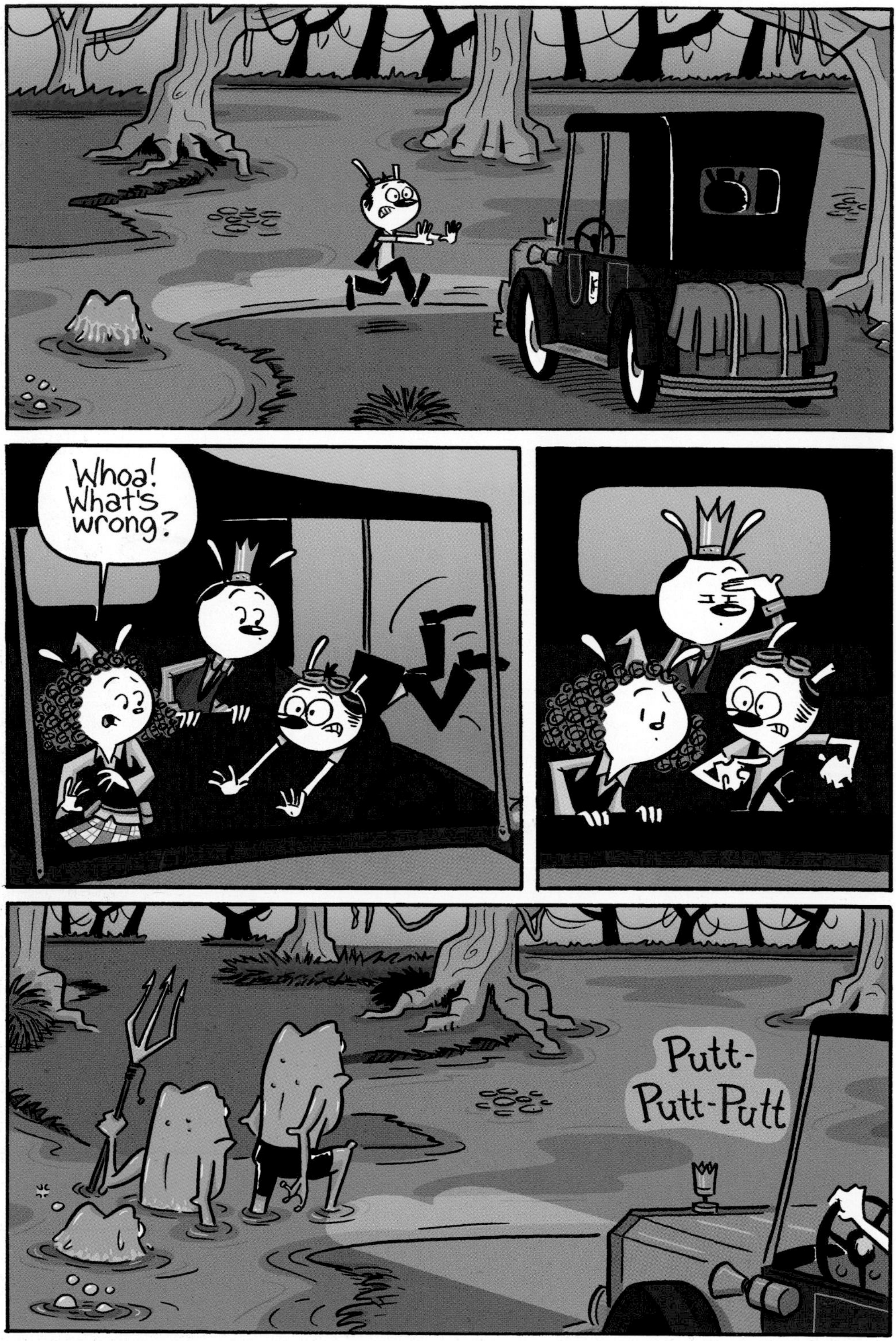
Whoa! What's wrong?
Putt-Putt-Putt

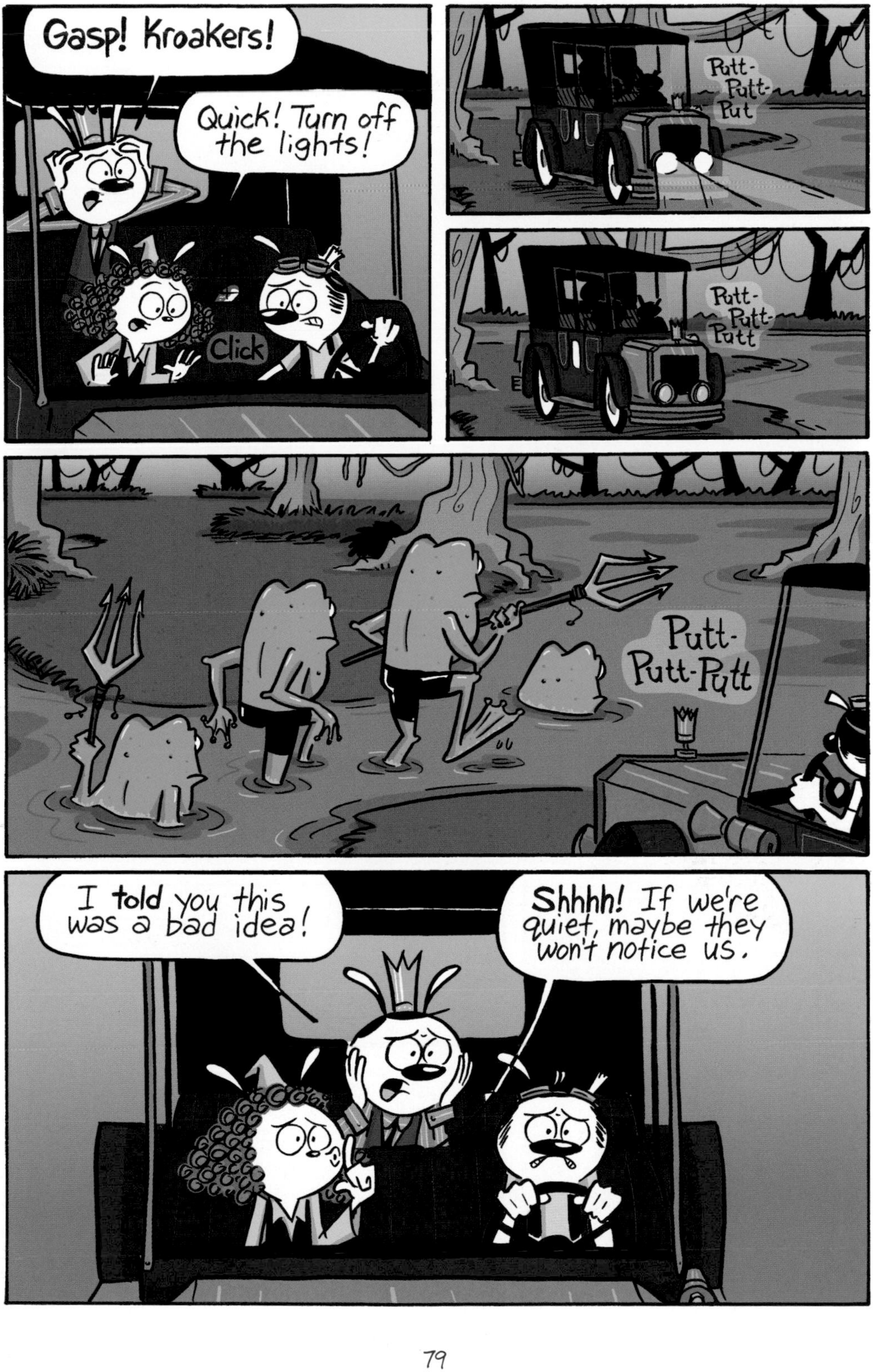
Gasp! Kroakers!
Quick! Turn off the lights!
Click
Putt-Putt-Put
Putt-Putt-Putt
Putt-Putt-Putt
I told you this was a bad idea!
Shhhh! If we're quiet, maybe they won't notice us.

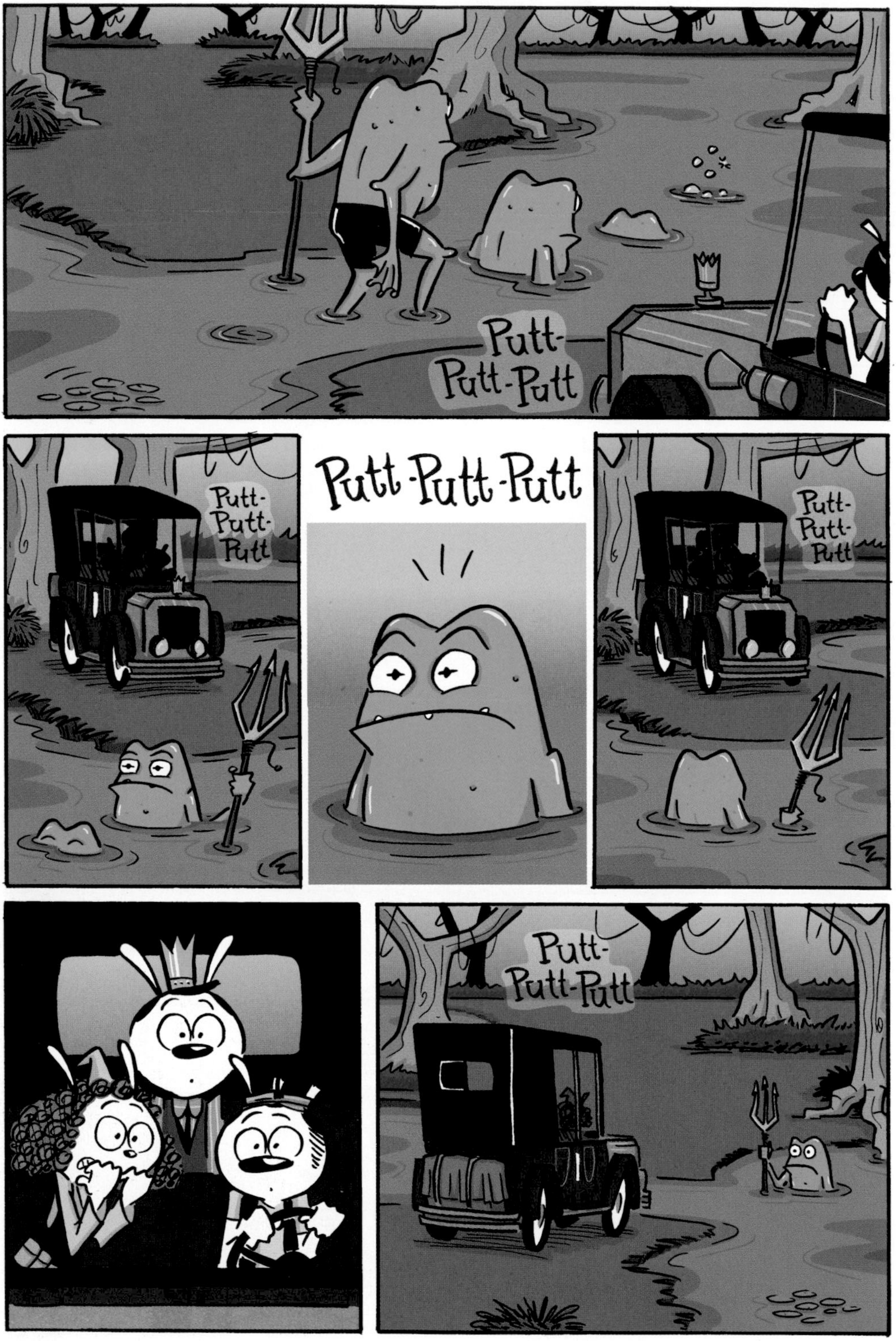
Putt-
Putt-Putt
Putt-
Putt-
Putt
Putt-Putt-Putt
Putt-
Putt-
Putt
Putt-
Putt-Putt

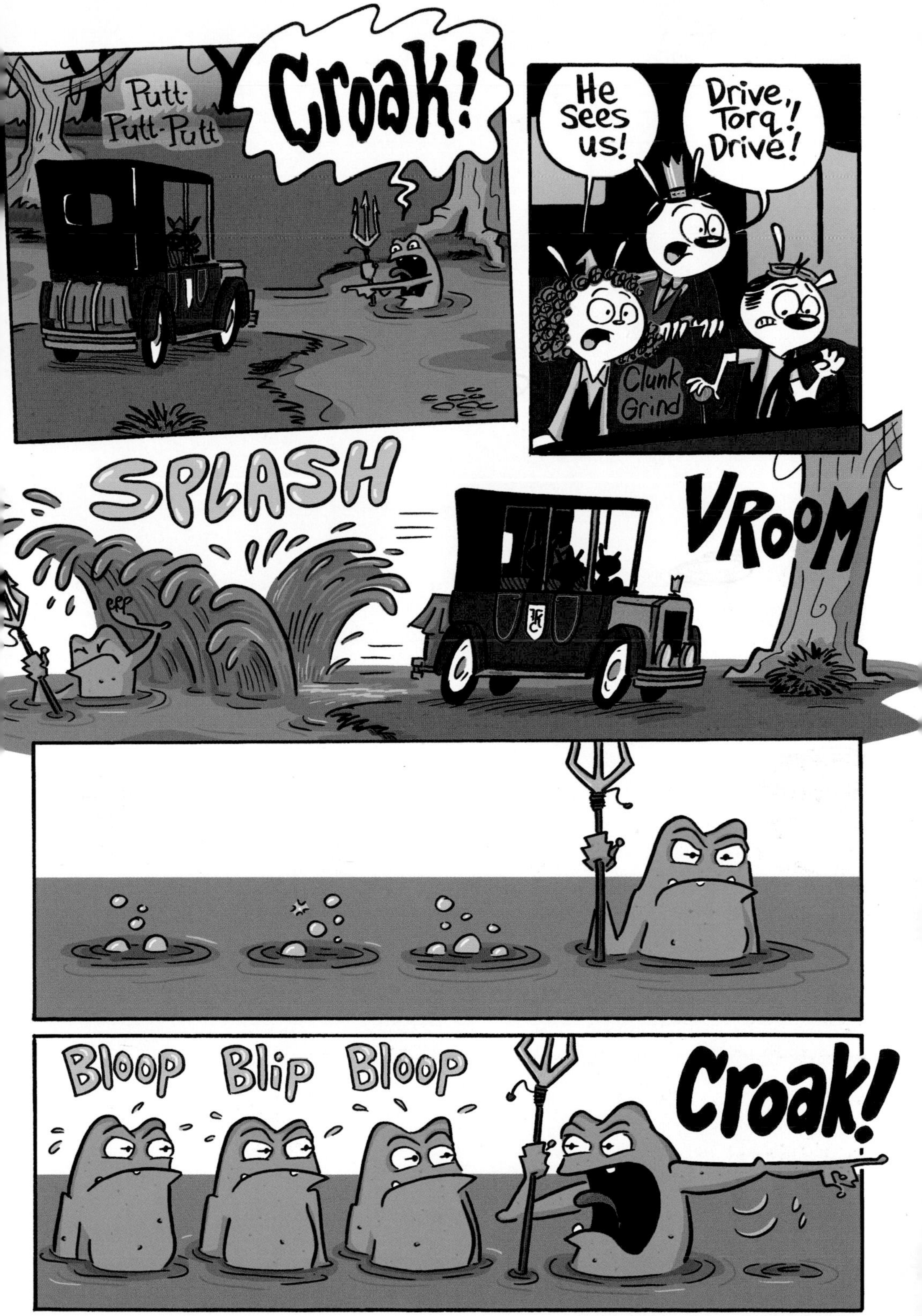
Putt-Putt-Putt
Croak!
He sees us!
Drive, Torq! Drive!
Clunk Grind
SPLASH
VROOM
Bloop Blip Bloop
Croak!

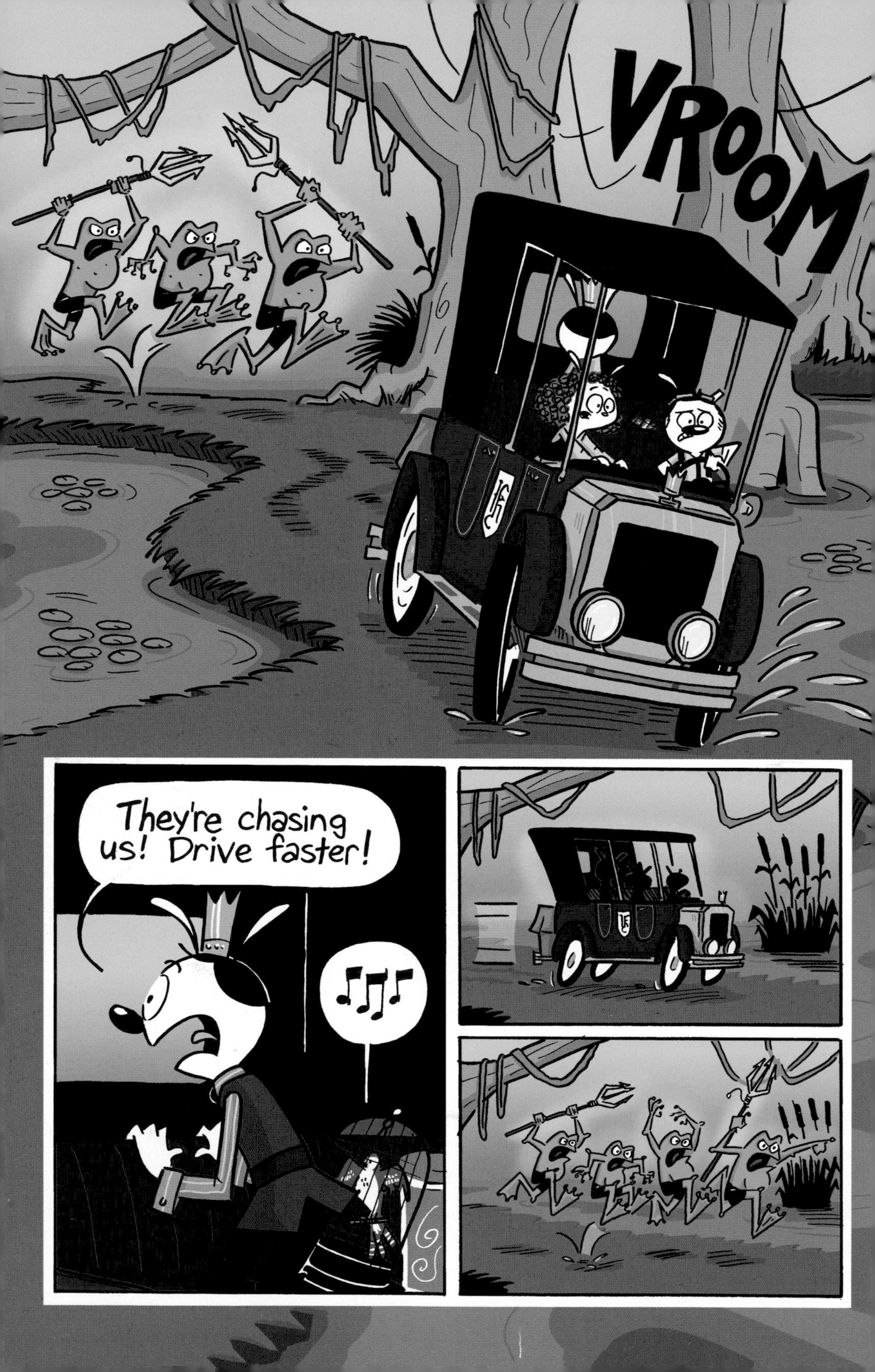
VROOM
They're chasing us! Drive faster!

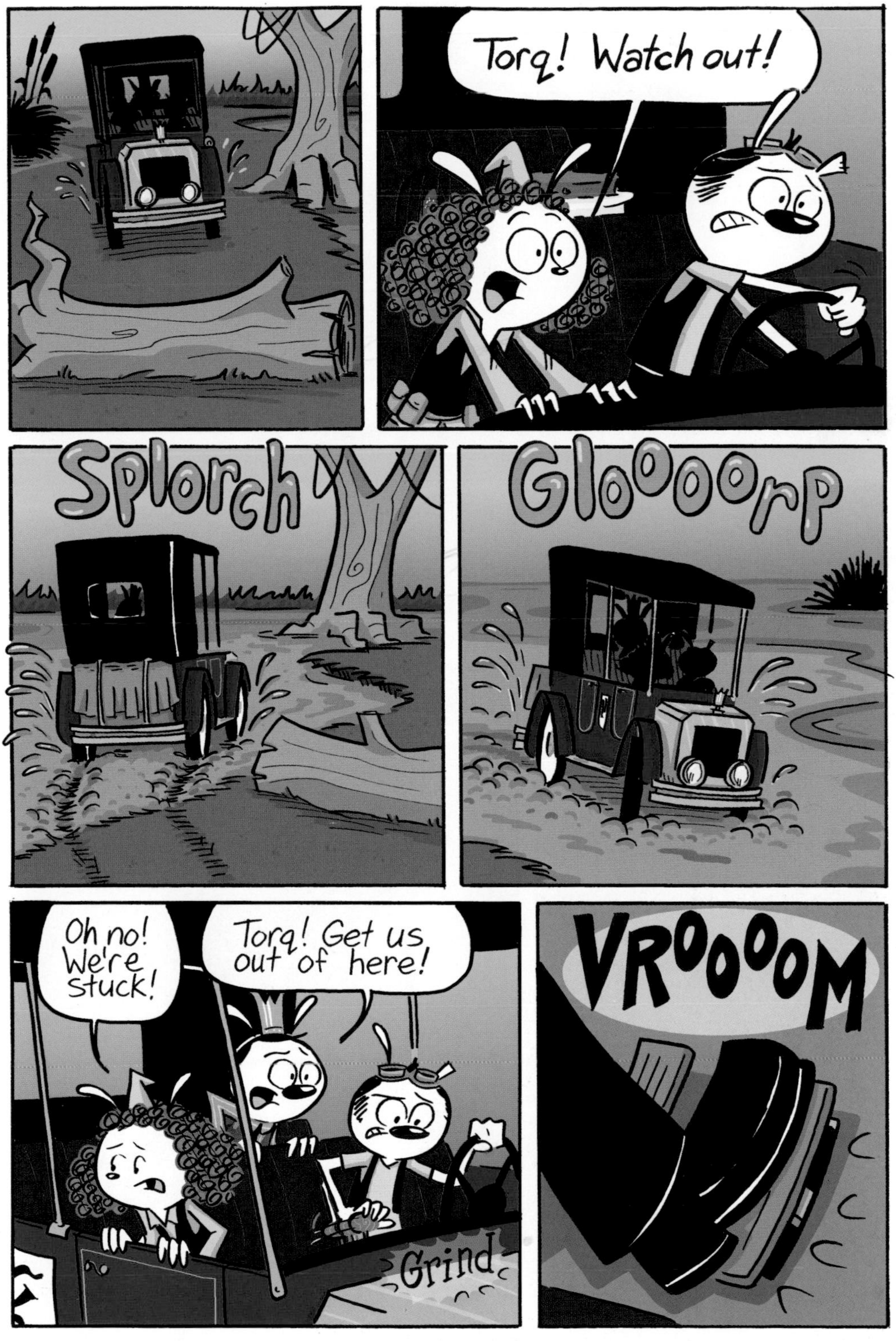
Torq! Watch out!
Splorch
Gloooorp
Oh no! We're stuck!
Torq! Get us out of here!
Grind
VROOOOM

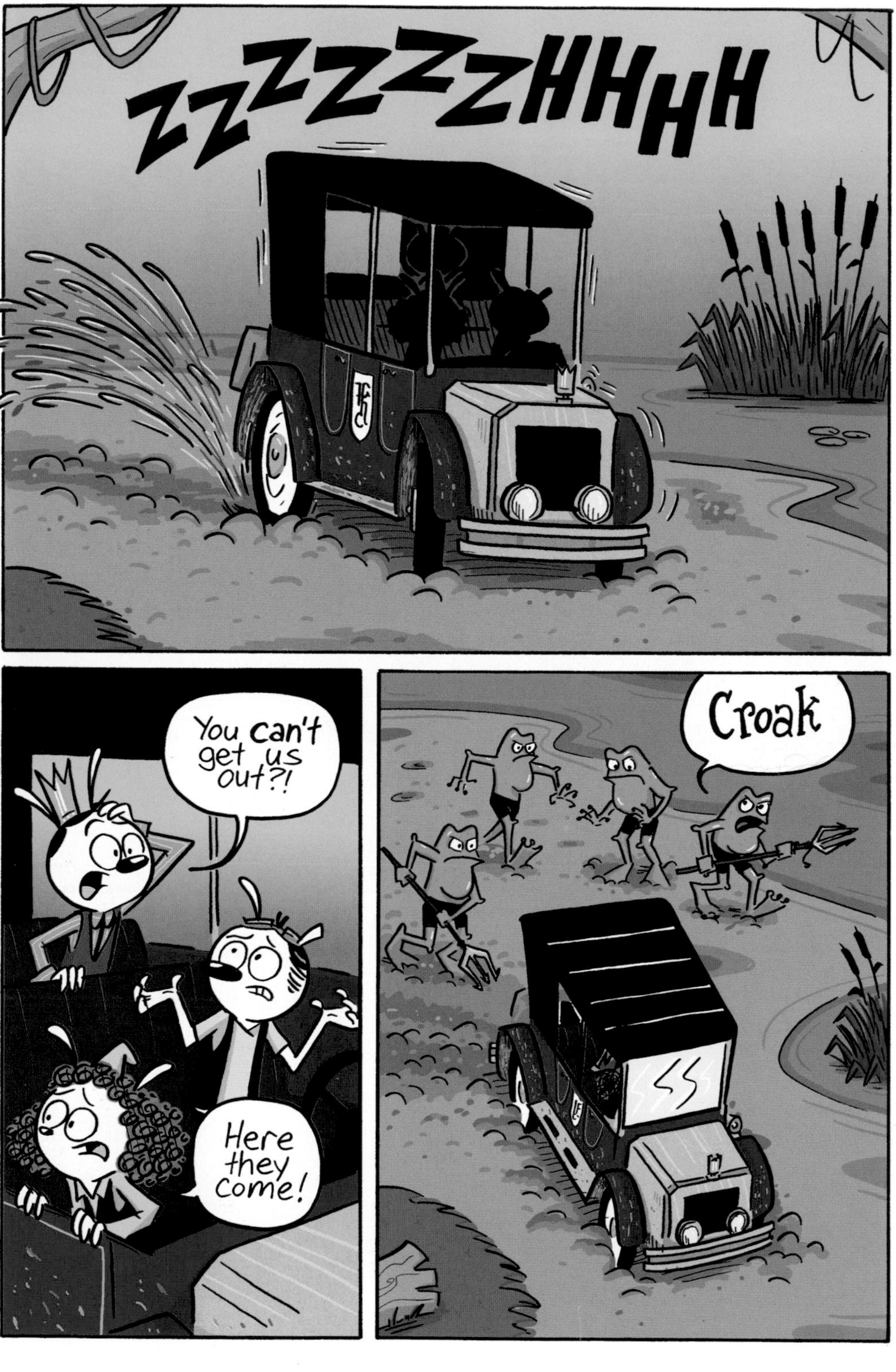
ZZZZZZZHHHHH
You can't get us out?!
Here they come!
Croak

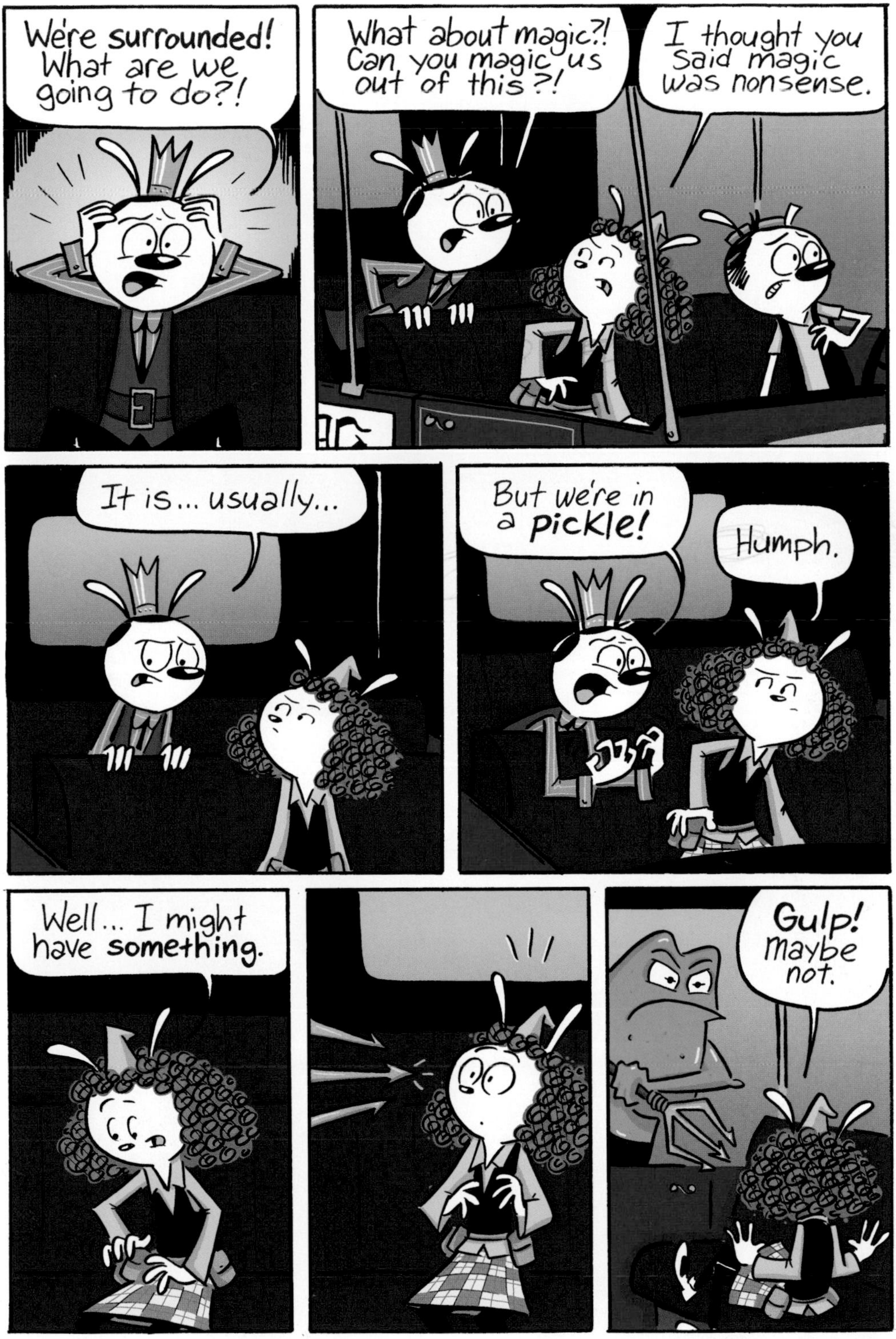
We're surrounded! What are we going to do?!
What about magic?! Can you magic us out of this?!
I thought you said magic was nonsense.
It is... usually...
But we're in a pickle!
Humph.
Well... I might have something.
Gulp! Maybe not.

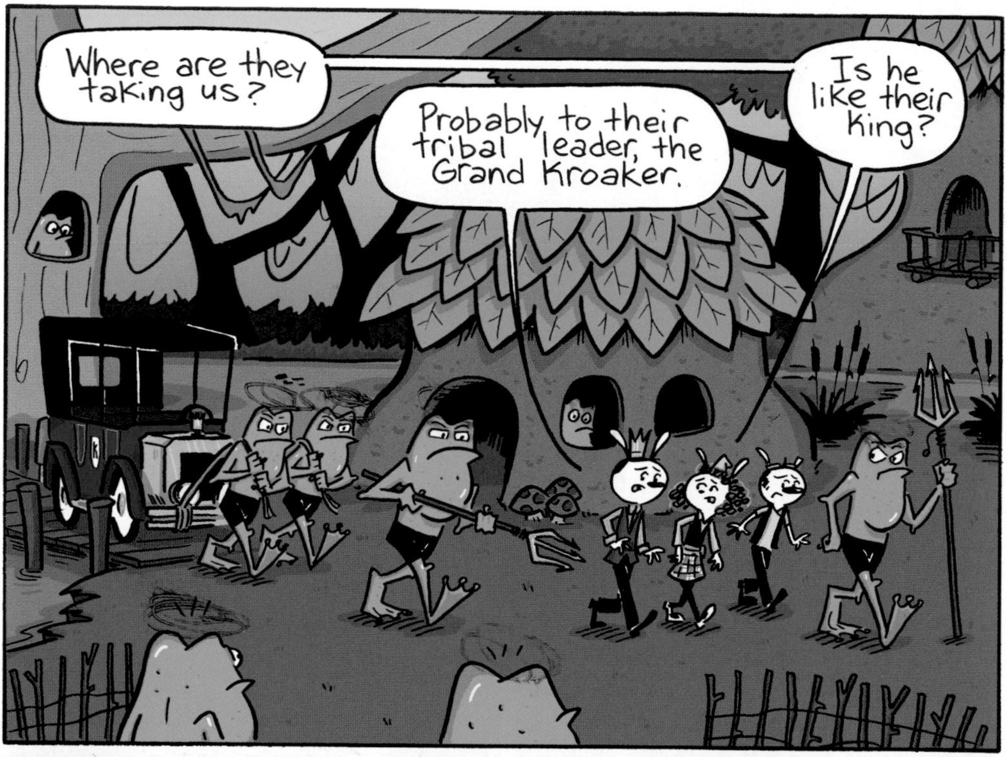
Where are they taking us?
Probably to their tribal leader, the Grand Kroaker.
Is he like their King?

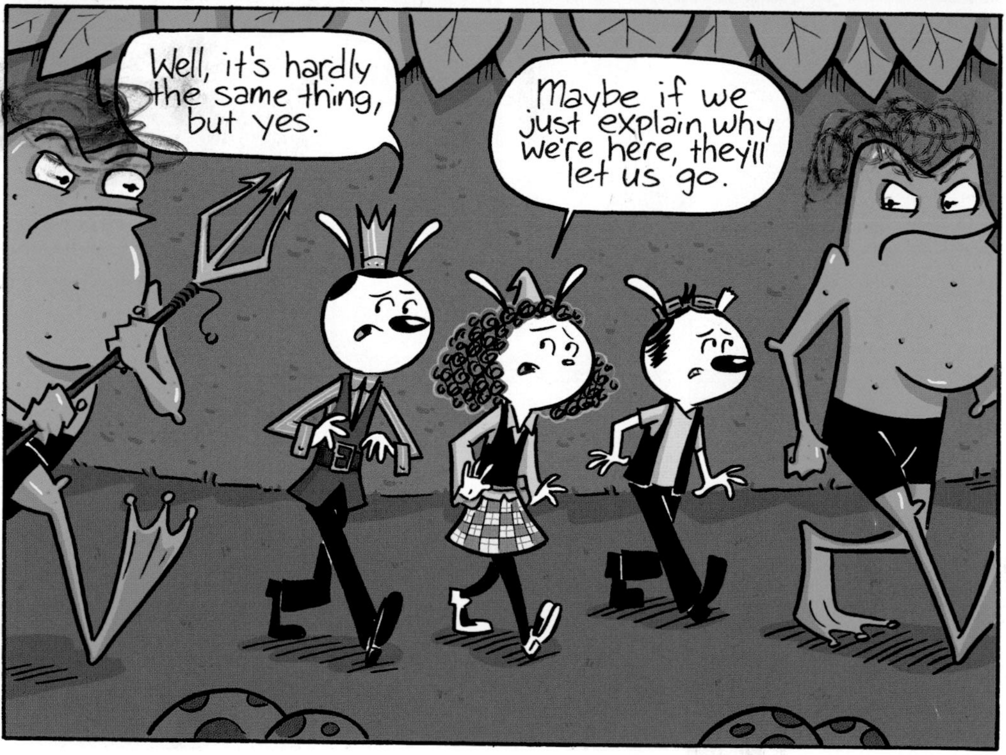
Well, it's hardly the same thing, but yes.
Maybe if we just explain why we're here, they'll let us go.

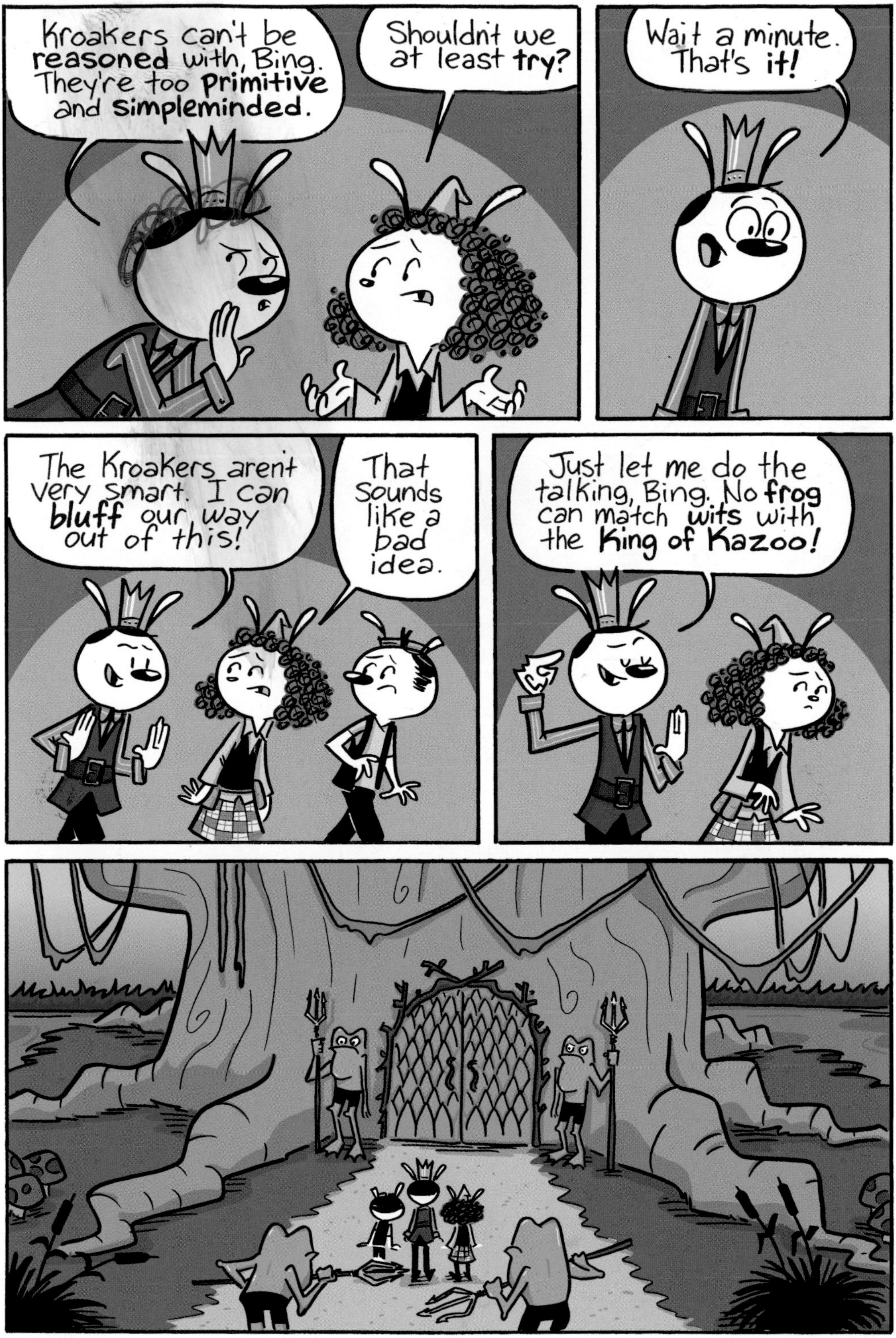
Kroakers can't be **reasoned** with, Bing. They're too **primitive** and **simpleminded**.
Shouldn't we at least **try**?
Wait a minute. That's **it**!
The Kroakers aren't very smart. I can **bluff** our way out of this!
That sounds like a bad idea.
Just let me do the talking, Bing. No **frog** can match **wits** with the **King of Kazoo**!

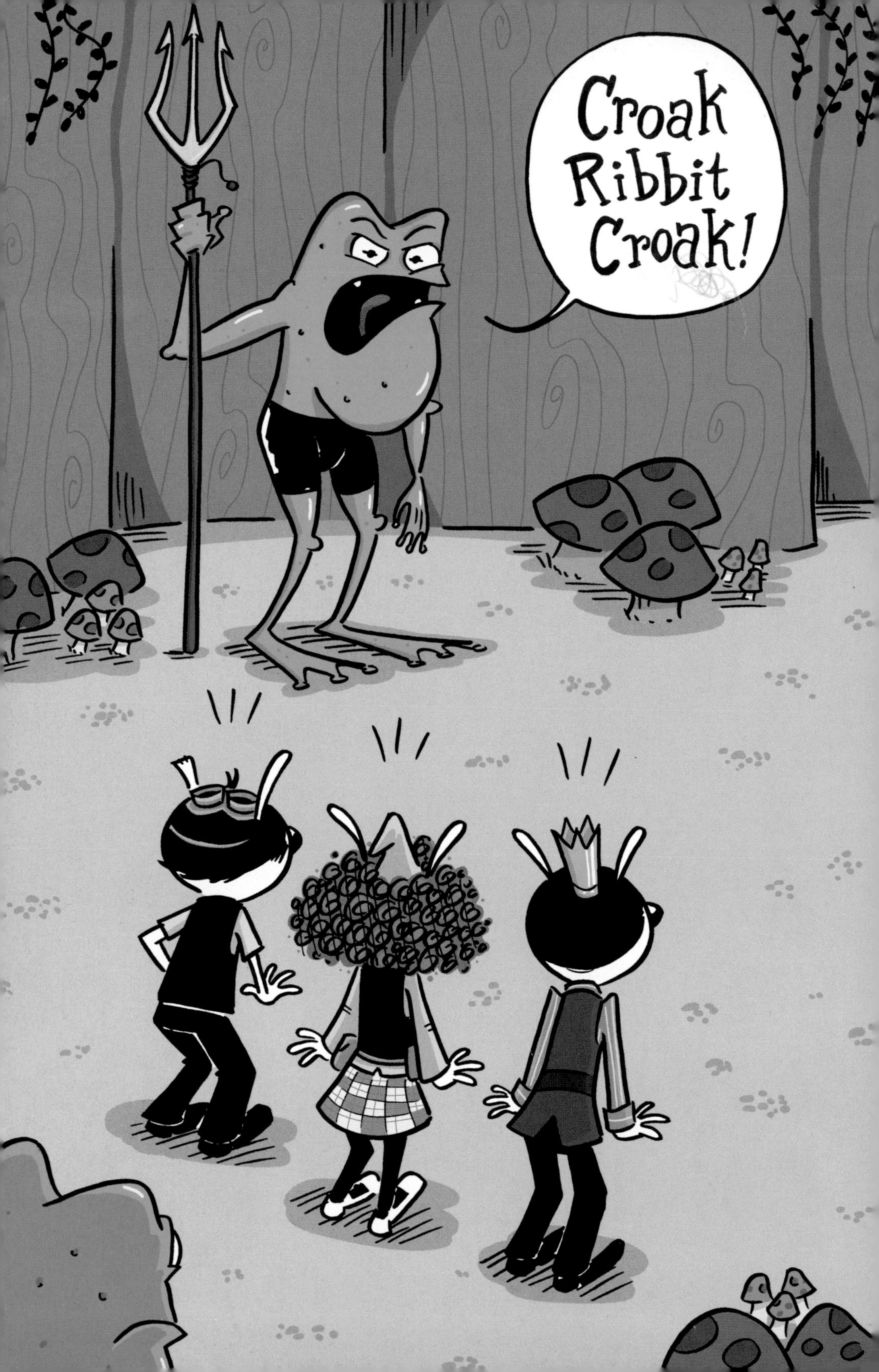
Croak Ribbit Croak!

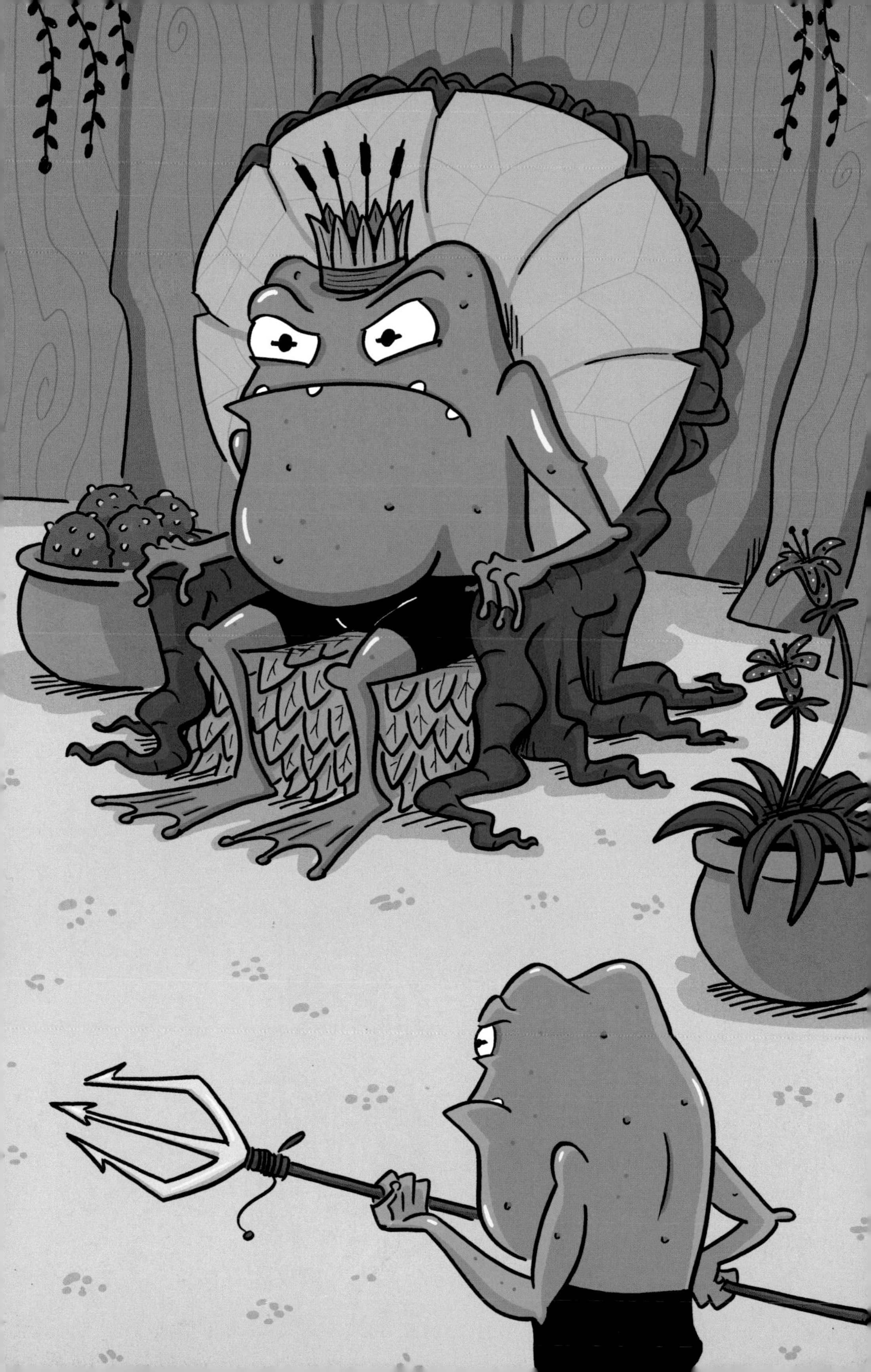

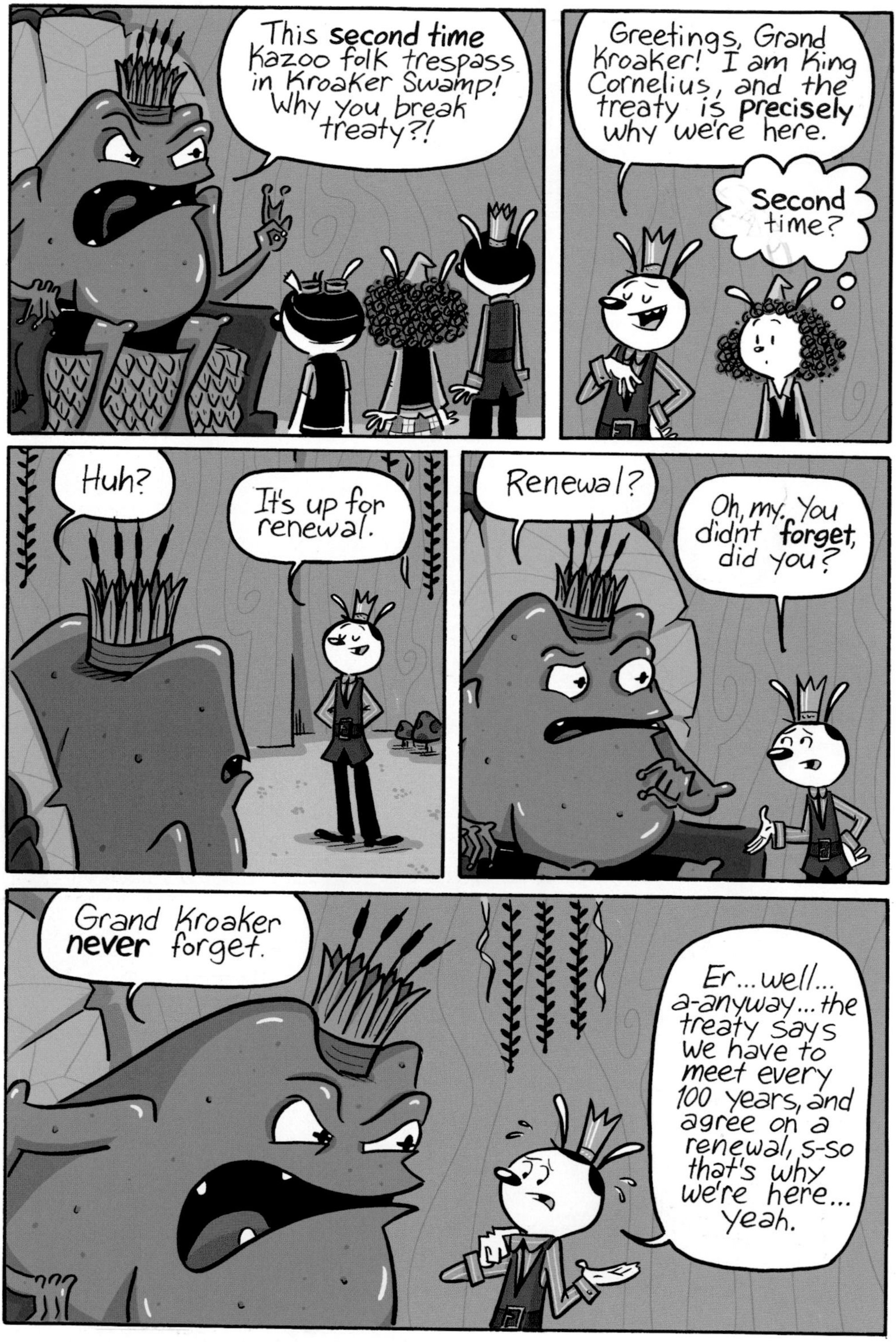
This **second time** Kazoo folk trespass in Kroaker Swamp! Why you break treaty?!
Greetings, Grand Kroaker! I am King Cornelius, and the treaty is **precisely** why we're here.
Second time?
Huh?
It's up for renewal.
Renewal?
Oh, my. You didnt **forget**, did you?
Grand Kroaker **never** forget.
Er... well... a-anyway... the treaty says we have to meet every 100 years, and agree on a renewal, s-so that's why we're here... Yeah.

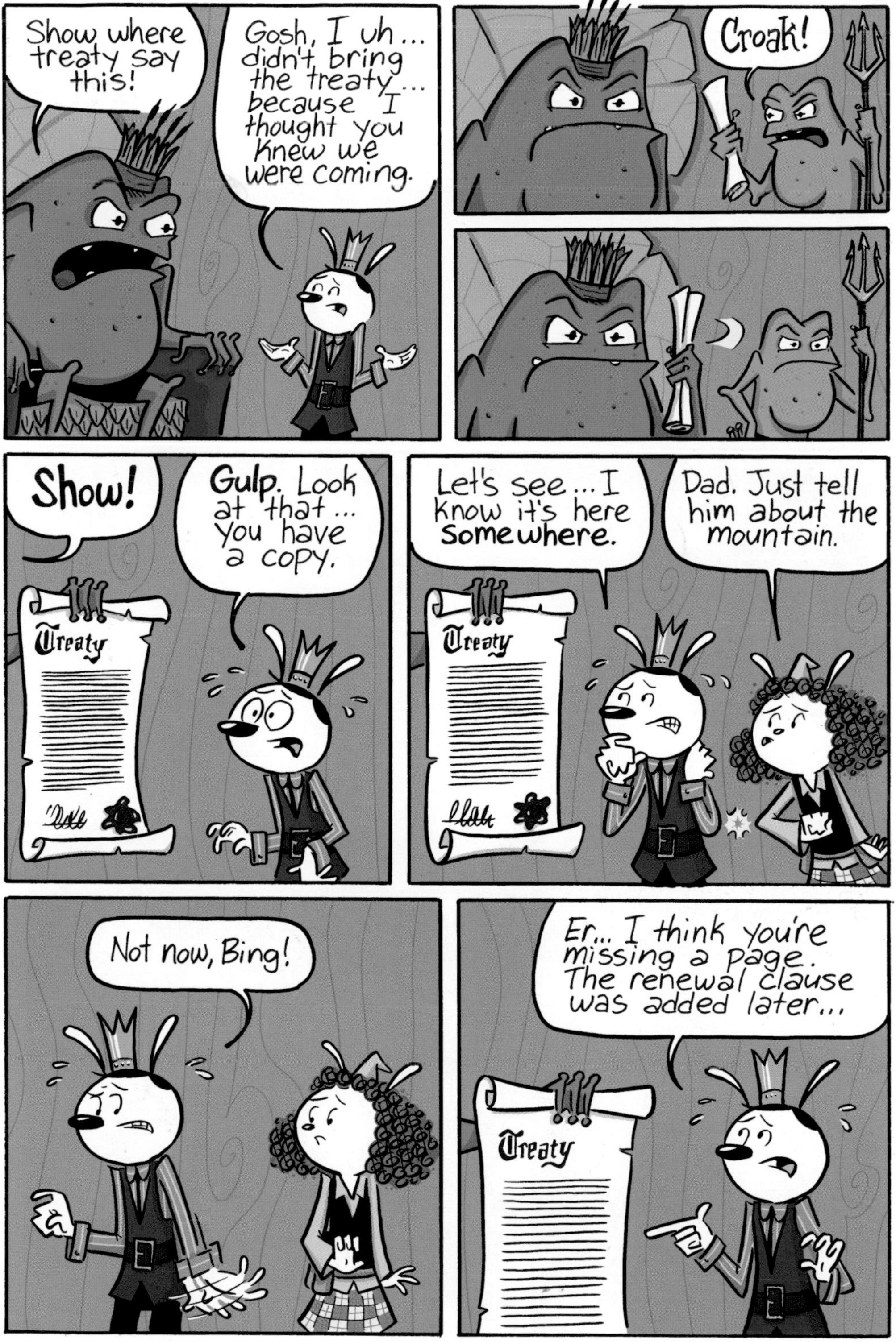

Show where treaty say this!
Gosh, I uh... didn't bring the treaty... because I thought you knew we were coming.
Croak!
Show!
Gulp. Look at that... you have a copy.
Treaty
Let's see... I know it's here somewhere.
Dad. Just tell him about the mountain.
Treaty
Not now, Bing!
Er... I think you're missing a page. The renewal clause was added later...
Treaty

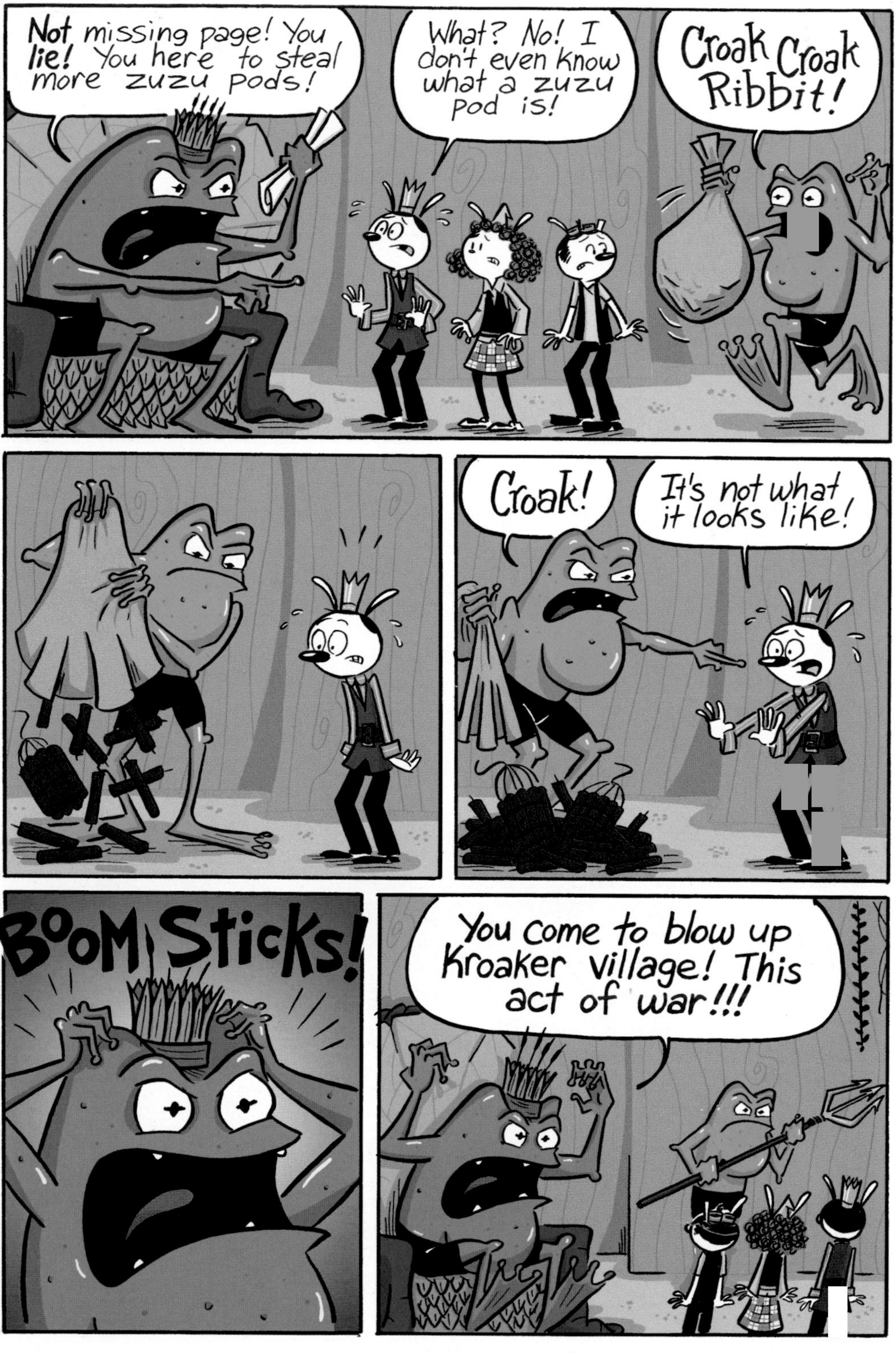
Not missing page! You lie! You here to steal more zuzu pods!
What? No! I don't even know what a zuzu pod is!
Croak Croak Ribbit!
Croak!
It's not what it looks like!
BOOM Sticks!
You come to blow up Kroaker village! This act of war!!!

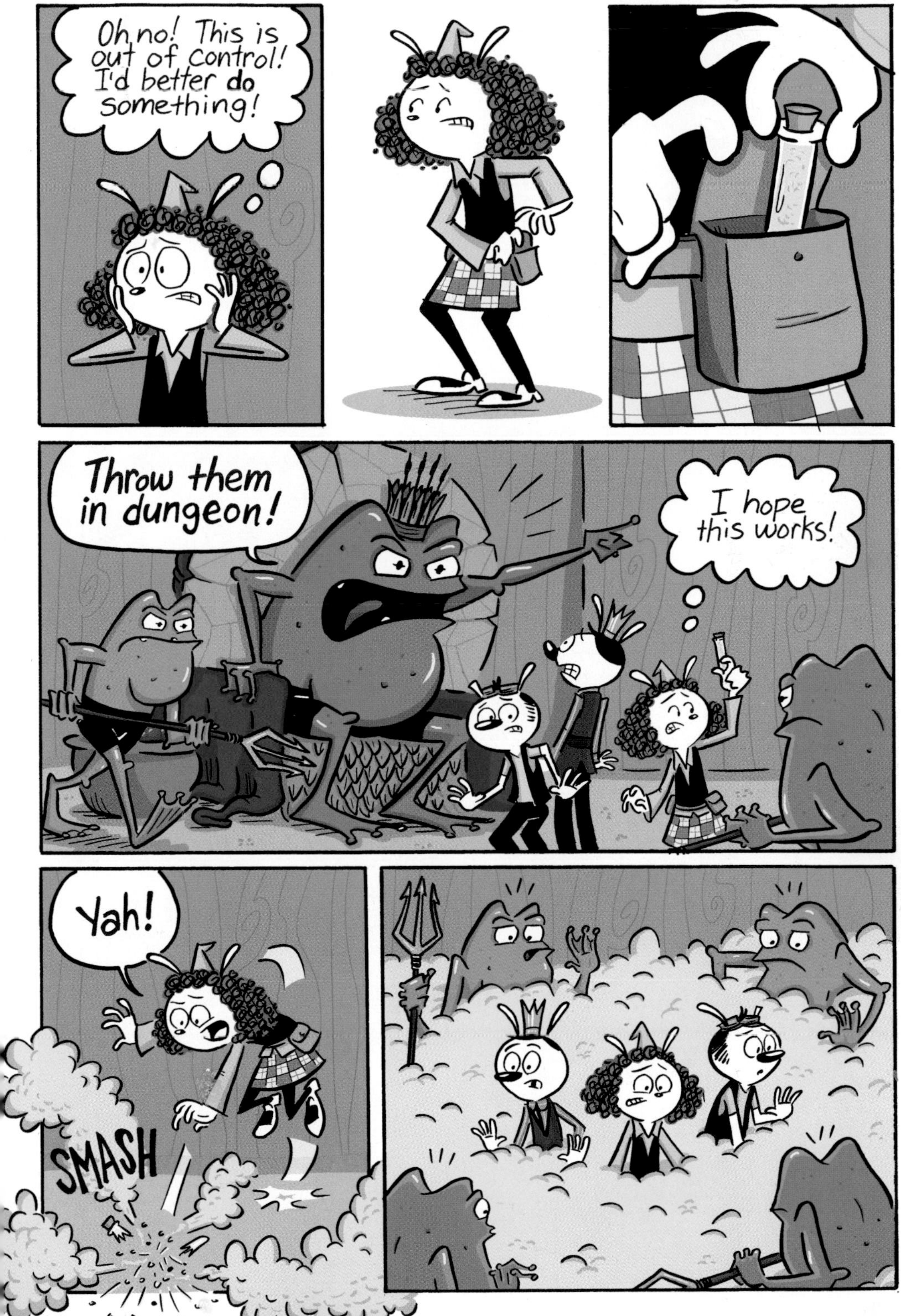
Oh no! This is out of control! I'd better do something!
Throw them in dungeon!
I hope this works!
Yah!
SMASH

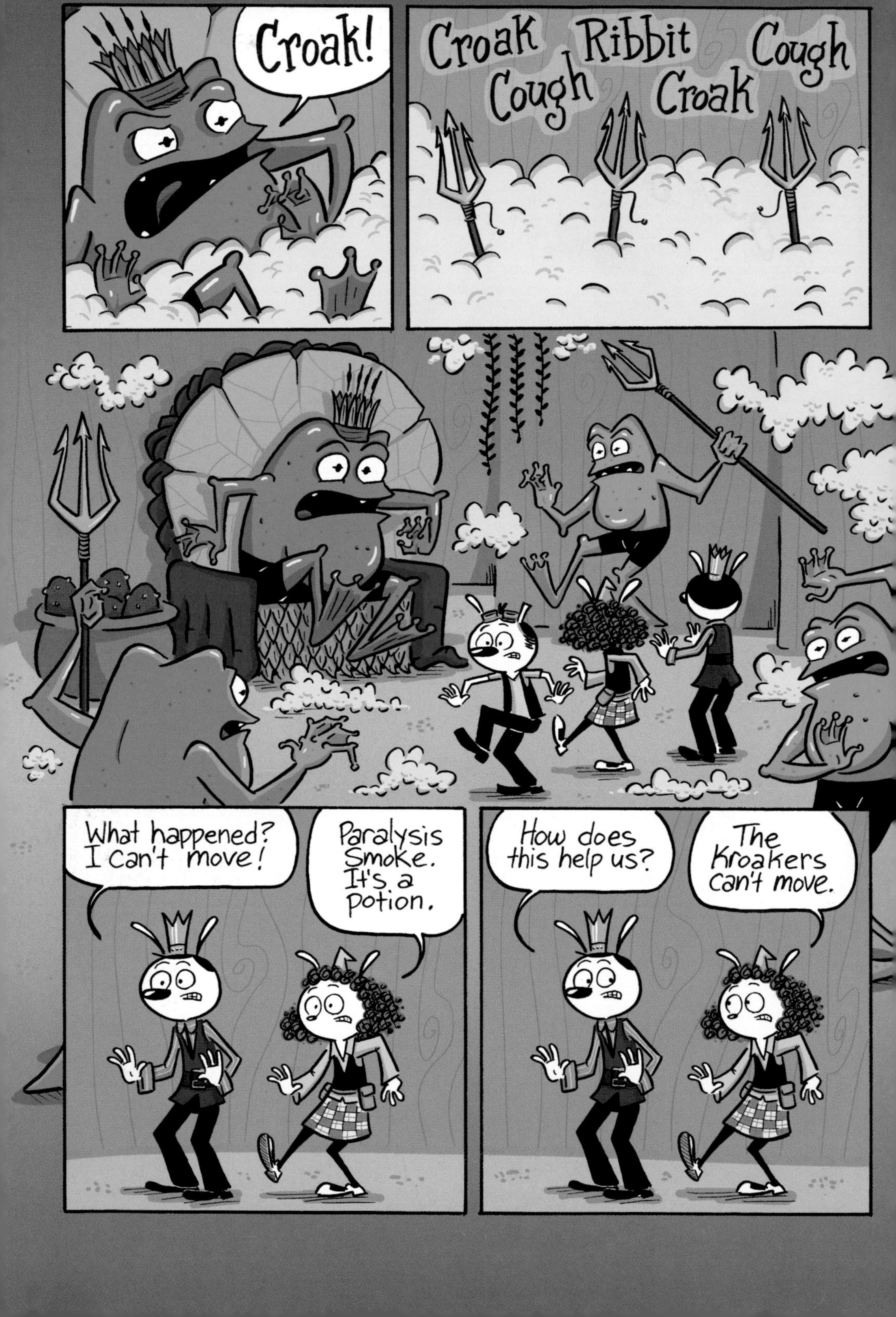
Croak!
Croak Ribbit Cough
Cough Croak
What happened? I can't move!
Paralysis Smoke. It's a potion.
How does this help us?
The Kroakers can't move.

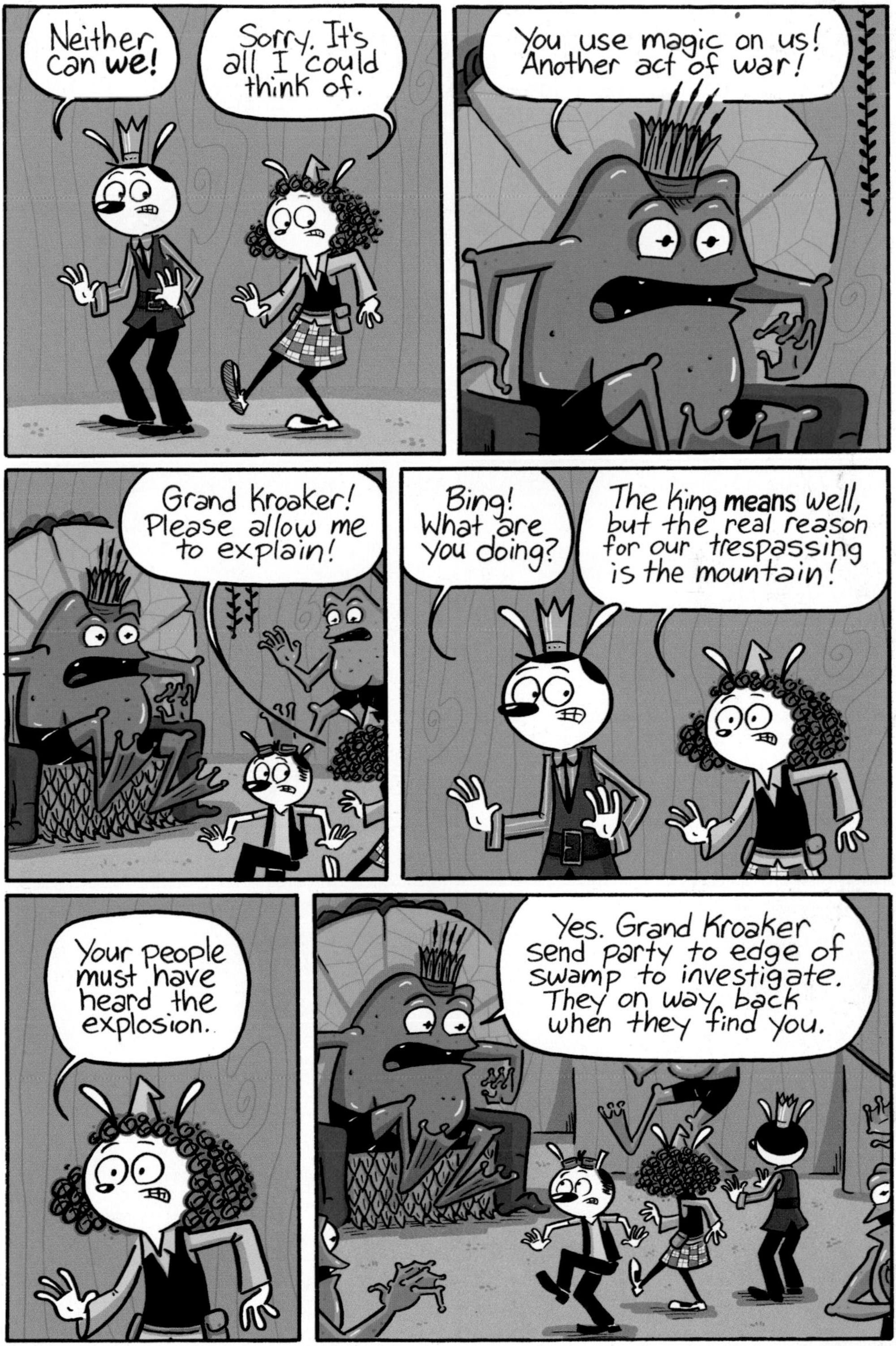
Neither can **we**!
Sorry. It's all I could think of.
You use magic on us! Another act of war!
Grand Kroaker! Please allow me to explain!
Bing! What are you doing?
The king **means** well, but the real reason for our trespassing is the mountain!
Your people must have heard the explosion.
Yes. Grand Kroaker send party to edge of swamp to investigate. They on way back when they find you.

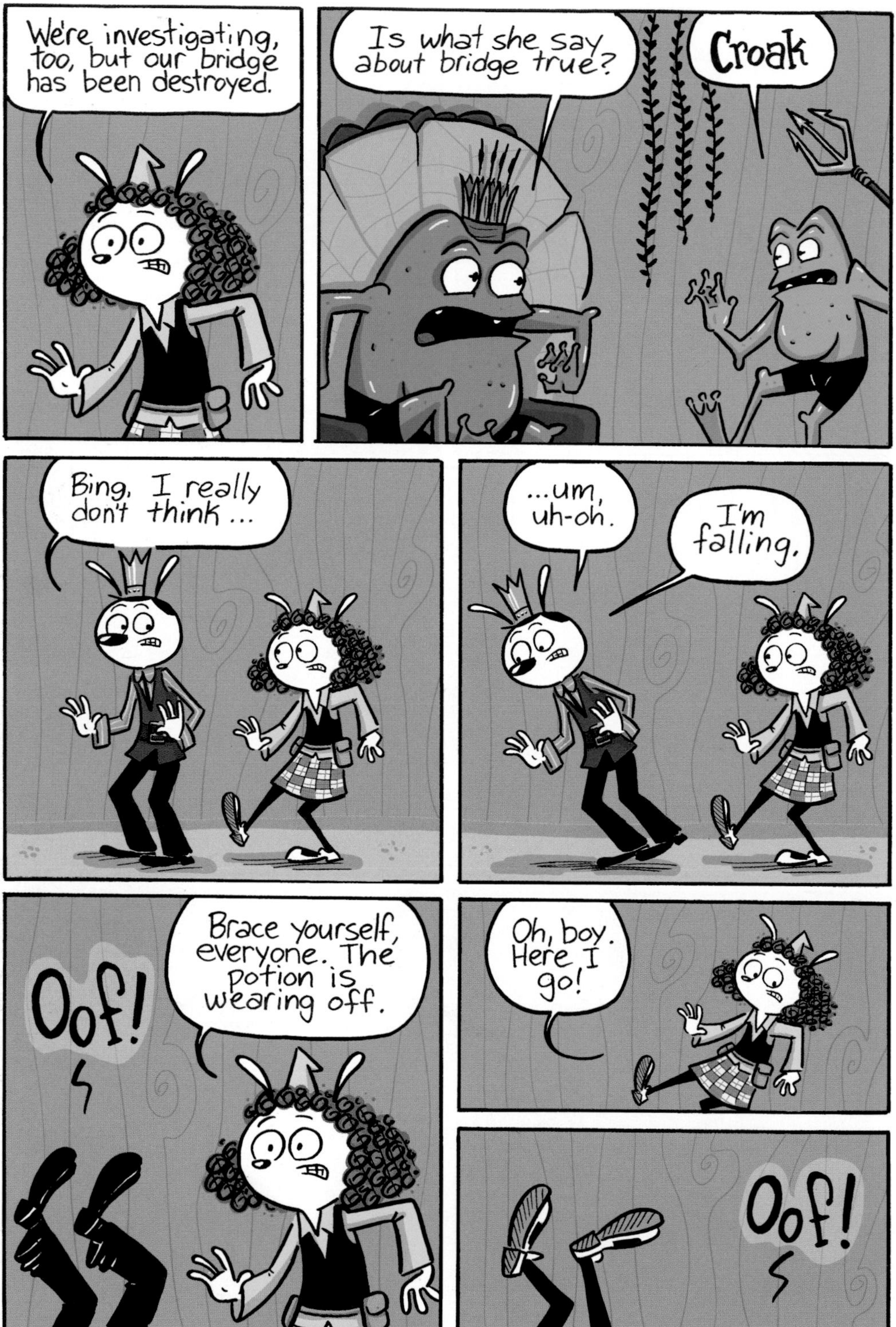
We're investigating, too, but our bridge has been destroyed.
Is what she say about bridge true?
Croak
Bing, I really don't think ...
...um, uh-oh.
I'm falling.
Oof!
Brace yourself, everyone. The potion is wearing off.
Oh, boy. Here I go!
Oof!

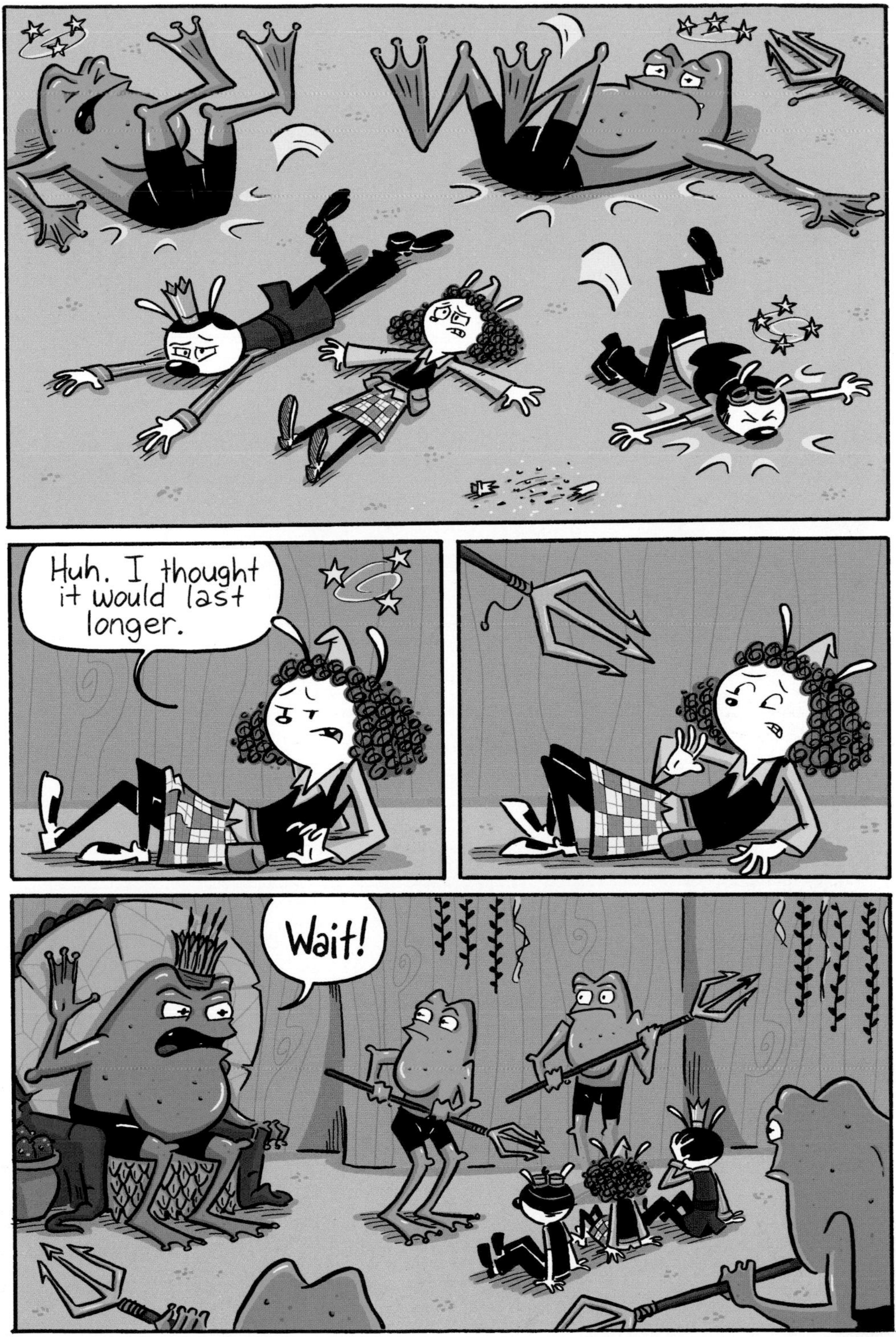
Huh. I thought it would last longer.
Wait!

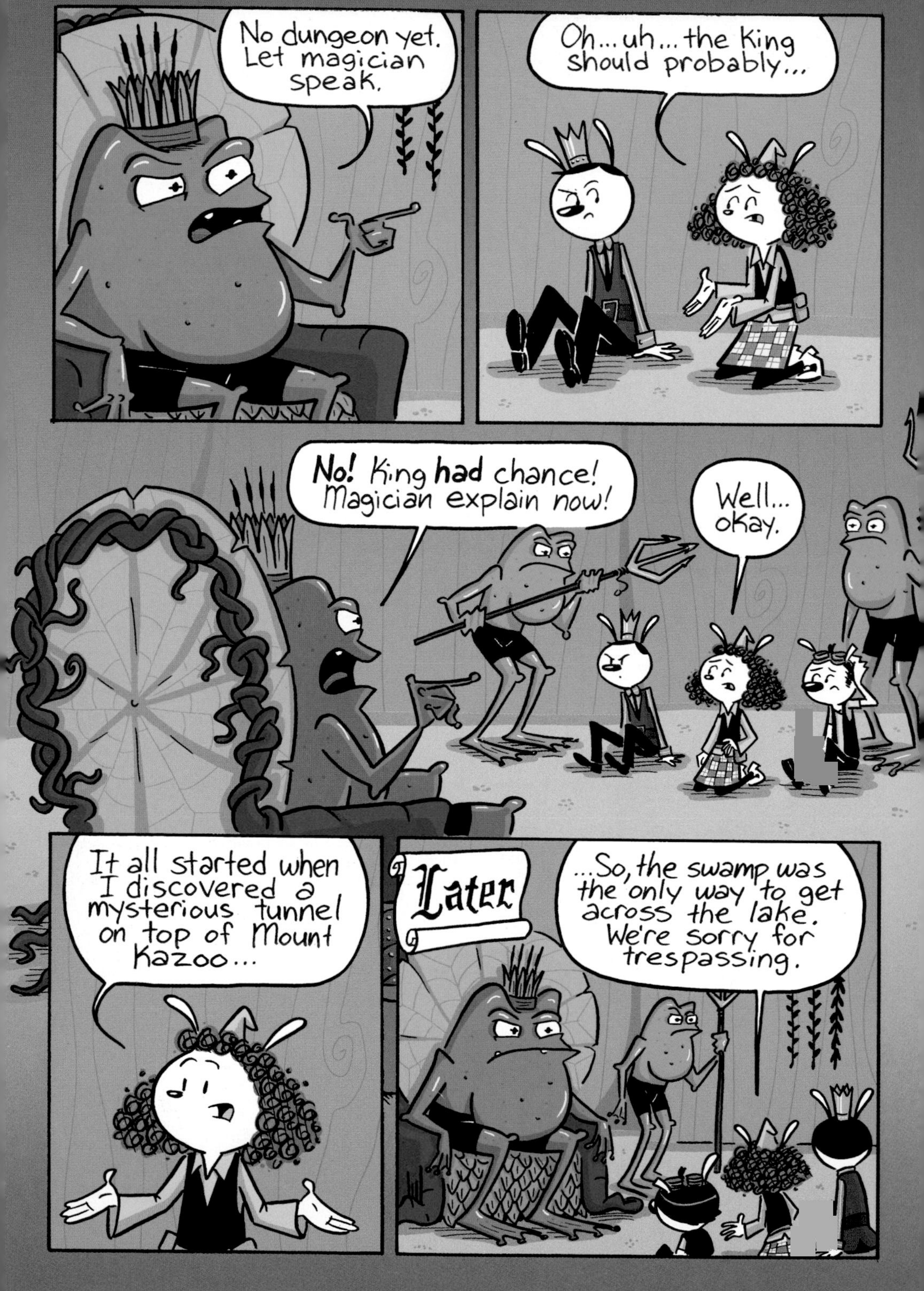
No dungeon yet. Let magician speak.
Oh... uh... the King should probably...
No! King had chance! Magician explain now!
Well... okay.
It all started when I discovered a mysterious tunnel on top of Mount Kazoo...
Later
...So, the swamp was the only way to get across the lake. We're sorry for trespassing.

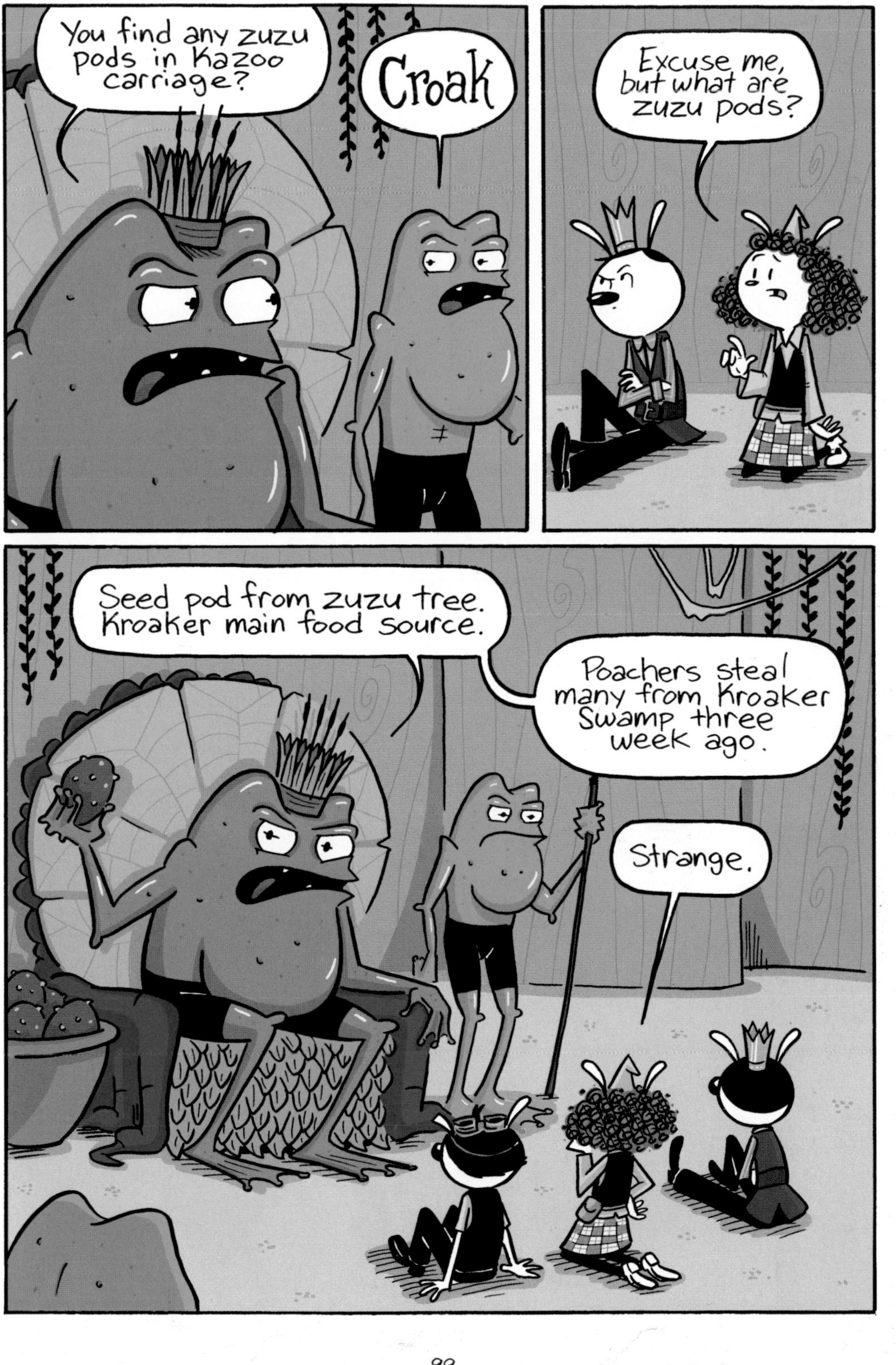
You find any zuzu pods in Kazoo carriage?
Croak
Excuse me, but what are zuzu pods?
Seed pod from zuzu tree. Kroaker main food source.
Poachers steal many from Kroaker Swamp three week ago.
Strange.

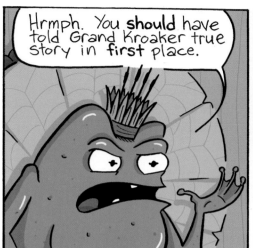

Hrmph. You **should** have told Grand Kroaker true story in **first** place.

I wanted to, but... er... I guess we were scared.

You should listen to advisor. **Good** leader know how to **listen**.

She's not my advisor, she's my daughter. A **good** King doesn't **need** an advisor.

Maybe not, but **you** do.

Croak
Ribbit

Ribbit
Croak

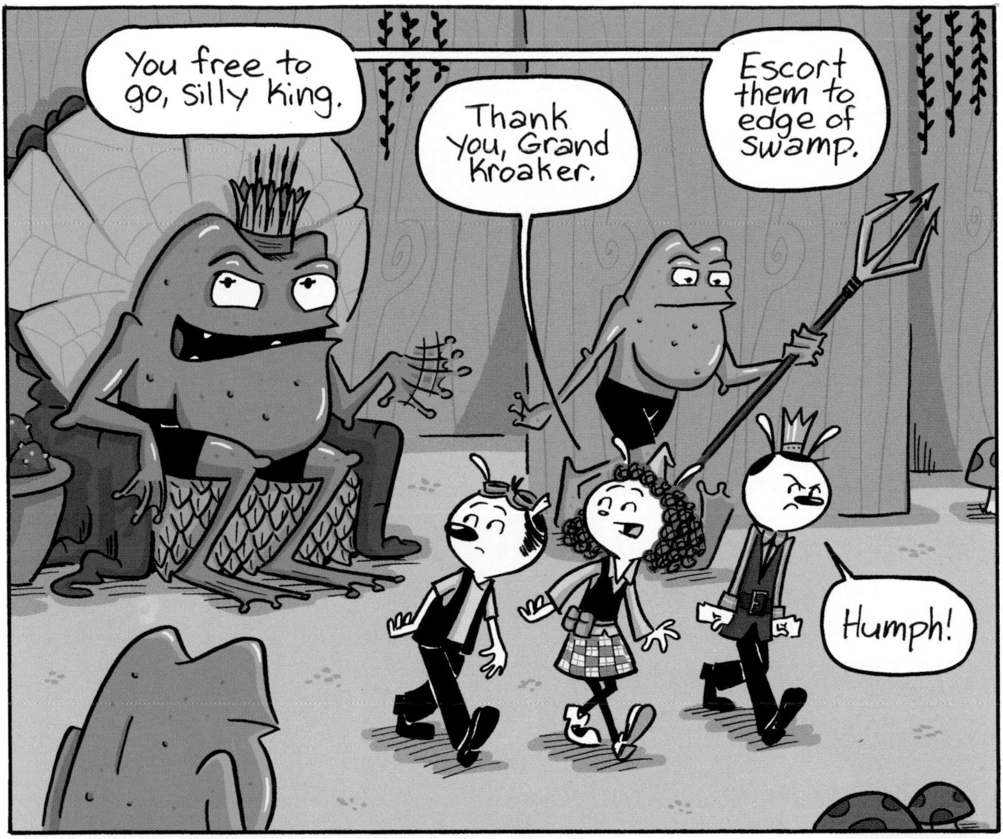
You free to go, silly King.
Thank you, Grand Kroaker.
Escort them to edge of swamp.
Humph!
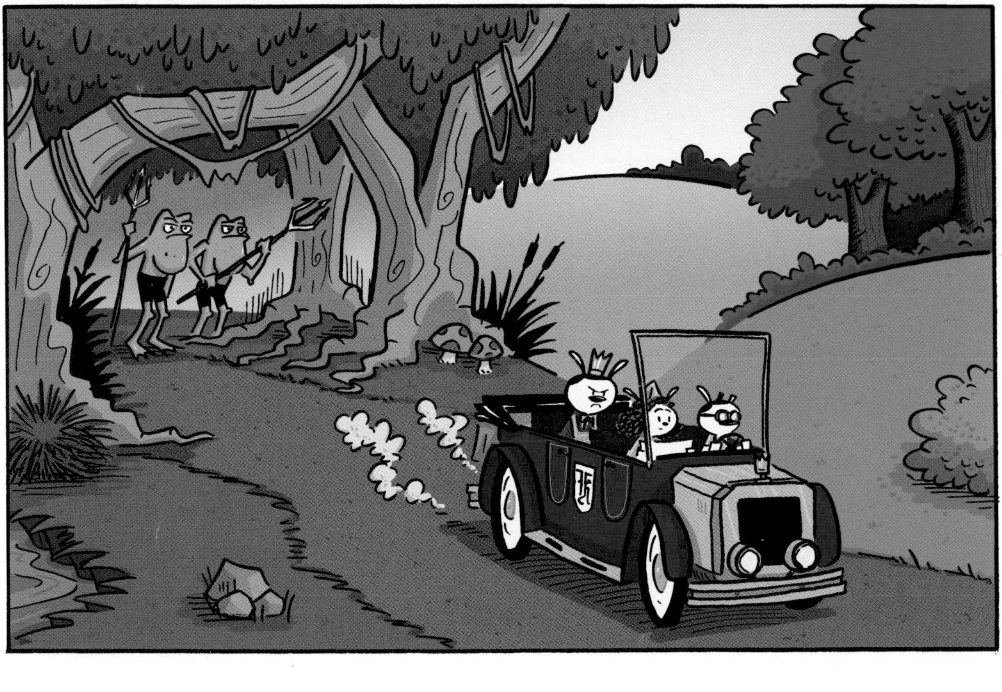

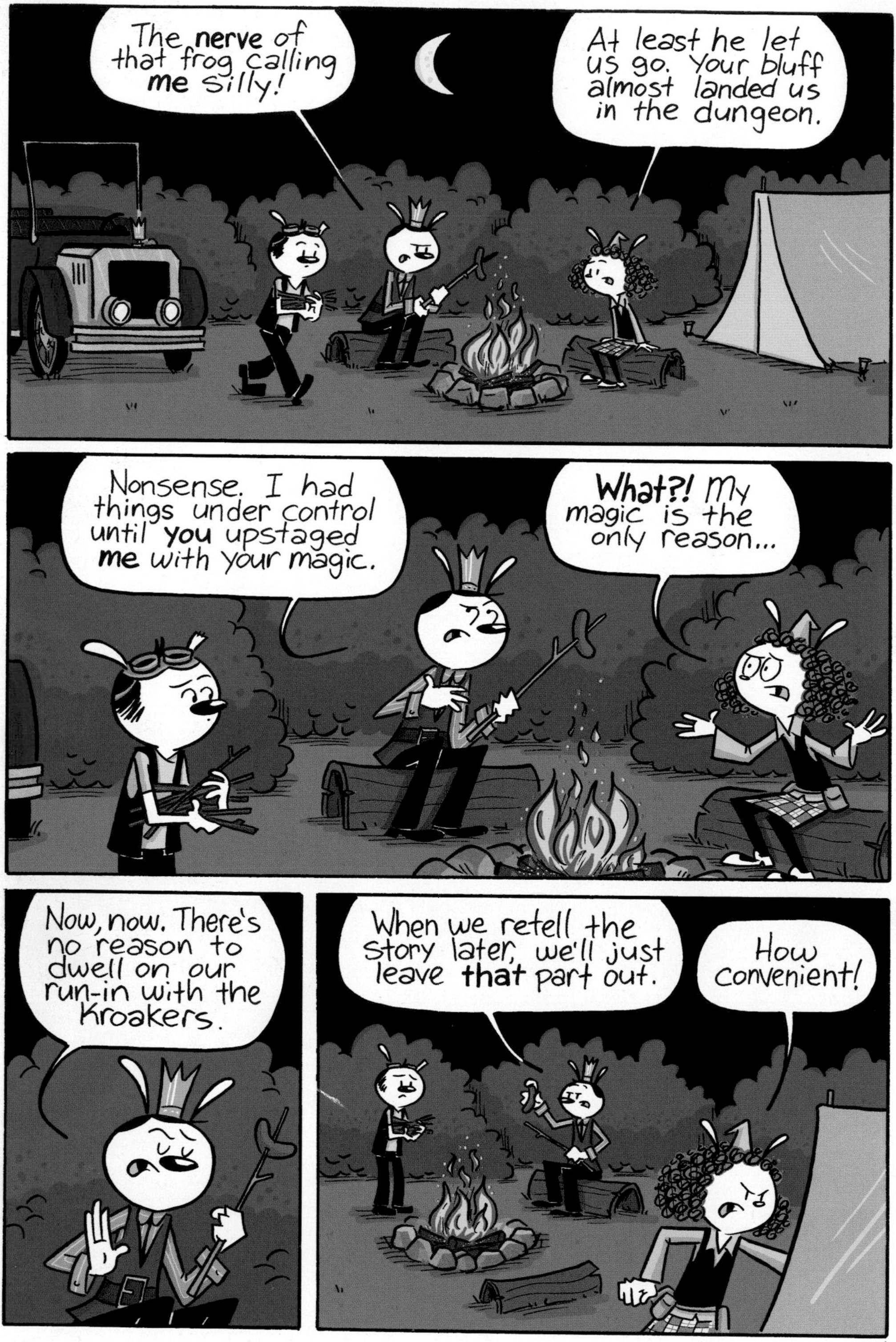
The **nerve** of that frog calling **me** silly!
At least he let us go. Your bluff almost landed us in the dungeon.
Nonsense. I had things under control until **you** upstaged **me** with your magic.
What?! My magic is the only reason...
Now, now. There's no reason to dwell on our run-in with the Kroakers.
When we retell the story later, we'll just leave **that** part out.
How convenient!

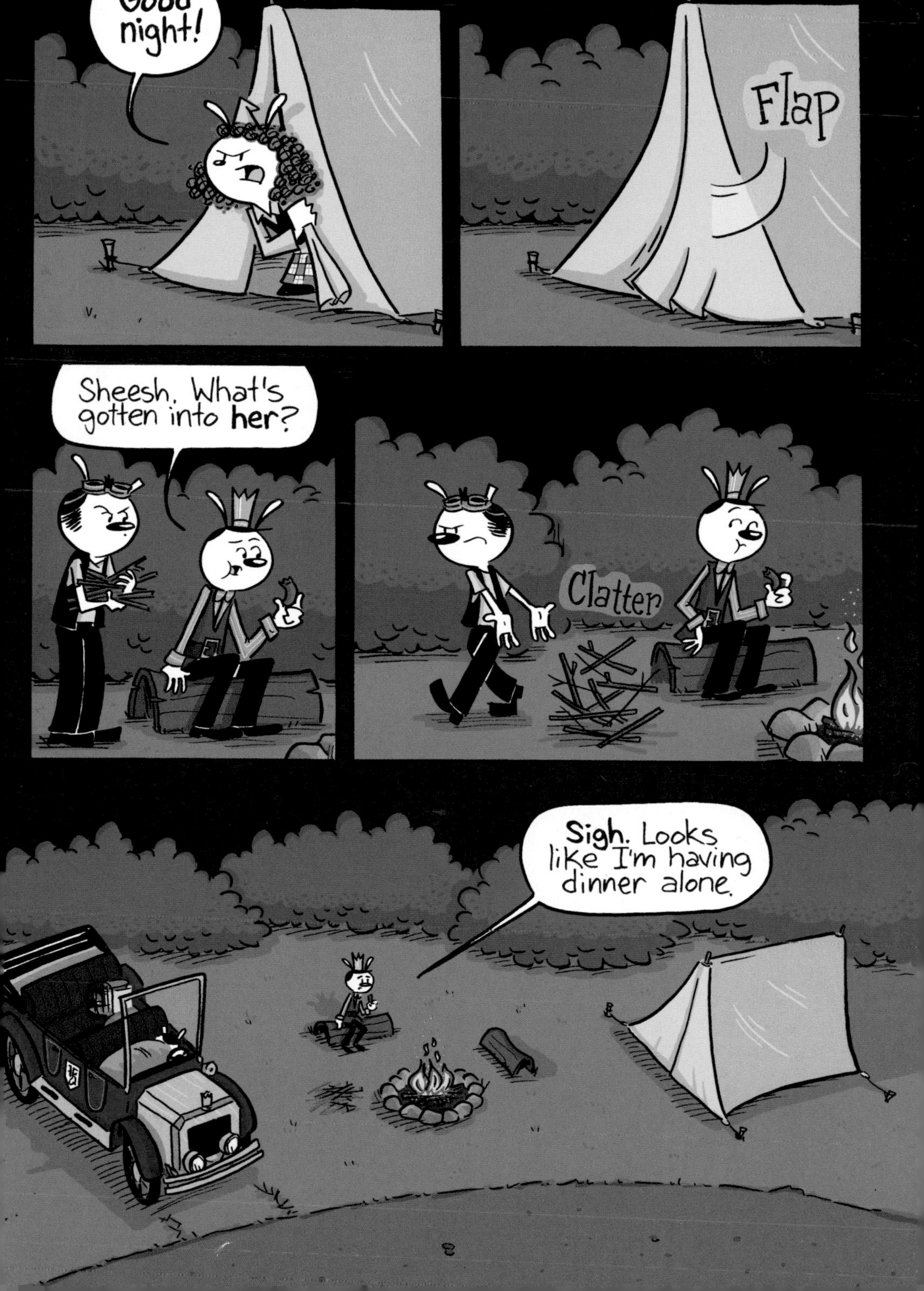
Good night!
Flap
Sheesh. What's gotten into her?
Clatter
Sigh. Looks like I'm having dinner alone.

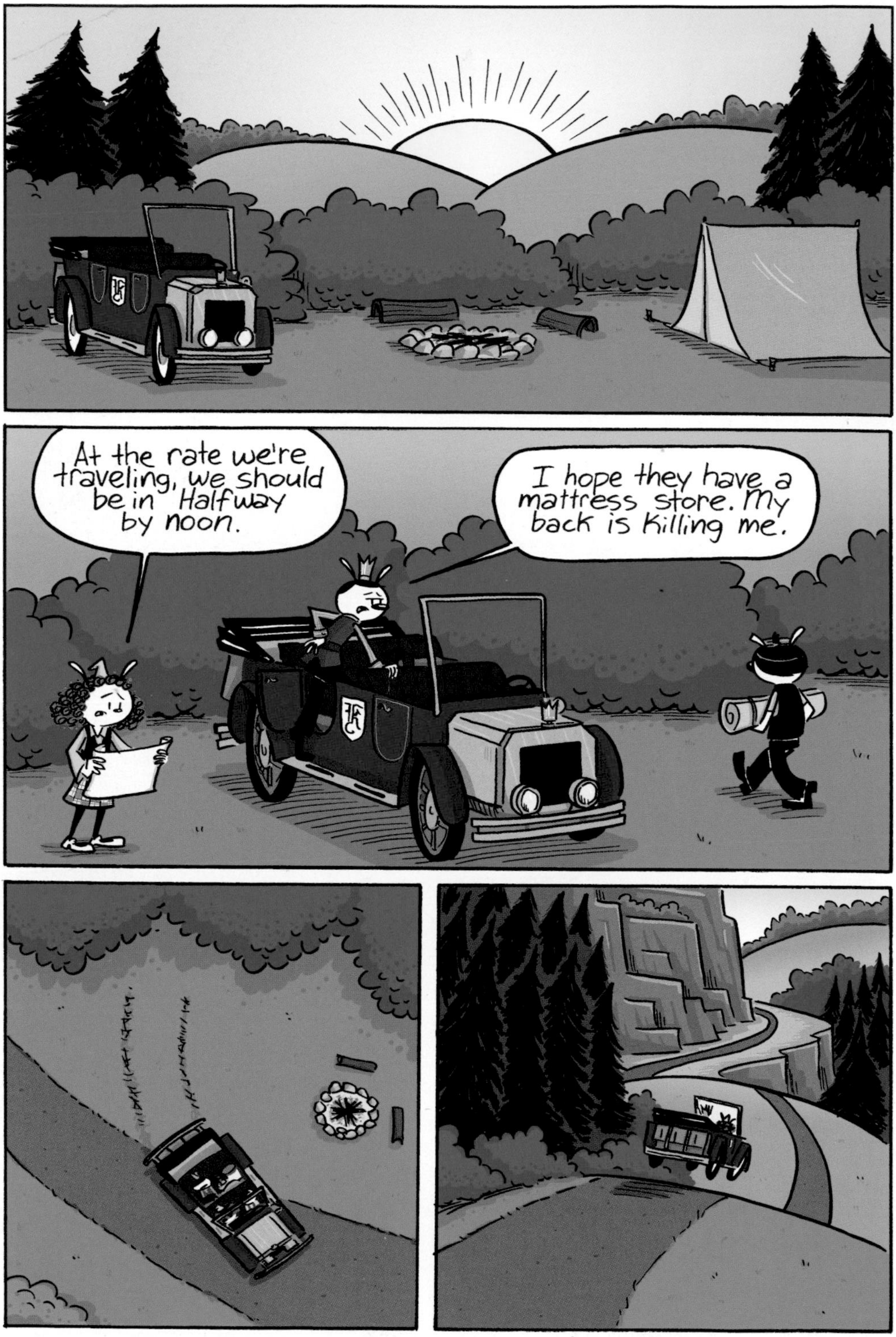
At the rate we're traveling, we should be in Halfway by noon.
I hope they have a mattress store. My back is killing me.

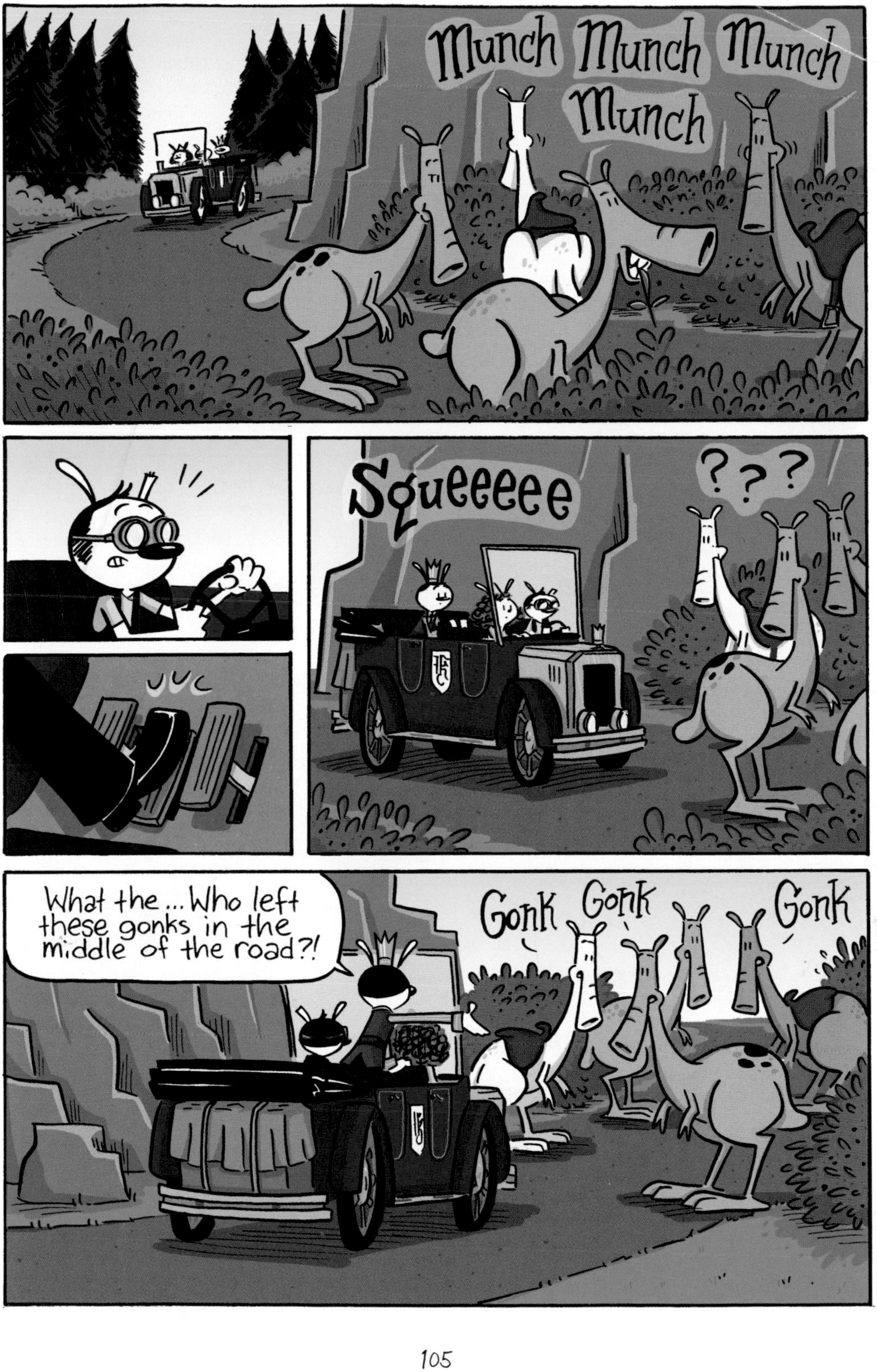
Munch Munch Munch
Munch
Squeeeee
???
What the... Who left these gonks in the middle of the road?!
Gonk
Gonk
Gonk

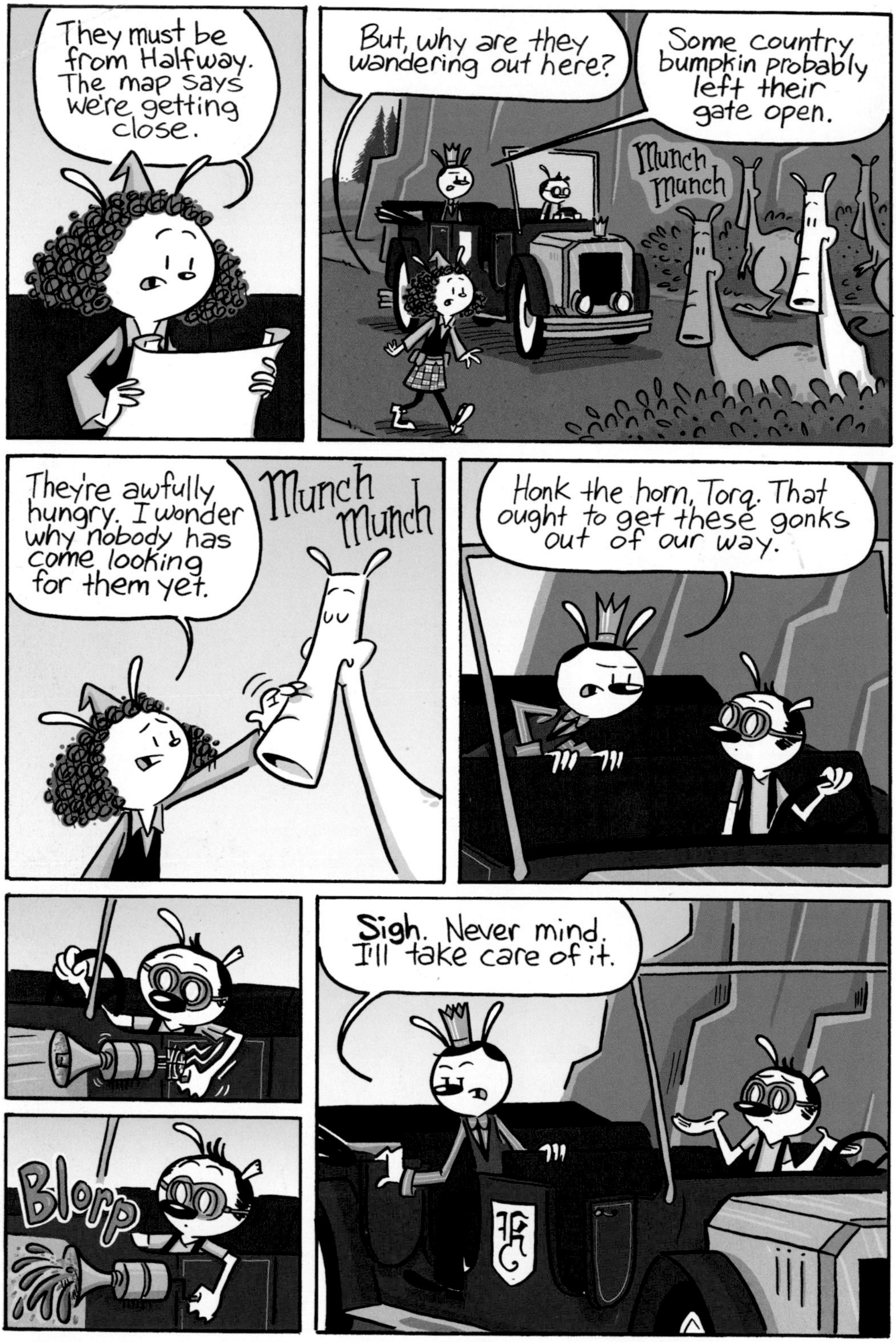
They must be from Halfway. The map says we're getting close.
But, why are they wandering out here?
Some country bumpkin probably left their gate open.
Munch munch
They're awfully hungry. I wonder why nobody has come looking for them yet.
Munch munch
Honk the horn, Torq. That ought to get these gonks out of our way.
Blorp
Sigh. Never mind. I'll take care of it.

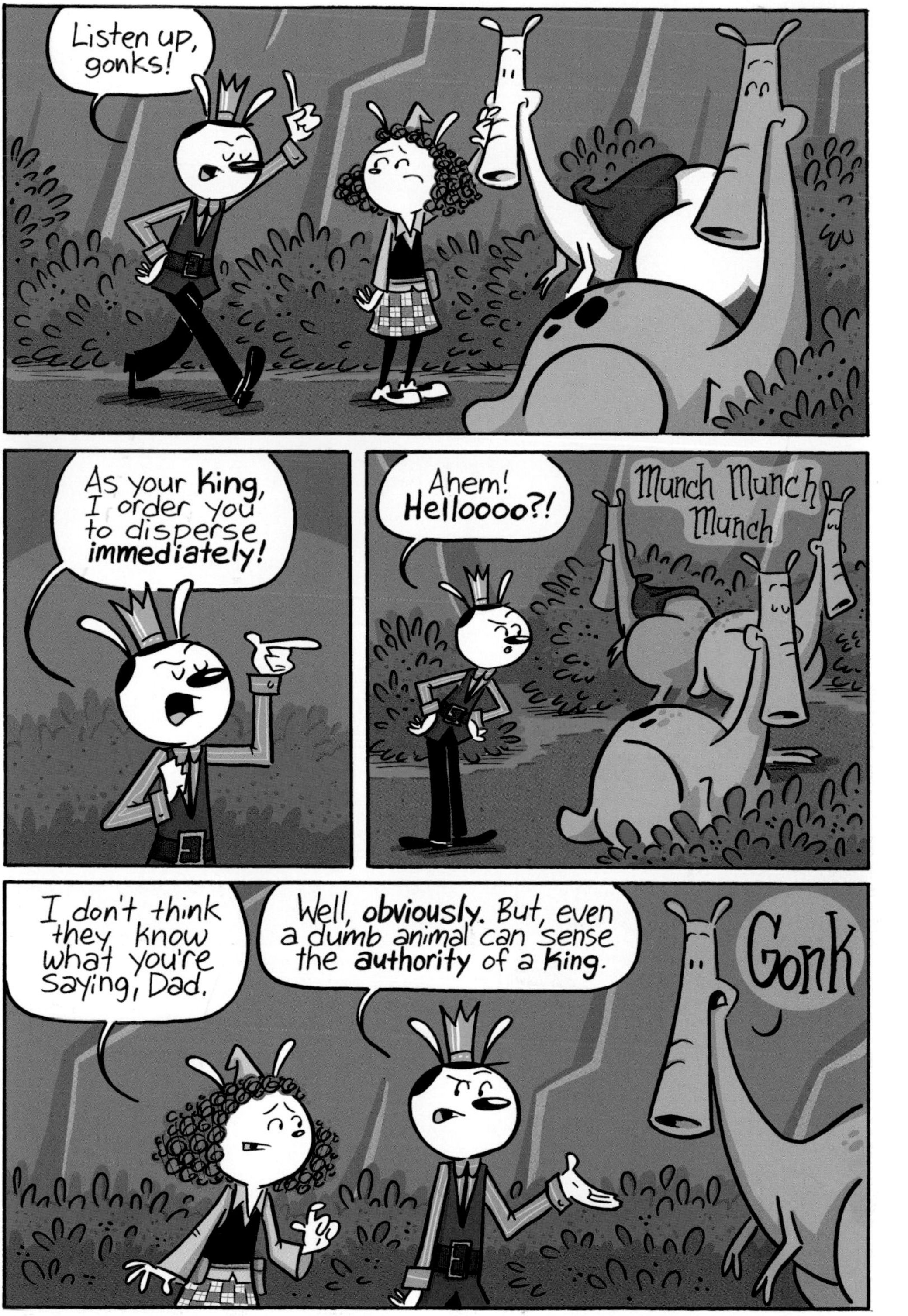
Listen up, gonks!
As your **King**, I order you to disperse **immediately**!
Ahem! **Helloooo?!**
Munch Munch Munch
I don't think they know what you're saying, Dad.
Well, **obviously**. But, even a dumb animal can sense the **authority** of a **King**.
Gonk

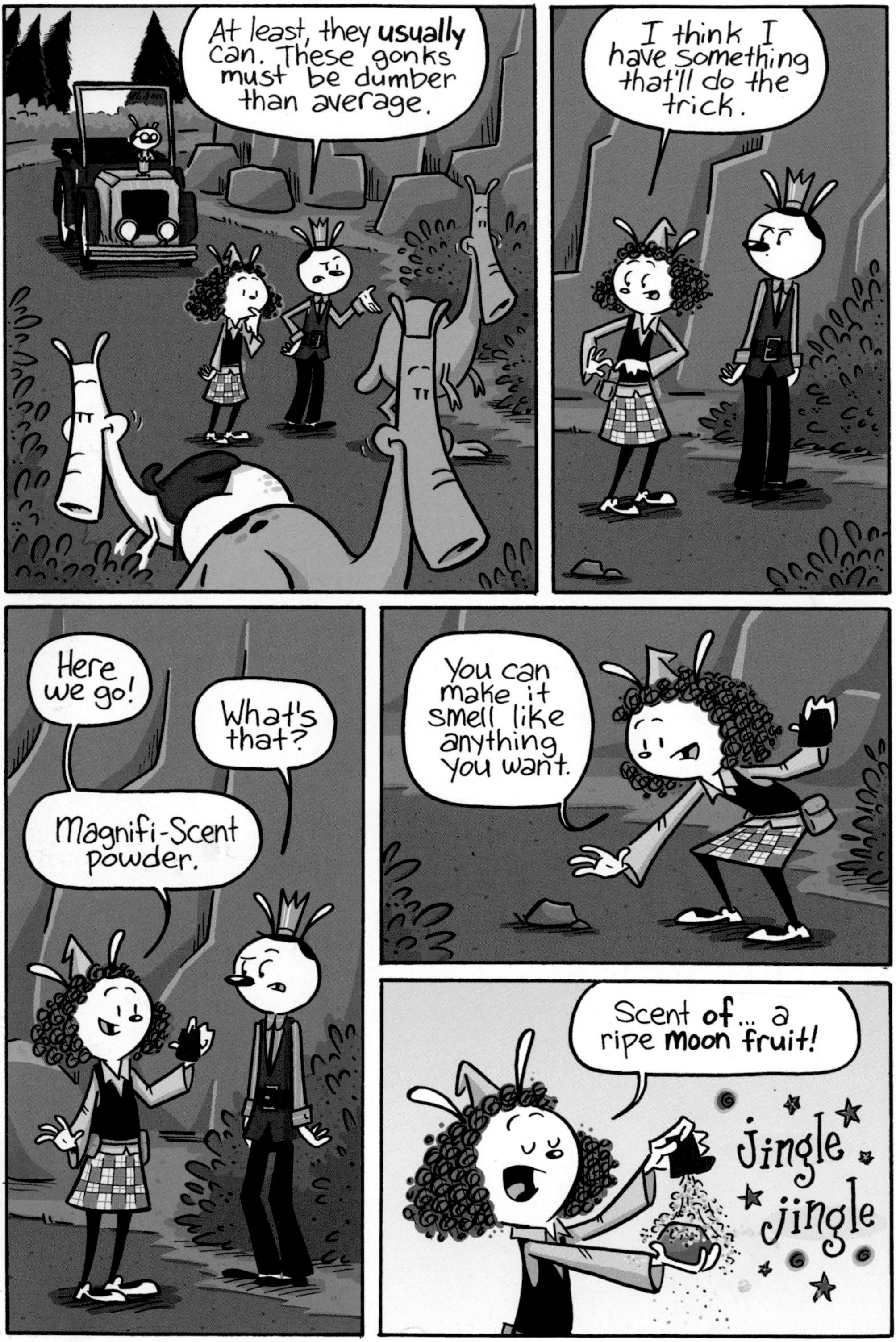
At least, they **usually** can. These gonks must be dumber than average.
I think I have something that'll do the trick.
Here we go!
What's that?
Magnifi-Scent powder.
You can make it smell like anything you want.
Scent **of**... a ripe **moon fruit**!
Jingle jingle

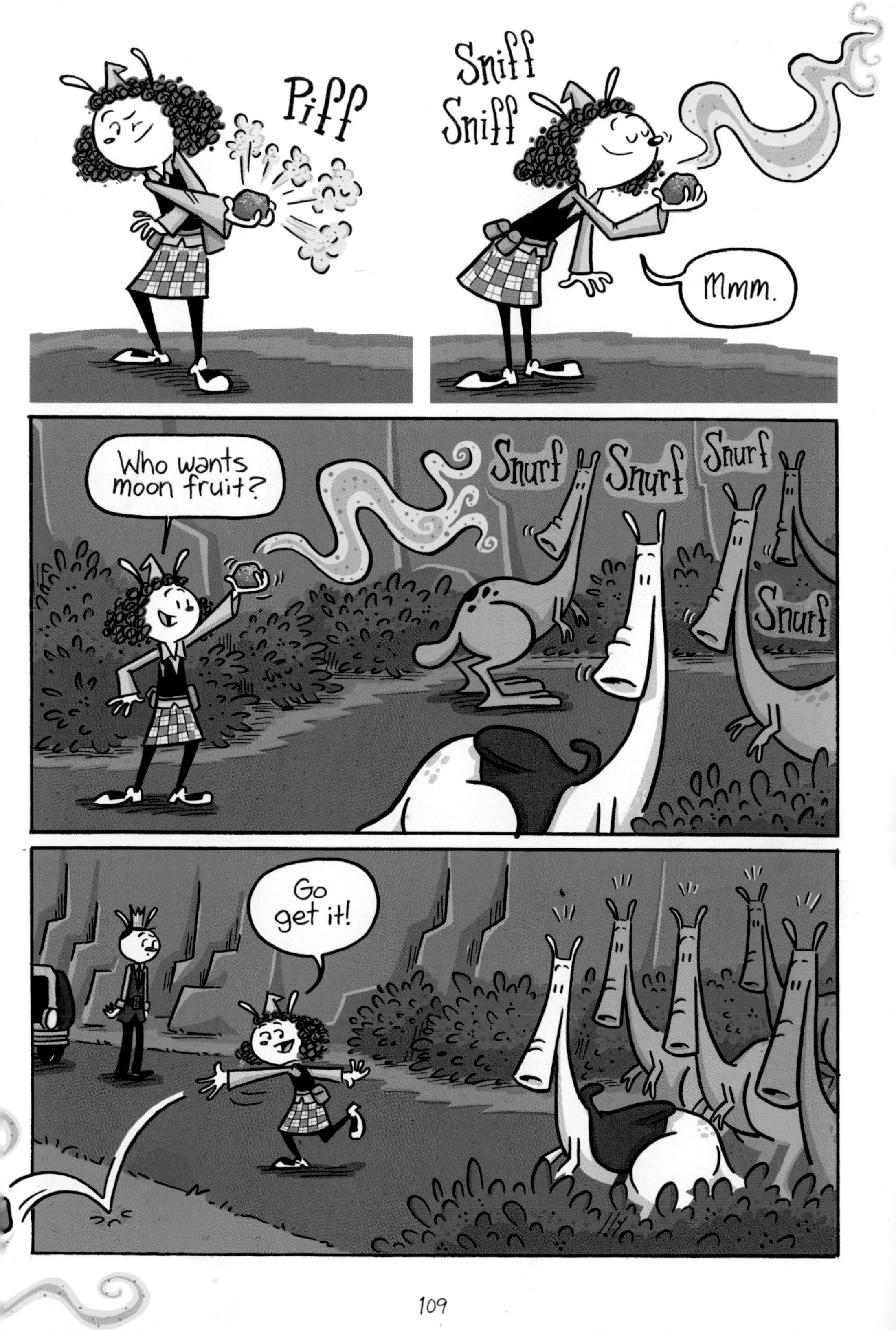
Piff
Sniff
Sniff
Mmm.
Who wants moon fruit?
Snurf
Snurf
Snurf
Snurf
Go get it!

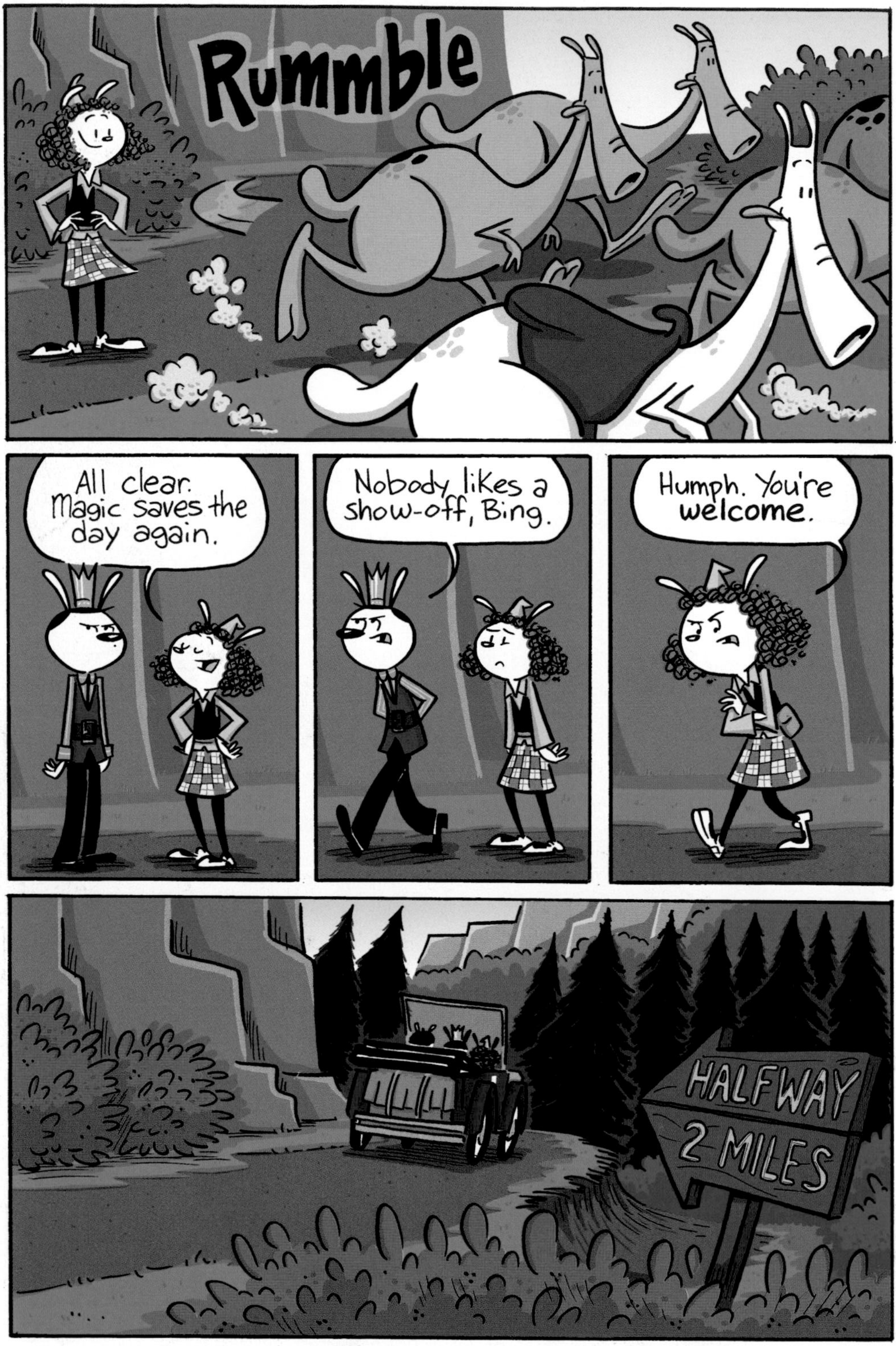
Rummble
All clear. Magic saves the day again.
Nobody likes a show-off, Bing.
Humph. You're **welcome**.
HALFWAY
2 MILES

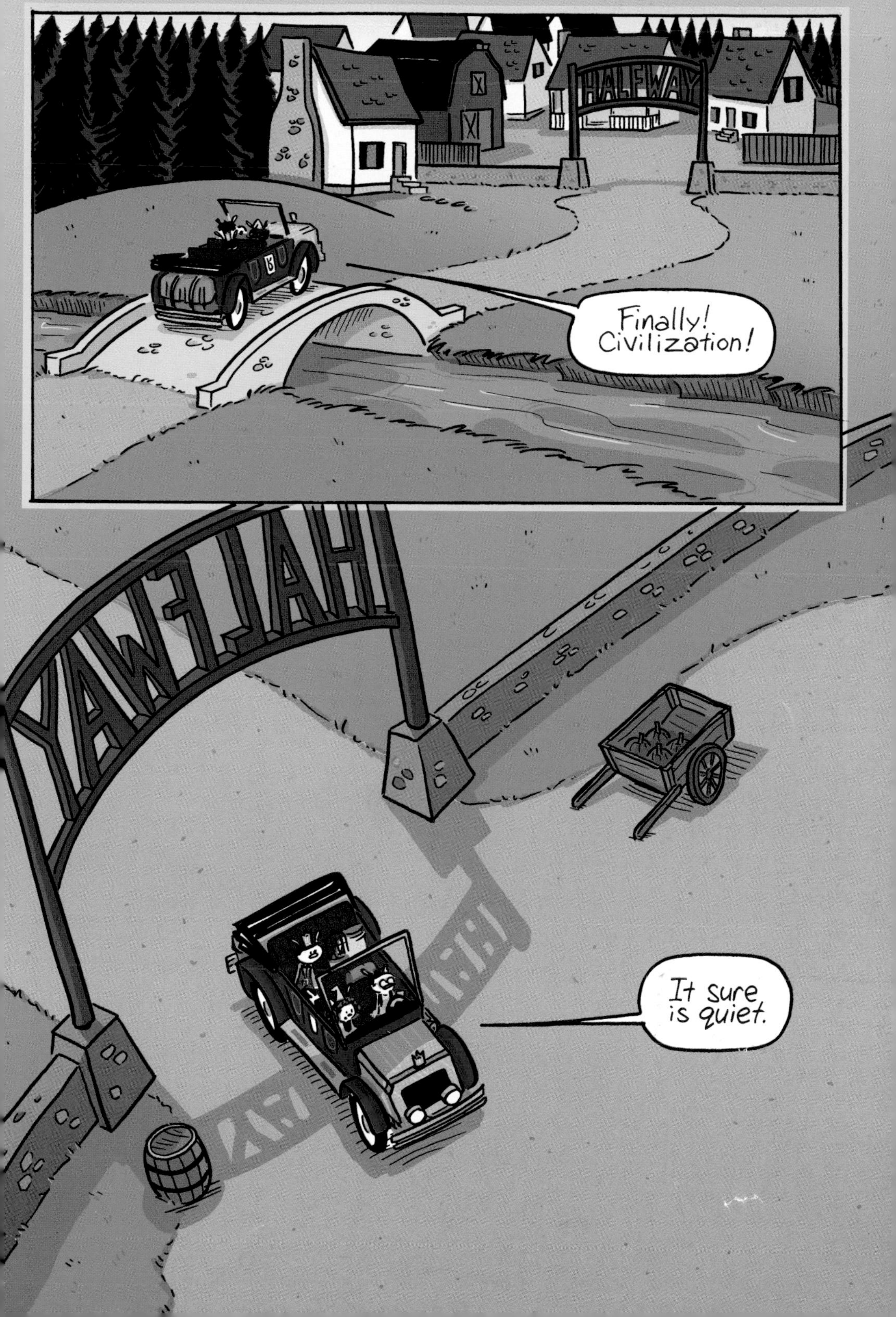
HALFWAY
Finally! Civilization!
HALFWAY
It sure is quiet.

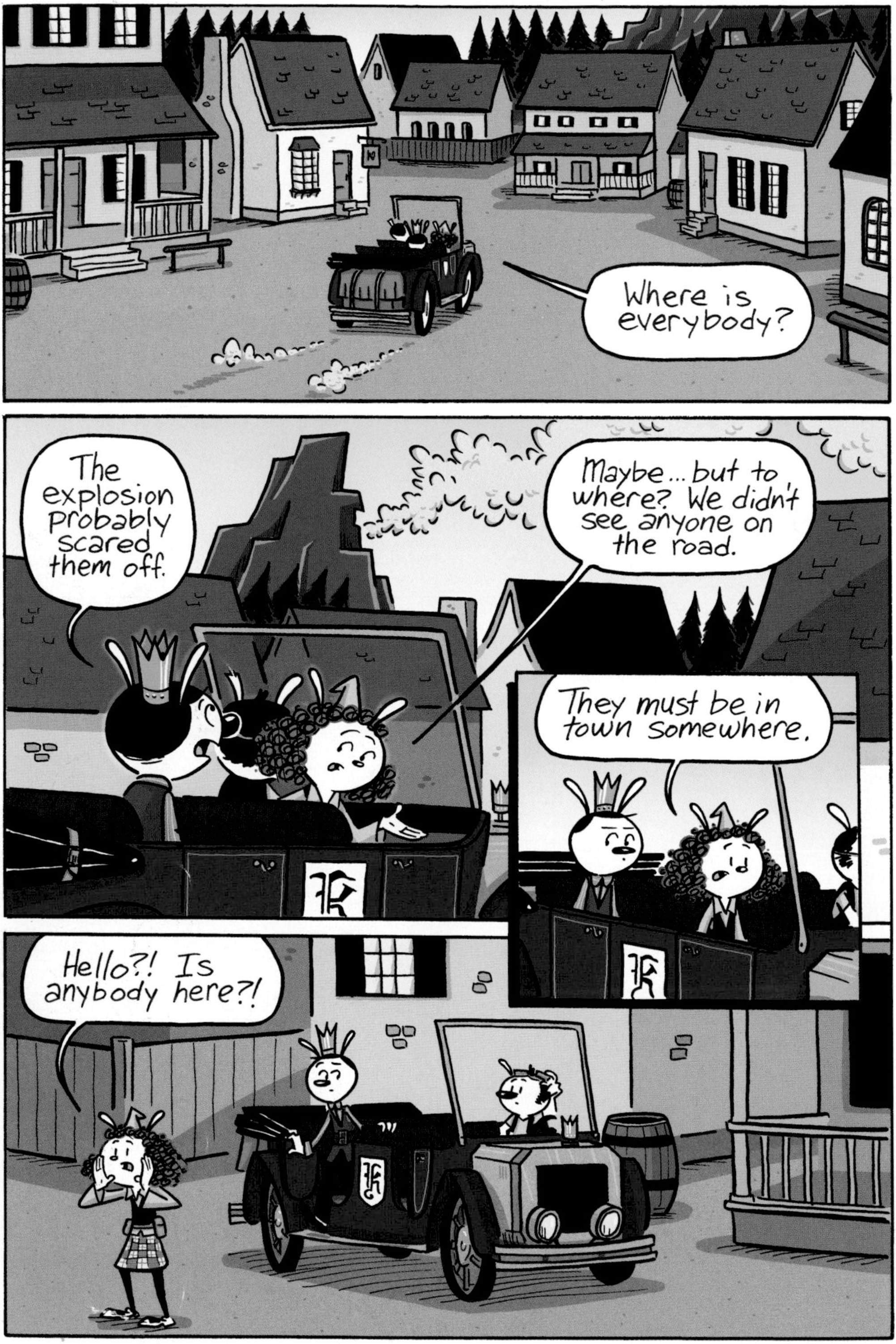
Where is everybody?
The explosion probably scared them off.
Maybe... but to where? We didn't see anyone on the road.
They must be in town somewhere.
Hello?! Is anybody here?!

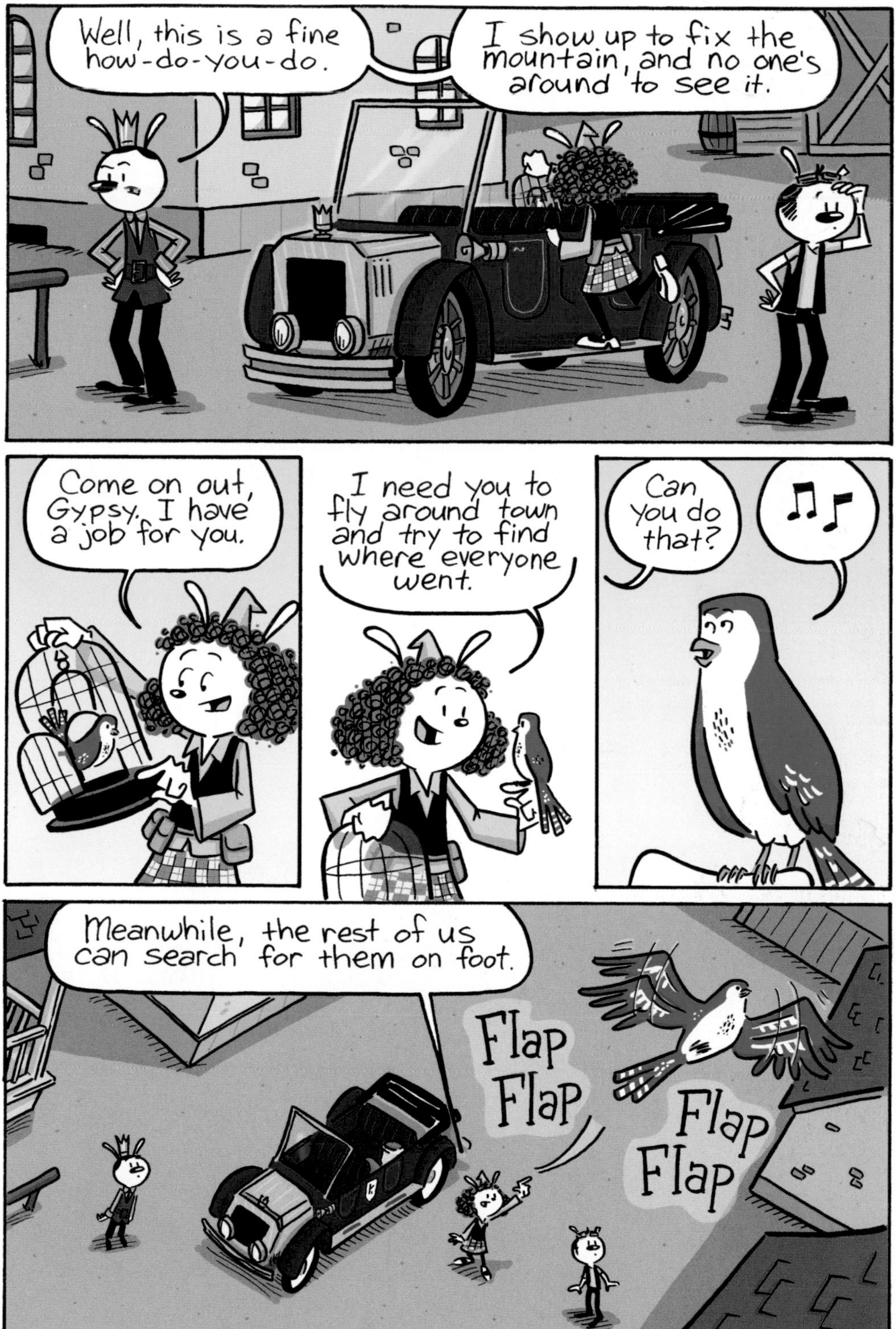
Well, this is a fine how-do-you-do.
I show up to fix the mountain, and no one's around to see it.
Come on out, Gypsy. I have a job for you.
I need you to fly around town and try to find where everyone went.
Can you do that?
♫♪
Meanwhile, the rest of us can search for them on foot.
Flap Flap
Flap Flap

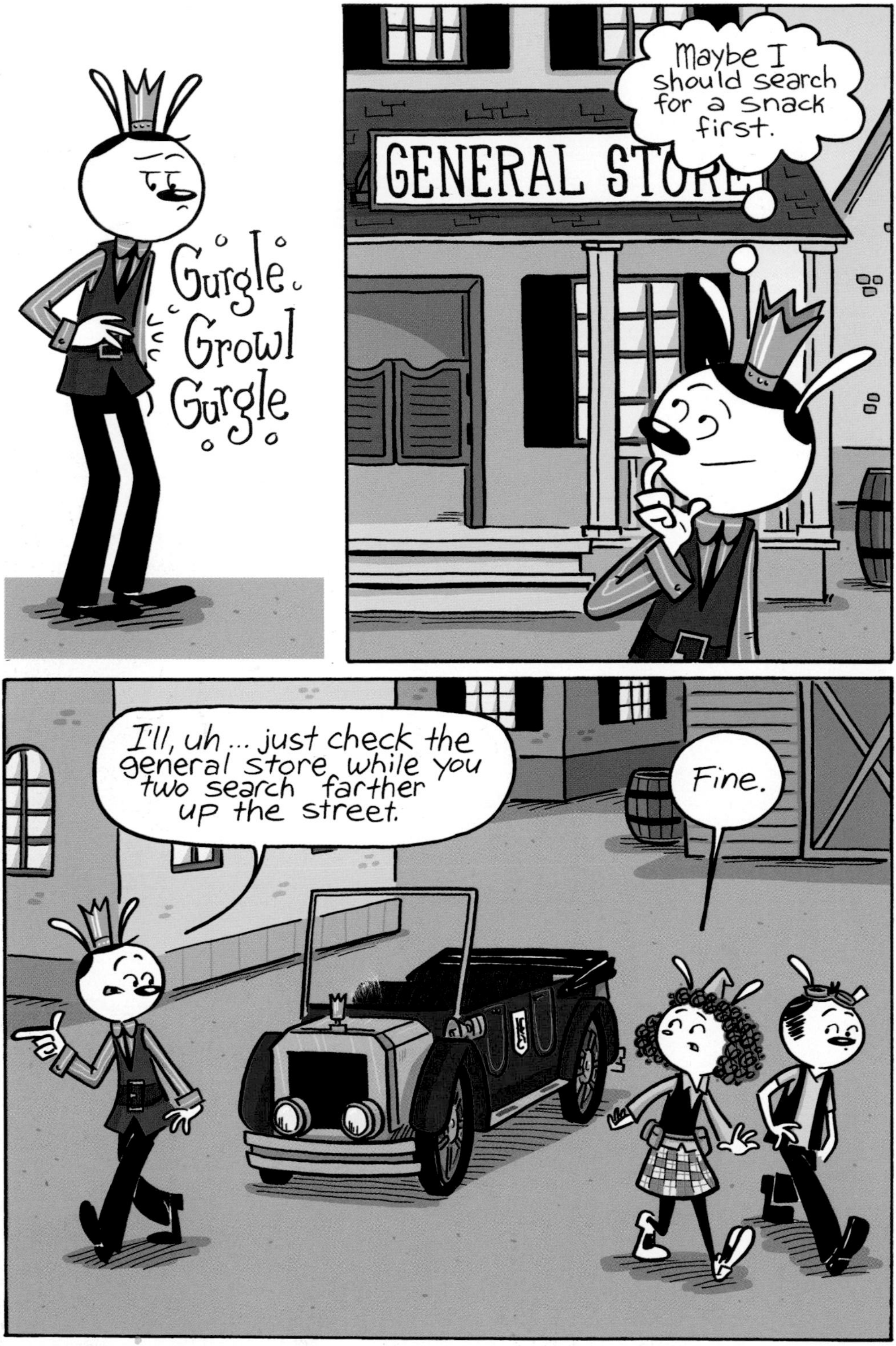
Gurgle
Growl
Gurgle
Maybe I should search for a snack first.
GENERAL STORE
I'll, uh ... just check the general store while you two search farther up the street.
Fine.

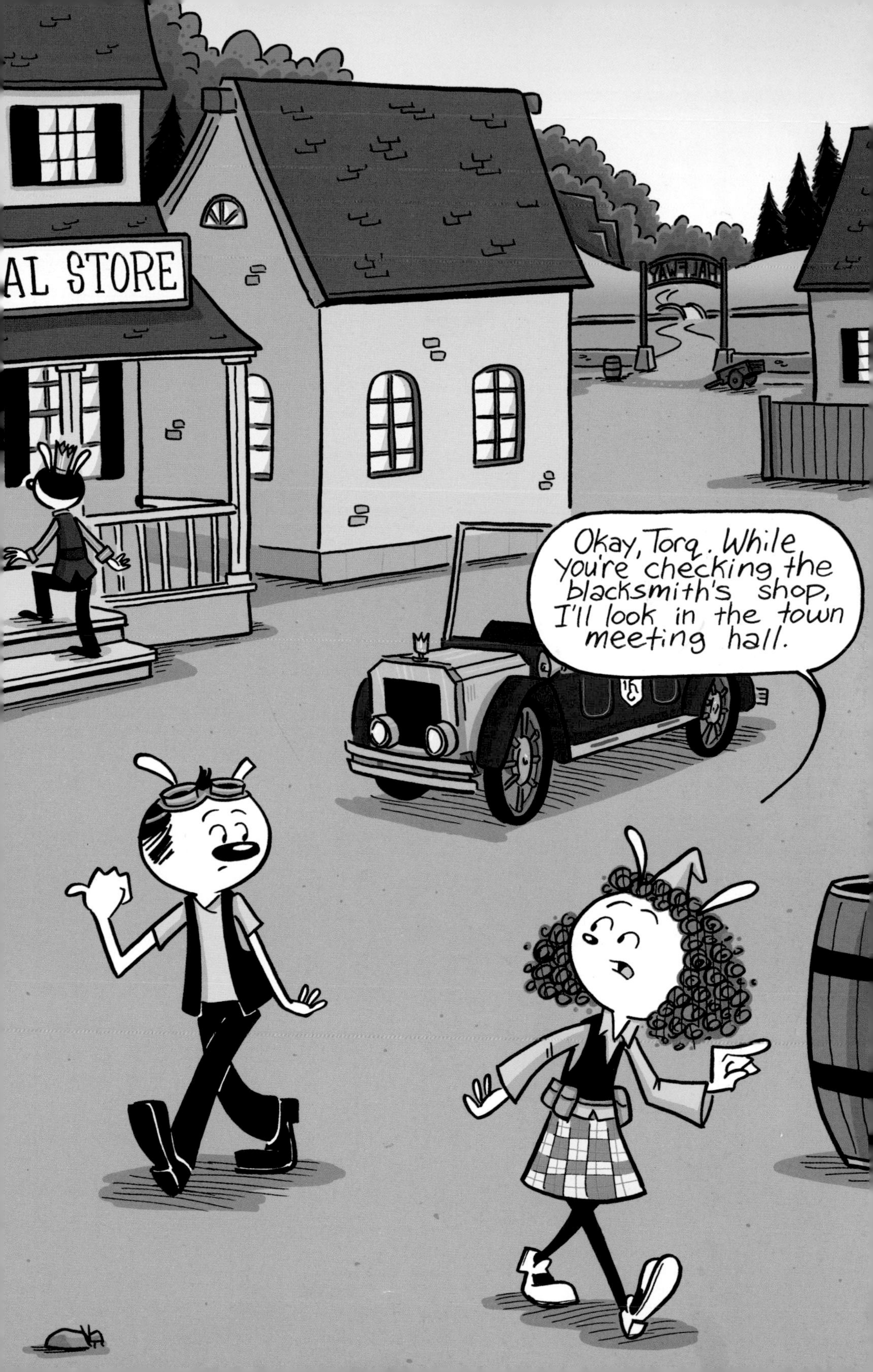
AL STORE
HALFWAY
Okay, Torq. While you're checking the blacksmith's shop, I'll look in the town meeting hall.

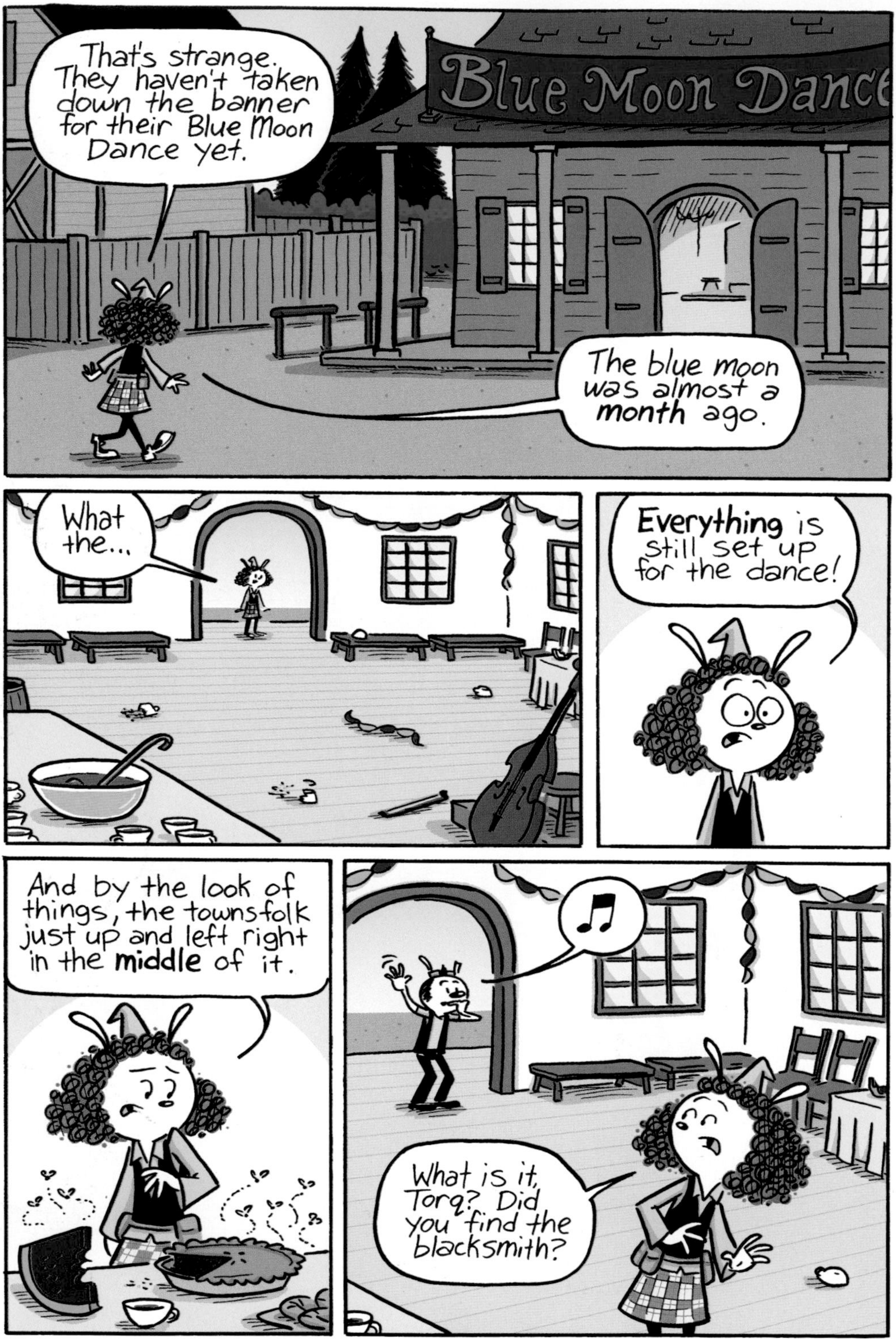
Blue Moon Dance
That's strange. They haven't taken down the banner for their Blue Moon Dance yet.
The blue moon was almost a **month** ago.
What the...
Everything is still set up for the dance!
And by the look of things, the townsfolk just up and left right in the **middle** of it.
♫
What is it, Torq? Did you find the blacksmith?

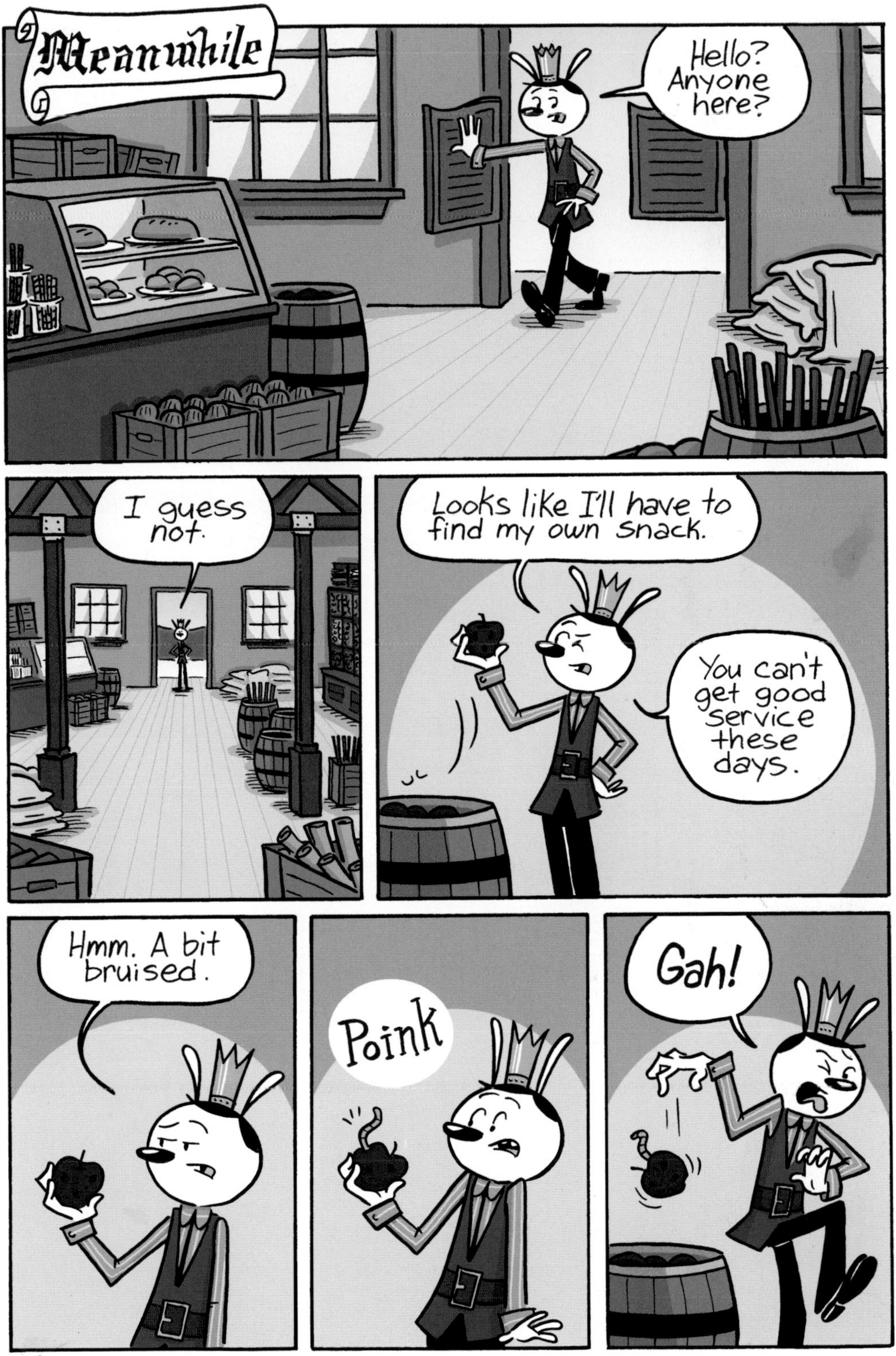
Meanwhile
Hello? Anyone here?
I guess not.
Looks like I'll have to find my own snack.
You can't get good service these days.
Hmm. A bit bruised.
Poink
Gah!

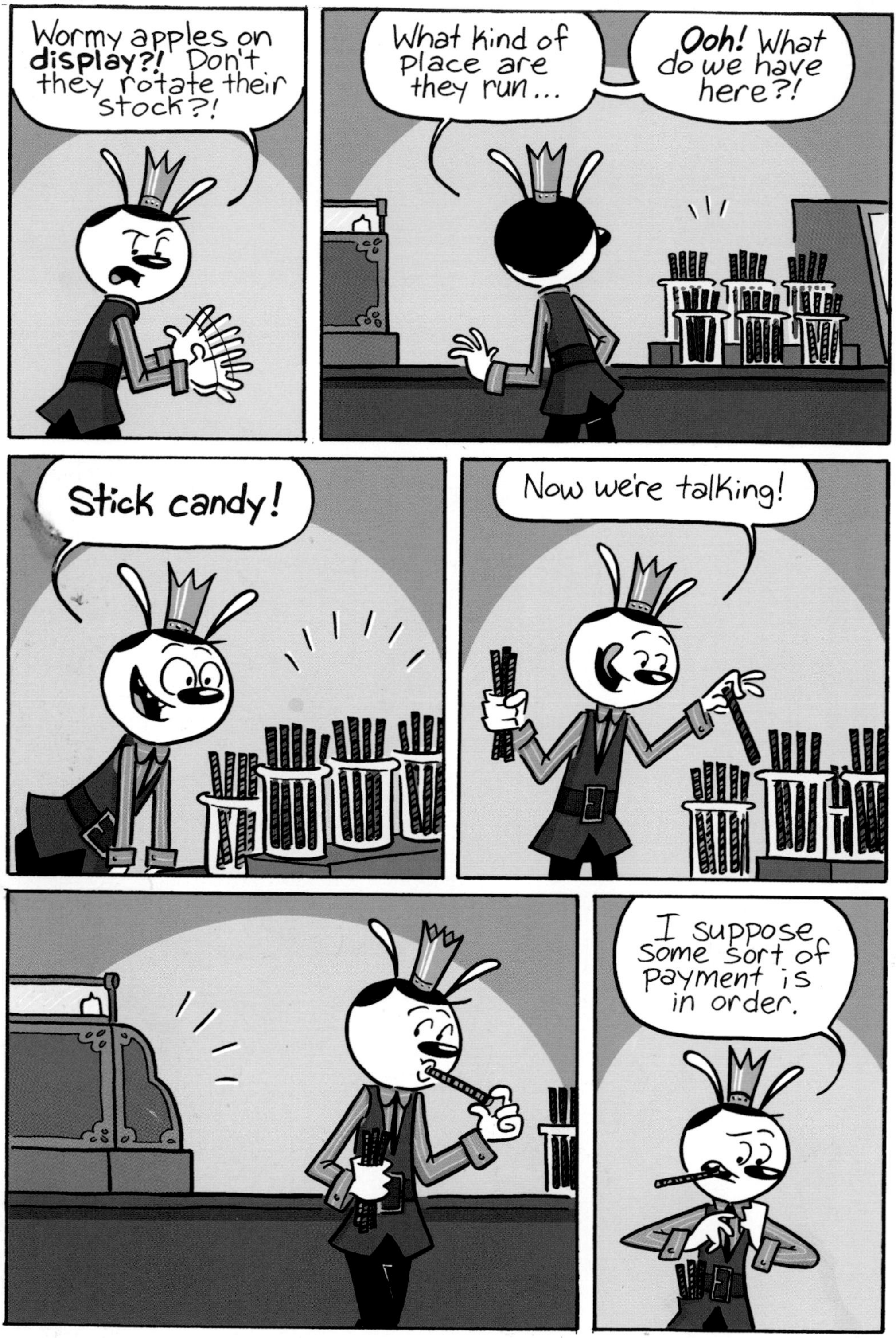
Wormy apples on **display?!** Don't they rotate their stock?!
What kind of place are they run...
Ooh! What do we have here?!
Stick candy!
Now we're talking!
I suppose some sort of payment is in order.

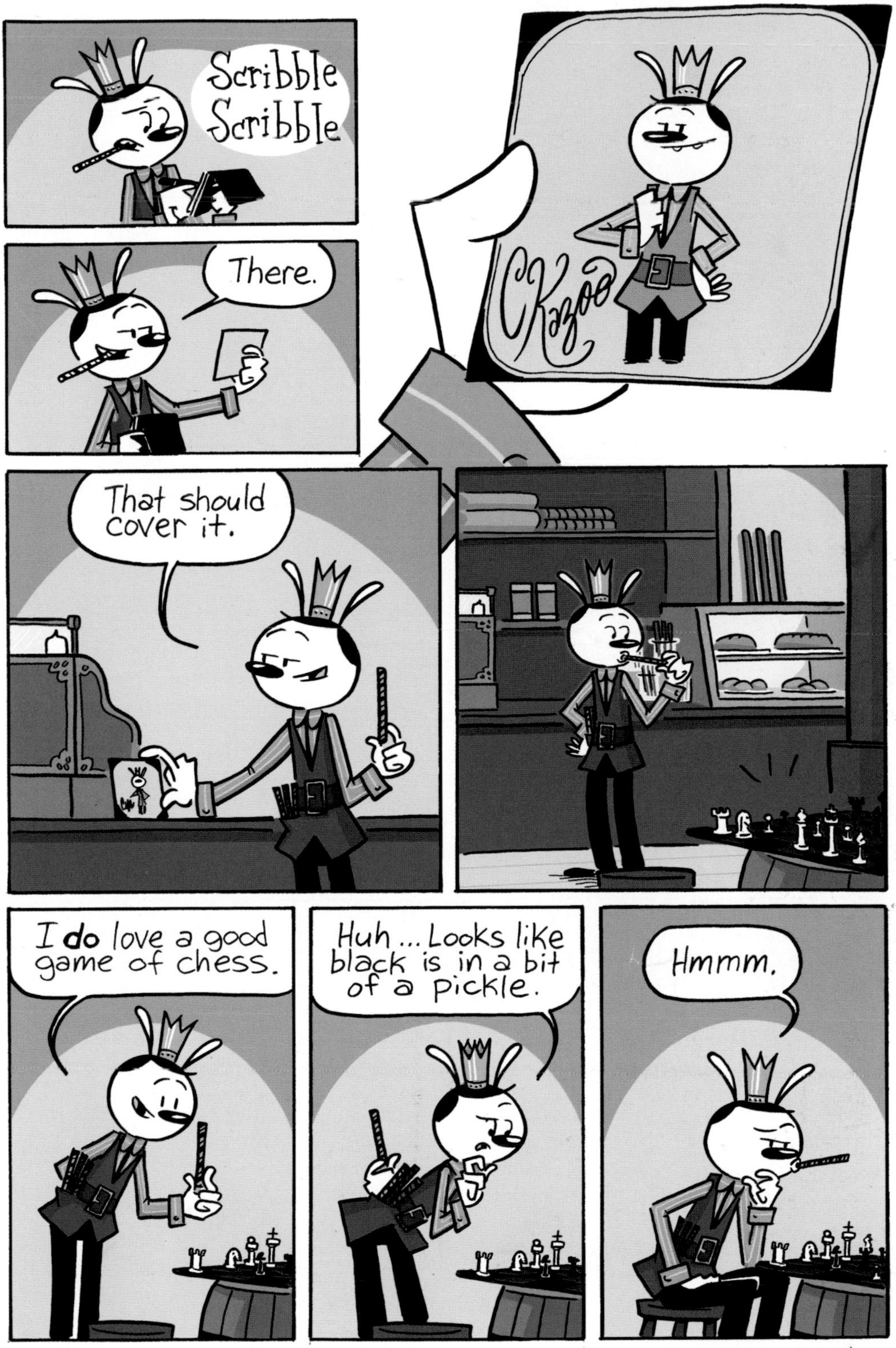
Scribble Scribble
There.
That should cover it.
I **do** love a good game of chess.
Huh ... Looks like black is in a bit of a pickle.
Hmmm.

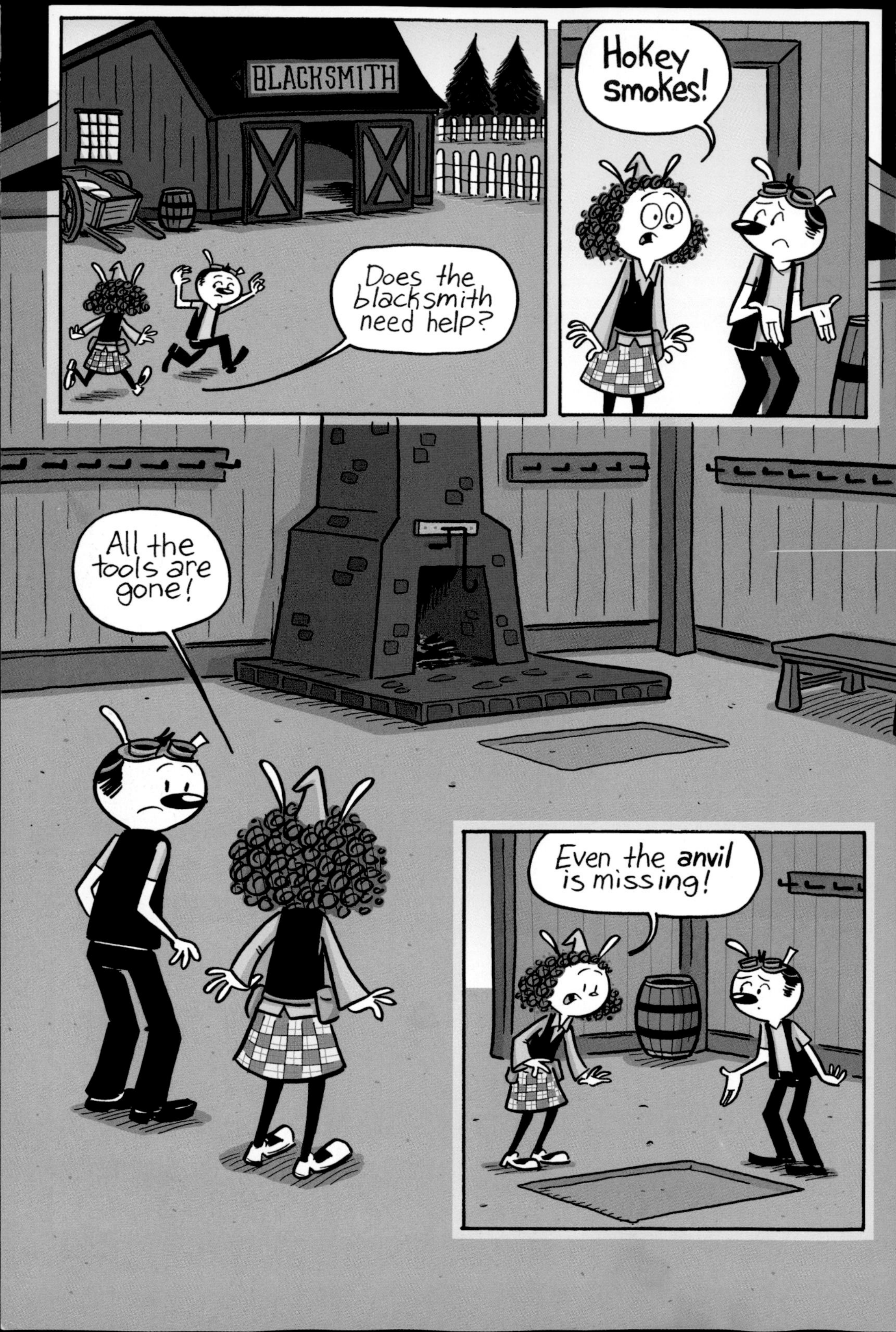
BLACKSMITH
Does the blacksmith need help?
Hokey smokes!
All the tools are gone!
Even the anvil is missing!

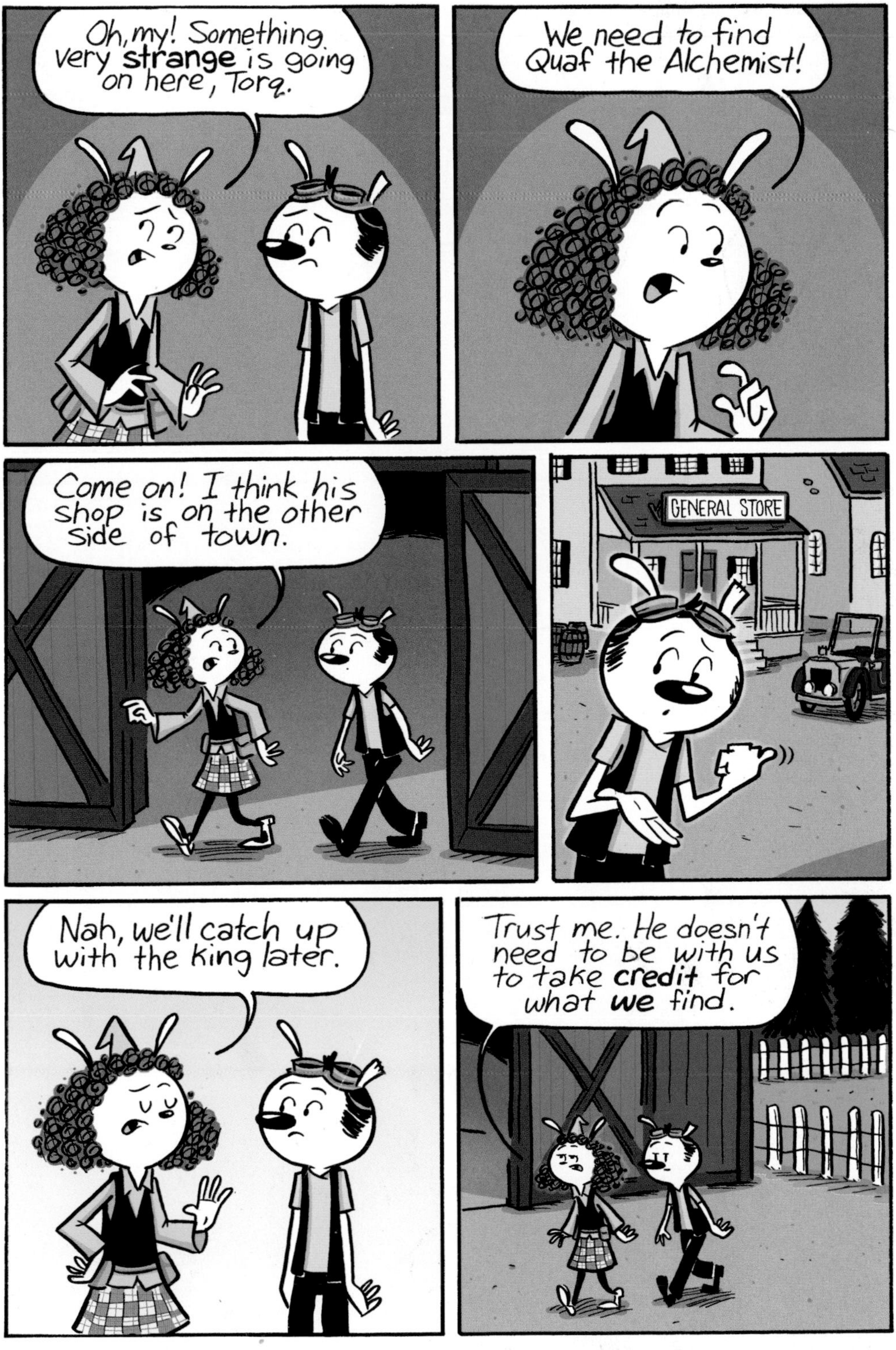
Oh, my! Something very **strange** is going on here, Torq.
We need to find Quaf the Alchemist!
Come on! I think his shop is on the other side of town.
GENERAL STORE
Nah, we'll catch up with the king later.
Trust me. He doesn't need to be with us to take **credit** for what **we** find.

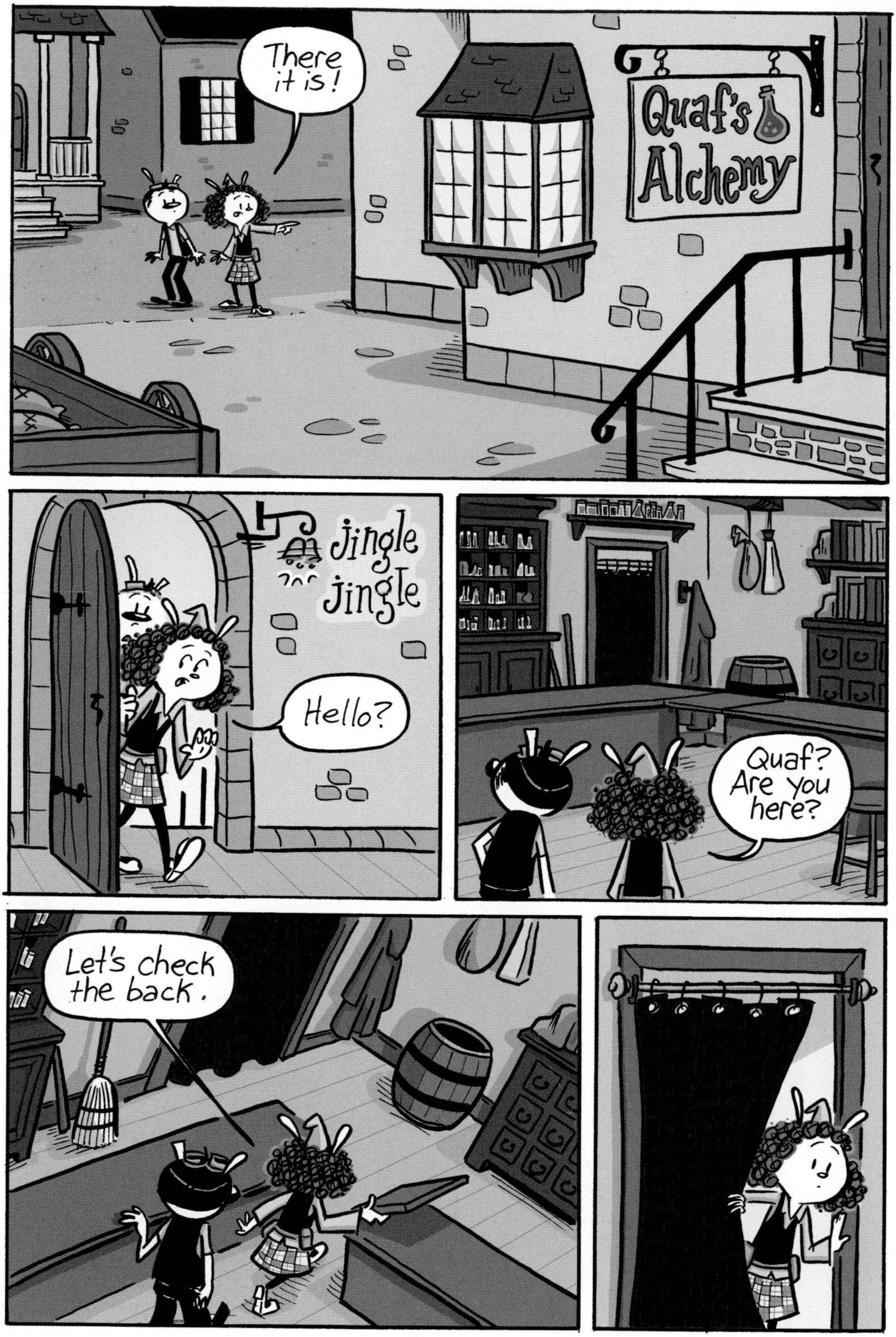
There it is!
Quaf's Alchemy
jingle jingle
Hello?
Quaf? Are you here?
Let's check the back.

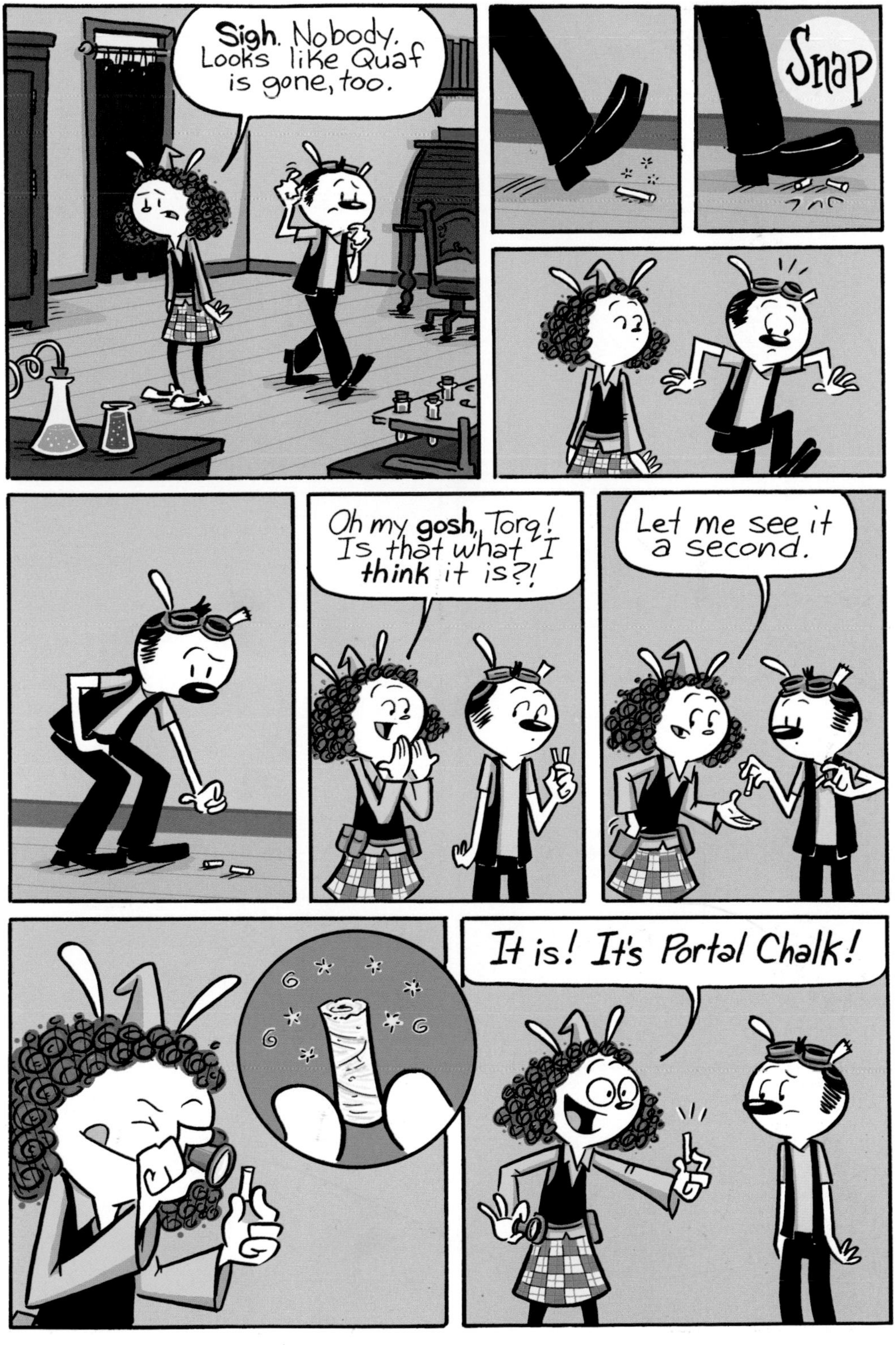
Sigh. Nobody. Looks like Quaf is gone, too.
Snap
Oh my gosh, Torq! Is that what I think it is?!
Let me see it a second.
It is! It's Portal Chalk!

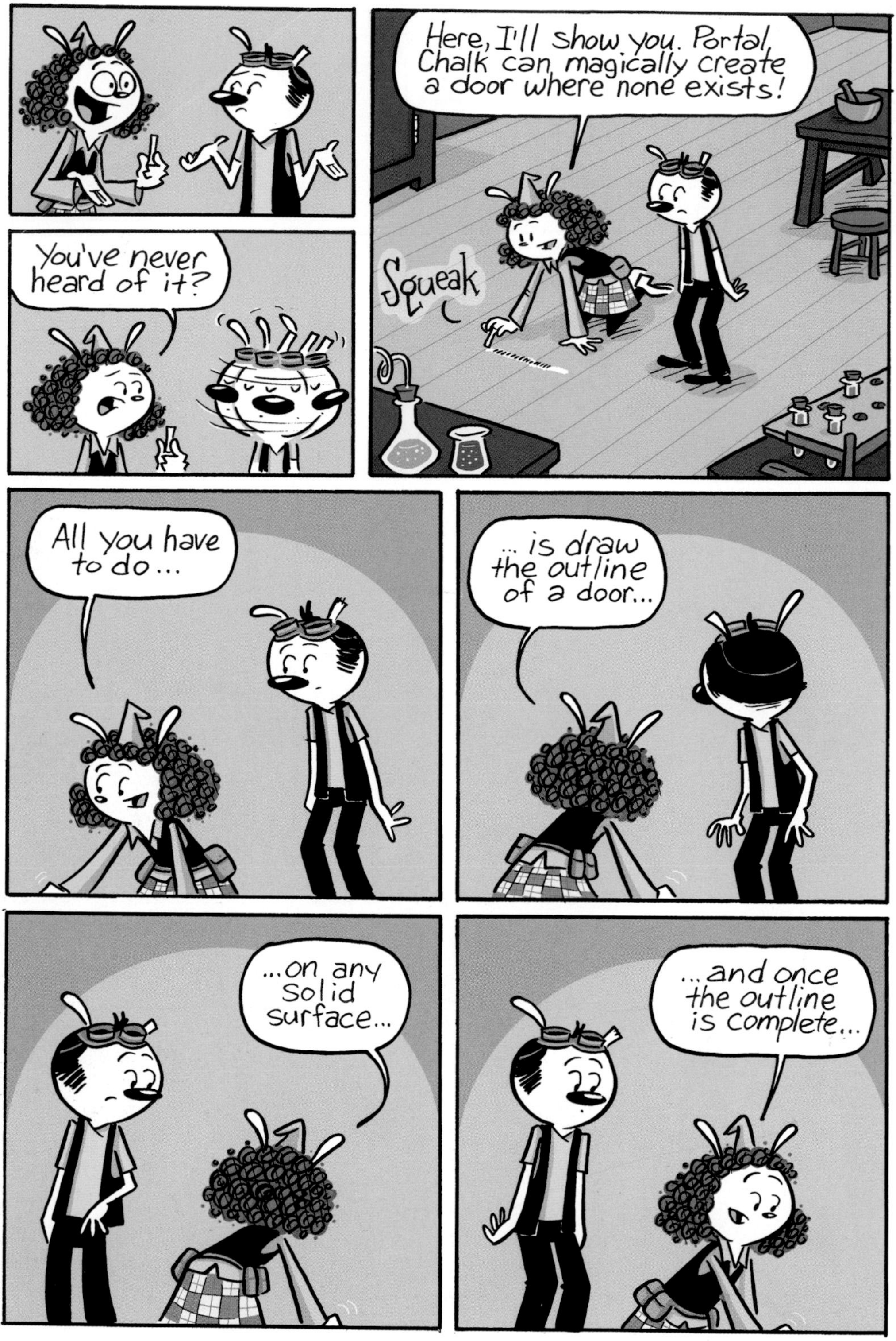
Here, I'll show you. Portal Chalk can magically create a door where none exists!
You've never heard of it?
Squeak
All you have to do...
... is draw the outline of a door...
...on any solid surface...
...and once the outline is complete...

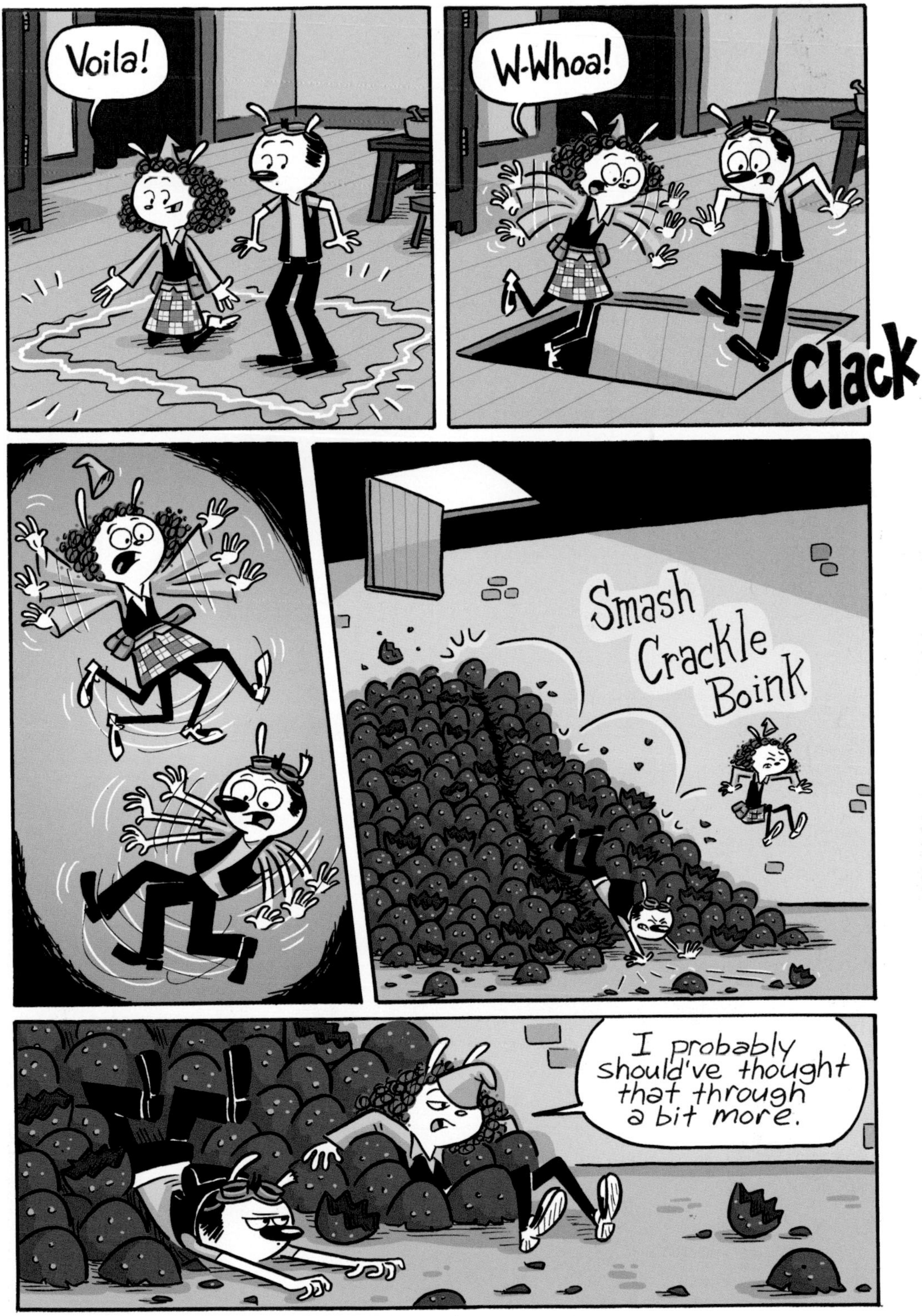
Voila!
W-Whoa!
Clack
Smash
Crackle
Boink
I probably should've thought that through a bit more.

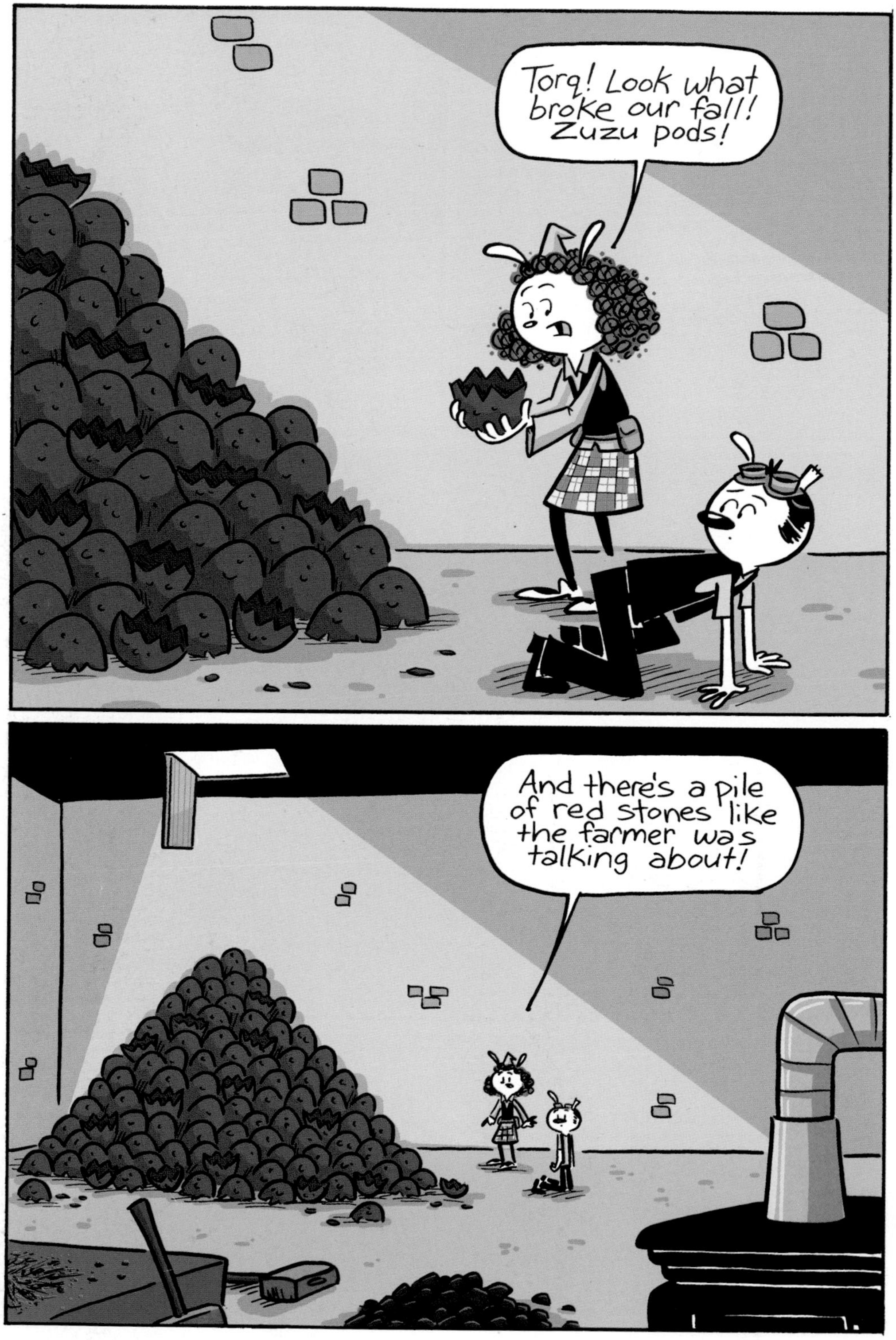
Torq! Look what broke our fall! Zuzu pods!
And there's a pile of red stones like the farmer was talking about!

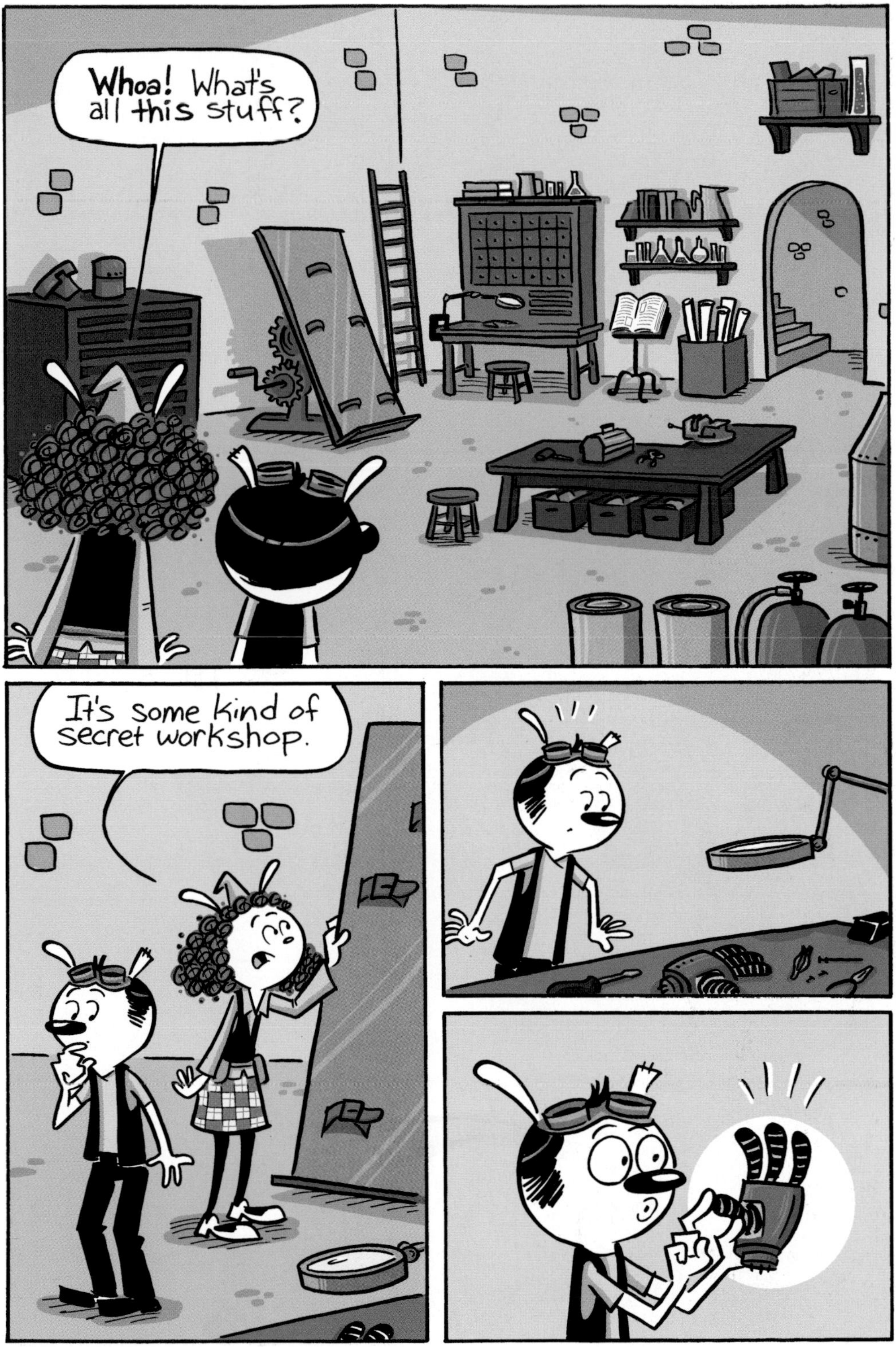
Whoa! What's all this stuff?
It's some kind of secret workshop.

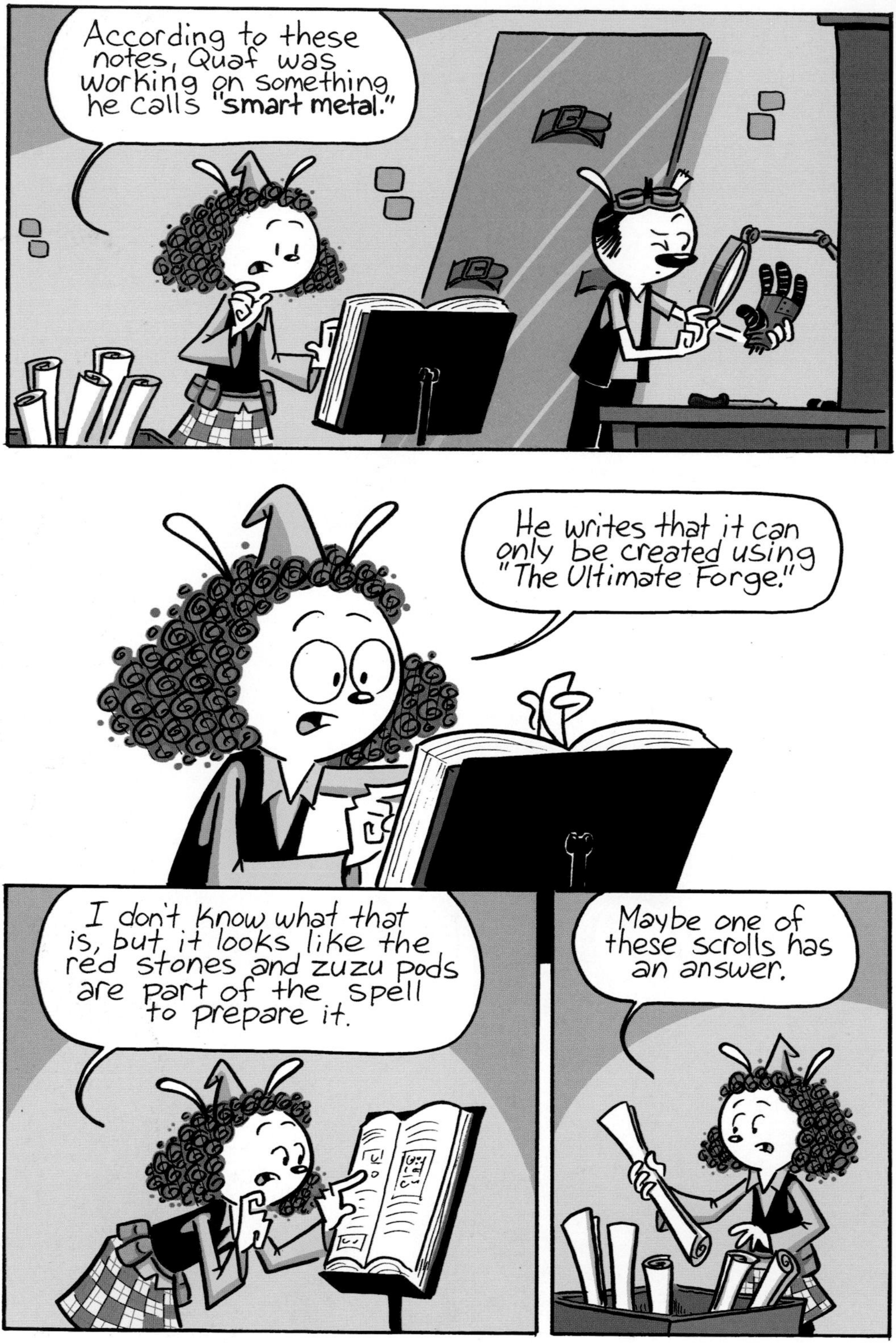
According to these notes, Quaf was working on something he calls "smart metal."
He writes that it can only be created using "The Ultimate Forge."
I don't know what that is, but it looks like the red stones and zuzu pods are part of the spell to prepare it.
Maybe one of these scrolls has an answer.

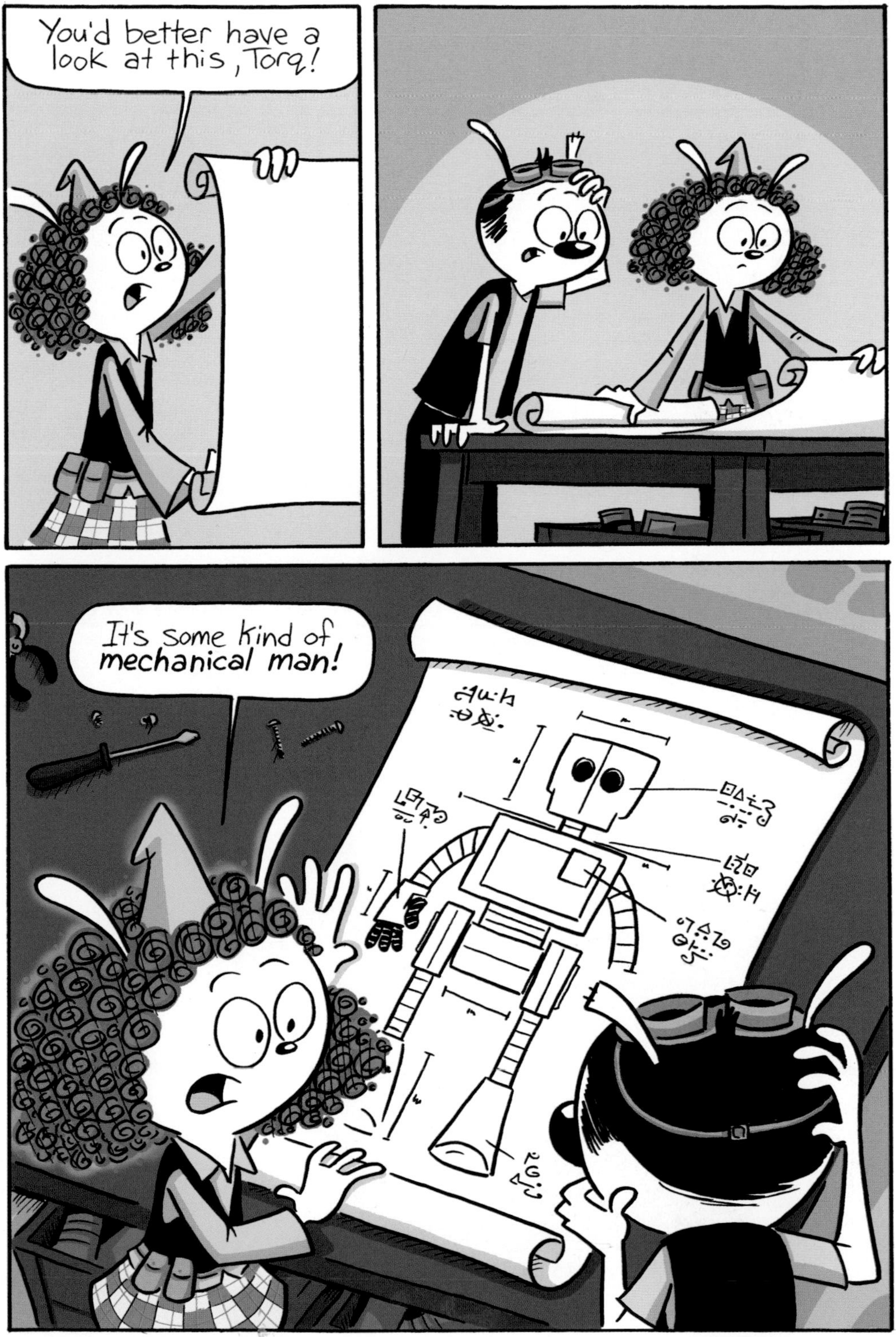
You'd better have a look at this, Torq!
It's some kind of **mechanical man!**

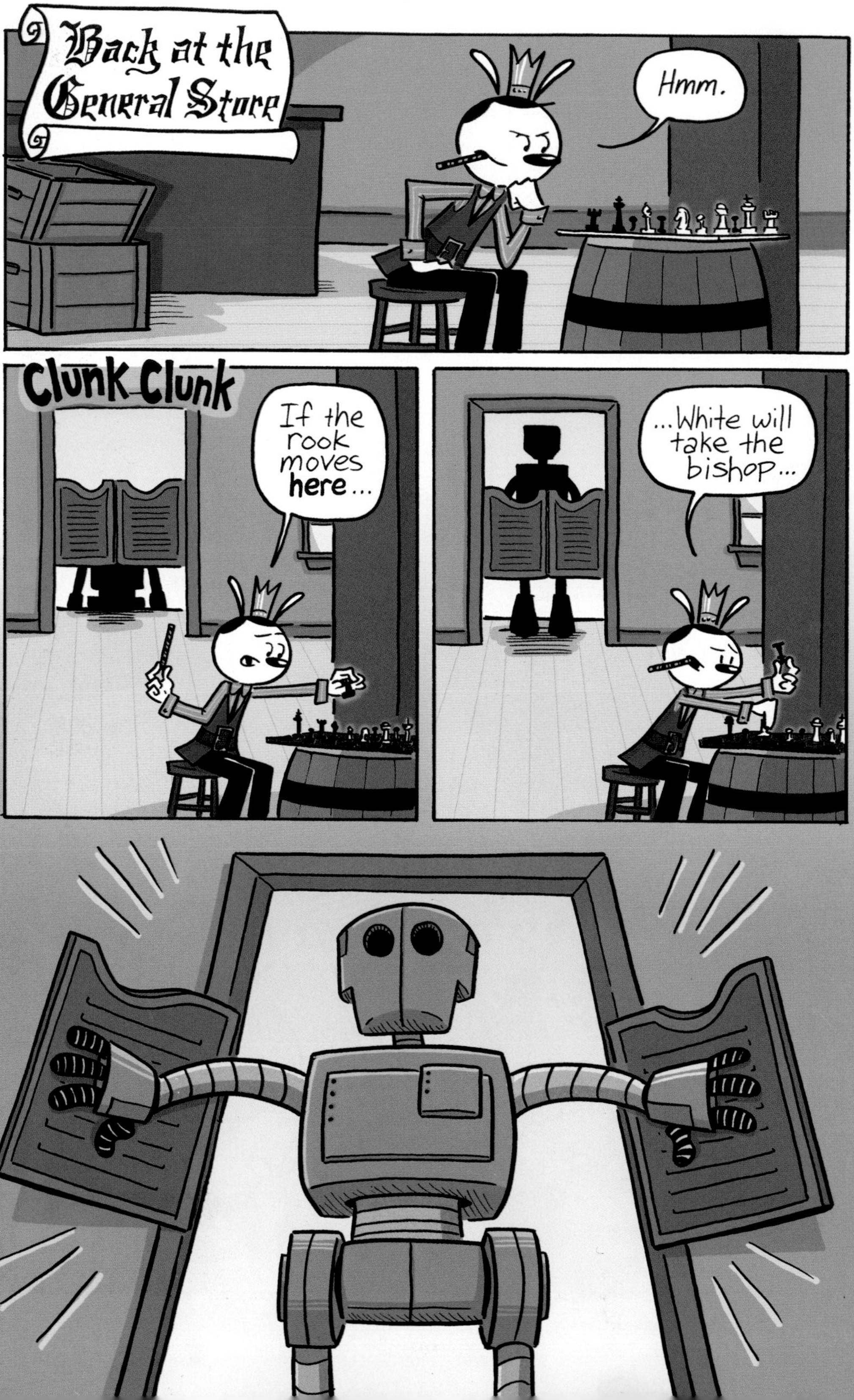
Back at the General Store
Hmm.
Clunk Clunk
If the rook moves **here**...
...White will take the bishop...

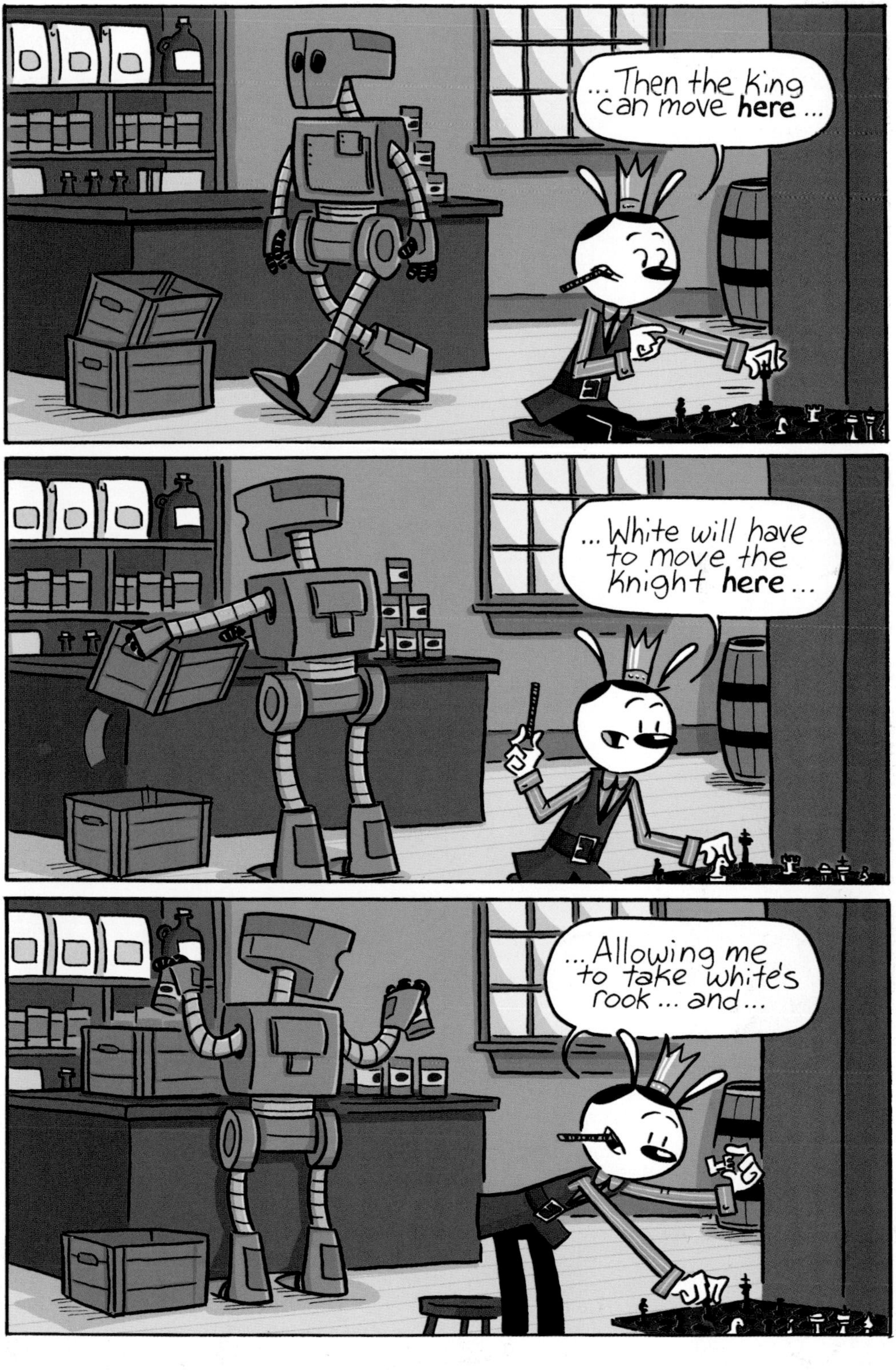
...Then the King can move **here**...
...White will have to move the Knight **here**...
...Allowing me to take white's rook... and...

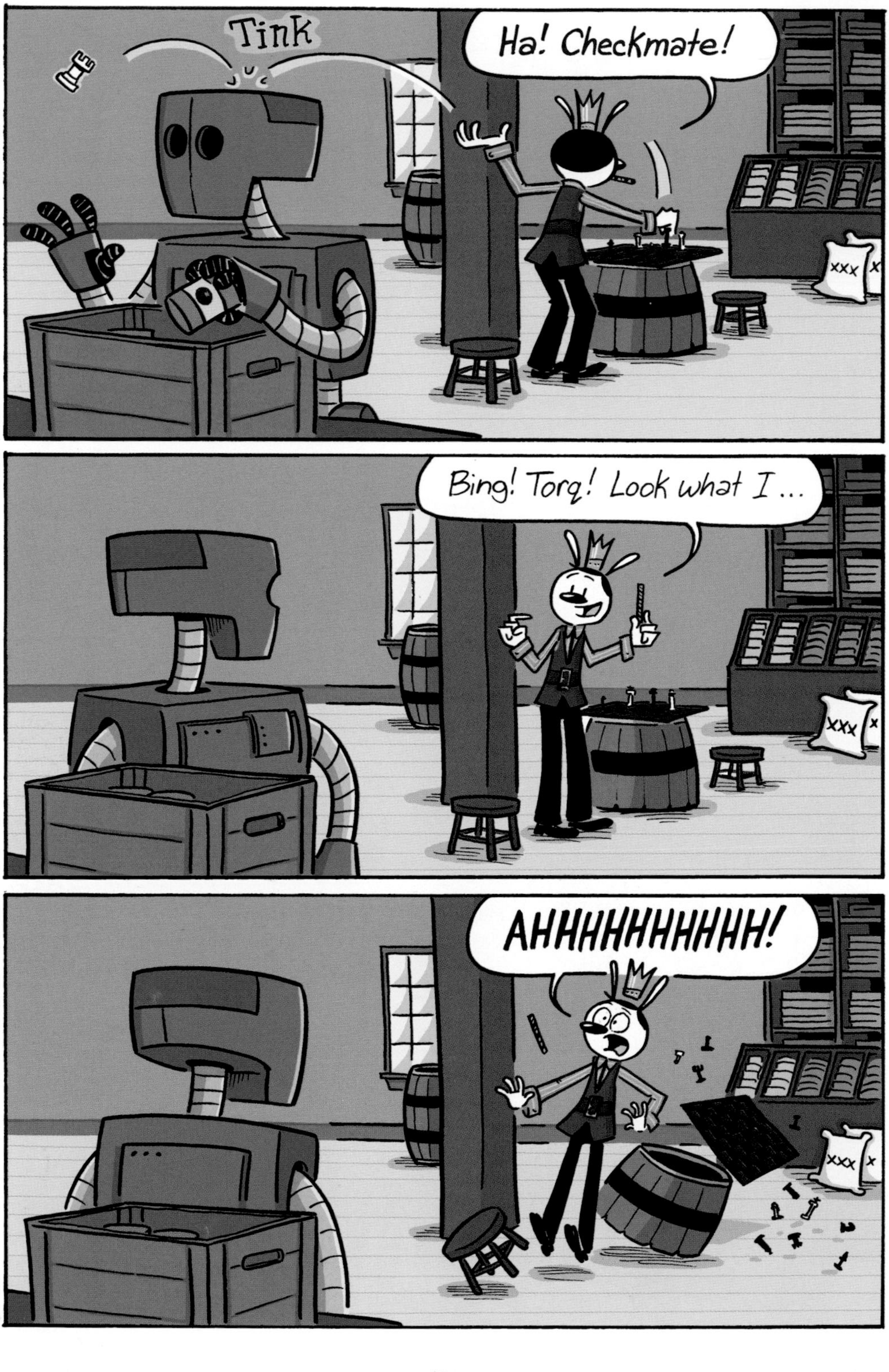
TINK
Ha! Checkmate!
Bing! Torq! Look what I...
AHHHHHHHHHH!

AHHHHHHHHHHHHHHH!

WHAM

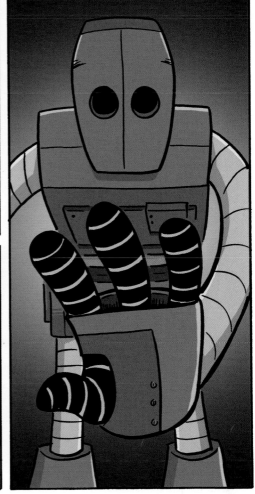

THUD

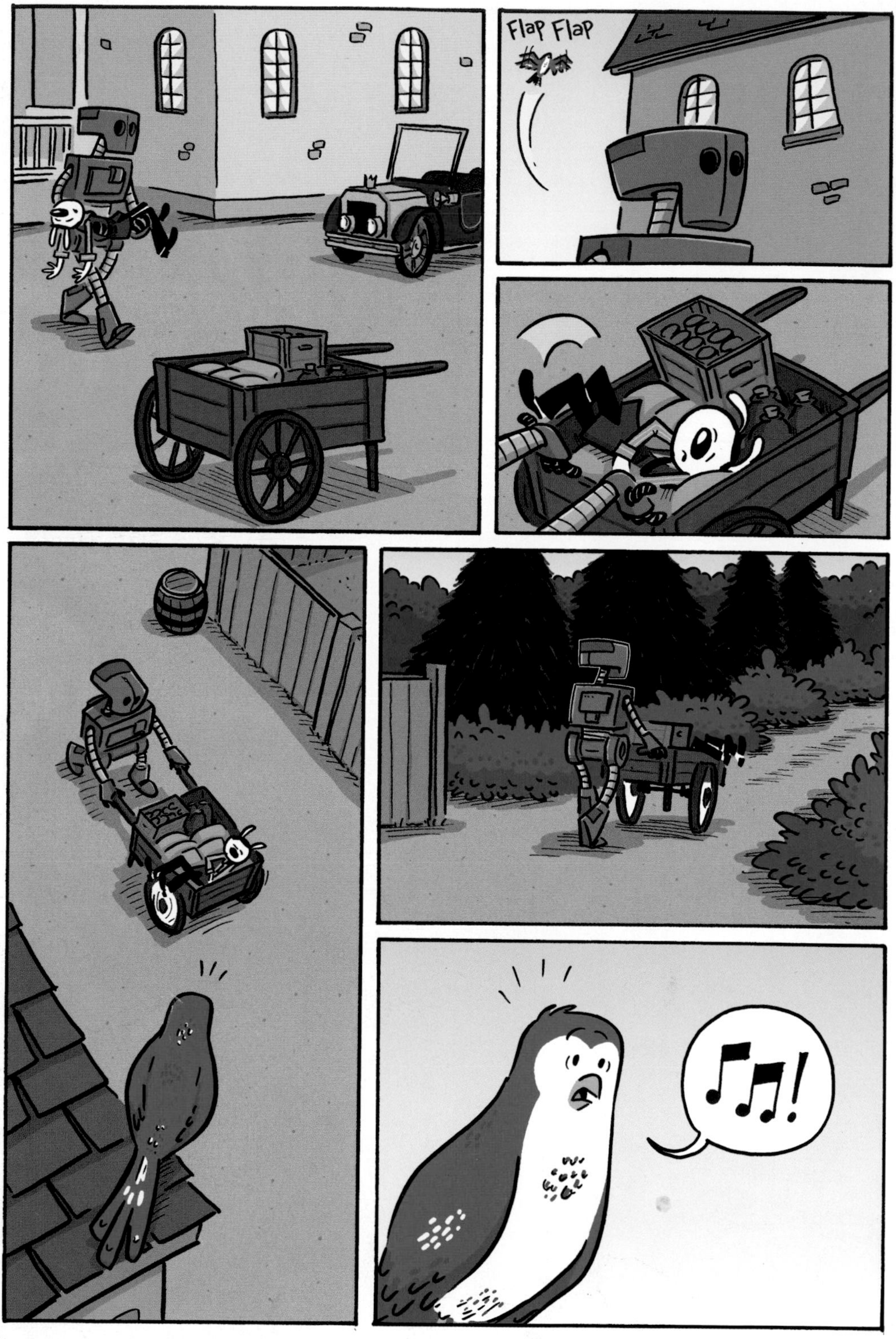
Flap Flap

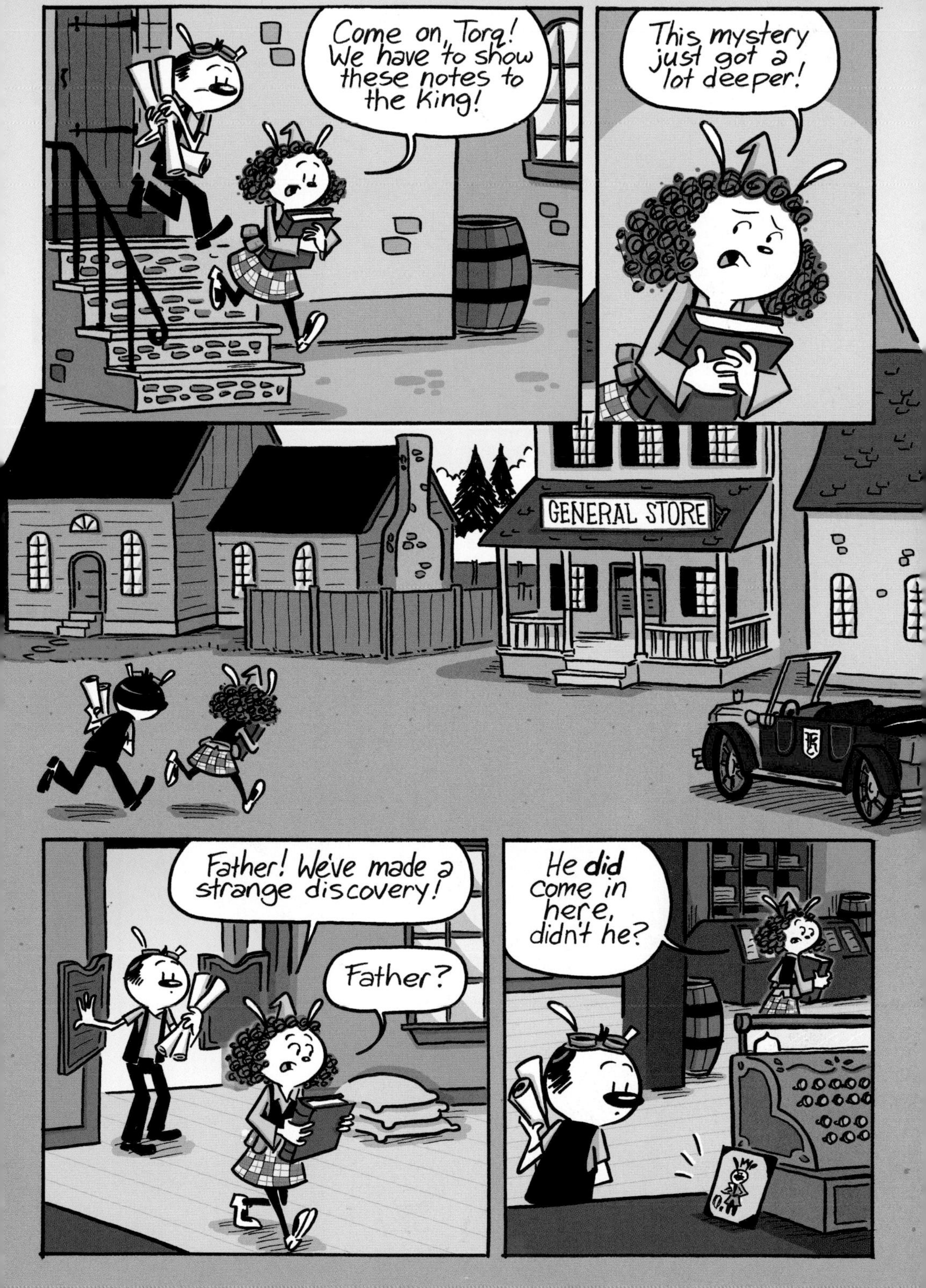
Come on, Torq! We have to show these notes to the King!
This mystery just got a lot deeper!
GENERAL STORE
Father! We've made a strange discovery!
Father?
He **did** come in here, didn't he?

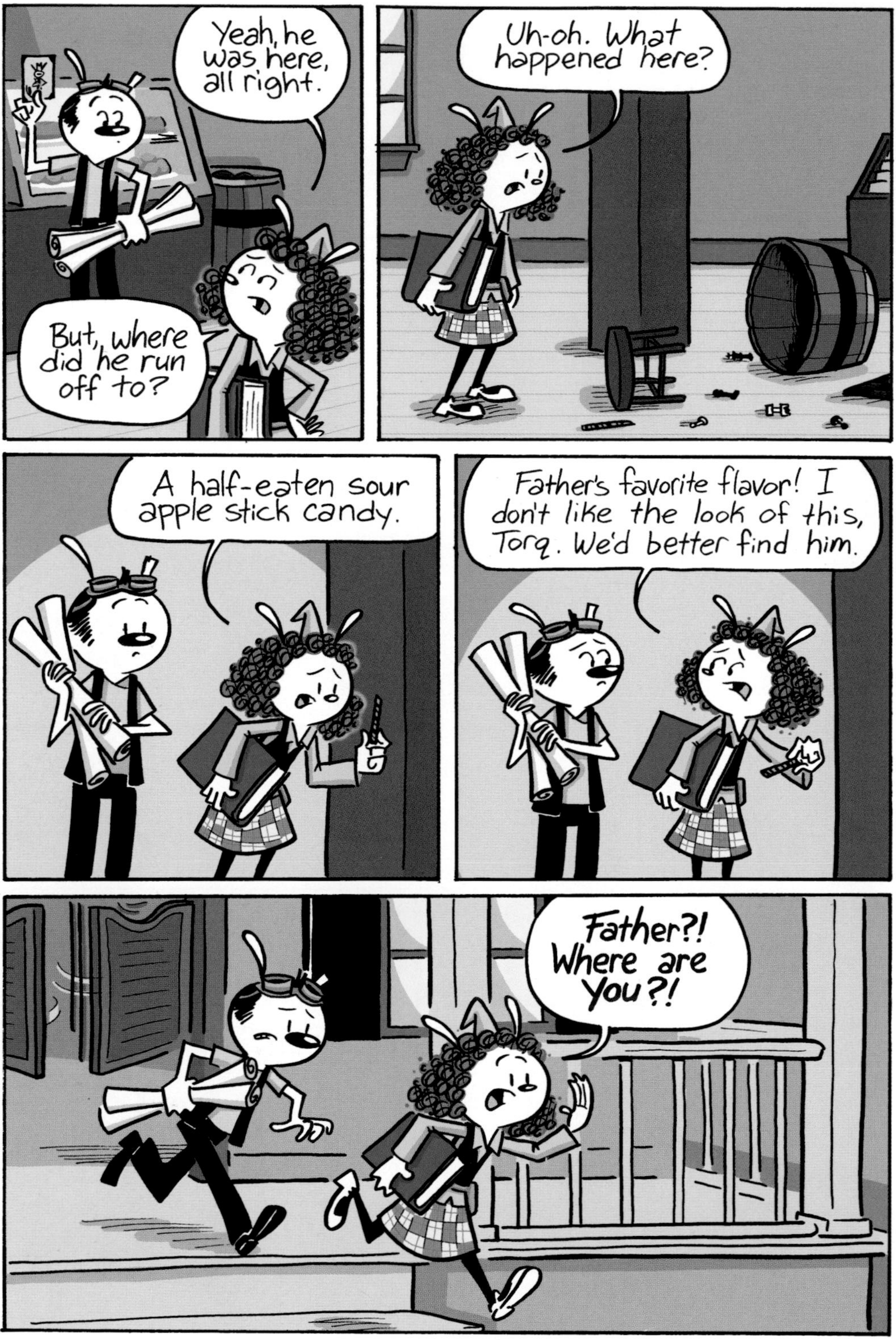
Yeah, he was here, all right.
But, where did he run off to?
Uh-oh. What happened here?
A half-eaten sour apple stick candy.
Father's favorite flavor! I don't like the look of this, Torq. We'd better find him.
Father?! Where are You?!

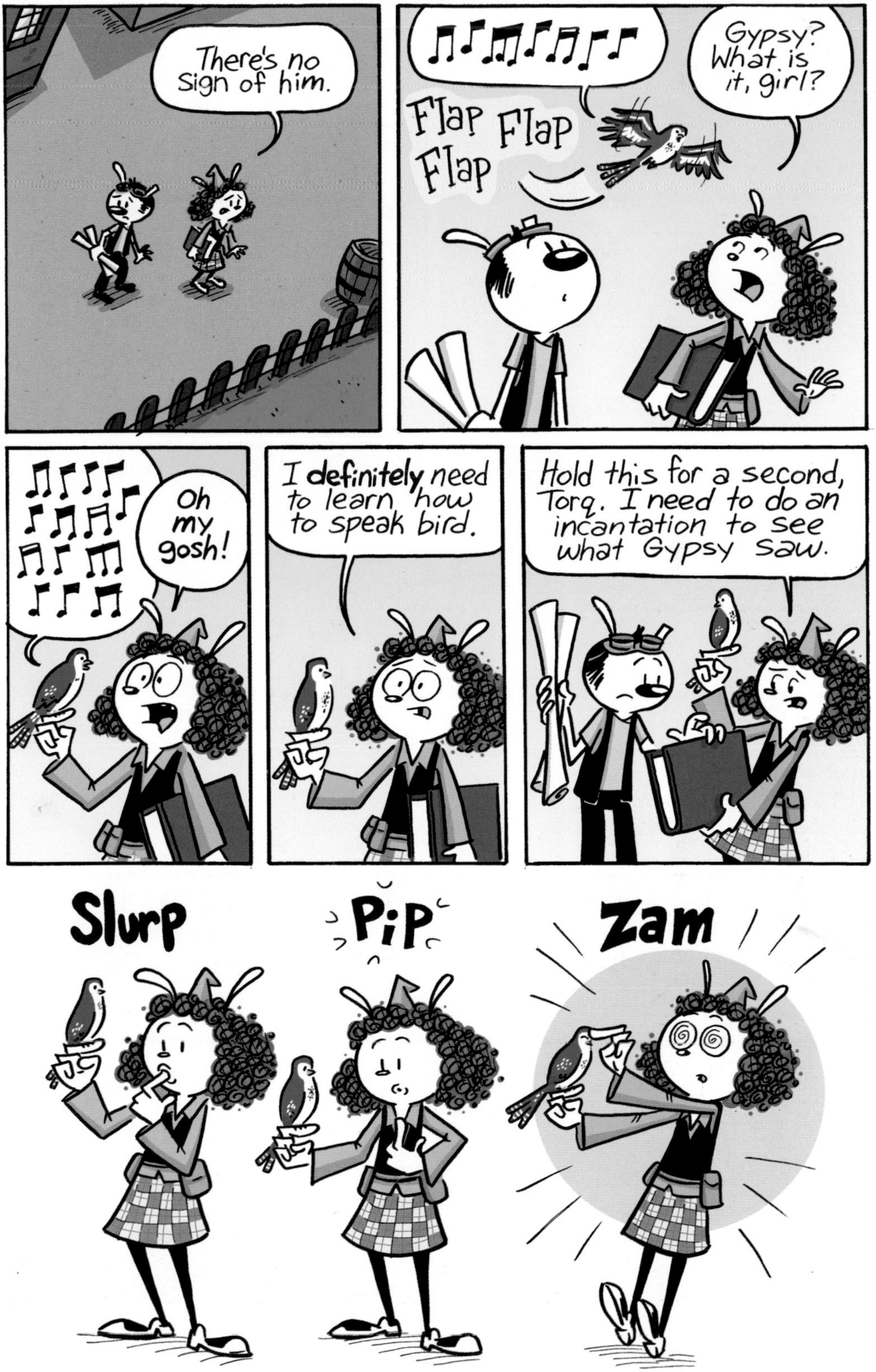
There's no sign of him.
Flap Flap Flap
Gypsy? What is it, girl?
Oh my gosh!
I **definitely** need to learn how to speak bird.
Hold this for a second, Torq. I need to do an incantation to see what Gypsy saw.
Slurp
Pip
Zam

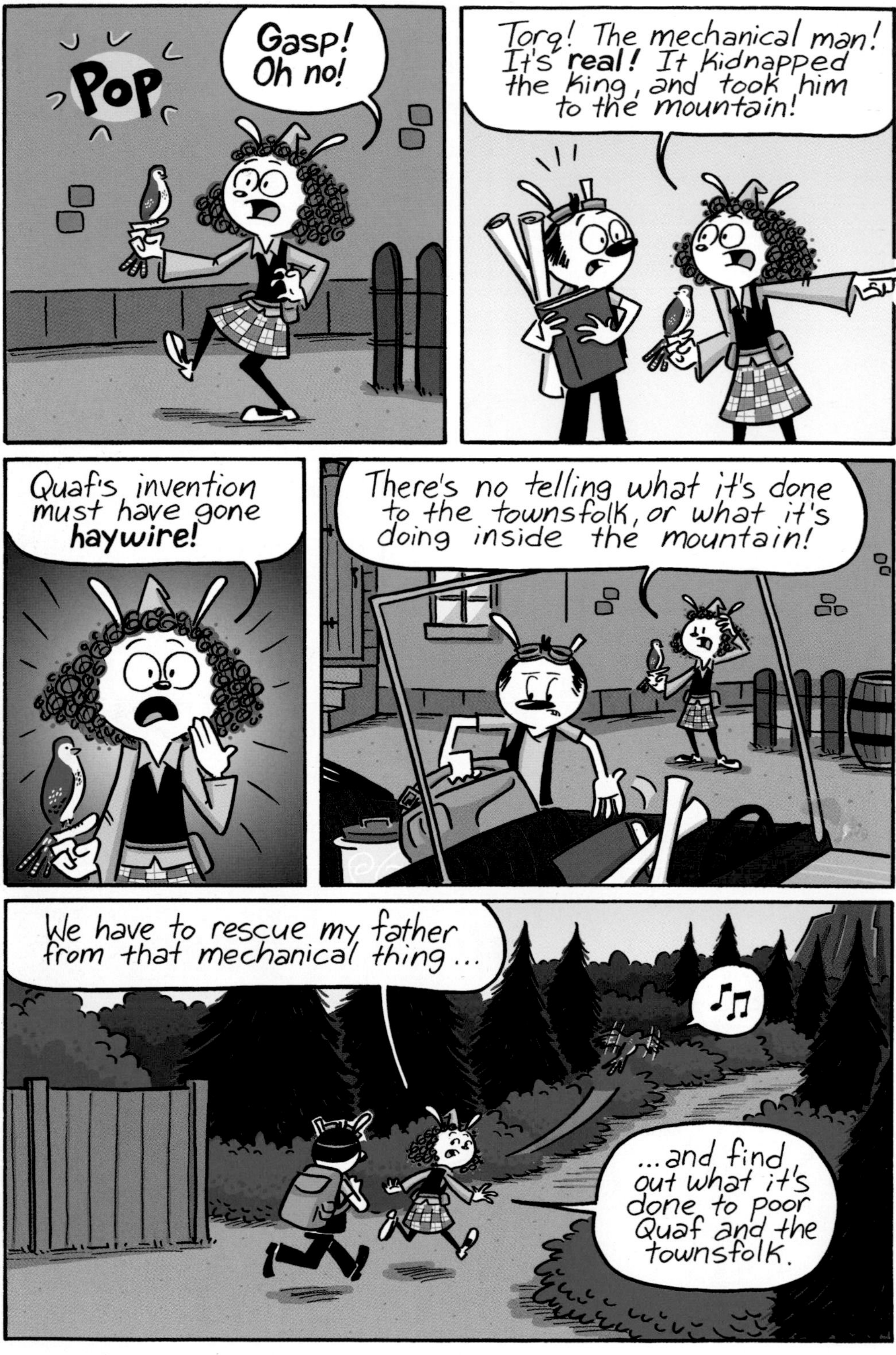
POP
Gasp! Oh no!
Torq! The mechanical man! It's **real!** It kidnapped the king, and took him to the mountain!
Quaf's invention must have gone **haywire!**
There's no telling what it's done to the townsfolk, or what it's doing inside the mountain!
We have to rescue my father from that mechanical thing...
...and find out what it's done to poor Quaf and the townsfolk.

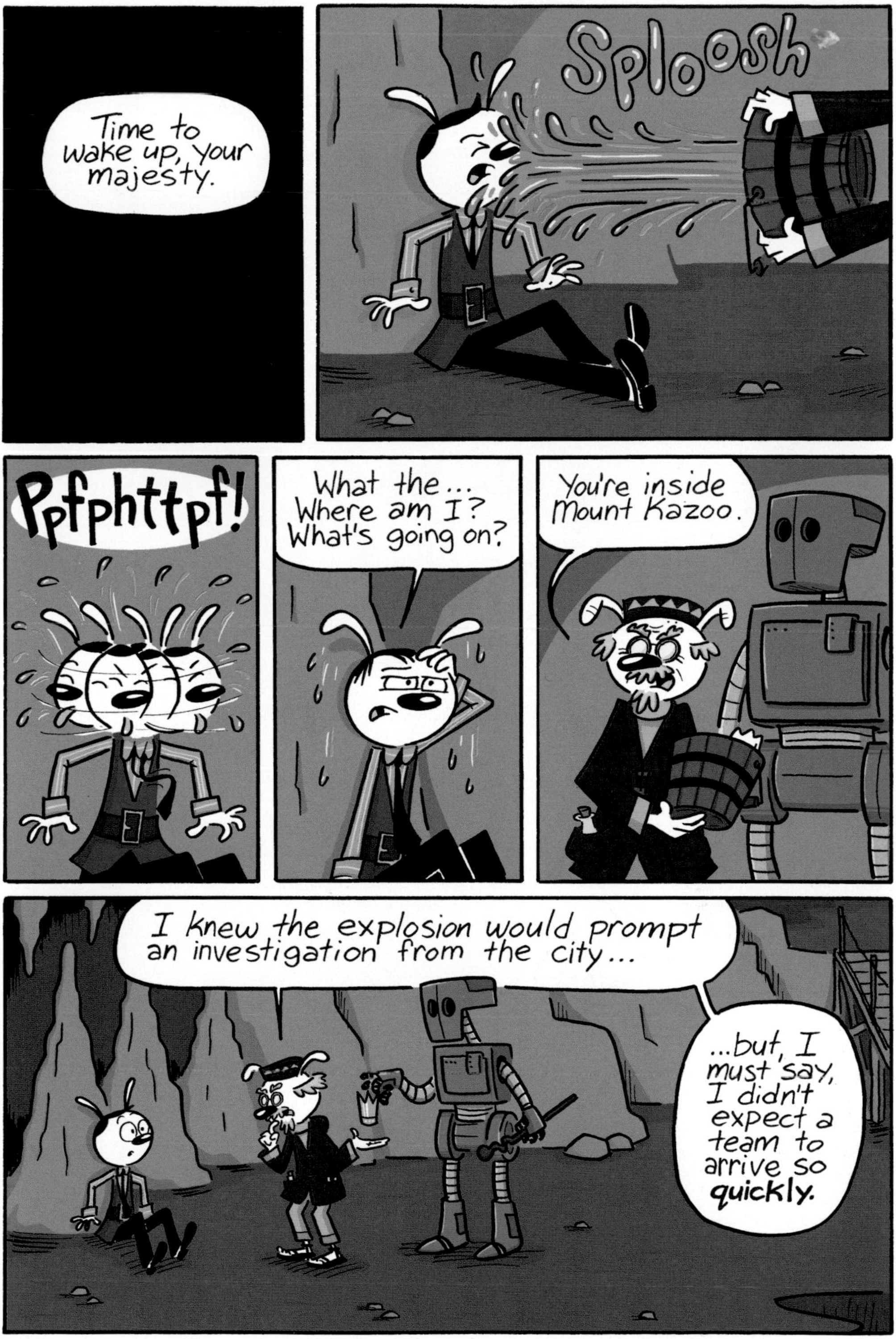
Time to wake up, your majesty.
Sploosh
Ppfphttpf!
What the... Where am I? What's going on?
You're inside Mount Kazoo.
I knew the explosion would prompt an investigation from the city...
...but, I must say, I didn't expect a team to arrive so **quickly.**

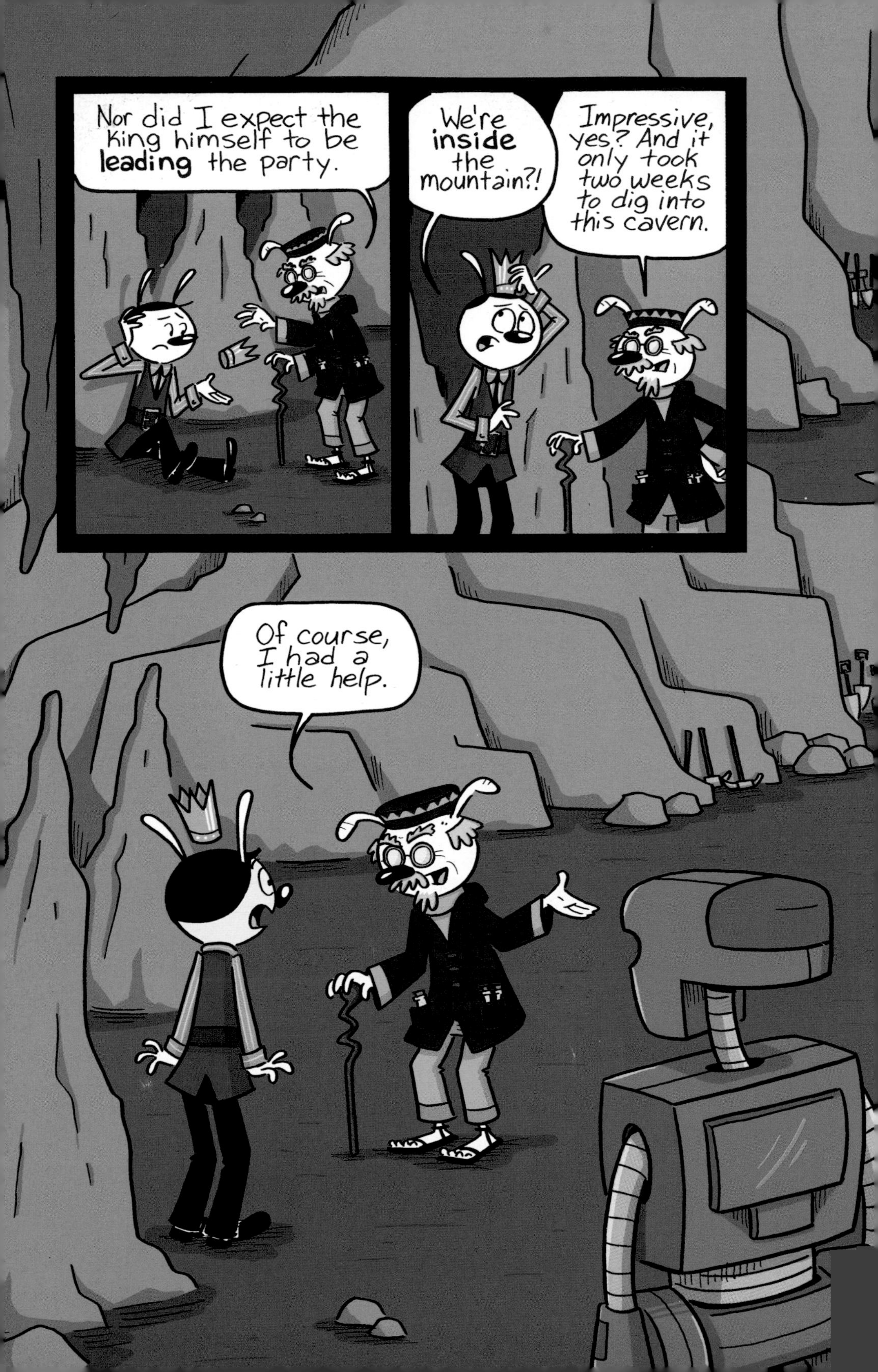
Nor did I expect the King himself to be **leading** the party.
We're **inside** the mountain?!
Impressive, yes? And it only took two weeks to dig into this cavern.
Of course, I had a little help.

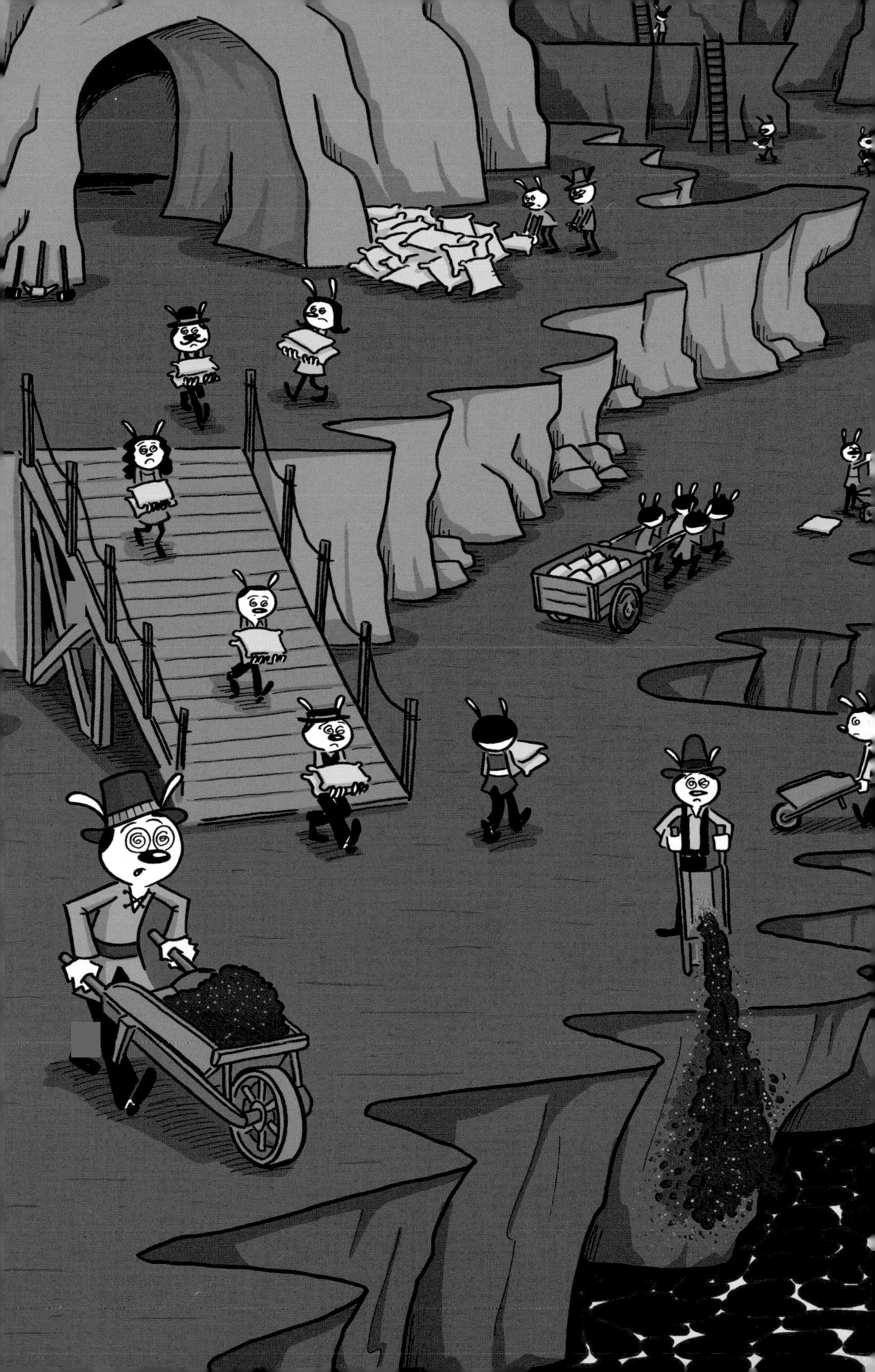

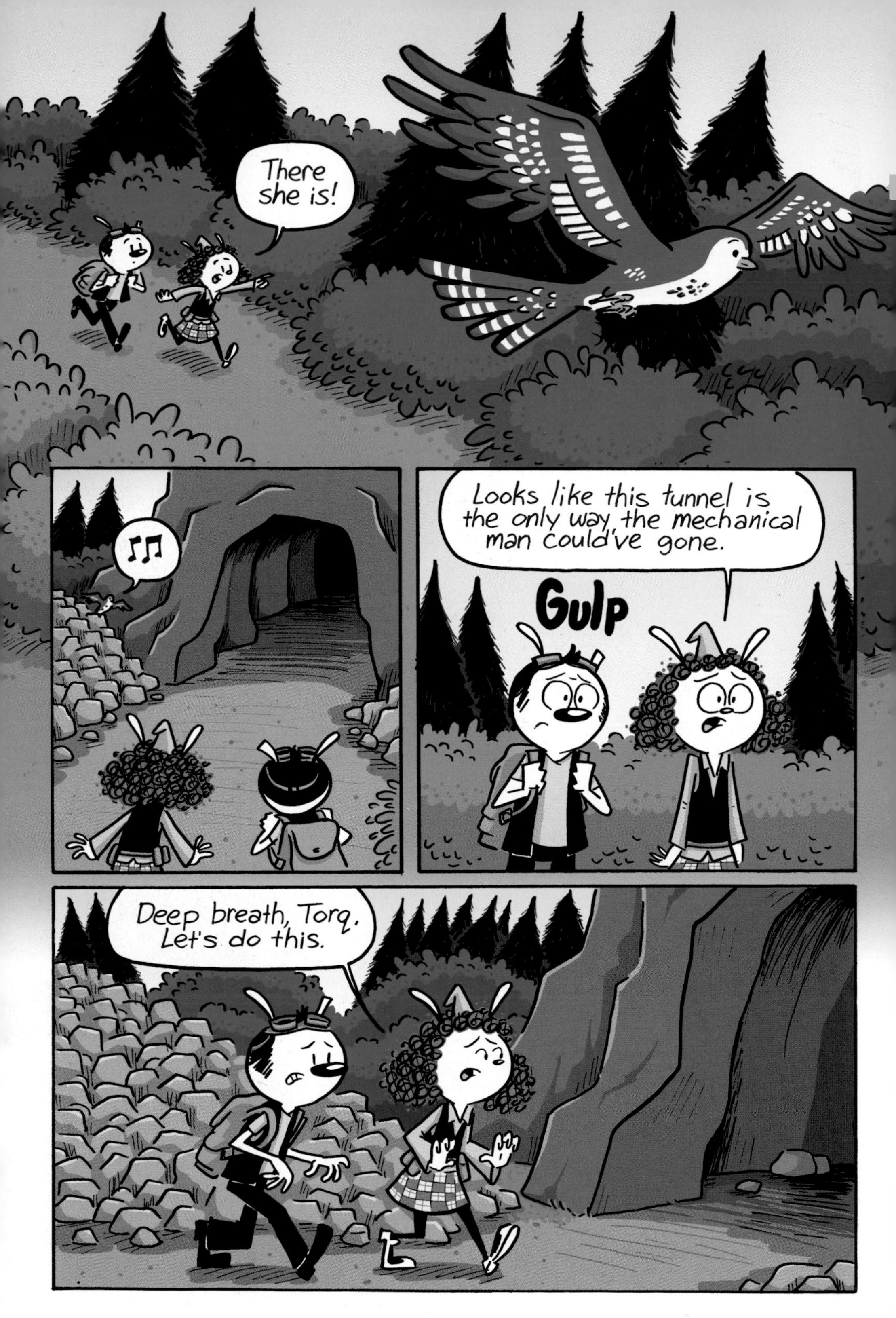
There she is!
♫
Looks like this tunnel is the only way the mechanical man could've gone.
GULP
Deep breath, Torq. Let's do this.

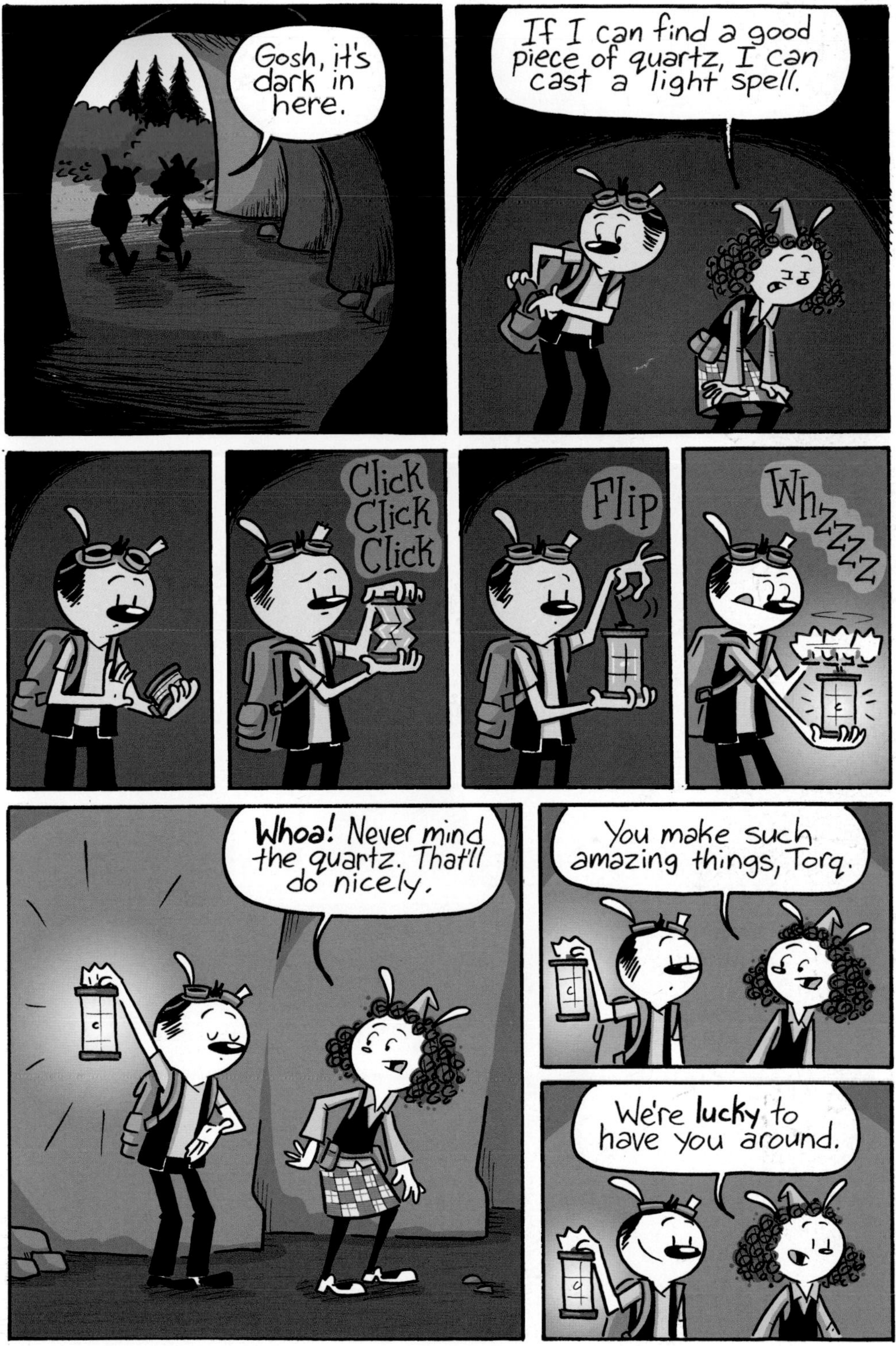
Gosh, it's dark in here.
If I can find a good piece of quartz, I can cast a light spell.
Click Click Click
Flip
Whzzzz
Whoa! Never mind the quartz. That'll do nicely.
You make such amazing things, Torq.
We're **lucky** to have you around.

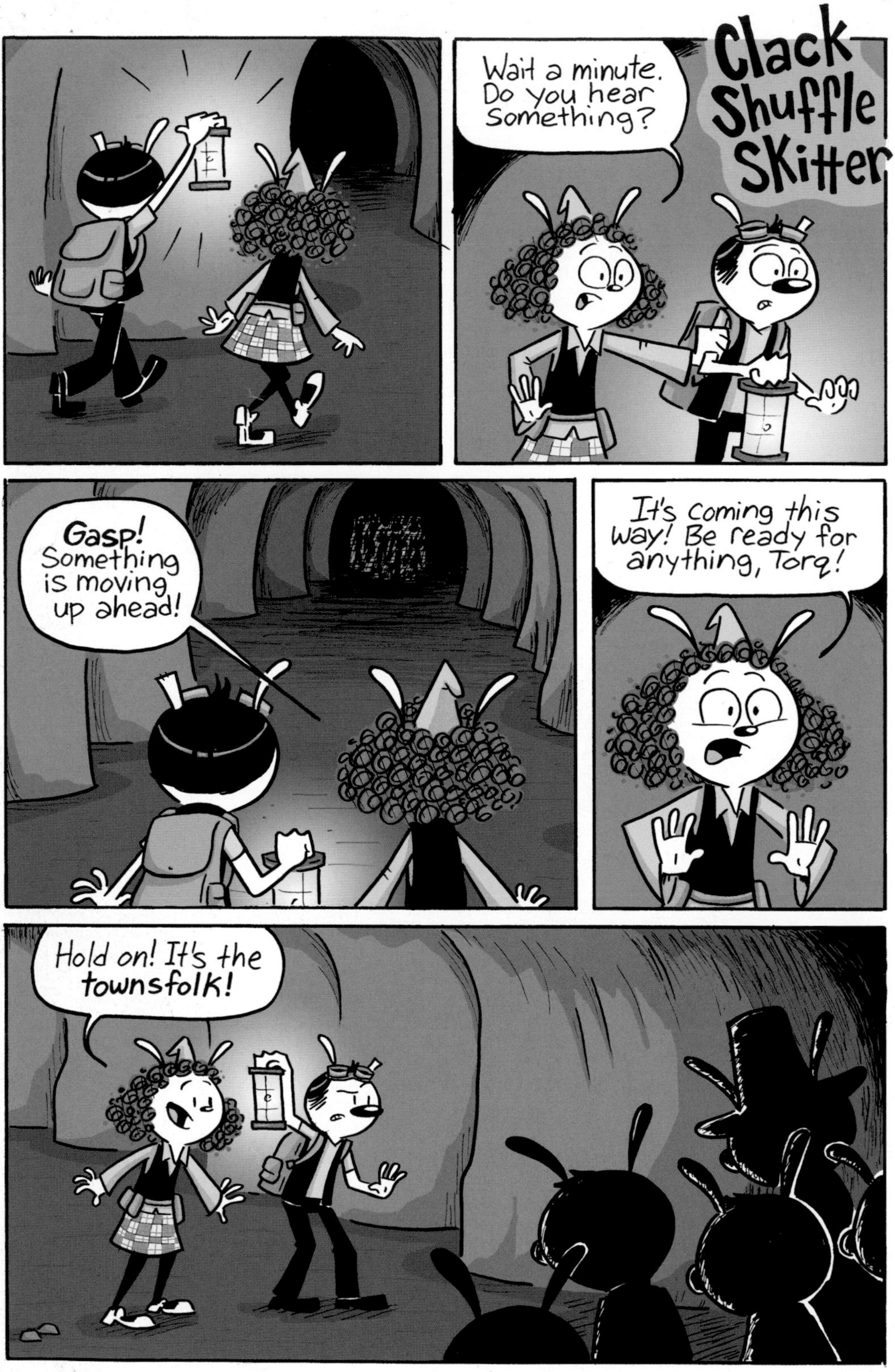
Wait a minute. Do you hear Something?
Clack Shuffle Skitter
Gasp! Something is moving up ahead!
It's coming this way! Be ready for anything, Torq!
Hold on! It's the townsfolk!

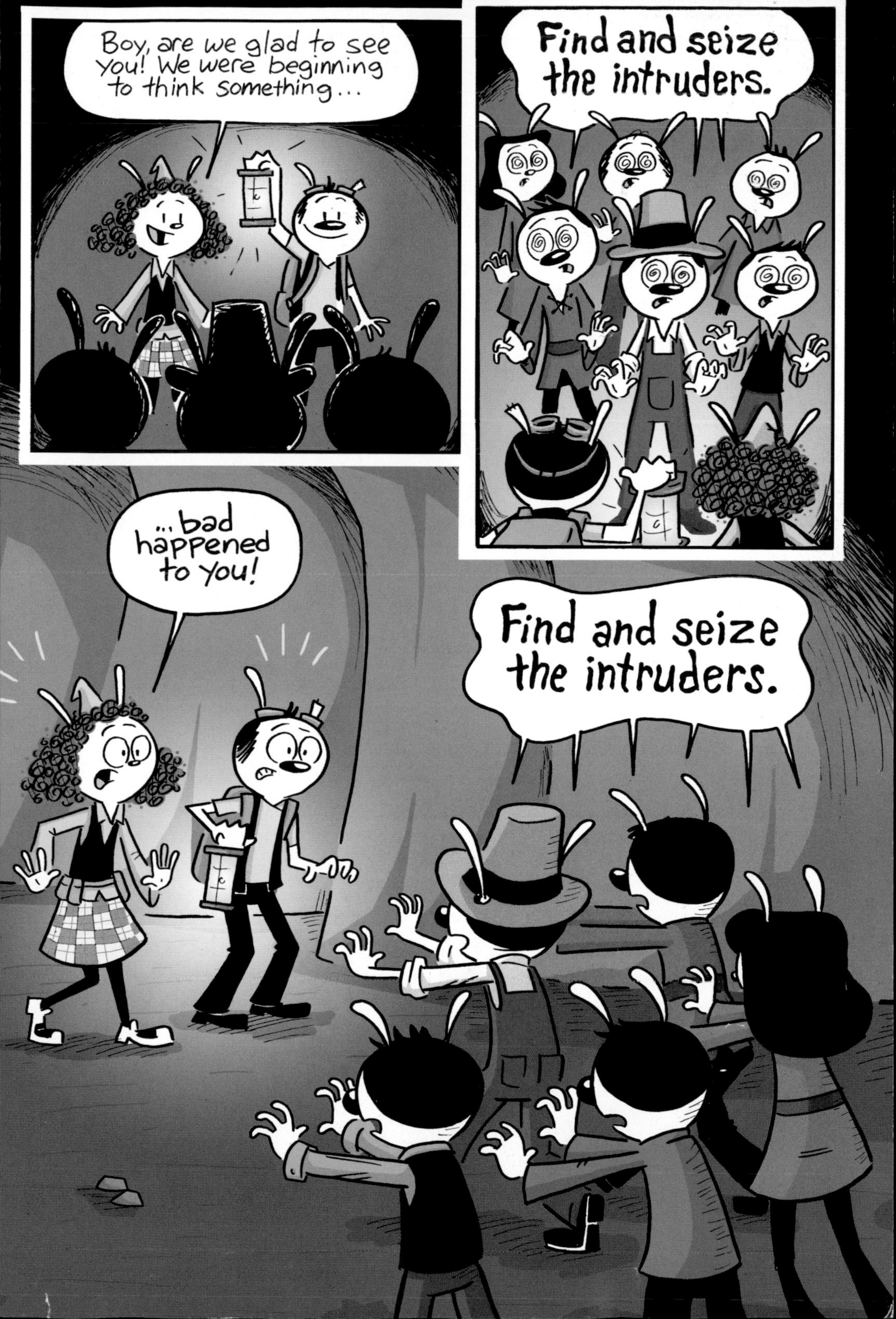
Boy, are we glad to see you! We were beginning to think something...
Find and seize the intruders.
...bad happened to you!
Find and seize the intruders.

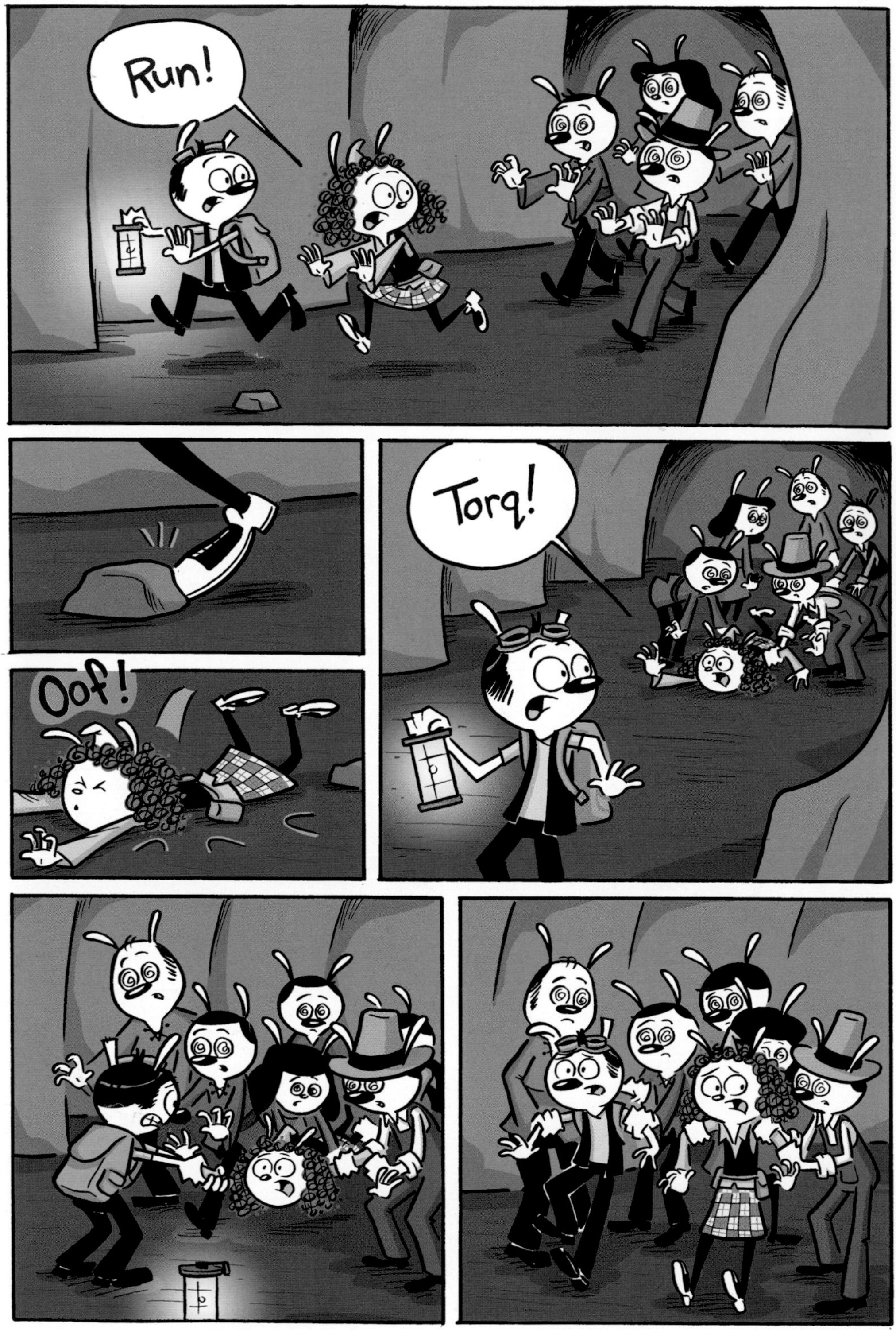
Run!
Torq!
Oof!

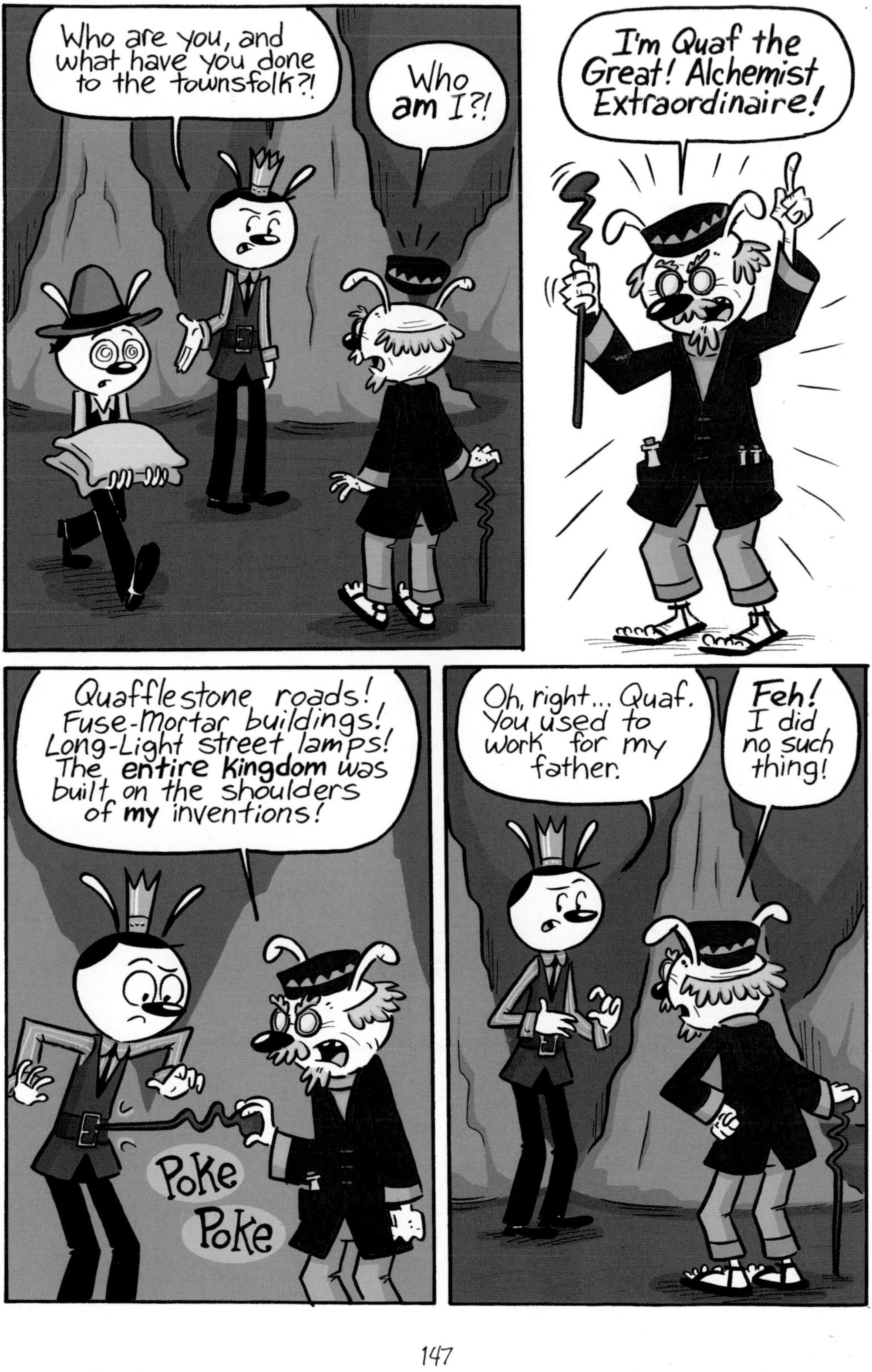

Who are you, and what have you done to the townsfolk?!
Who am I?!
I'm Quaf the Great! Alchemist Extraordinaire!
Quafflestone roads! Fuse-Mortar buildings! Long-Light street lamps! The **entire kingdom** was built on the shoulders of **my** inventions!
Poke
Poke
Oh, right... Quaf. You used to work for my father.
Feh! I did no such thing!

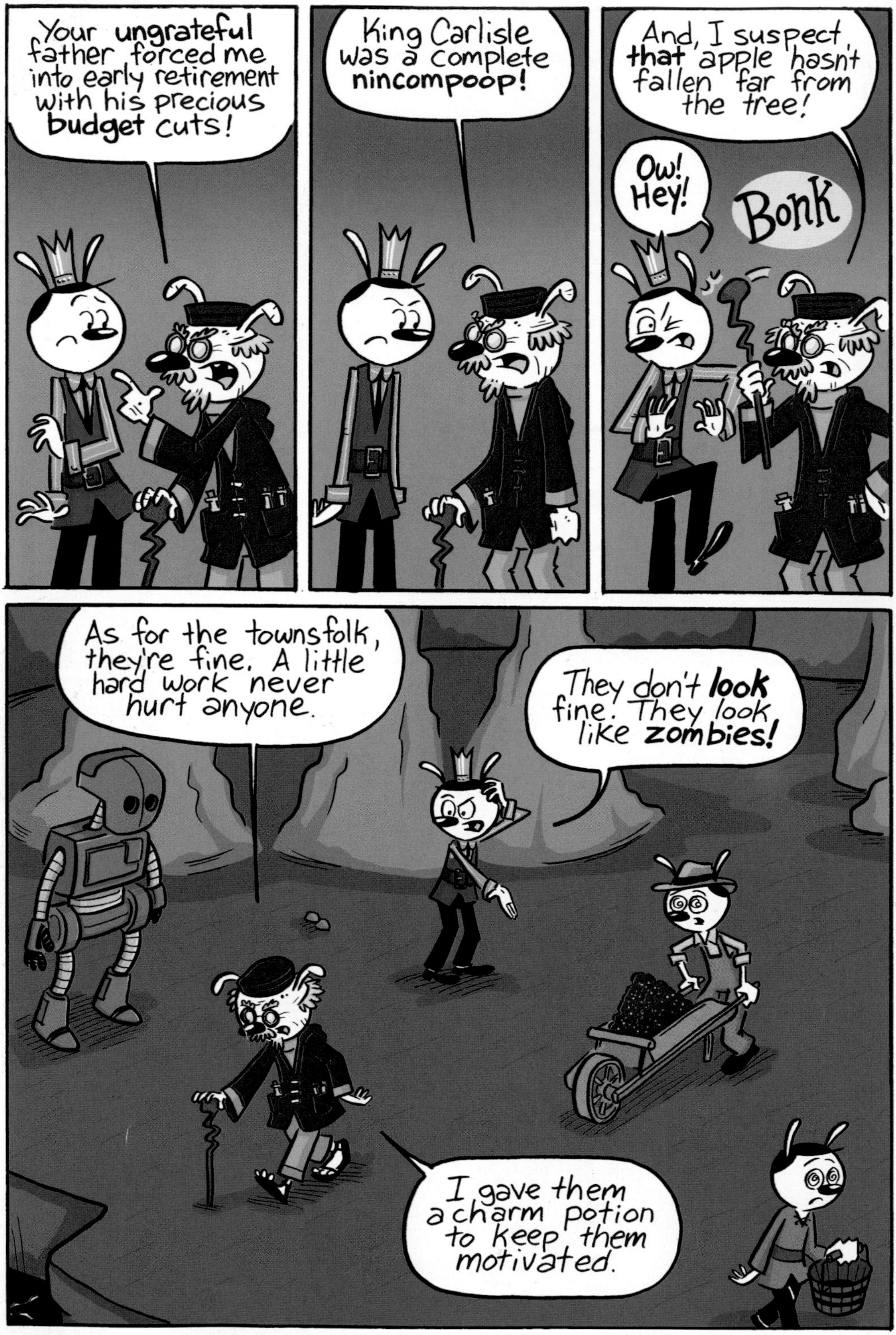
Your ungrateful father forced me into early retirement with his precious budget cuts!
King Carlisle was a complete nincompoop!
And, I suspect that apple hasn't fallen far from the tree!
Ow! Hey!
BONK
As for the townsfolk, they're fine. A little hard work never hurt anyone.
They don't look fine. They look like zombies!
I gave them a charm potion to keep them motivated.

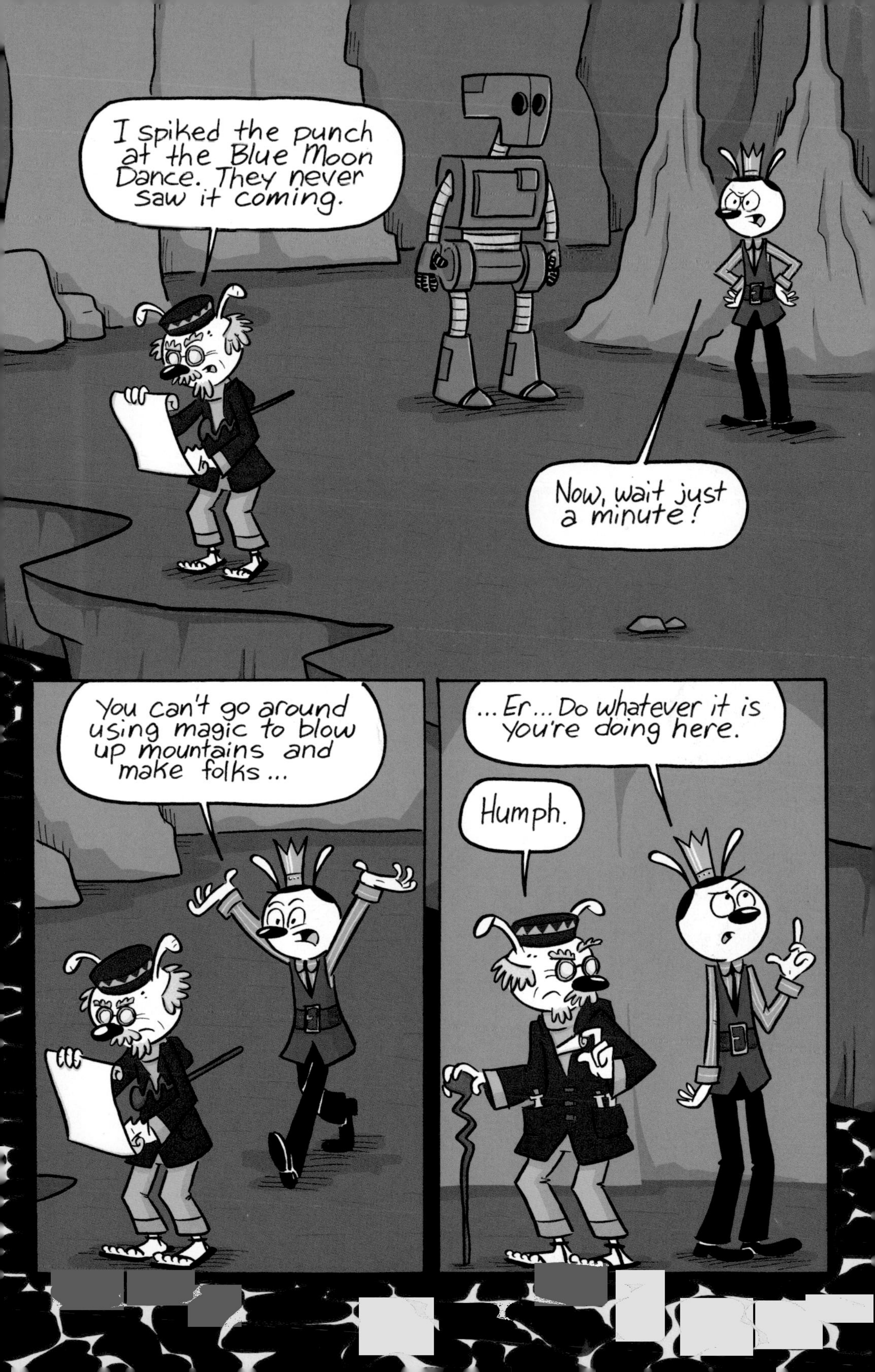
I spiked the punch at the Blue Moon Dance. They never saw it coming.
Now, wait just a minute!
You can't go around using magic to blow up mountains and make folks...
Humph.
...Er...Do whatever it is you're doing here.

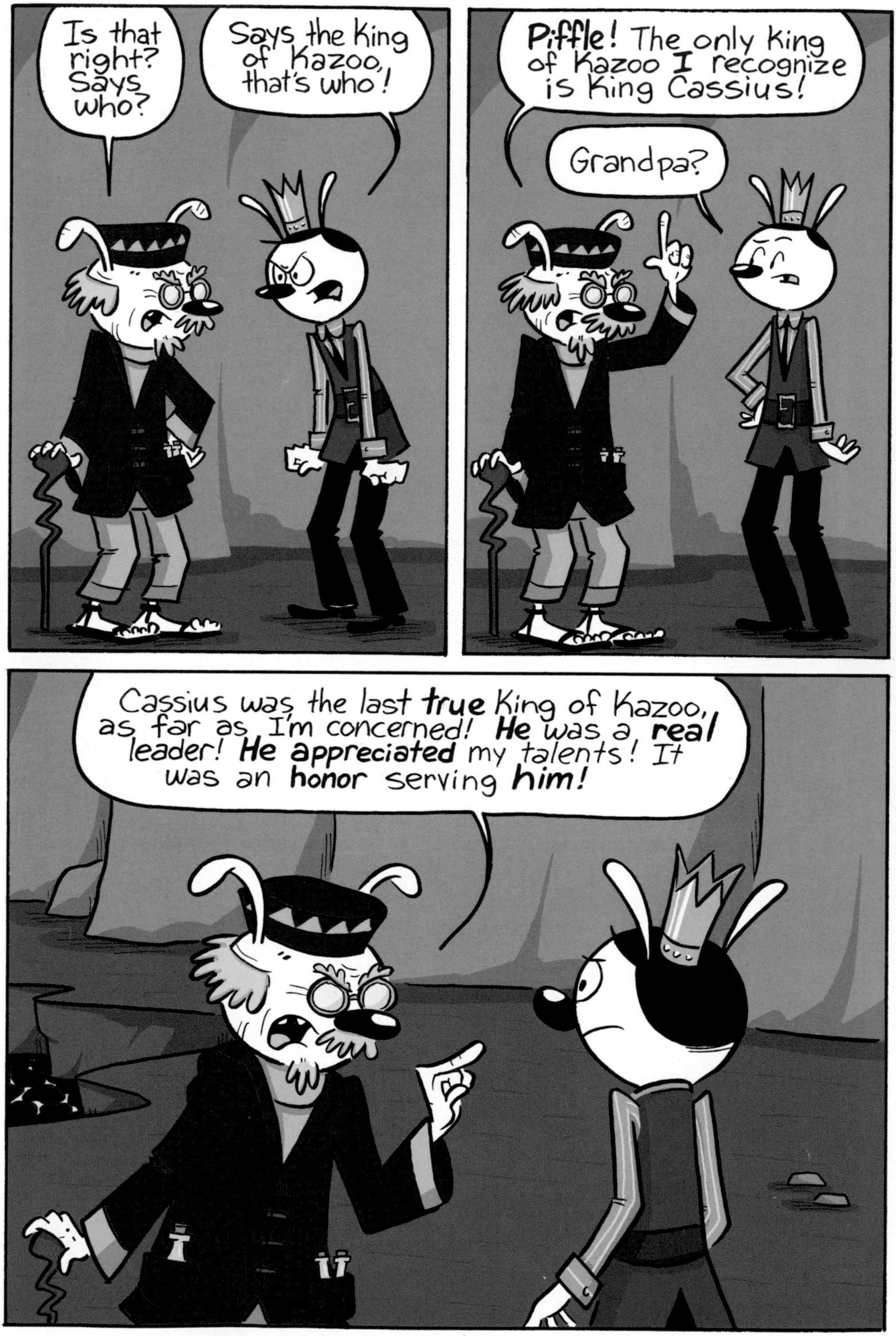
Is that right? Says who?
Says the King of Kazoo, that's who!
Piffle! The only King of Kazoo I recognize is King Cassius!
Grandpa?
Cassius was the last true King of Kazoo, as far as I'm concerned! He was a real leader! He appreciated my talents! It was an honor serving him!

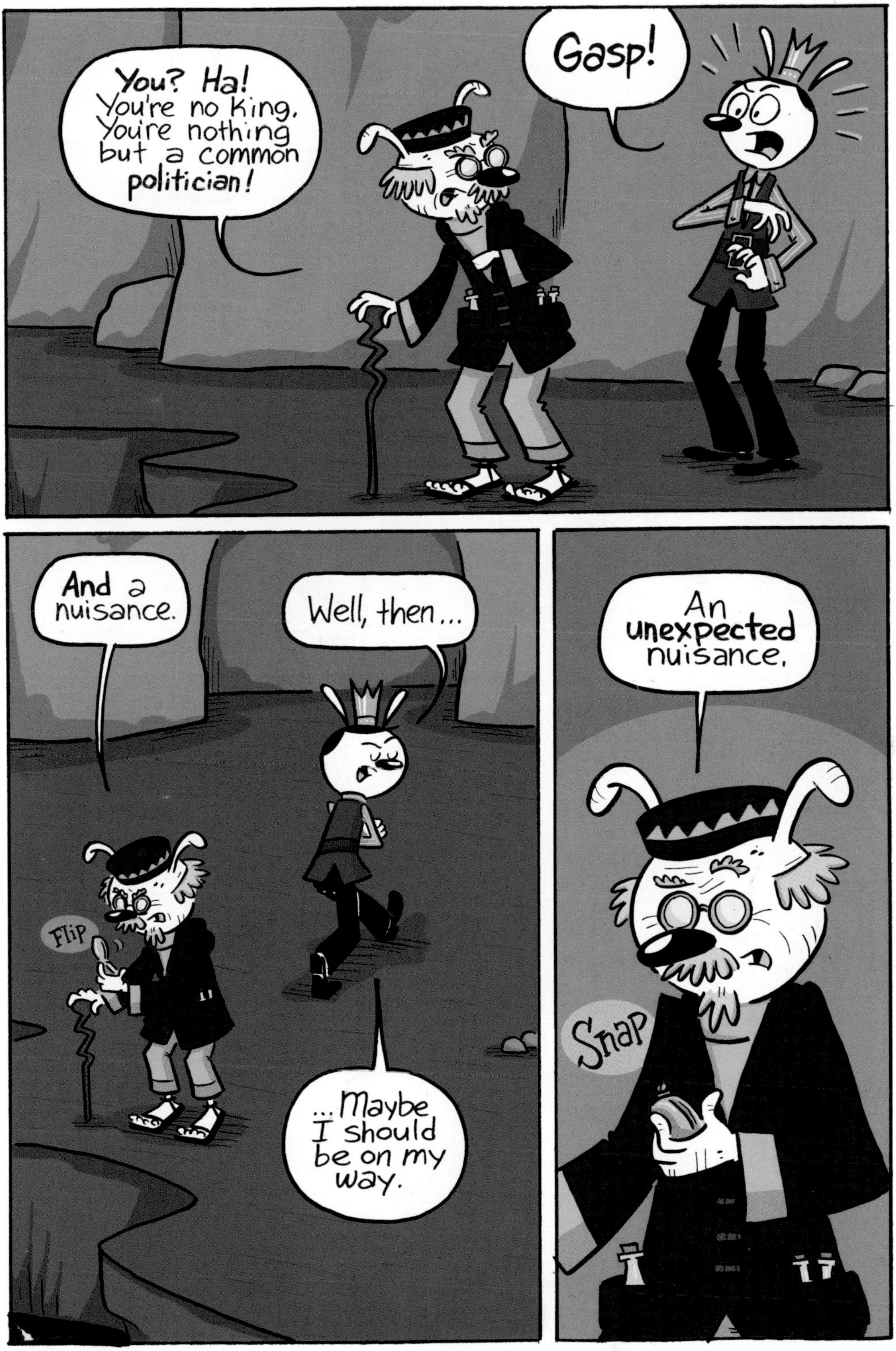
You? Ha! You're no king. You're nothing but a common politician!
Gasp!
And a nuisance.
Well, then...
...Maybe I should be on my way.
Flip
An unexpected nuisance.
Snap

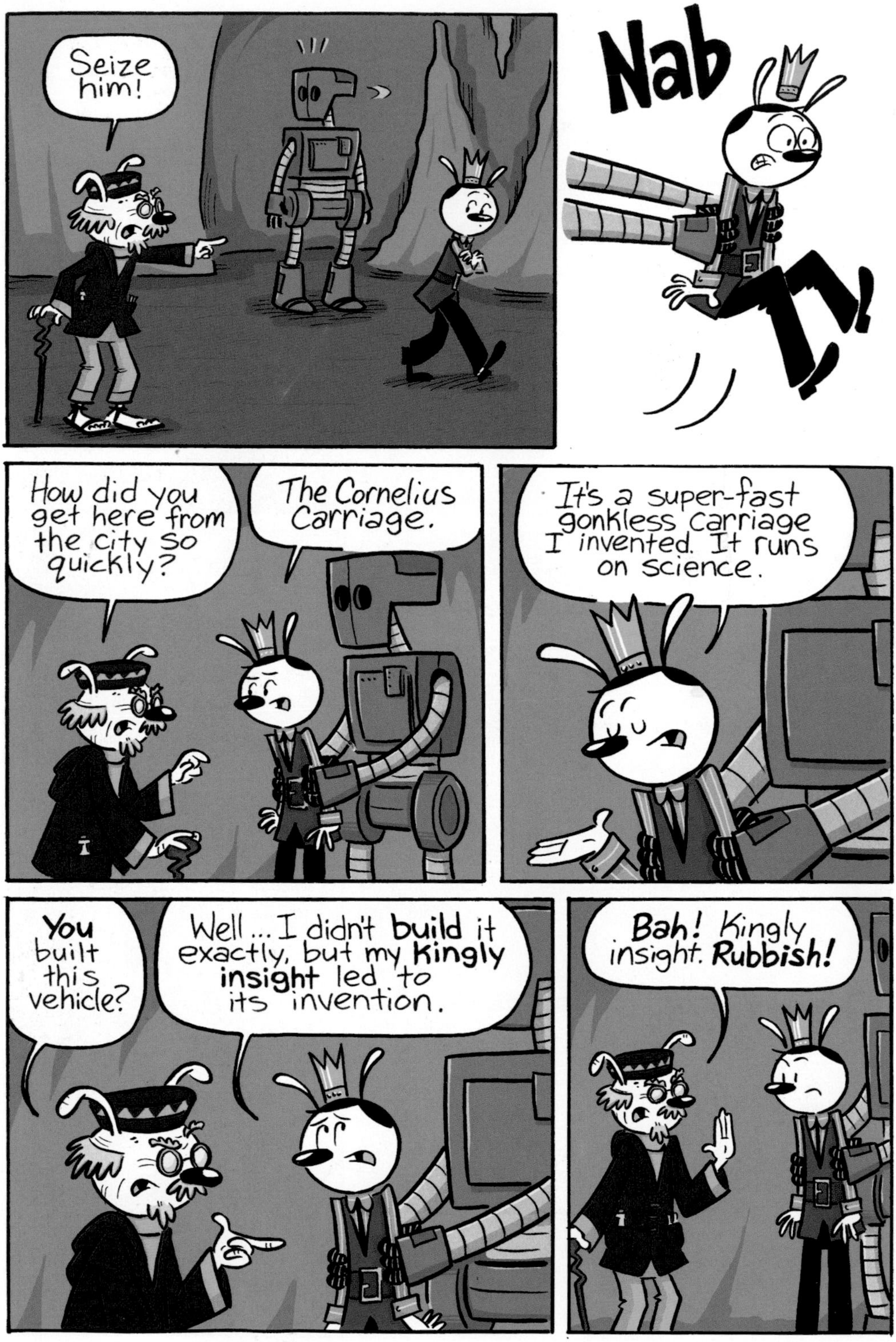
Seize him!
Nab
How did you get here from the city so quickly?
The Cornelius Carriage.
It's a super-fast gonkless carriage I invented. It runs on science.
You built this vehicle?
Well... I didn't build it exactly, but my Kingly insight led to its invention.
Bah! Kingly insight. Rubbish!

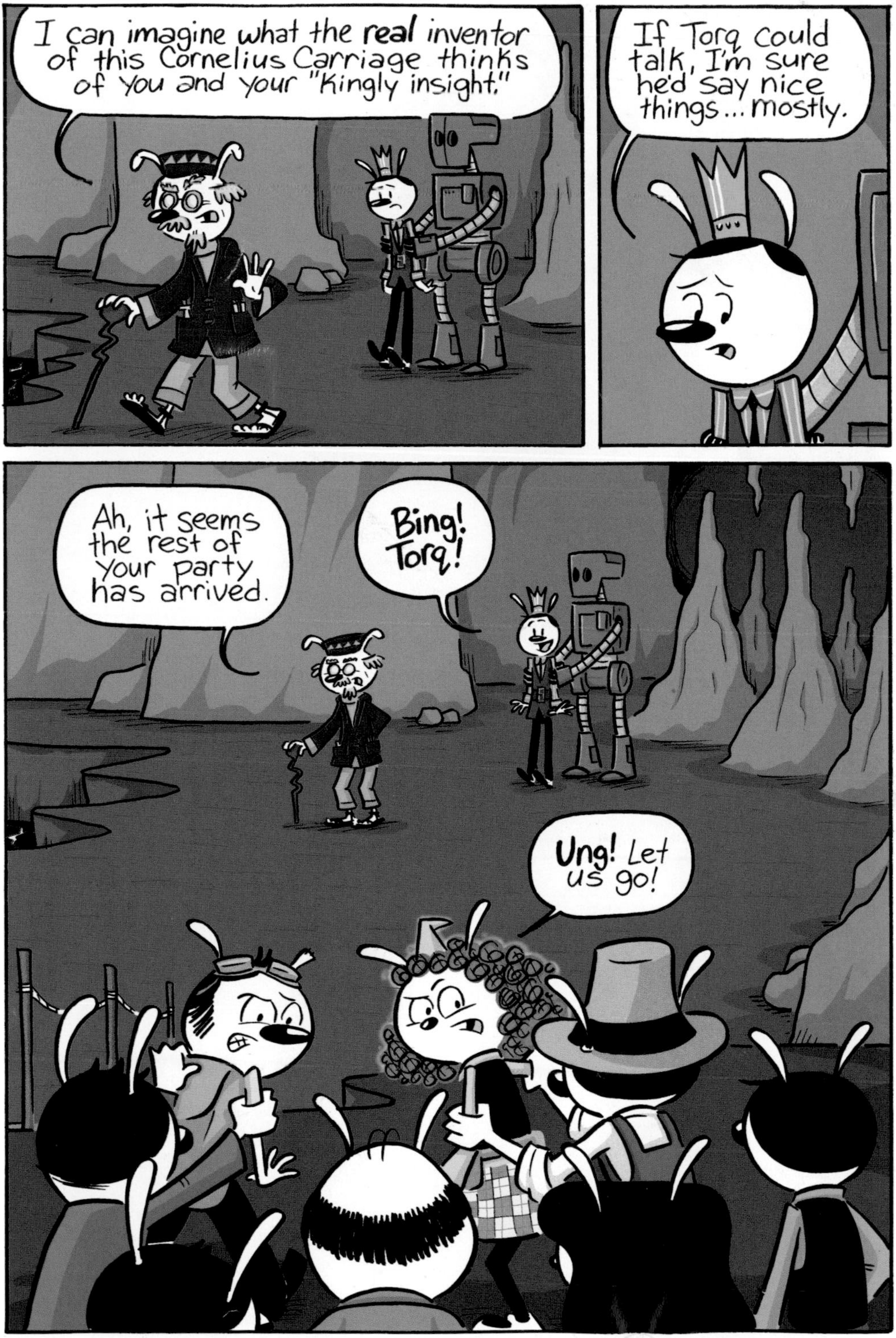
I can imagine what the **real** inventor of this Cornelius Carriage thinks of you and your "Kingly insight."
If Torq could talk, I'm sure he'd say nice things... mostly.
Ah, it seems the rest of your party has arrived.
Bing! Torq!
Ung! Let us go!

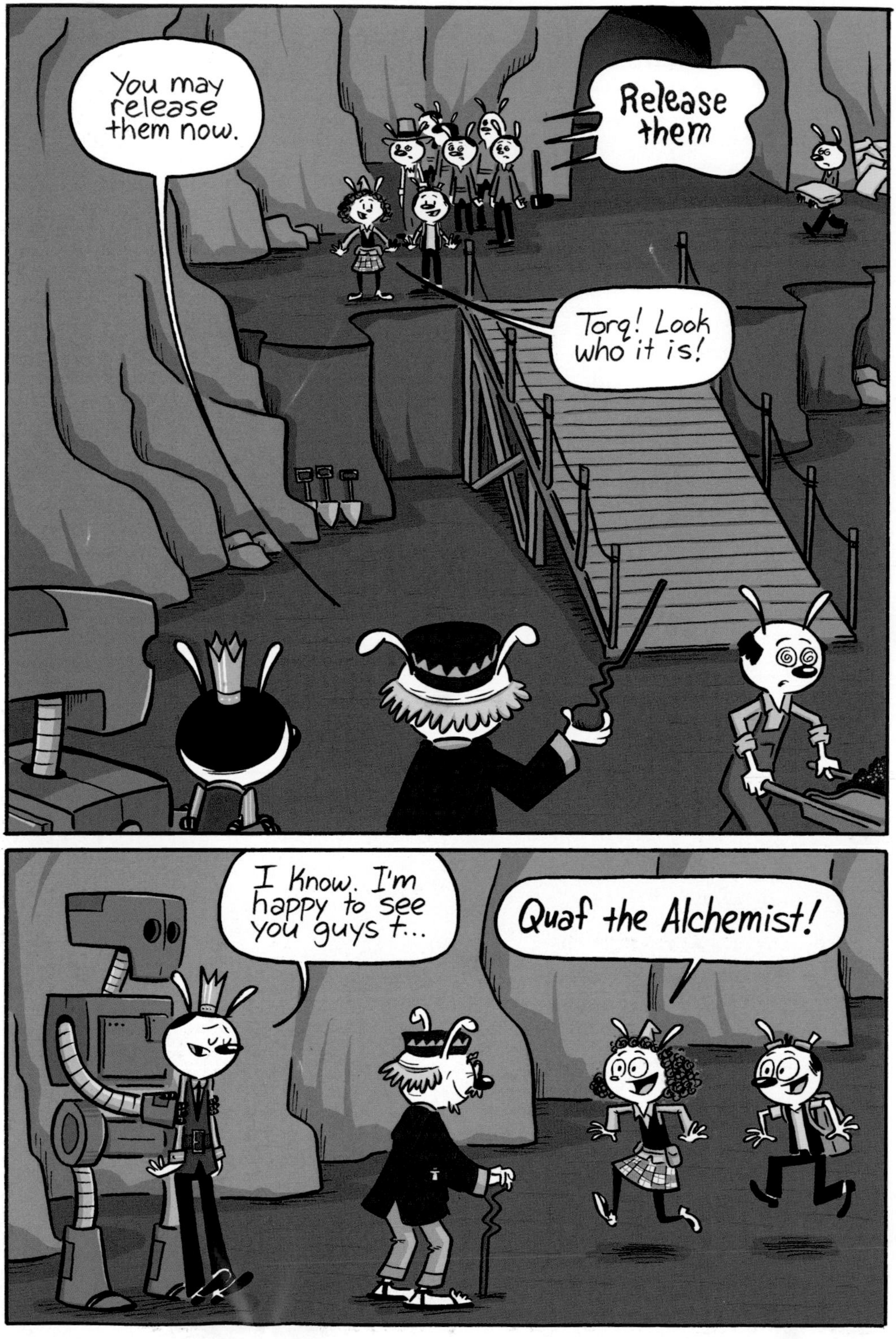
You may release them now.
Release them
Torq! Look who it is!
I know. I'm happy to see you guys t...
Quaf the Alchemist!

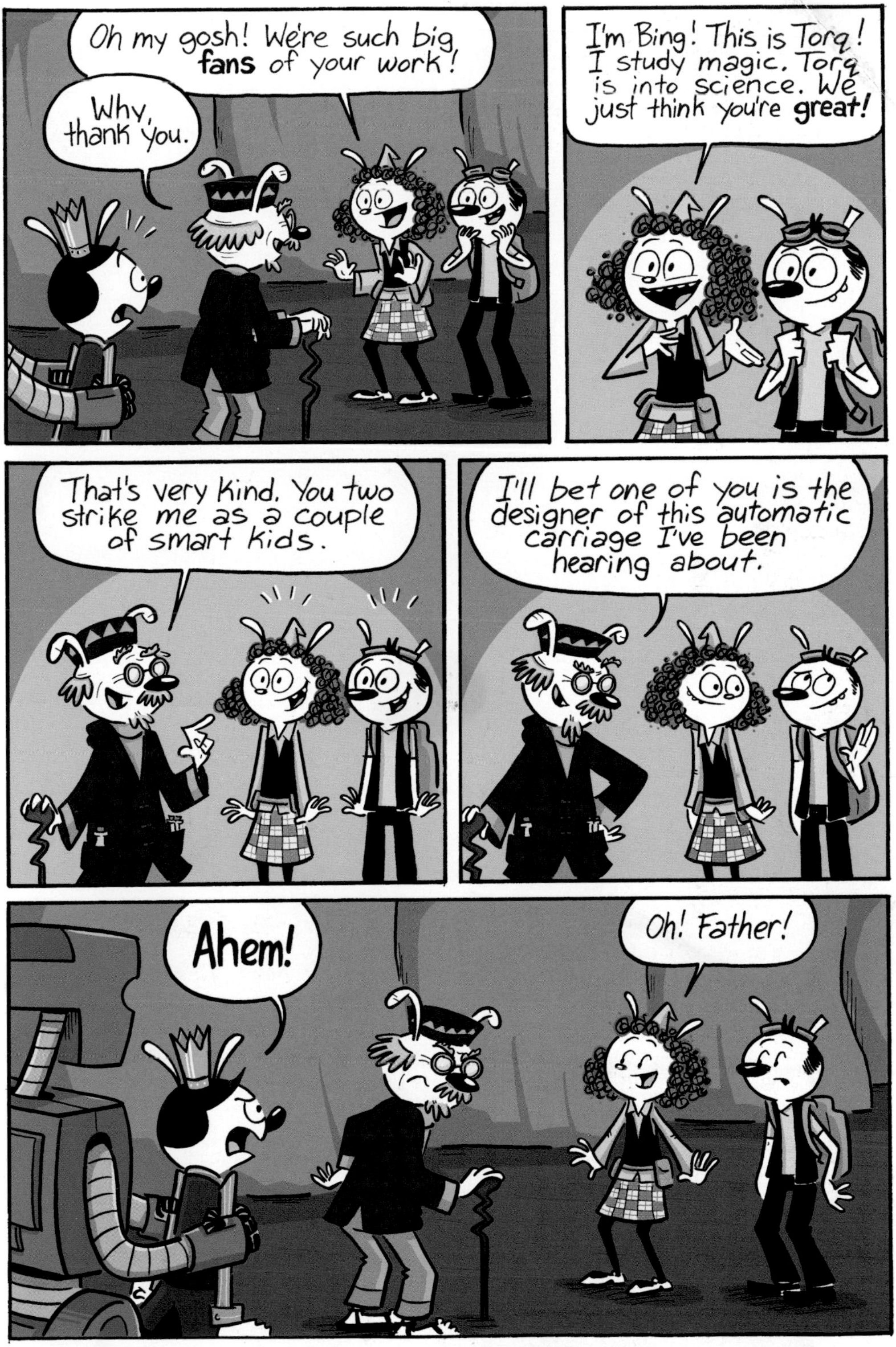
Oh my gosh! We're such big fans of your work!
Why, thank you.
I'm Bing! This is Torq! I study magic. Torq is into science. We just think you're great!
That's very kind. You two strike me as a couple of smart kids.
I'll bet one of you is the designer of this automatic carriage I've been hearing about.
Ahem!
Oh! Father!

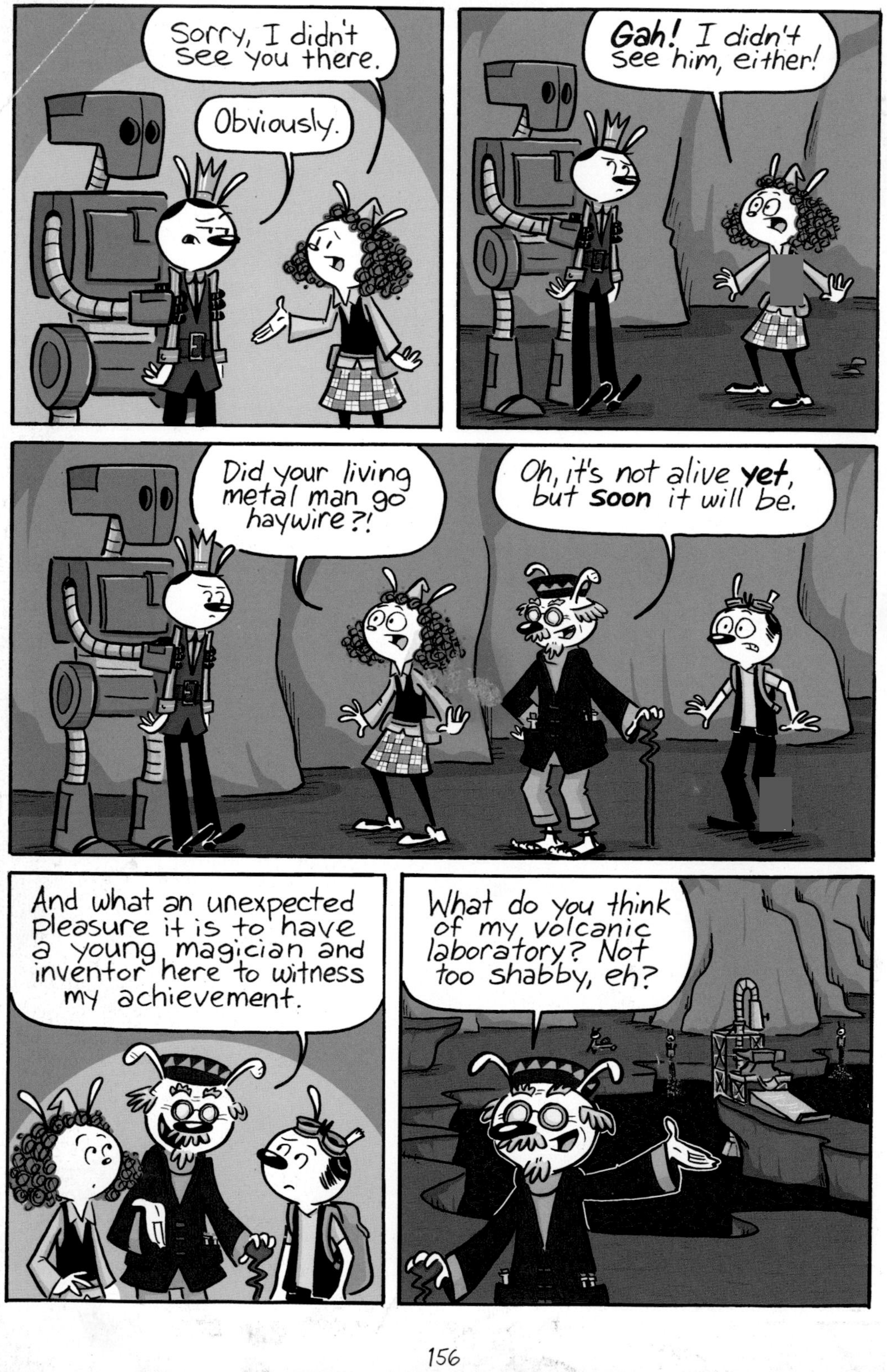

Sorry, I didn't see you there.
Obviously.
Gah! I didn't see him, either!
Did your living metal man go haywire?!
Oh, it's not alive yet, but soon it will be.
And what an unexpected pleasure it is to have a young magician and inventor here to witness my achievement.
What do you think of my volcanic laboratory? Not too shabby, eh?

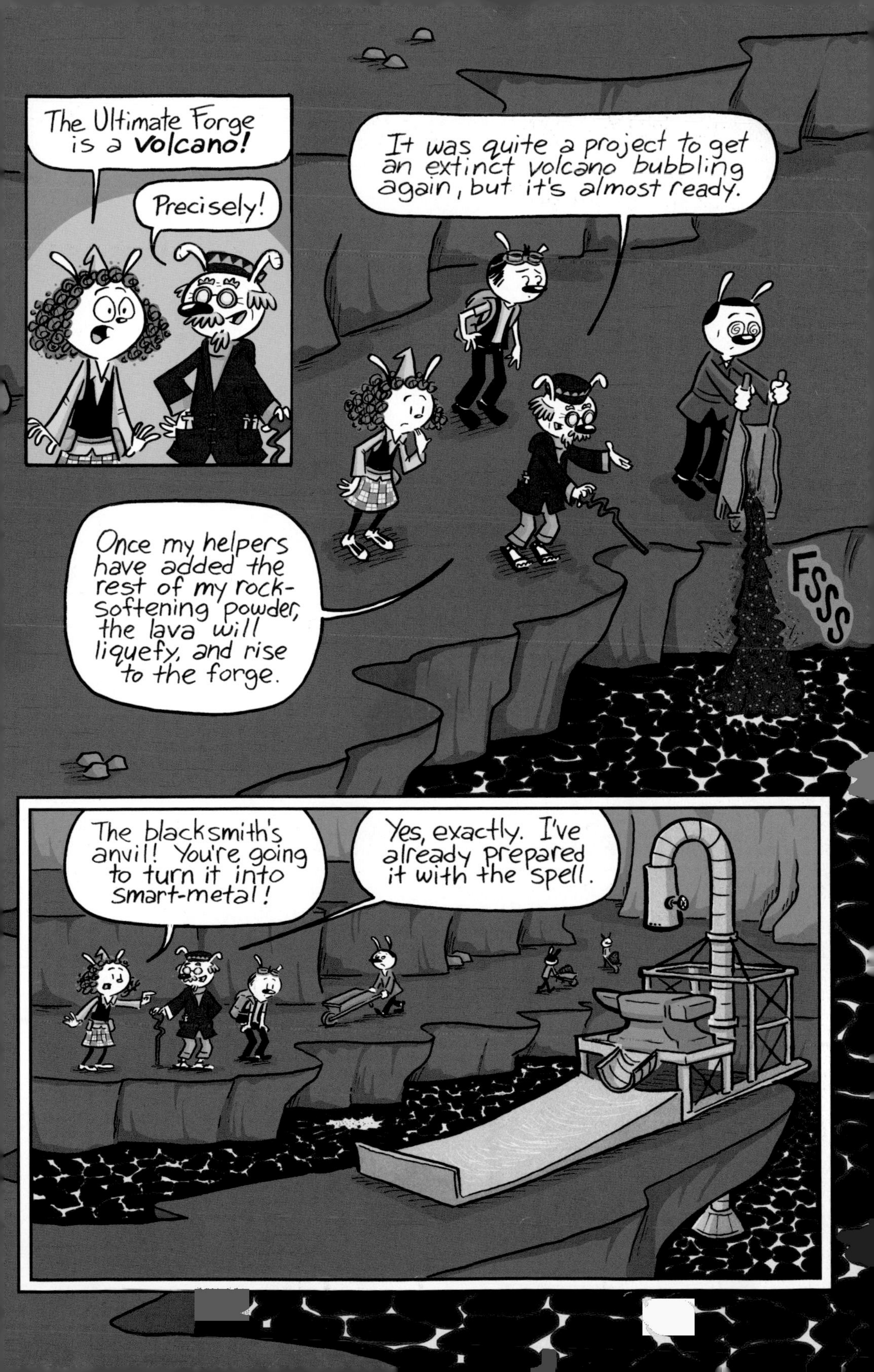
The Ultimate Forge is a **volcano!**
Precisely!
It was quite a project to get an extinct volcano bubbling again, but it's almost ready.
Once my helpers have added the rest of my rock-softening powder, the lava will liquefy, and rise to the forge.
FSSS
The blacksmith's anvil! You're going to turn it into smart-metal!
Yes, exactly. I've already prepared it with the spell.

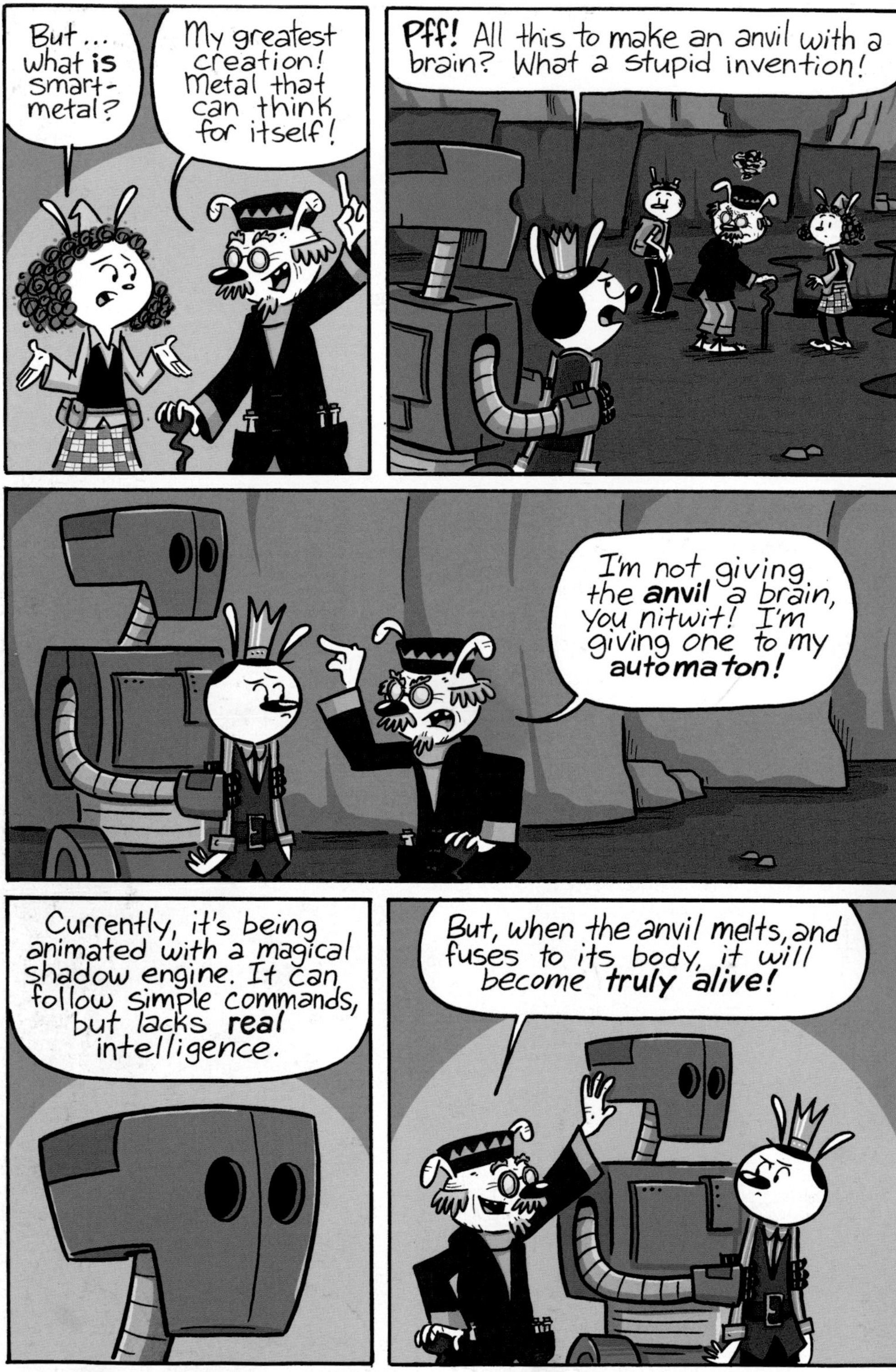
But... what **is** smart-metal?
My greatest creation! Metal that can think for itself!
Pff! All this to make an anvil with a brain? What a stupid invention!
I'm not giving the **anvil** a brain, you nitwit! I'm giving one to my **automaton!**
Currently, it's being animated with a magical shadow engine. It can follow simple commands, but lacks **real** intelligence.
But, when the anvil melts, and fuses to its body, it will become **truly alive!**

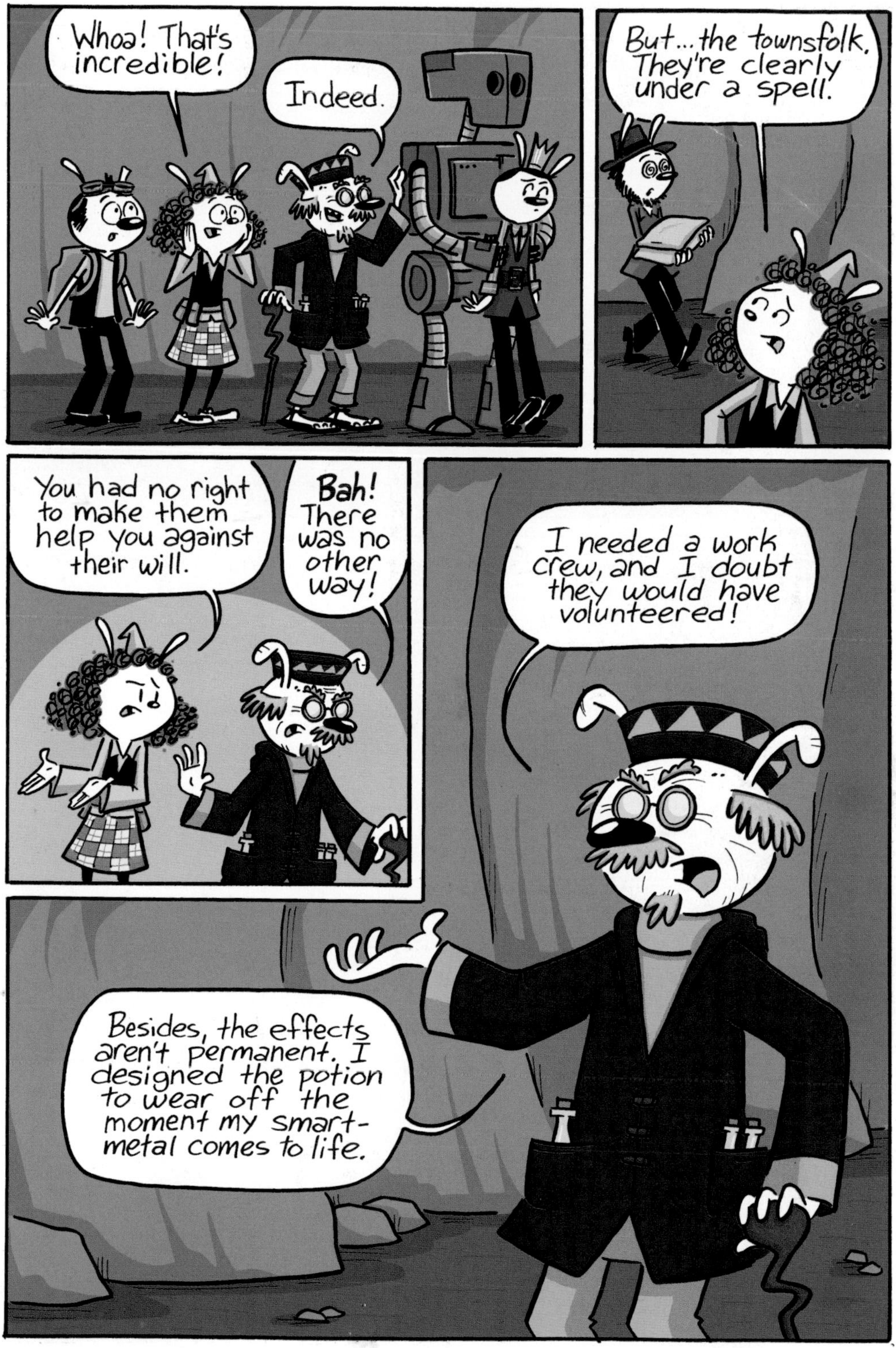
Whoa! That's incredible!
Indeed.
But... the townsfolk. They're clearly under a spell.
You had no right to make them help you against their will.
Bah! There was no other way!
I needed a work crew, and I doubt they would have volunteered!
Besides, the effects aren't permanent. I designed the potion to wear off the moment my smart-metal comes to life.

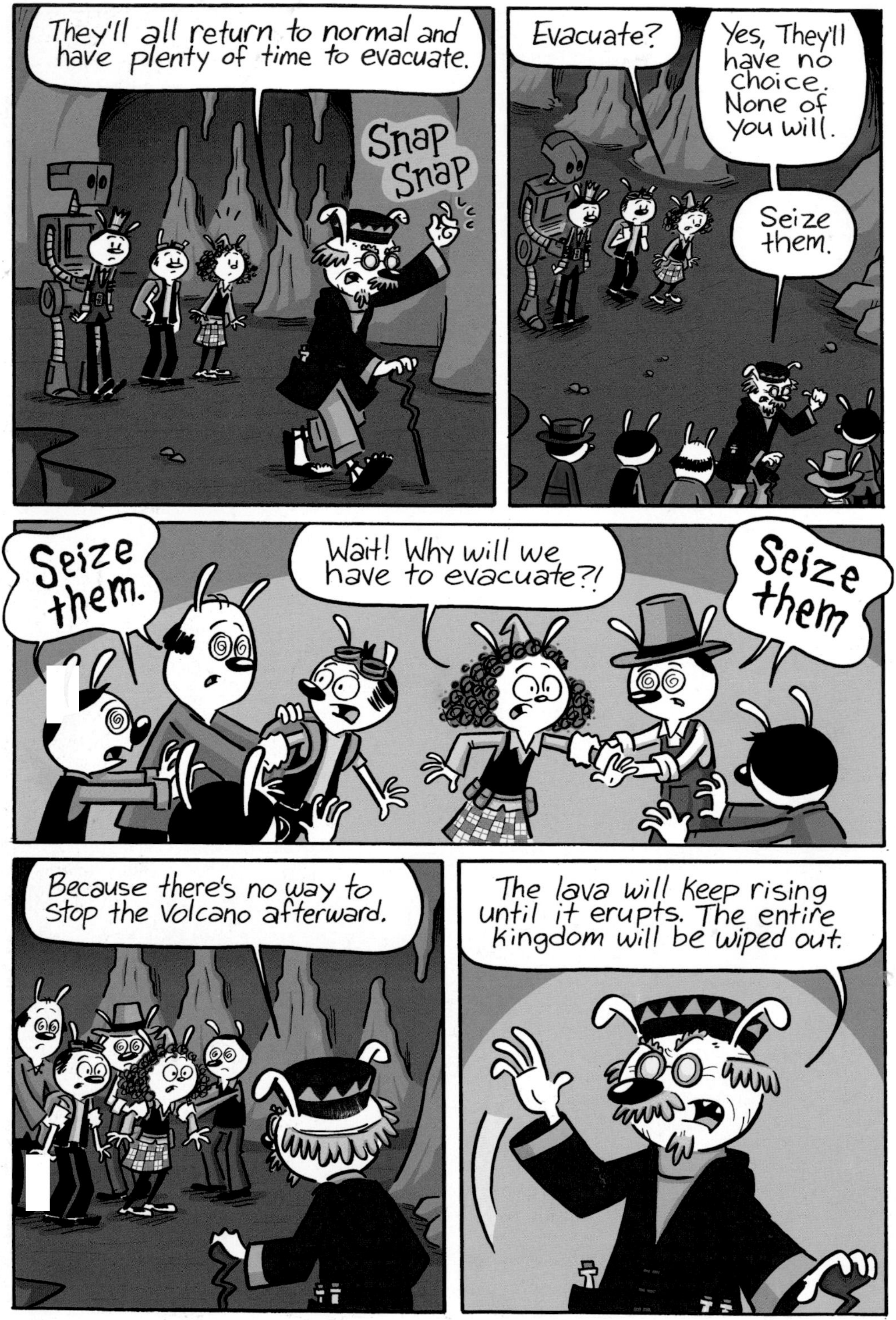
They'll all return to normal and have plenty of time to evacuate.
Snap Snap
Evacuate?
Yes, They'll have no choice. None of you will.
Seize them.
Seize them.
Wait! Why will we have to evacuate?!
Seize them
Because there's no way to stop the volcano afterward.
The lava will keep rising until it erupts. The entire kingdom will be wiped out.

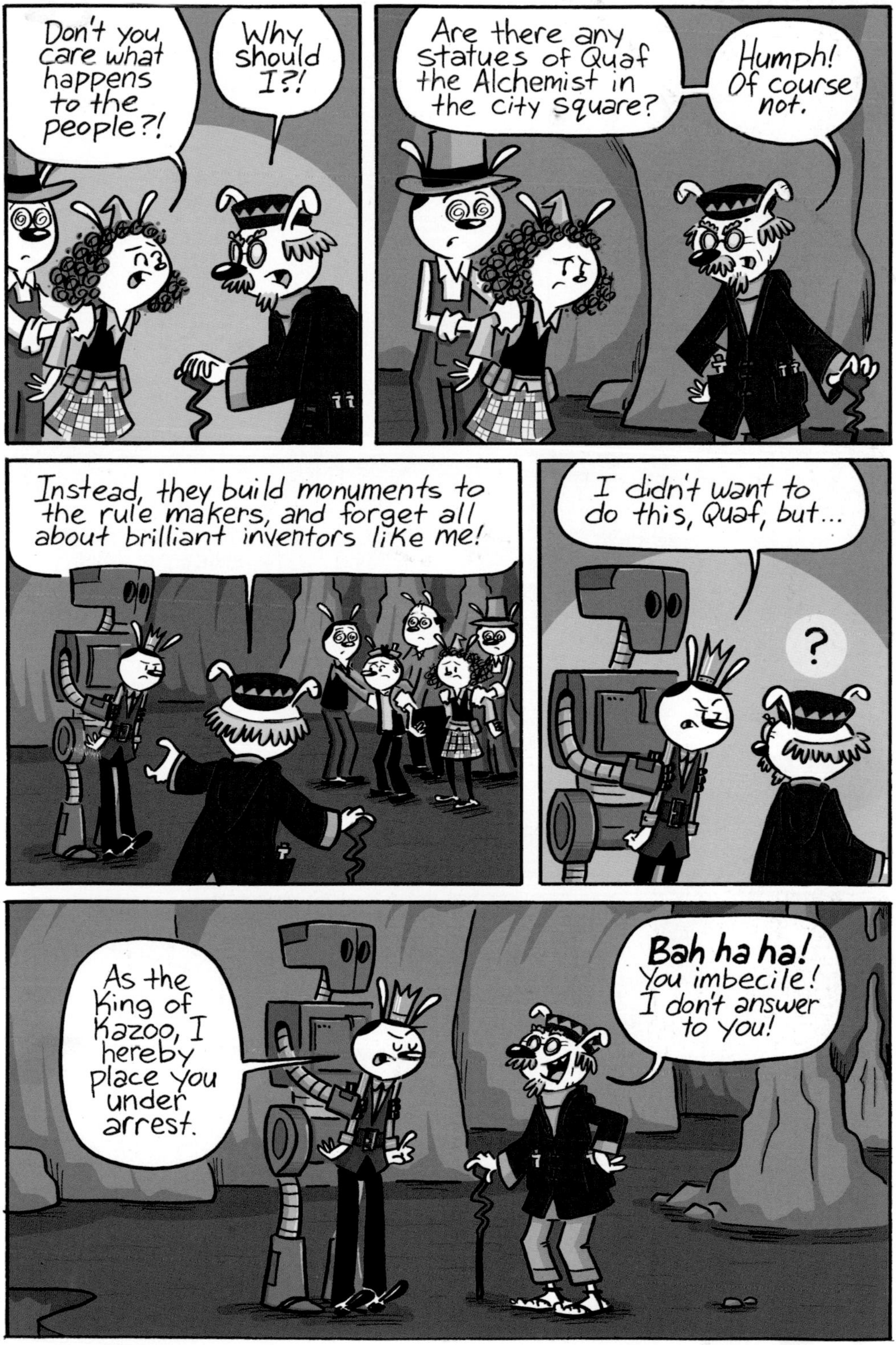
Don't you care what happens to the people?!
Why should I?!
Are there any statues of Quaf the Alchemist in the city square?
Humph! Of course not.
Instead, they build monuments to the rule makers, and forget all about brilliant inventors like me!
I didn't want to do this, Quaf, but...
?
As the King of Kazoo, I hereby place you under arrest.
Bah ha ha! You imbecile! I don't answer to you!

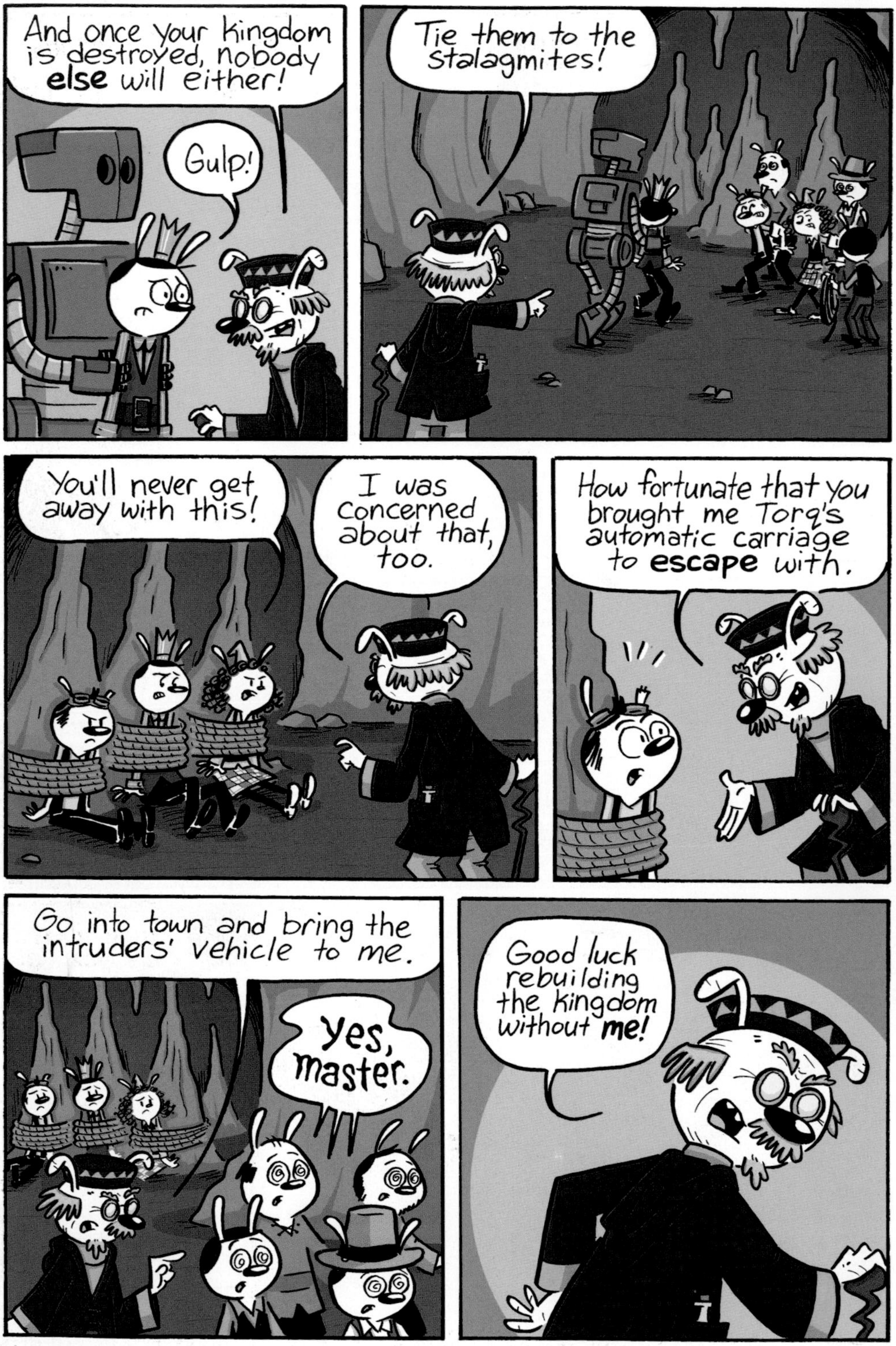
And once your kingdom is destroyed, nobody **else** will either!
Gulp!
Tie them to the stalagmites!
You'll never get away with this!
I was concerned about that, too.
How fortunate that you brought me Torq's automatic carriage to **escape** with.
Go into town and bring the intruders' vehicle to me.
Yes, master.
Good luck rebuilding the kingdom without **me**!

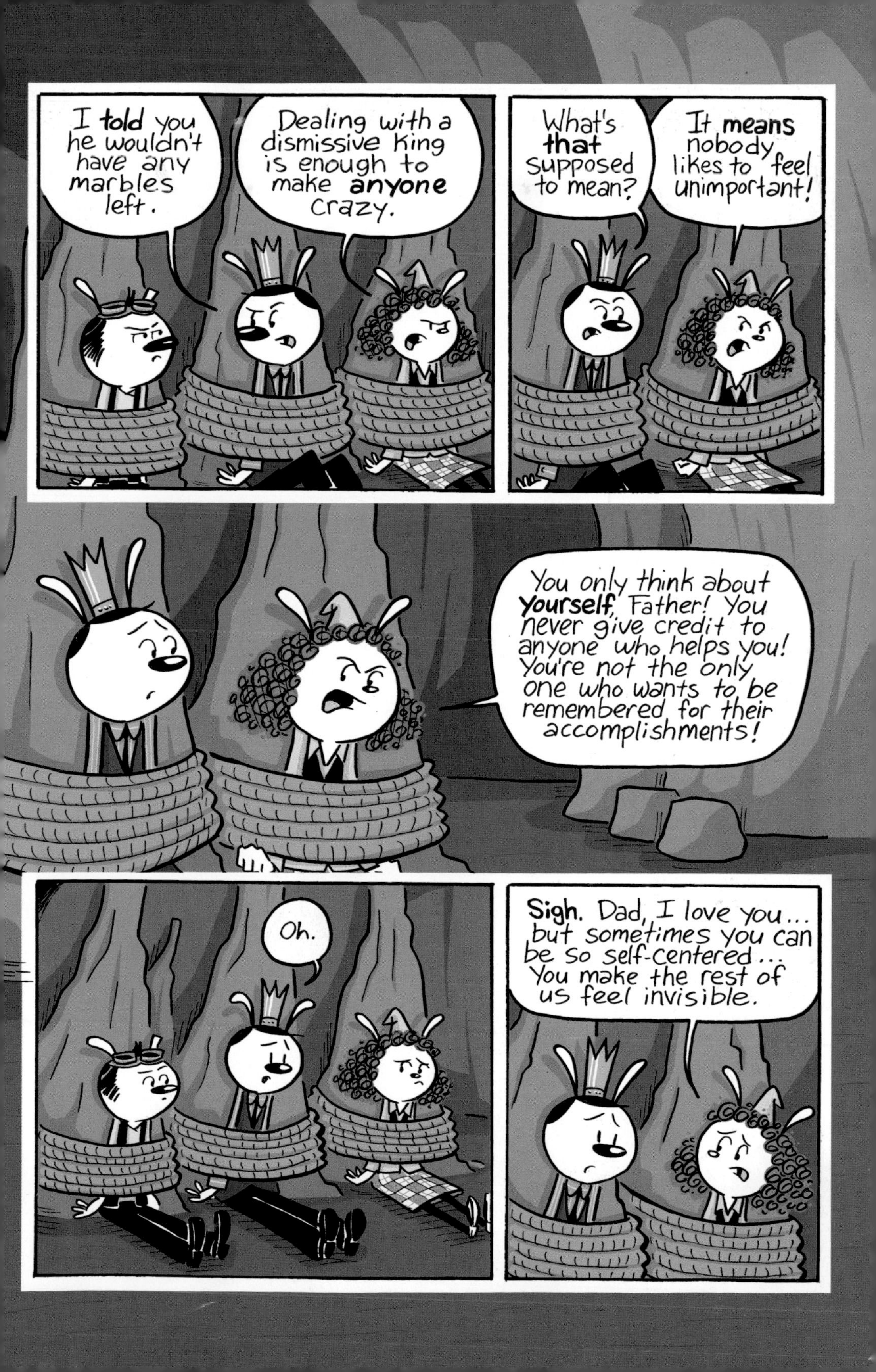
I told you he wouldn't have any marbles left.
Dealing with a dismissive king is enough to make anyone crazy.
What's that supposed to mean?
It means nobody likes to feel unimportant!
You only think about yourself, Father! You never give credit to anyone who helps you! You're not the only one who wants to be remembered for their accomplishments!
Oh.
Sigh. Dad, I love you... but sometimes you can be so self-centered... You make the rest of us feel invisible.

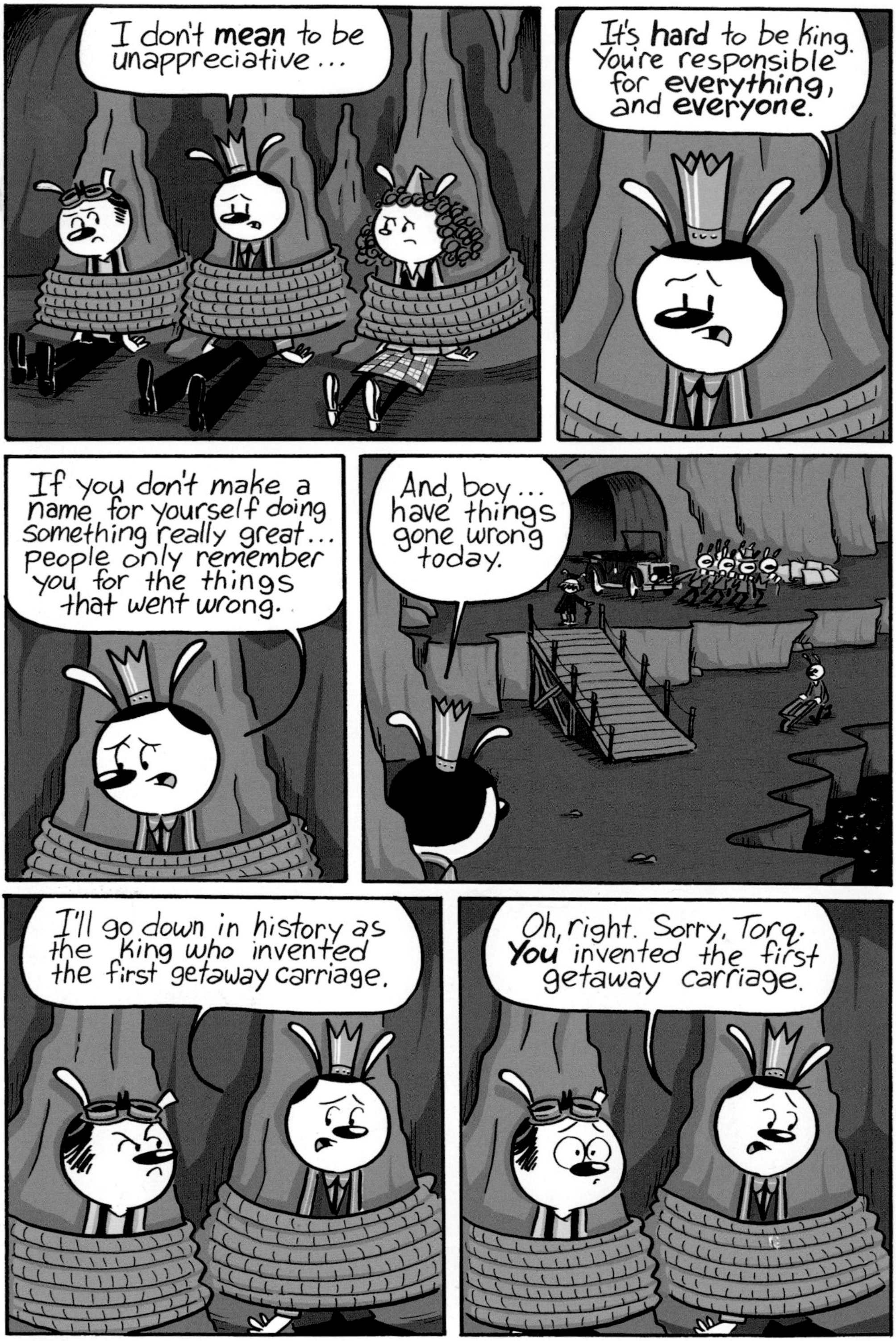
I don't **mean** to be unappreciative...
It's **hard** to be king. You're responsible for **everything**, and **everyone**.
If you don't make a name for yourself doing something really great... people only remember you for the things that went wrong.
And, boy... have things gone wrong today.
I'll go down in history as the king who invented the first getaway carriage.
Oh, right. Sorry, Torq. **You** invented the first getaway carriage.

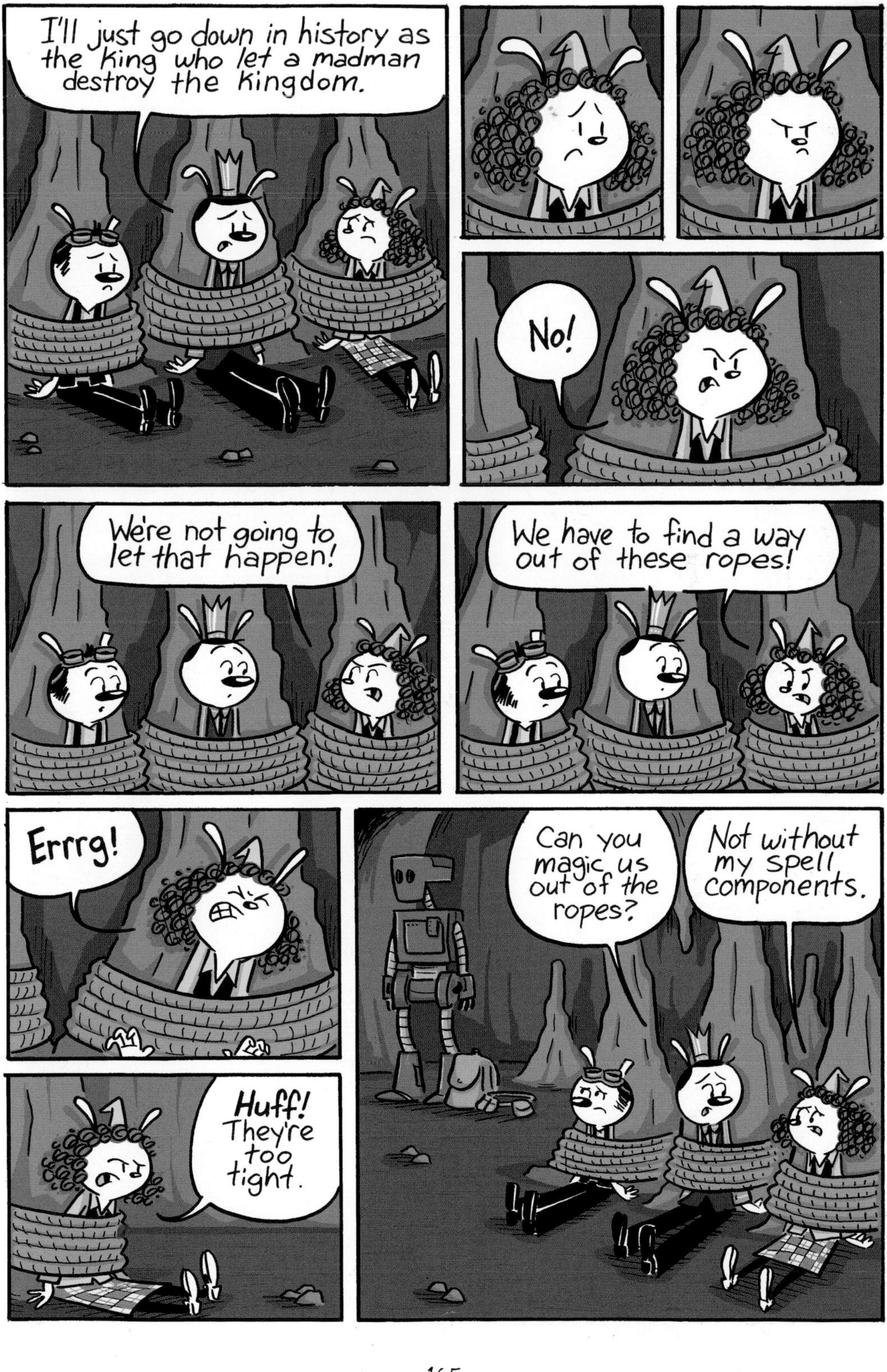
I'll just go down in history as the king who let a madman destroy the kingdom.
No!
We're not going to let that happen!
We have to find a way out of these ropes!
Errrg!
Huff! They're too tight.
Can you magic us out of the ropes?
Not without my spell components.

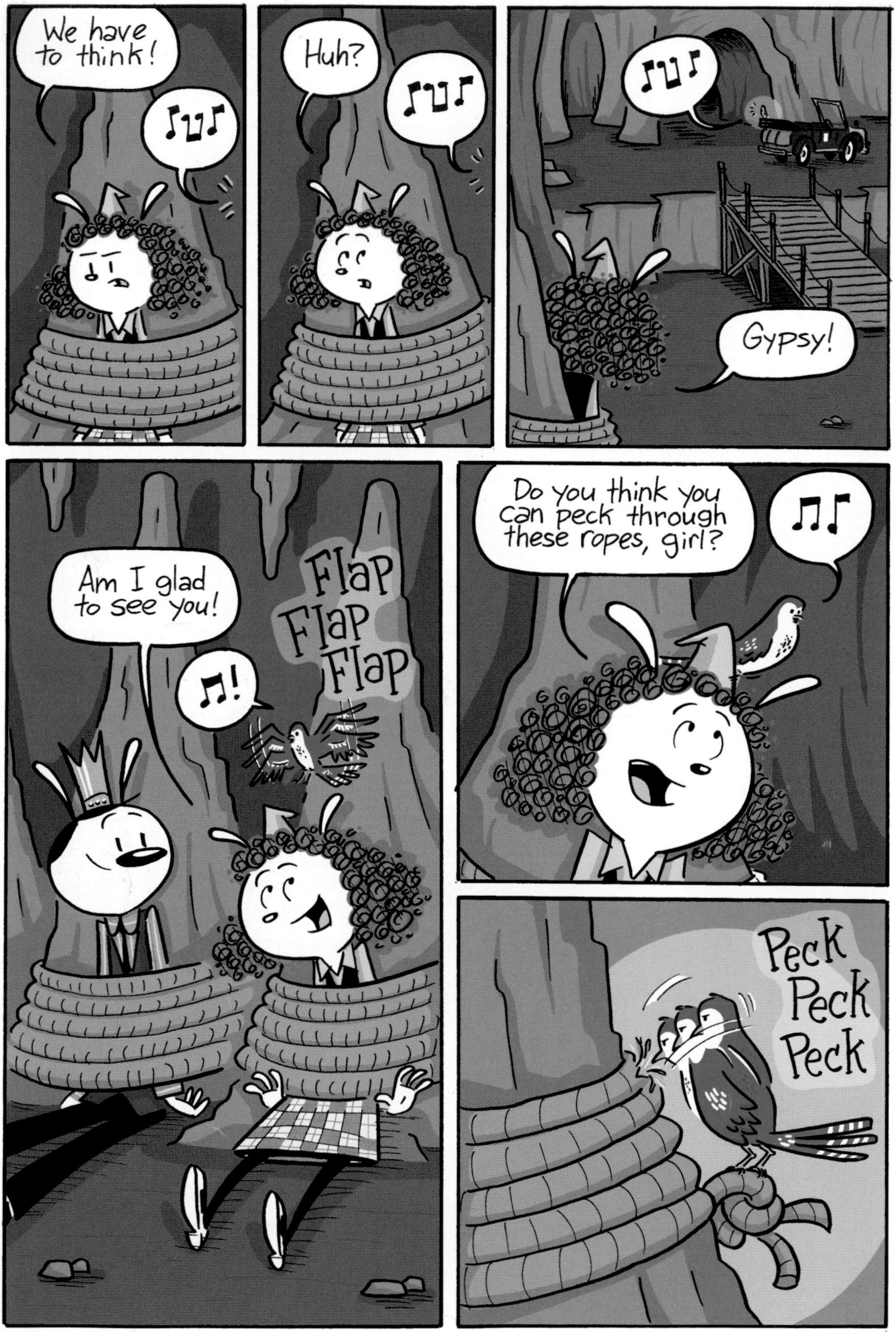
We have to think!
Huh?
Gypsy!
Am I glad to see you!
Flap
Flap
Flap
Do you think you can peck through these ropes, girl?
Peck
Peck
Peck

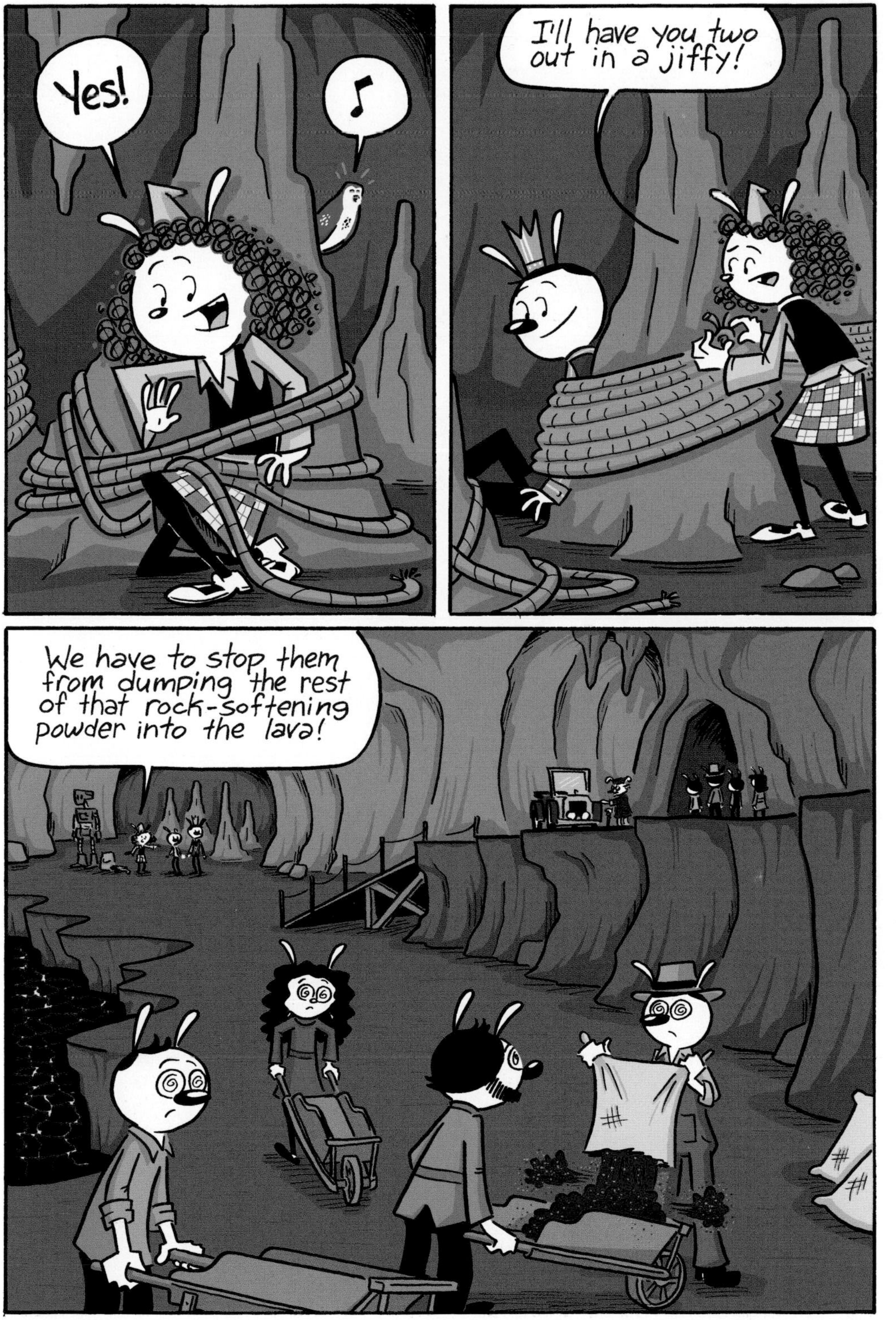
Yes!
♪
I'll have you two out in a jiffy!
We have to stop them from dumping the rest of that rock-softening powder into the lava!

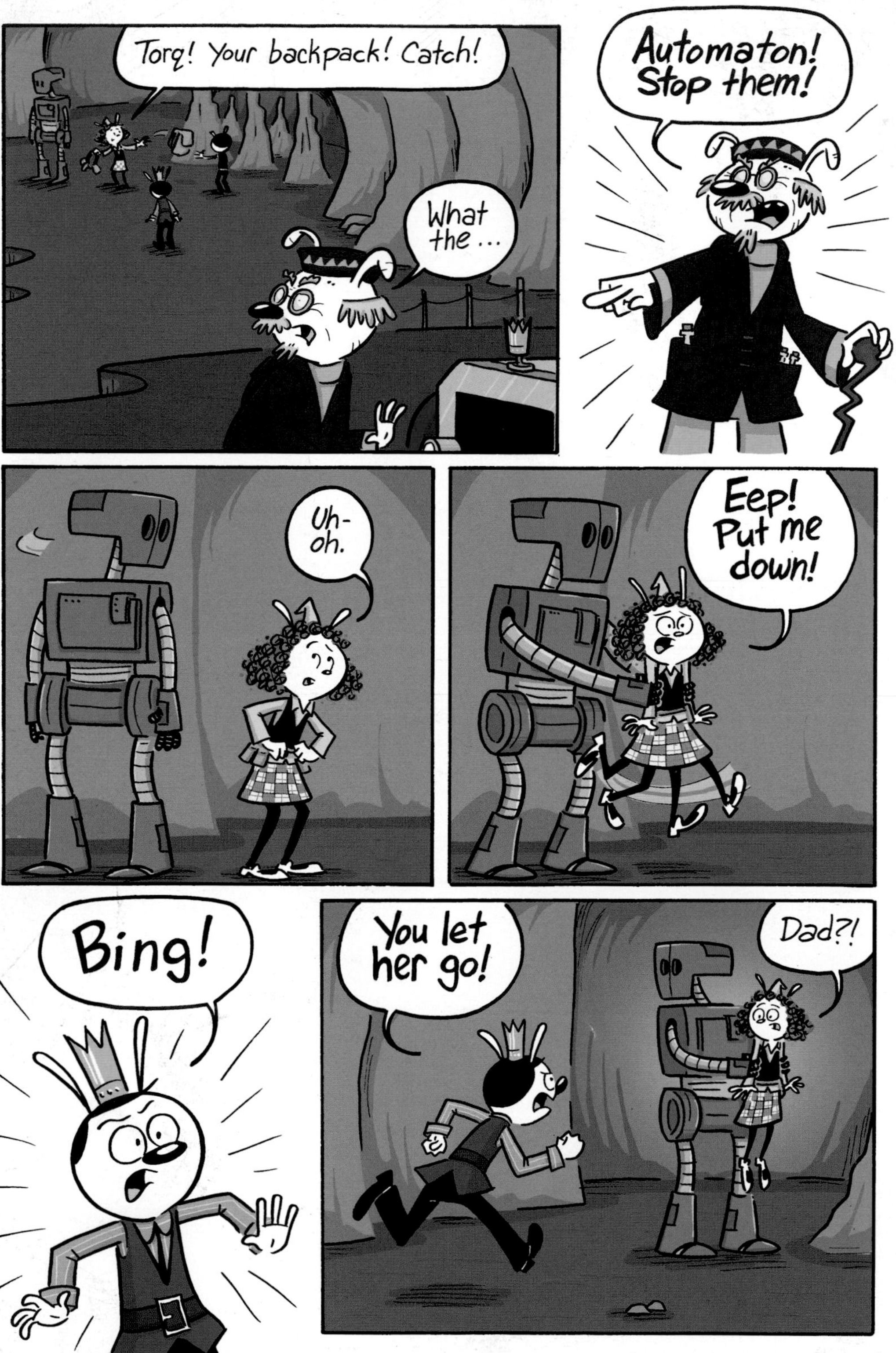
Torq! Your backpack! Catch!
What the...
Automaton! Stop them!
Uh-oh.
Eep! Put me down!
Bing!
You let her go!
Dad?!

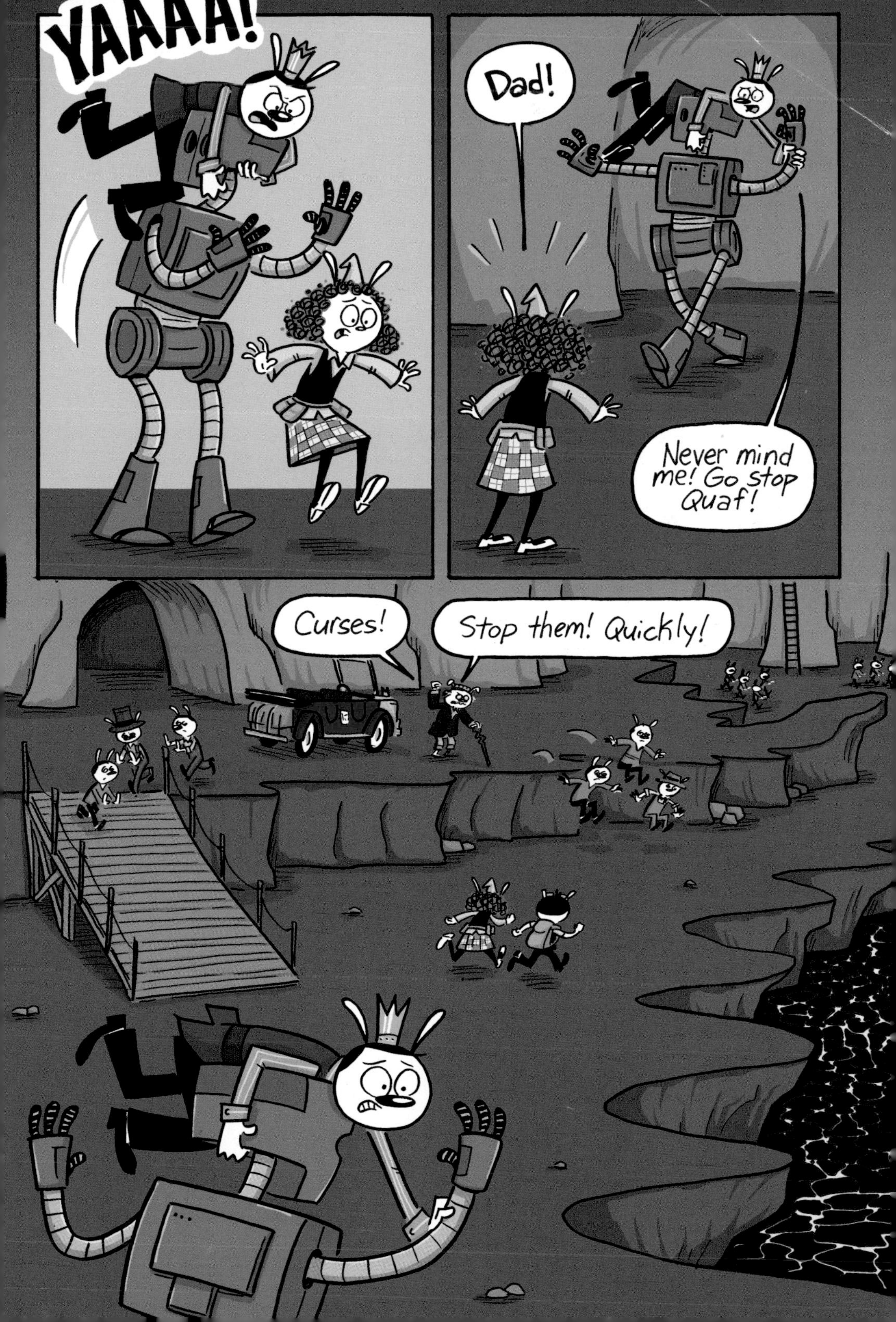
YAAAA!
Dad!
Never mind me! Go stop Quaf!
Curses!
Stop them! Quickly!

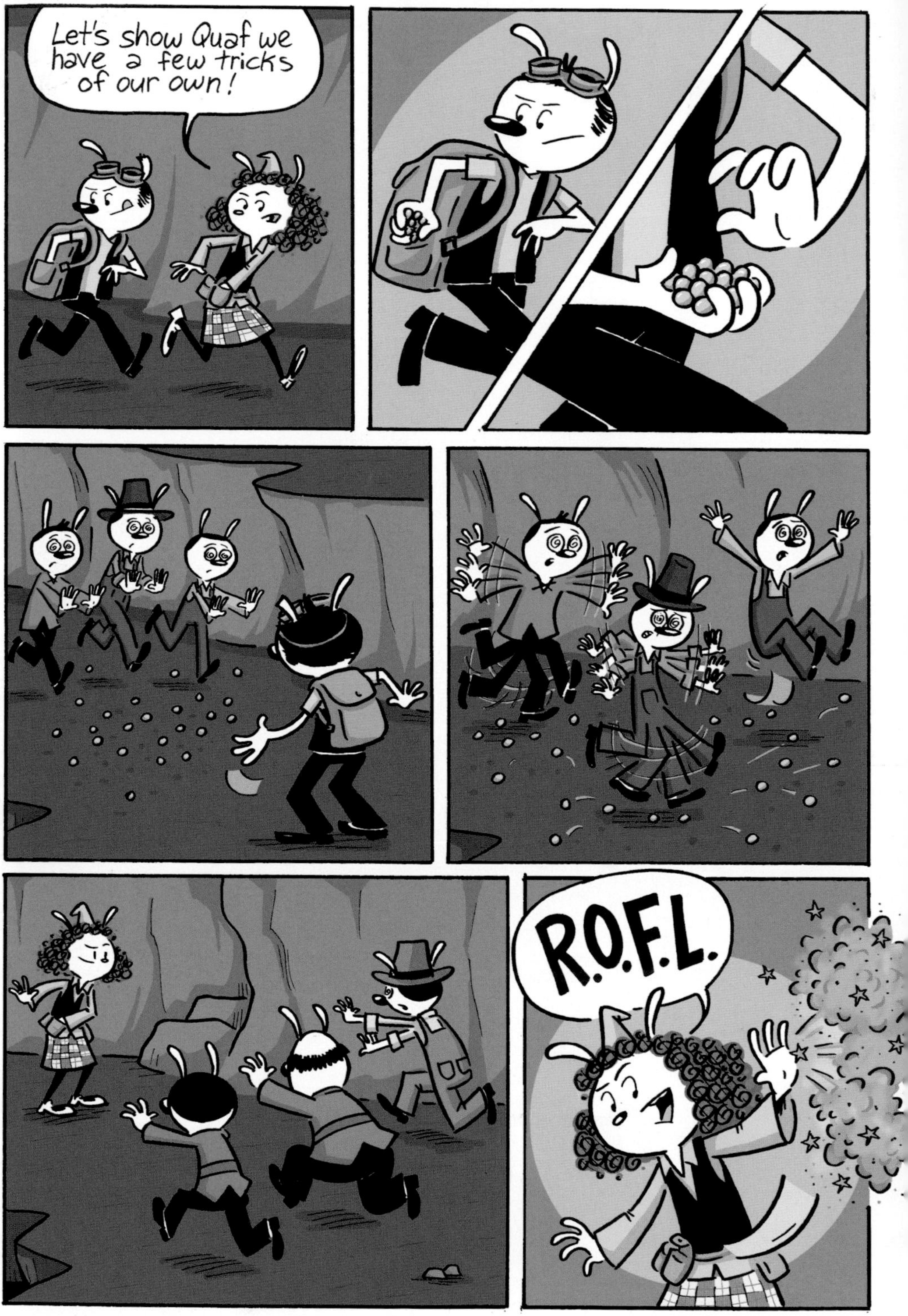
Let's show Quaf we have a few tricks of our own!
R.O.F.L.

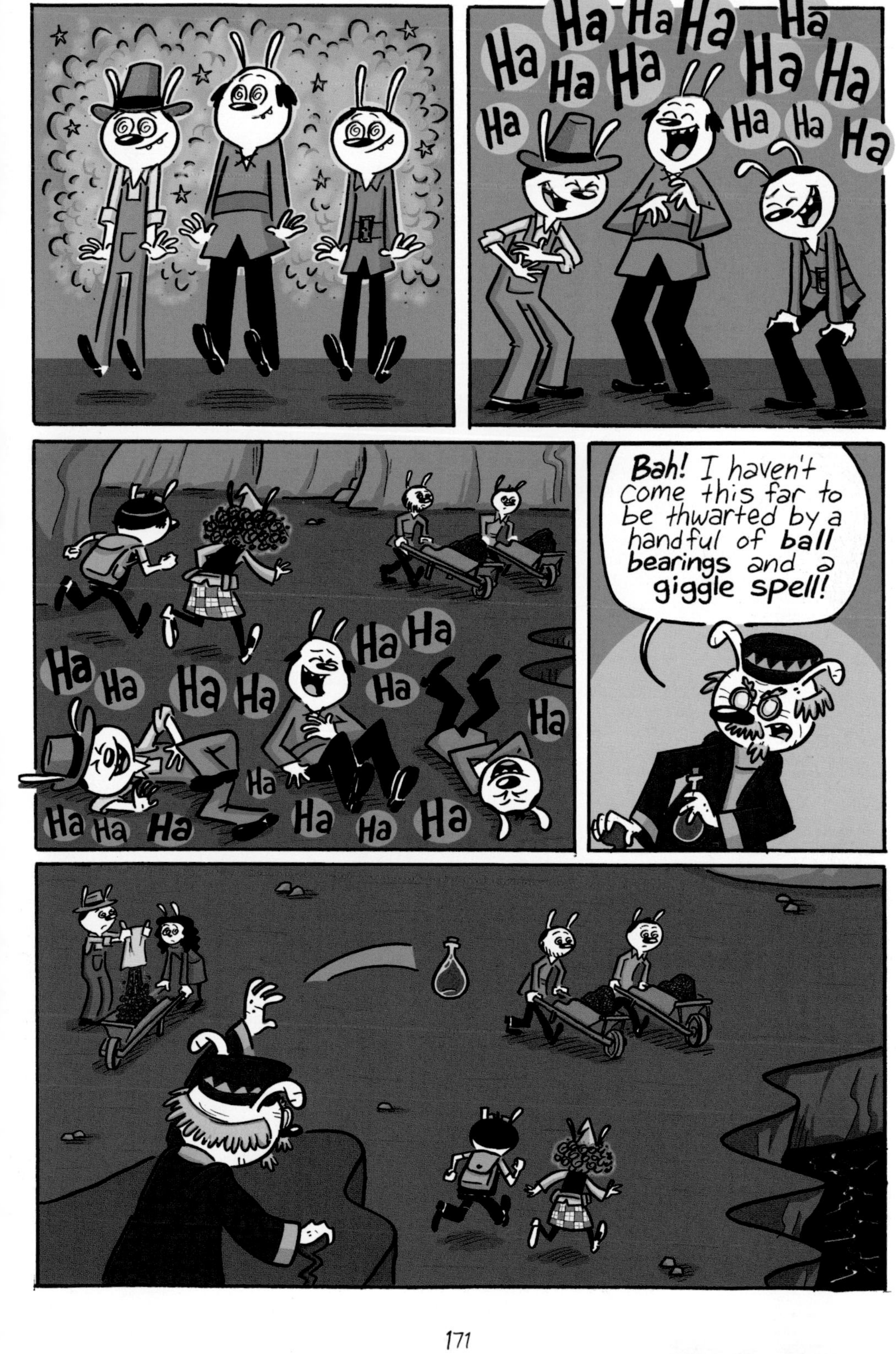
Ha Ha Ha Ha Ha
Ha Ha Ha Ha Ha
Ha Ha Ha Ha
Ha Ha
Ha Ha Ha Ha Ha
Ha Ha
Ha Ha Ha Ha Ha Ha
Bah! I haven't come this far to be thwarted by a handful of ball bearings and a giggle spell!

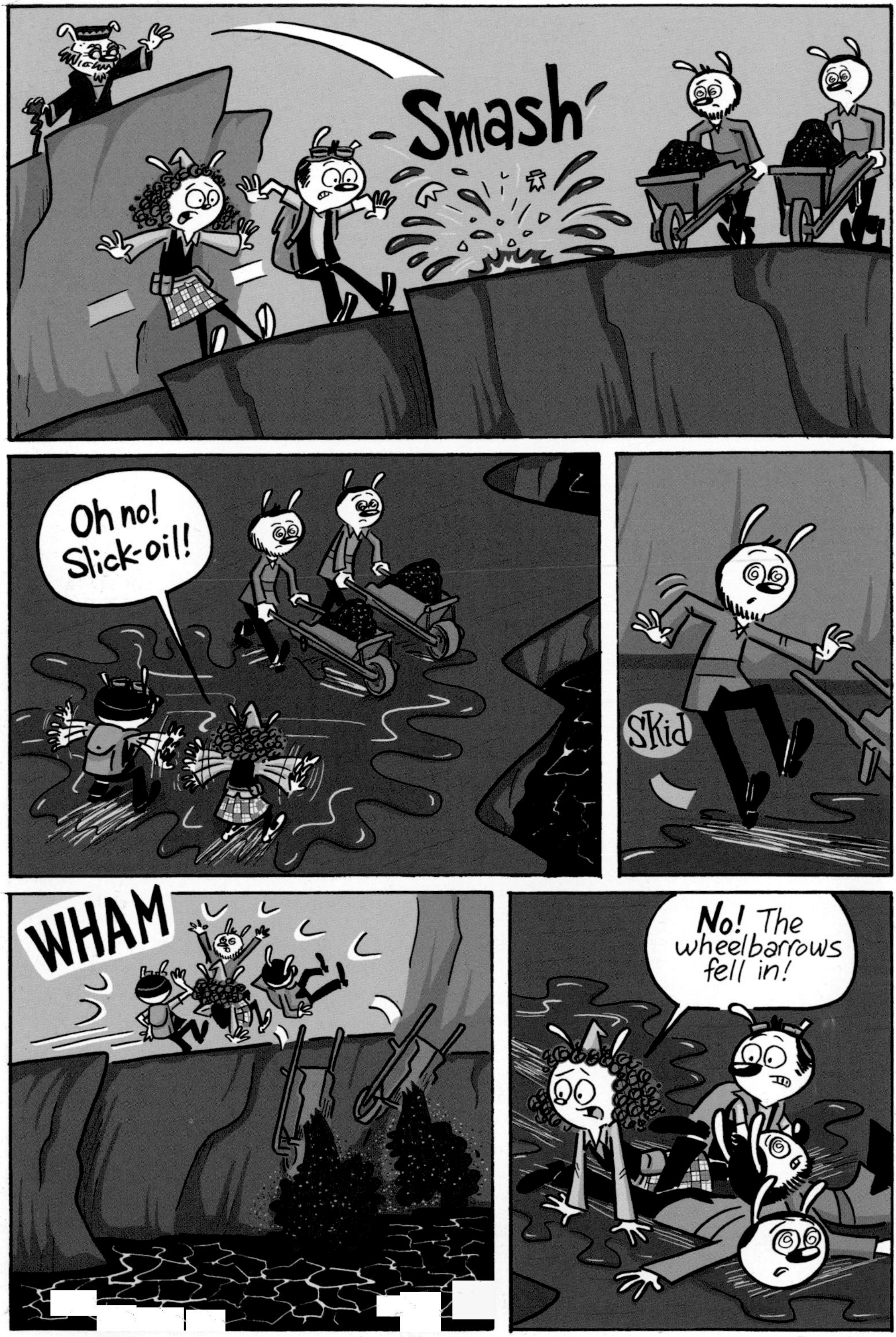
Smash
Oh no! Slick-oil!
SKid
WHAM
No! The wheelbarrows fell in!

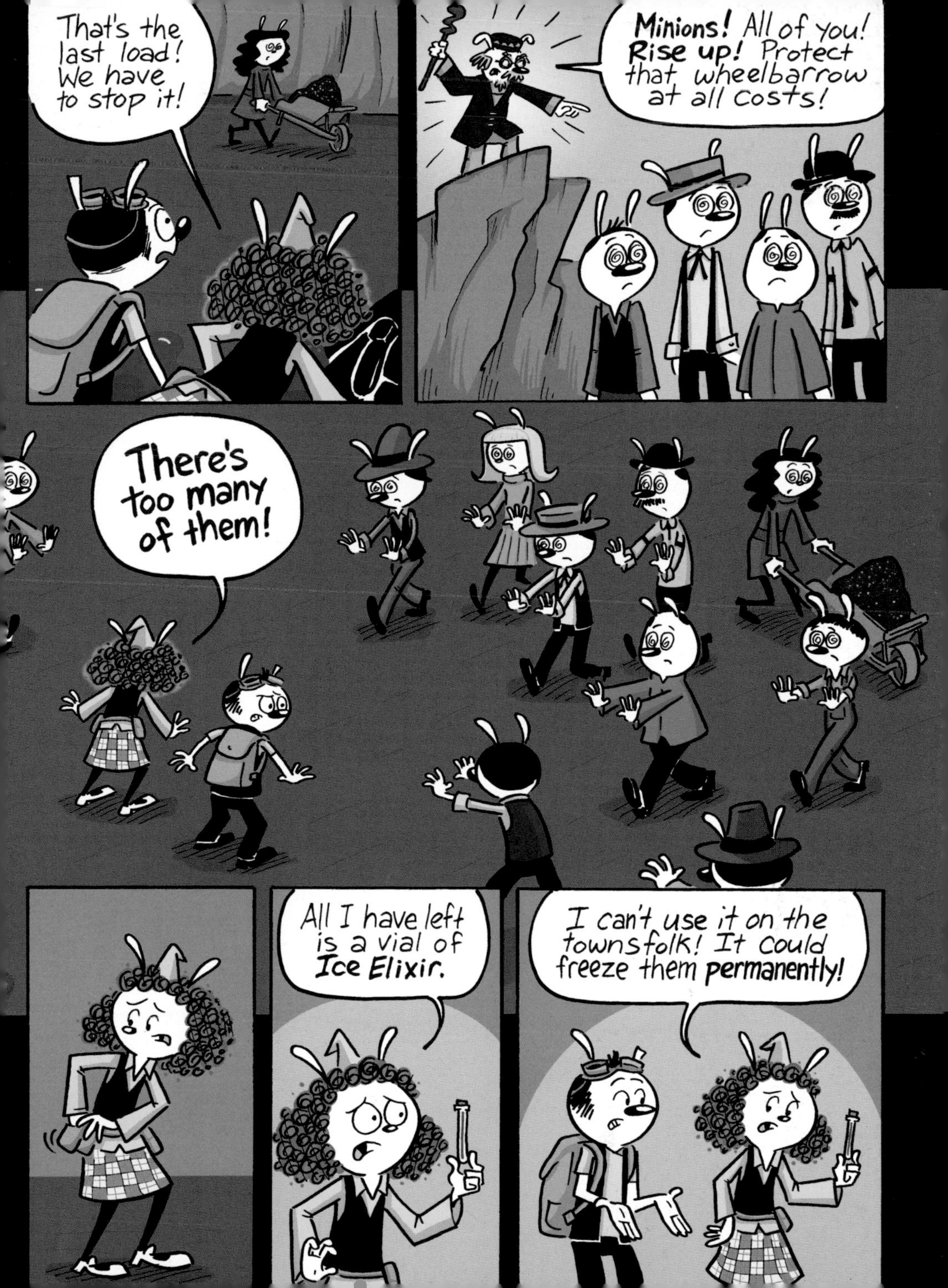
That's the last load! We have to stop it!
Minions! All of you! Rise up! Protect that wheelbarrow at all costs!
There's too many of them!
All I have left is a vial of Ice Elixir.
I can't use it on the townsfolk! It could freeze them permanently!

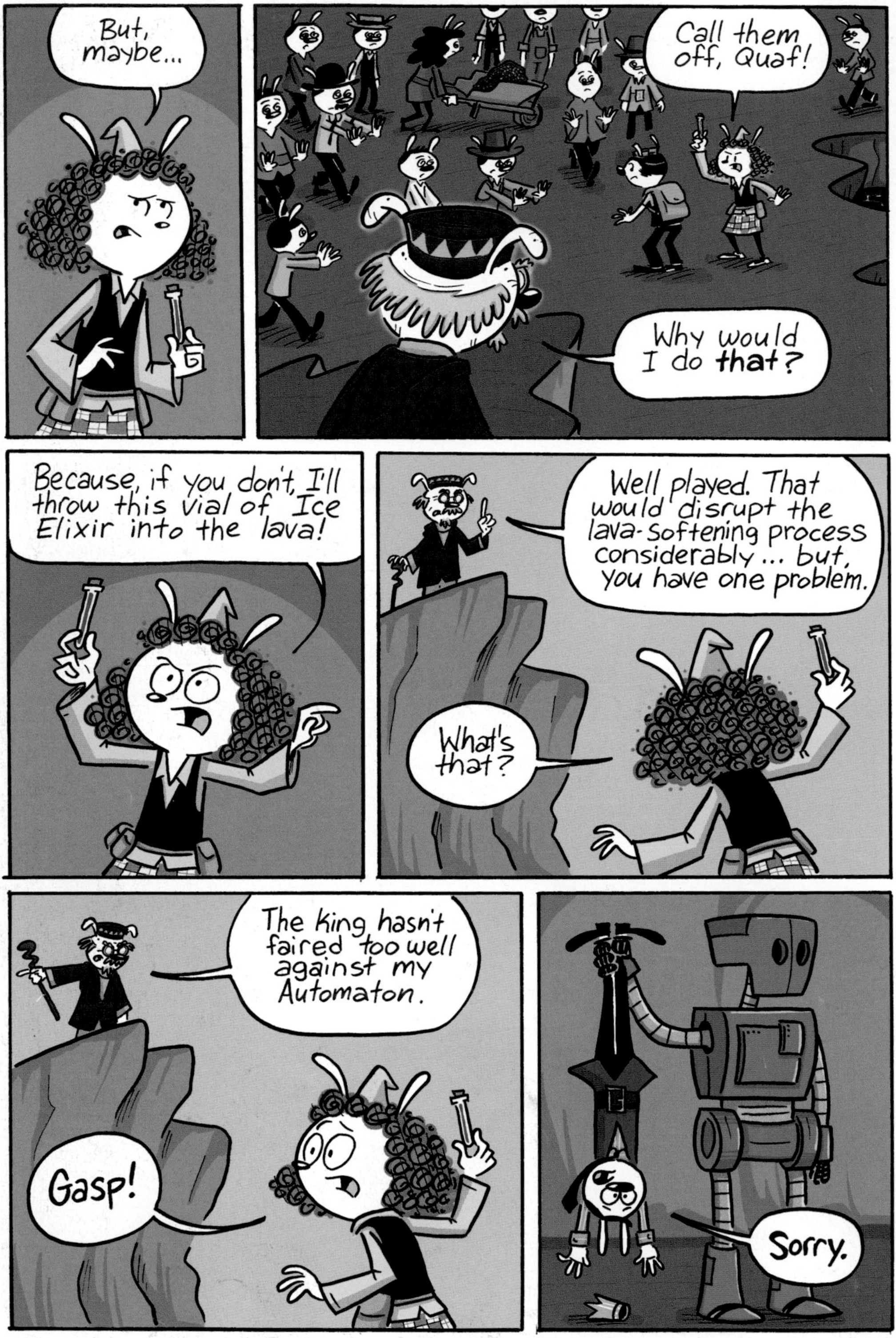
But, maybe...
Call them off, Quaf!
Why would I do **that?**
Because, if you don't, I'll throw this vial of Ice Elixir into the lava!
Well played. That would disrupt the lava-softening process considerably ... but, you have one problem.
What's that?
The King hasn't faired too well against my Automaton.
Gasp!
Sorry.

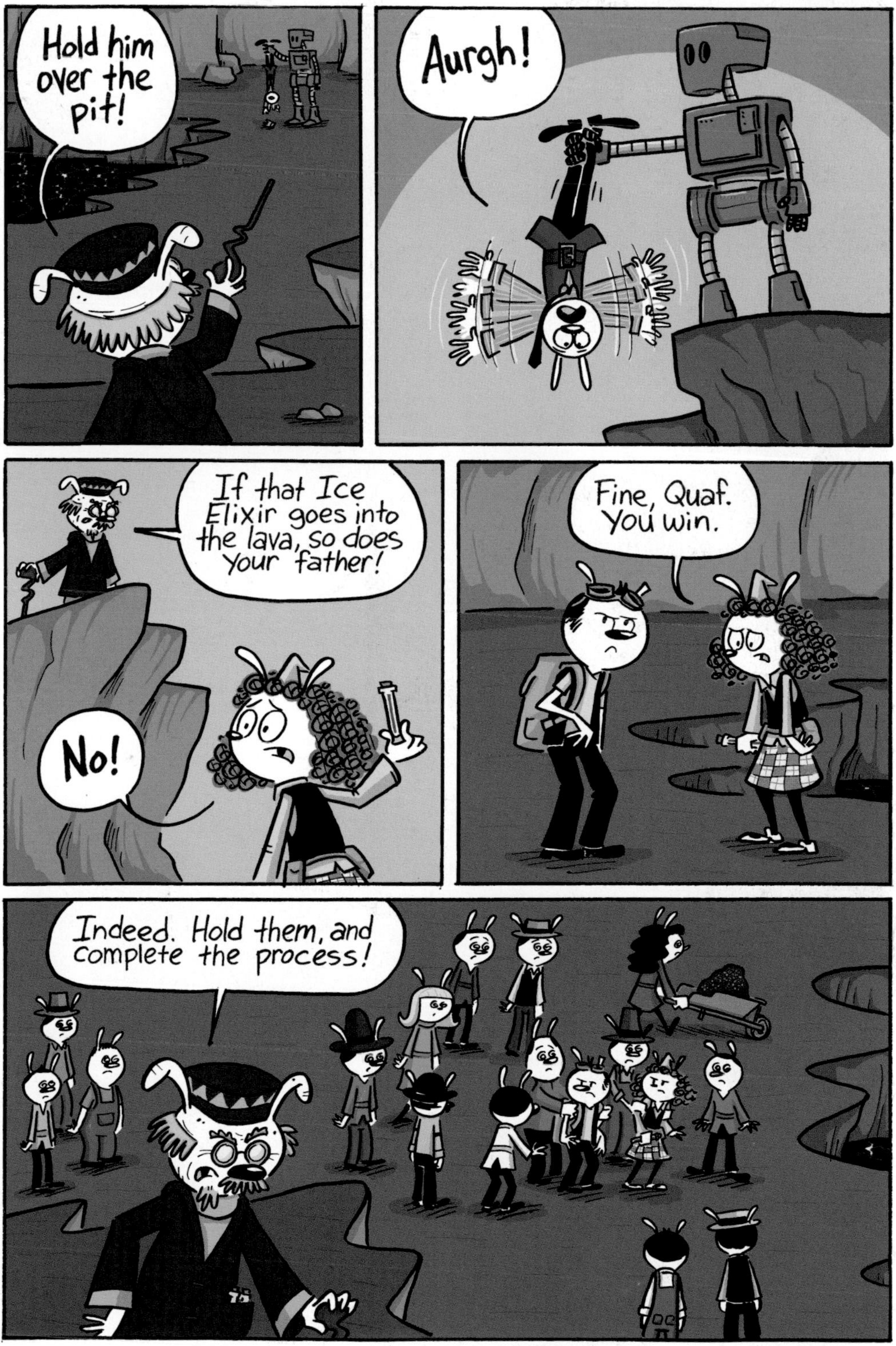

Hold him over the pit!
Aurgh!
If that Ice Elixir goes into the lava, so does your father!
No!
Fine, Quaf. You win.
Indeed. Hold them, and complete the process!

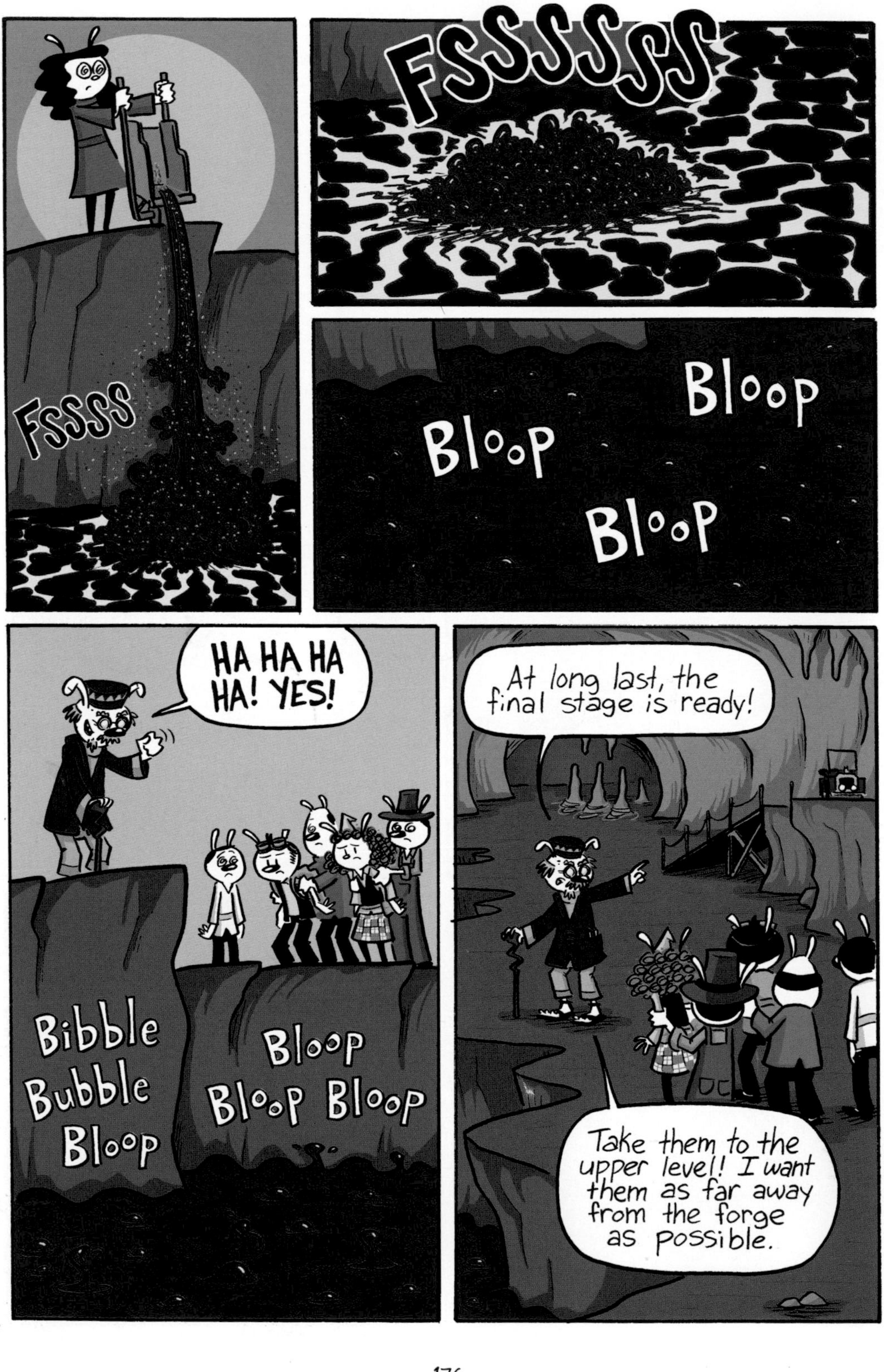
FSSSS
FSSSSSSS
Bloop
Bloop
Bloop
HA HA HA HA! YES!
Bibble Bubble Bloop
Bloop Bloop Bloop
At long last, the final stage is ready!
Take them to the upper level! I want them as far away from the forge as possible.

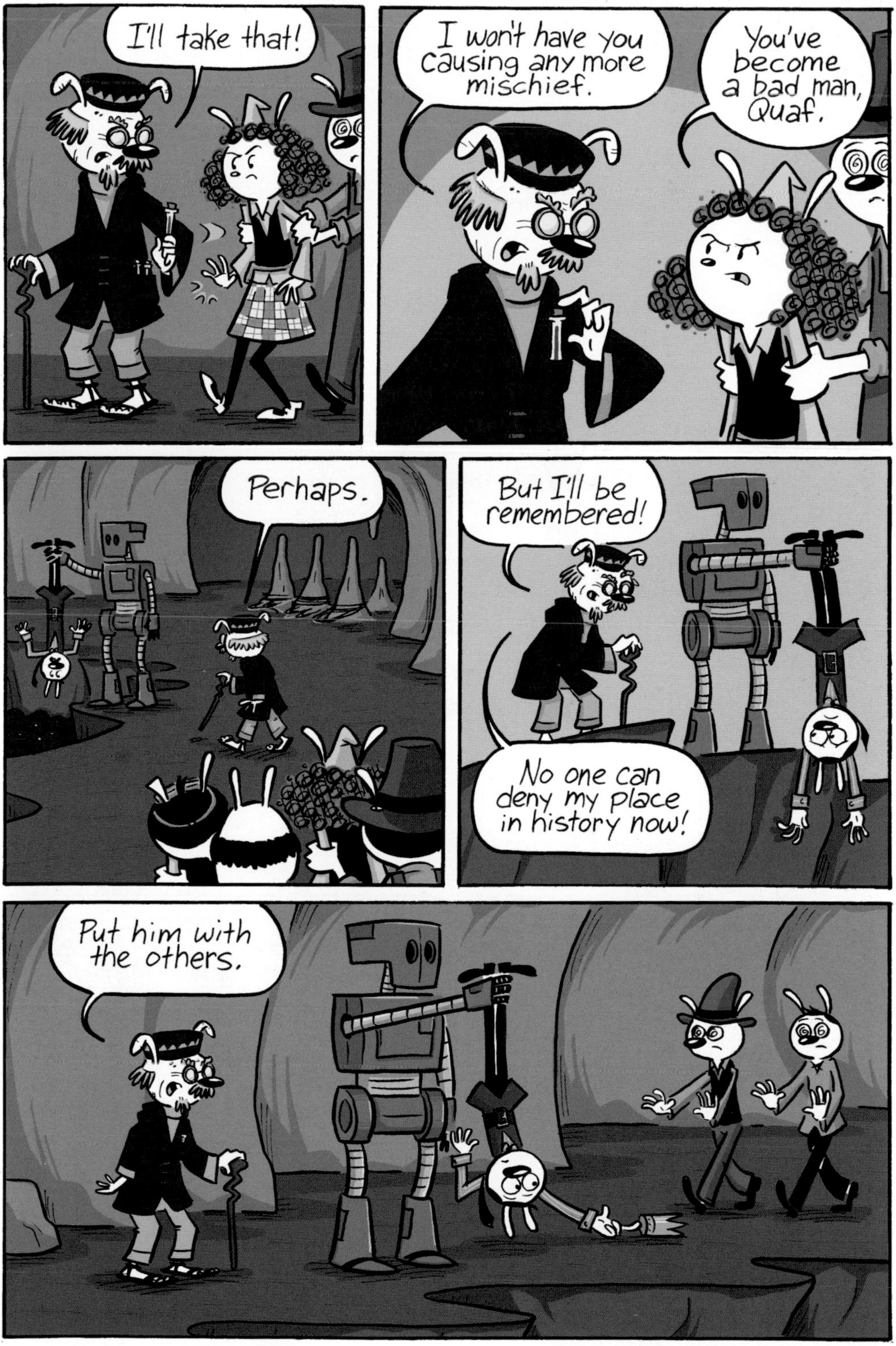
I'll take that!
I won't have you causing any more mischief.
You've become a bad man, Quaf.
Perhaps.
But I'll be remembered!
No one can deny my place in history now!
Put him with the others.

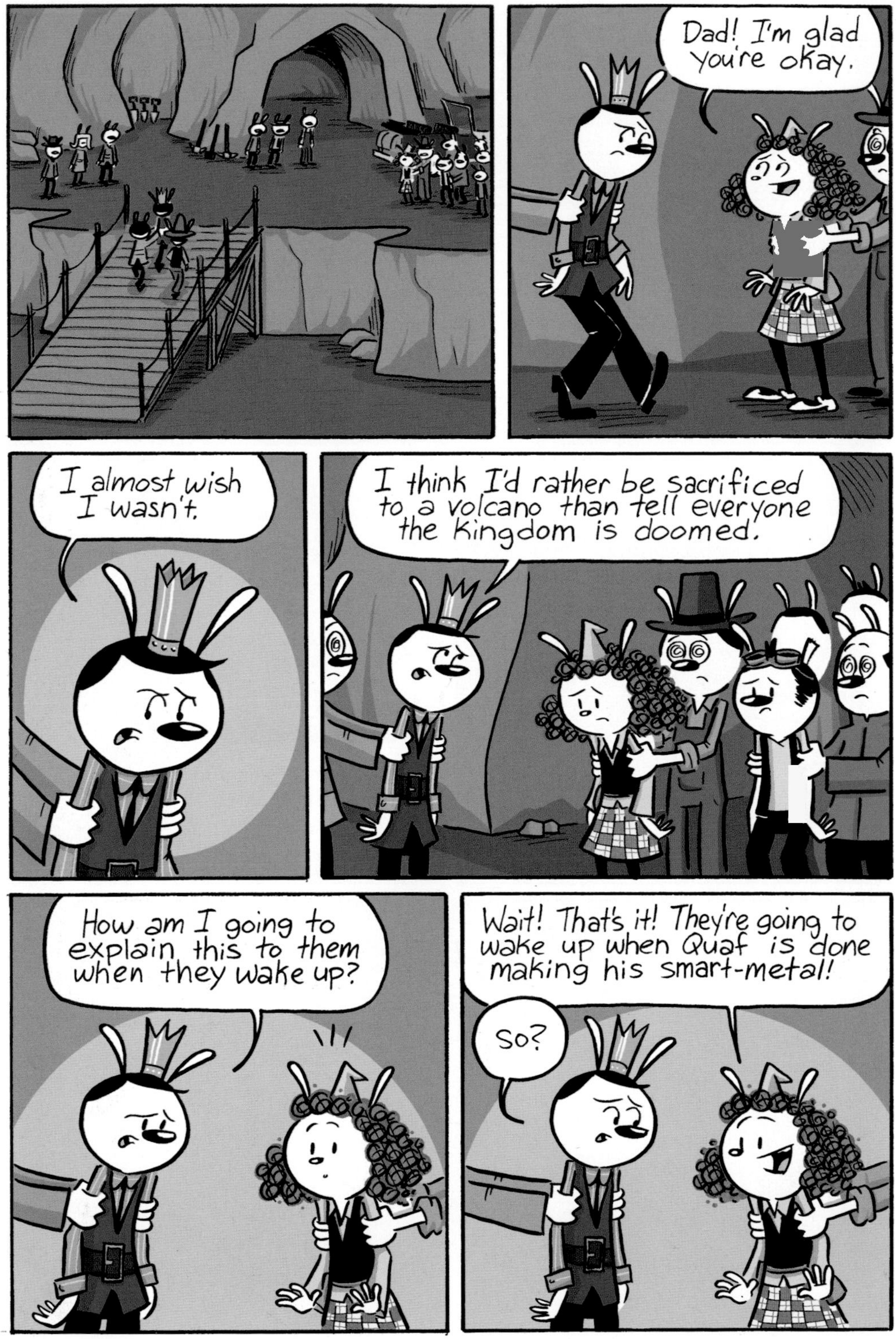
Dad! I'm glad you're okay.
I almost wish I wasn't.
I think I'd rather be sacrificed to a volcano than tell everyone the Kingdom is doomed.
How am I going to explain this to them when they wake up?
Wait! That's it! They're going to wake up when Quaf is done making his smart-metal!
So?

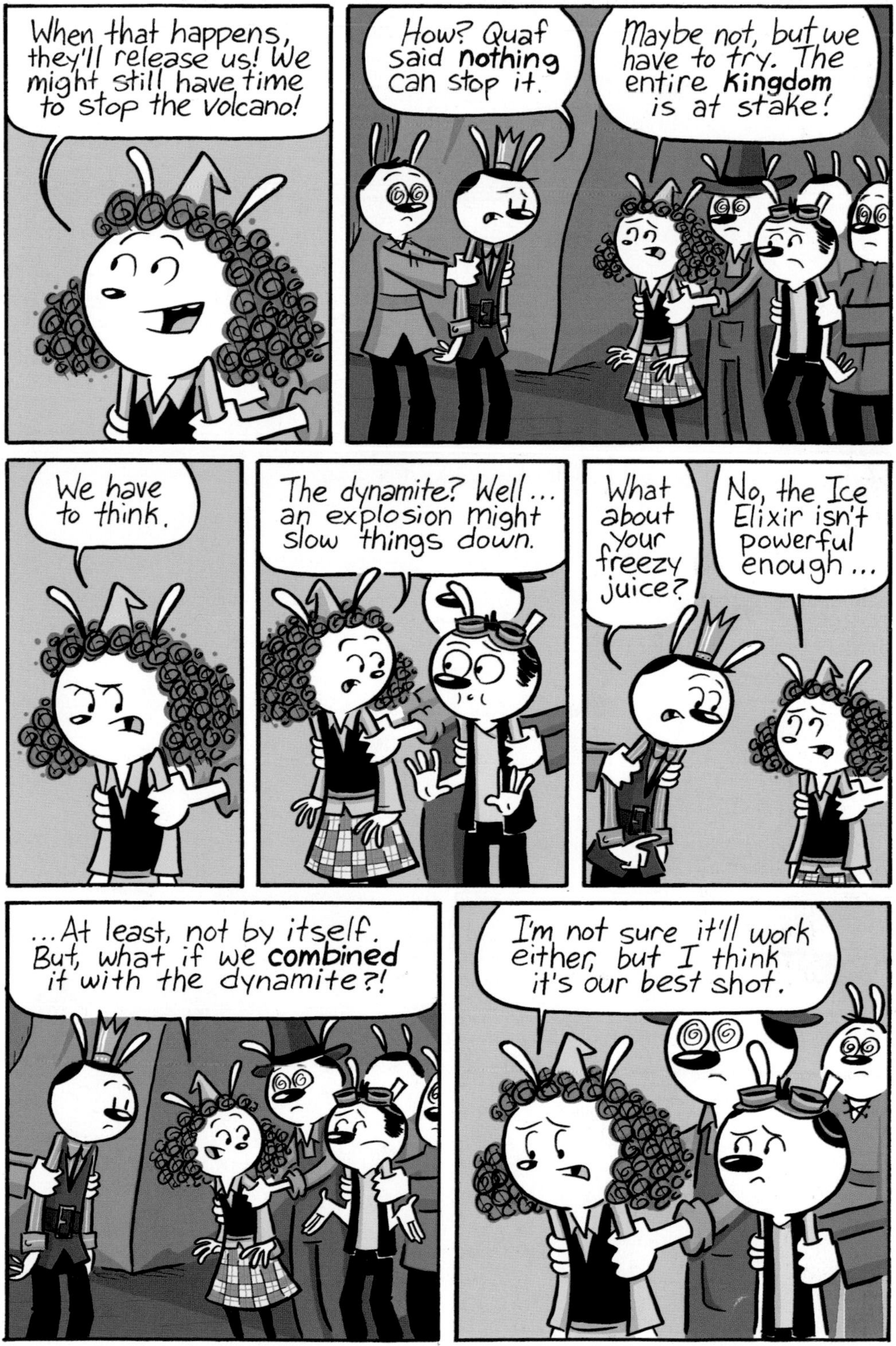
When that happens, they'll release us! We might still have time to stop the volcano!
How? Quaf said **nothing** can stop it.
Maybe not, but we have to try. The entire **Kingdom** is at stake!
We have to think.
The dynamite? Well... an explosion might slow things down.
What about your freezy juice?
No, the Ice Elixir isn't powerful enough...
...At least, not by itself. But, what if we **combined** it with the dynamite?!
I'm not sure it'll work either, but I think it's our best shot.

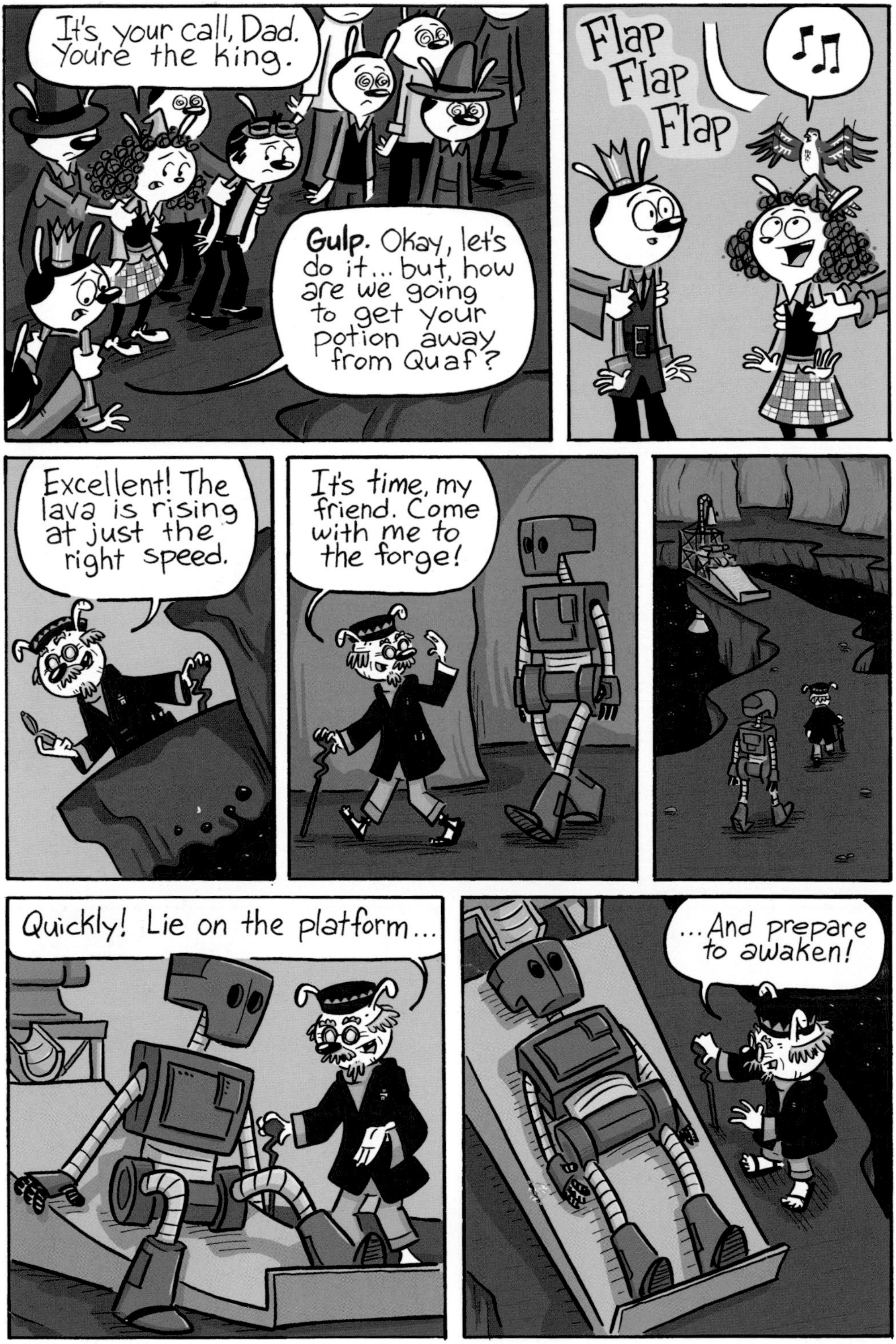
It's your call, Dad. You're the king.
Gulp. Okay, let's do it... but, how are we going to get your potion away from Quaf?
Flap Flap Flap
Excellent! The lava is rising at just the right speed.
It's time, my friend. Come with me to the forge!
Quickly! Lie on the platform...
...And prepare to awaken!

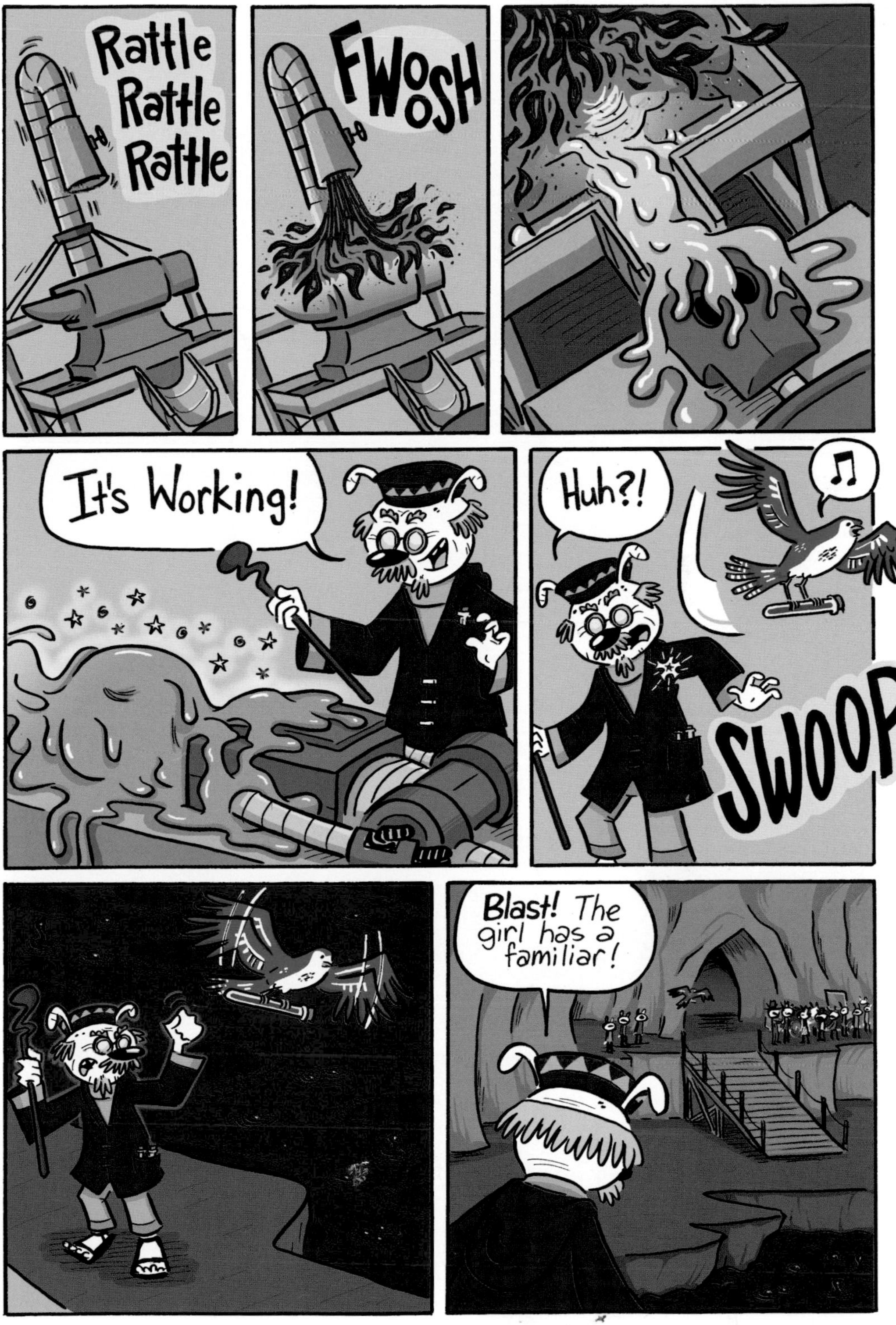
Rattle
Rattle
Rattle
FWOOSH
It's Working!
Huh?!
♫
SWOOP
Blast! The girl has a familiar!

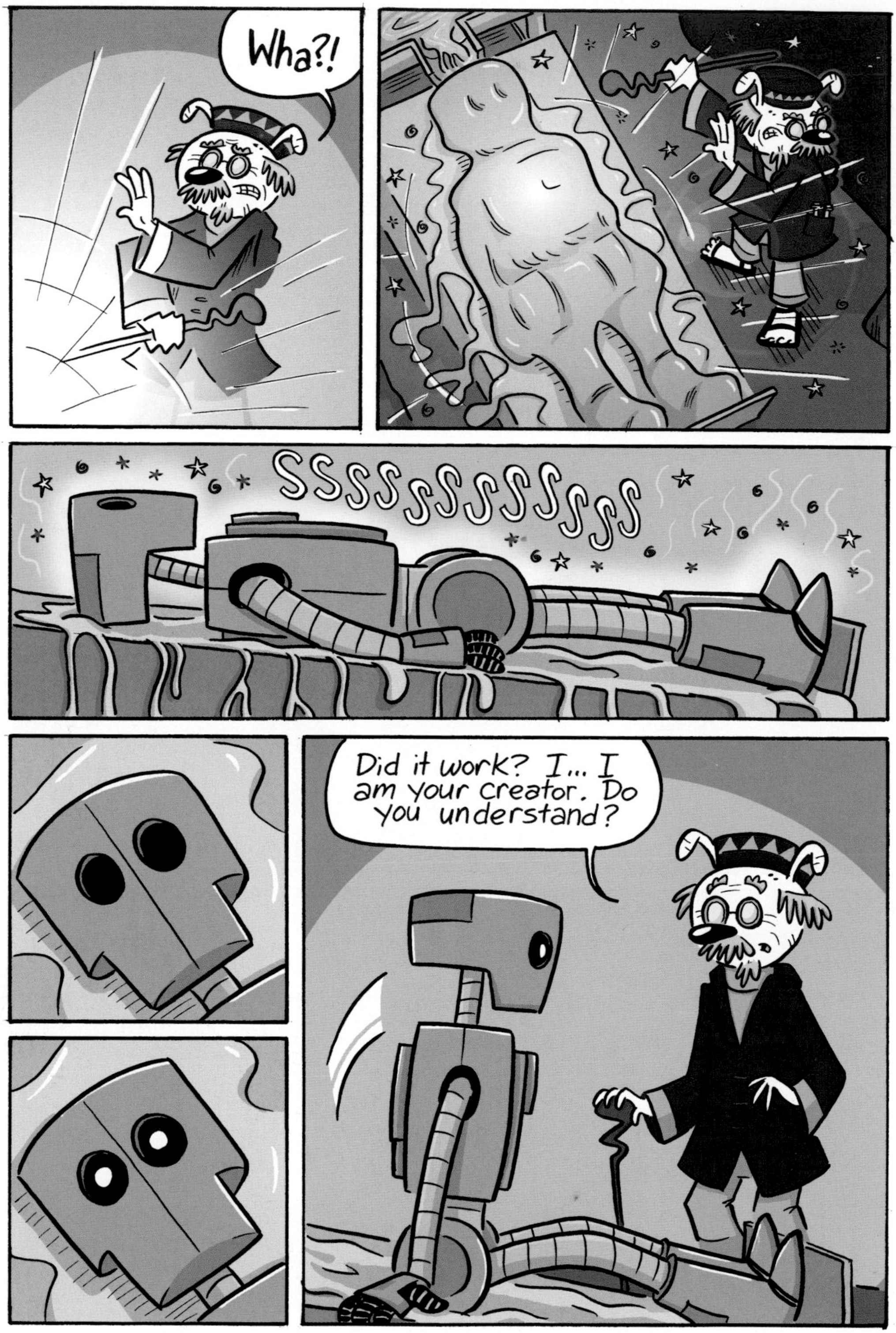
Wha?!
SSSSSSSSSSSSSS
Did it work? I... I am your creator. Do you understand?

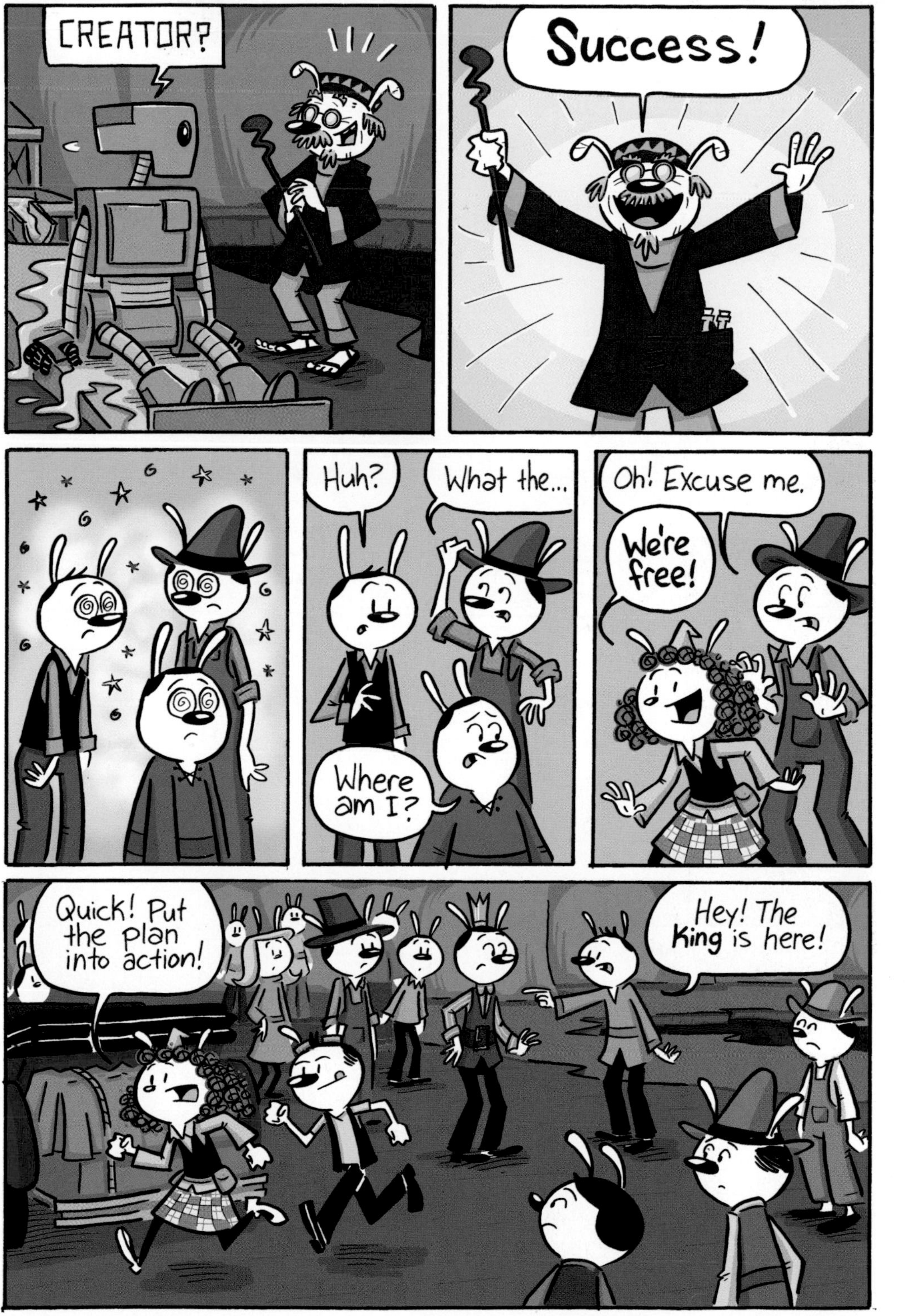
CREATOR?
Success!
Huh?
What the...
Where am I?
Oh! Excuse me.
We're free!
Quick! Put the plan into action!
Hey! The King is here!

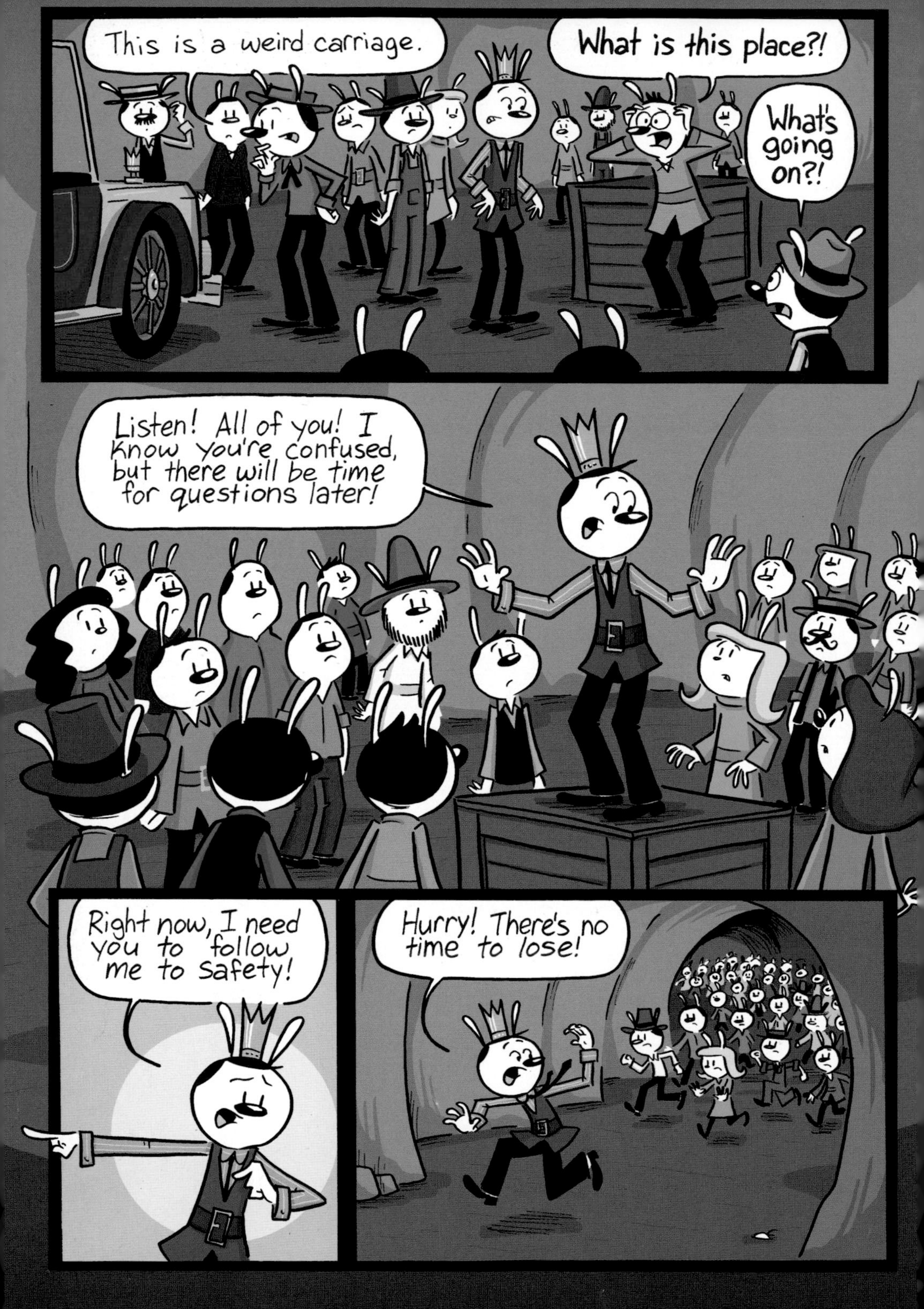
This is a weird carriage.
What is this place?!
What's going on?!
Listen! All of you! I know you're confused, but there will be time for questions later!
Right now, I need you to follow me to safety!
Hurry! There's no time to lose!

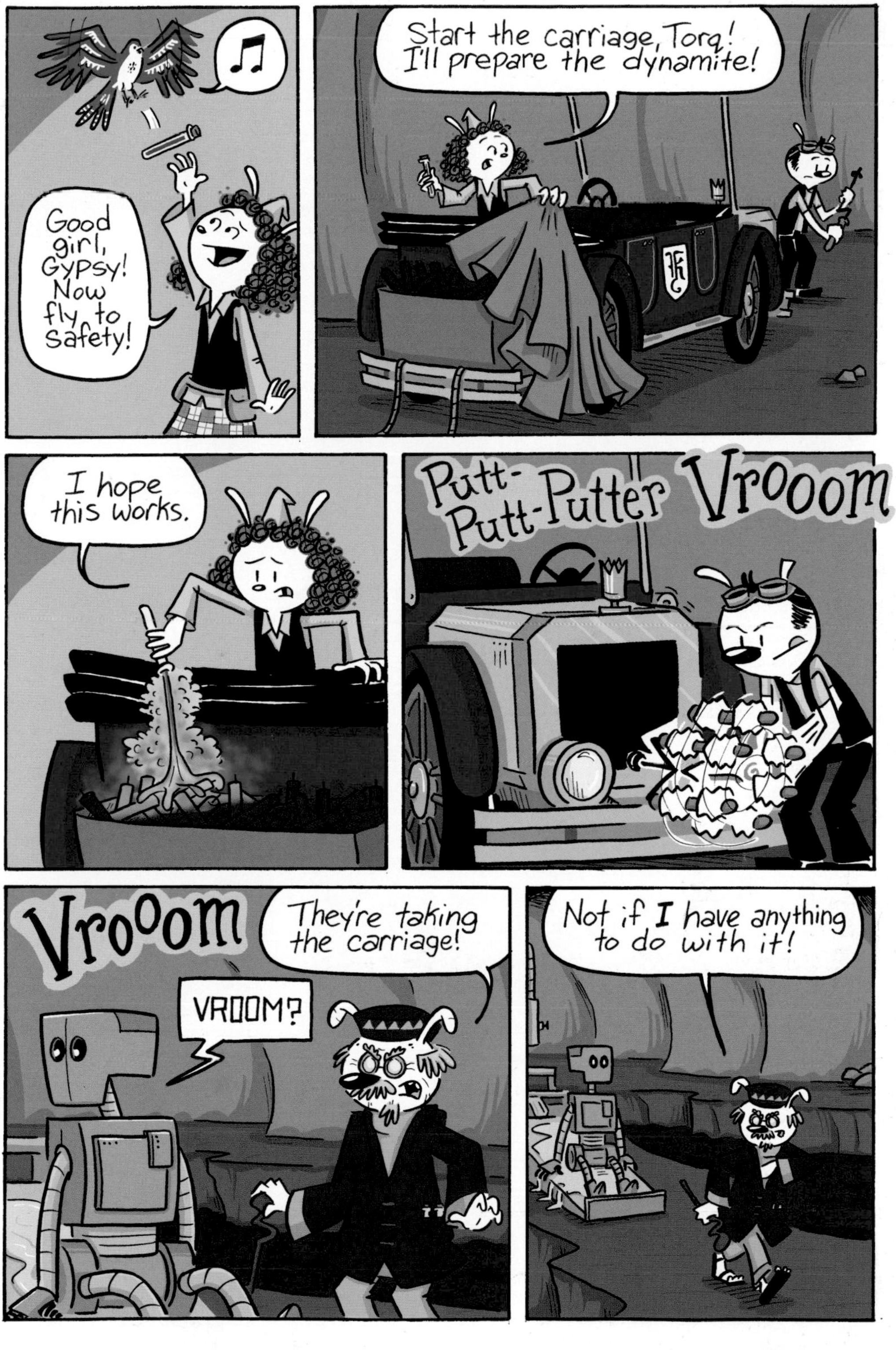
Good girl, Gypsy! Now fly to safety!
Start the carriage, Torq! I'll prepare the dynamite!
I hope this works.
Putt-Putt-Putter Vroooom
Vrooom
They're taking the carriage!
VROOM?
Not if I have anything to do with it!

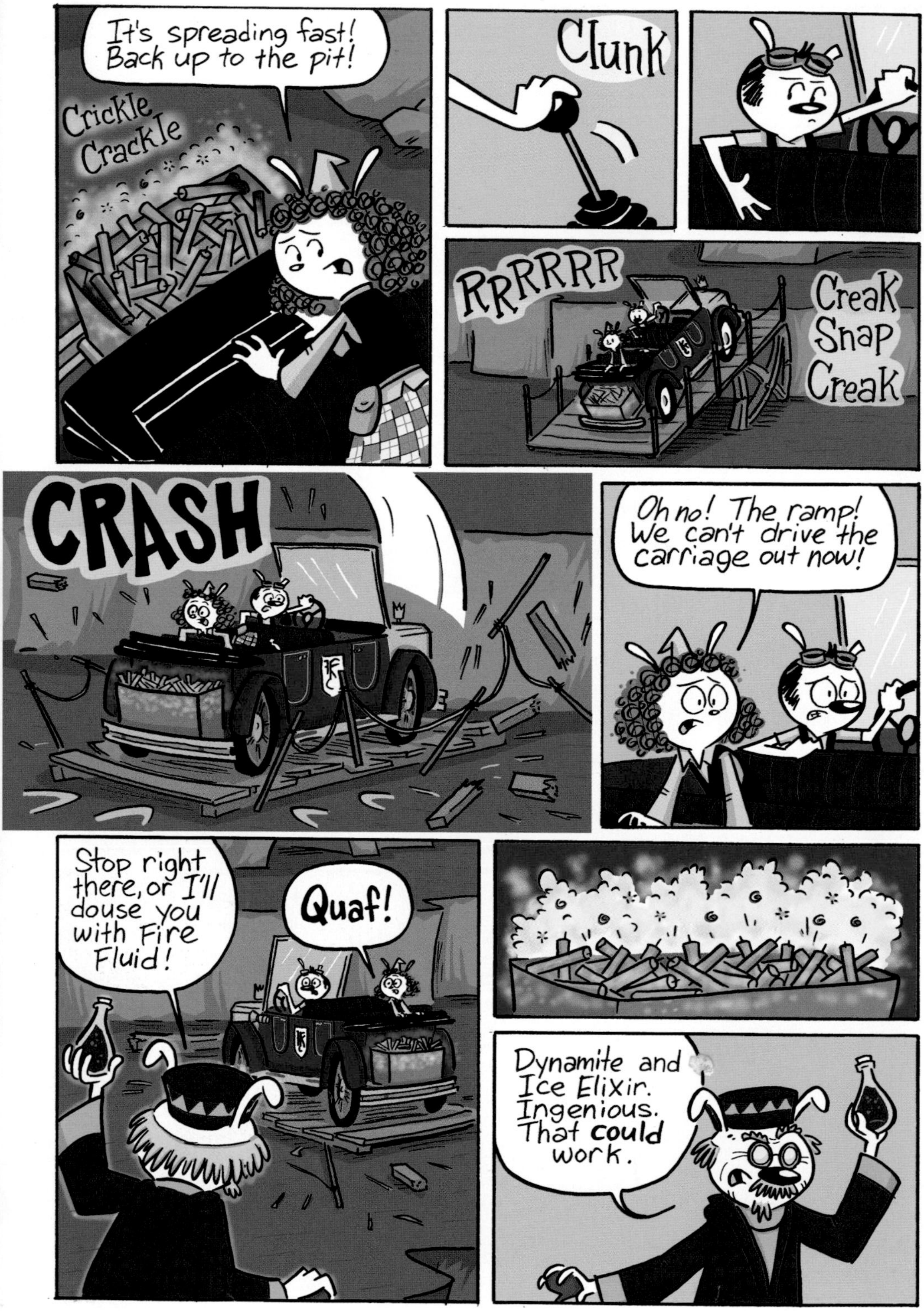
It's spreading fast! Back up to the pit!
Crickle Crackle
Clunk
RRRRRR
Creak Snap Creak
CRASH
Oh no! The ramp! We can't drive the carriage out now!
Stop right there, or I'll douse you with Fire Fluid!
Quaf!
Dynamite and Ice Elixir. Ingenious. That **could** work.

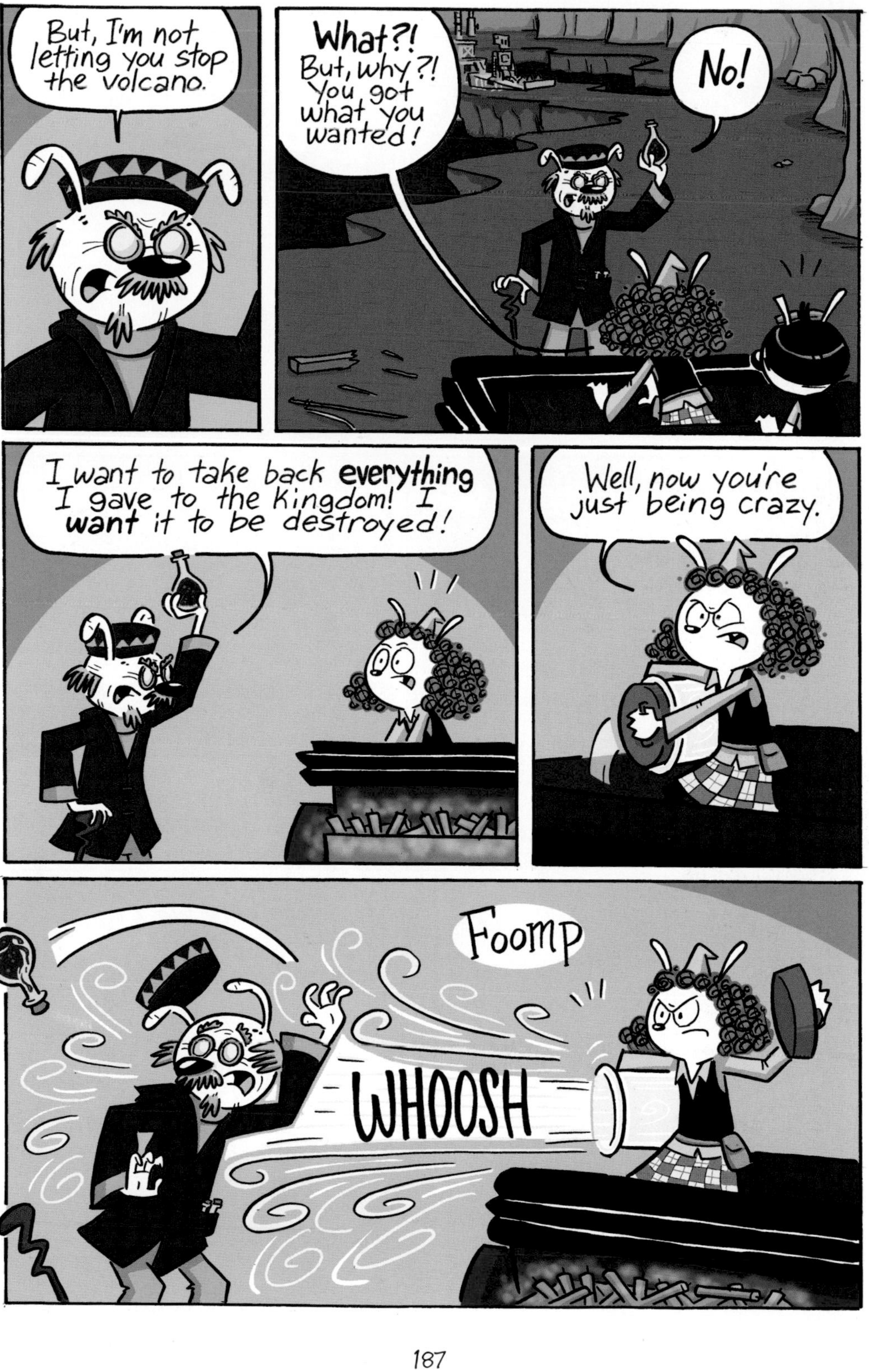
But, I'm not letting you stop the volcano.
What?! But, why?! You got what you wanted!
No!
I want to take back everything I gave to the Kingdom! I want it to be destroyed!
Well, now you're just being crazy.
Foomp
WHOOSH

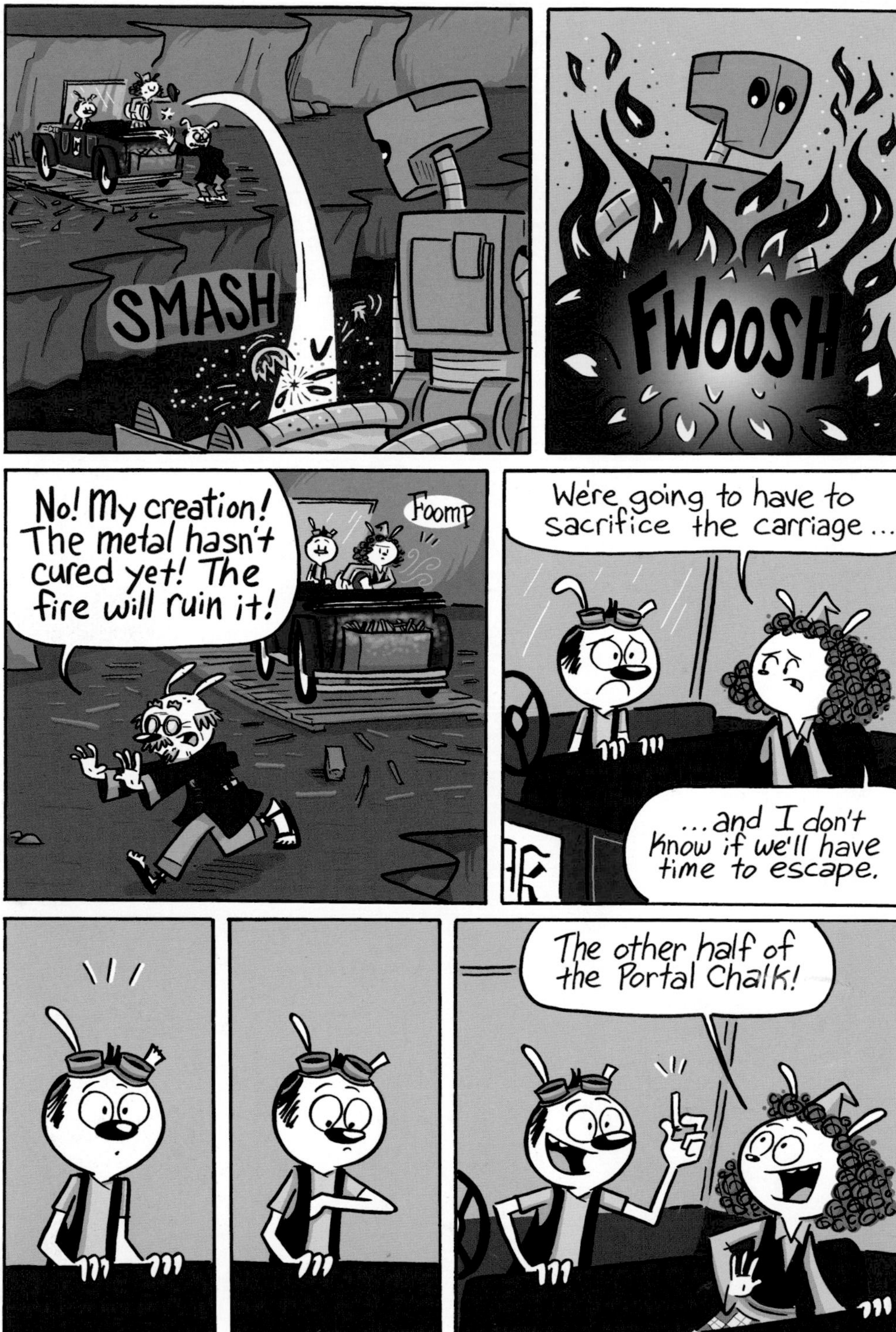
SMASH
FWOOSH
No! My creation! The metal hasn't cured yet! The fire will ruin it!
Foomp
We're going to have to sacrifice the carriage...
...and I don't know if we'll have time to escape.
The other half of the Portal Chalk!

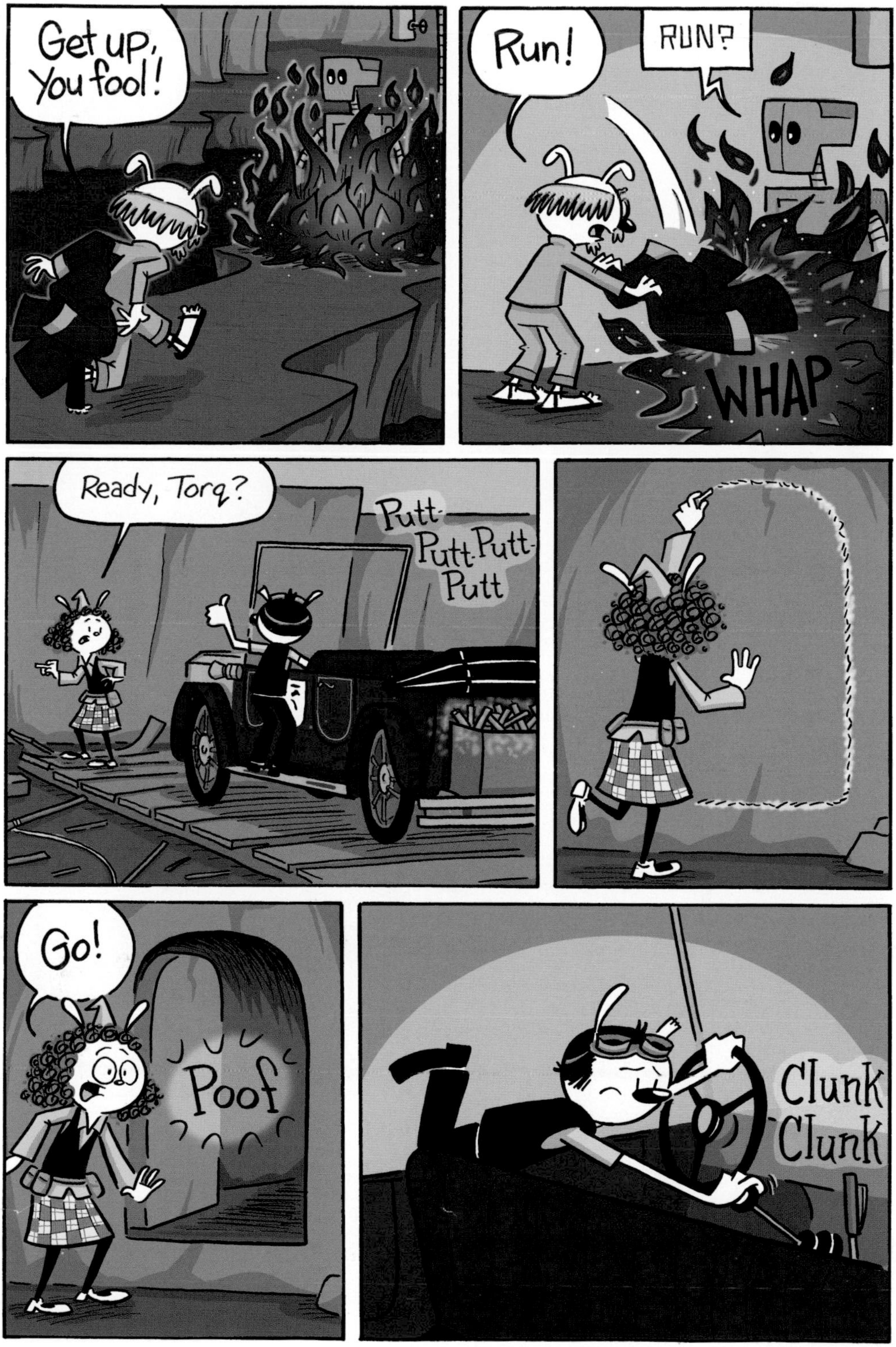
Get up, You fool!
Run!
RUN?
WHAP
Ready, Torq?
Putt-Putt-Putt-Putt
Go!
Poof
Clunk
Clunk

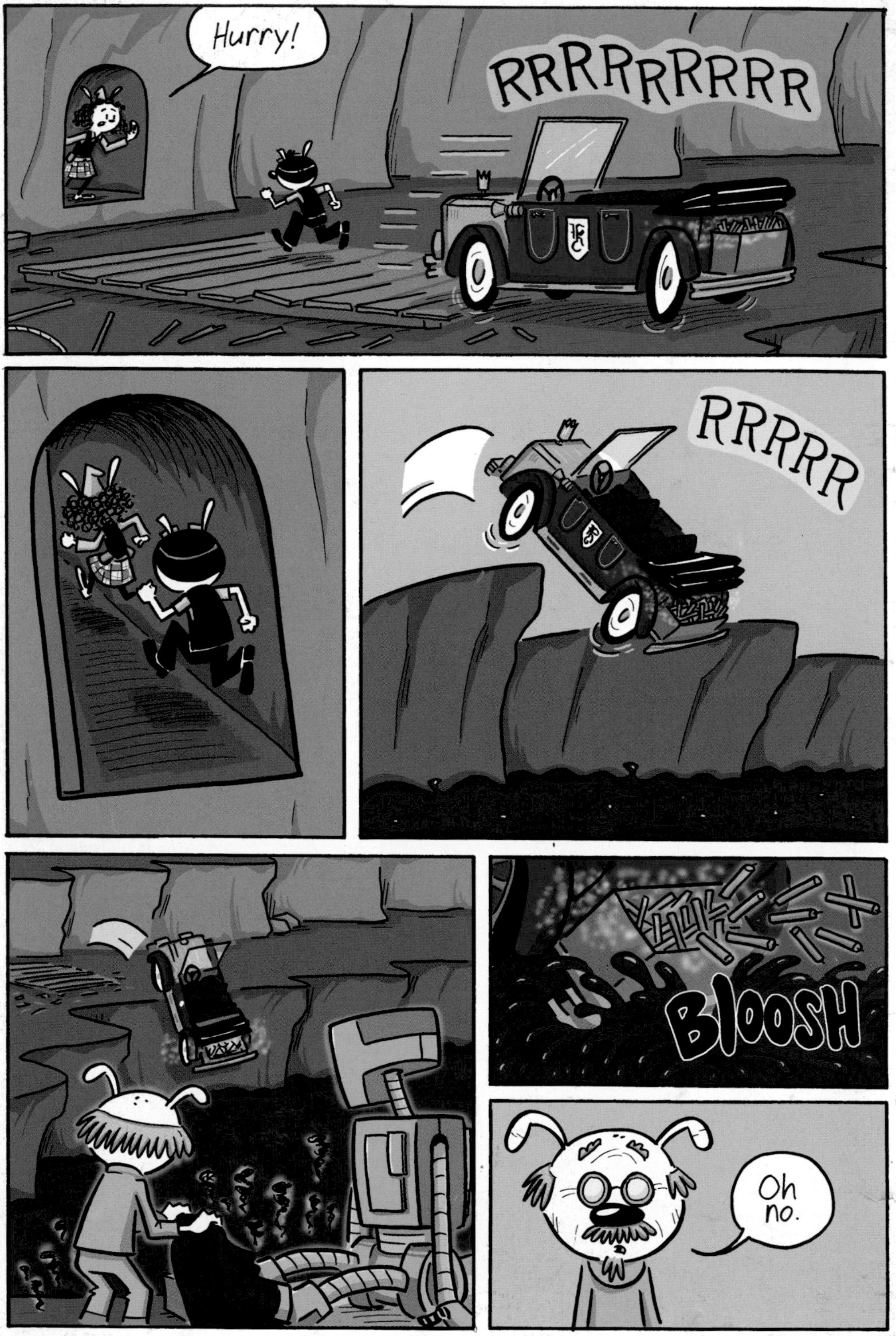
Hurry!
RRRRRRRRRR
RRRRR
BLOOSH
Oh no.

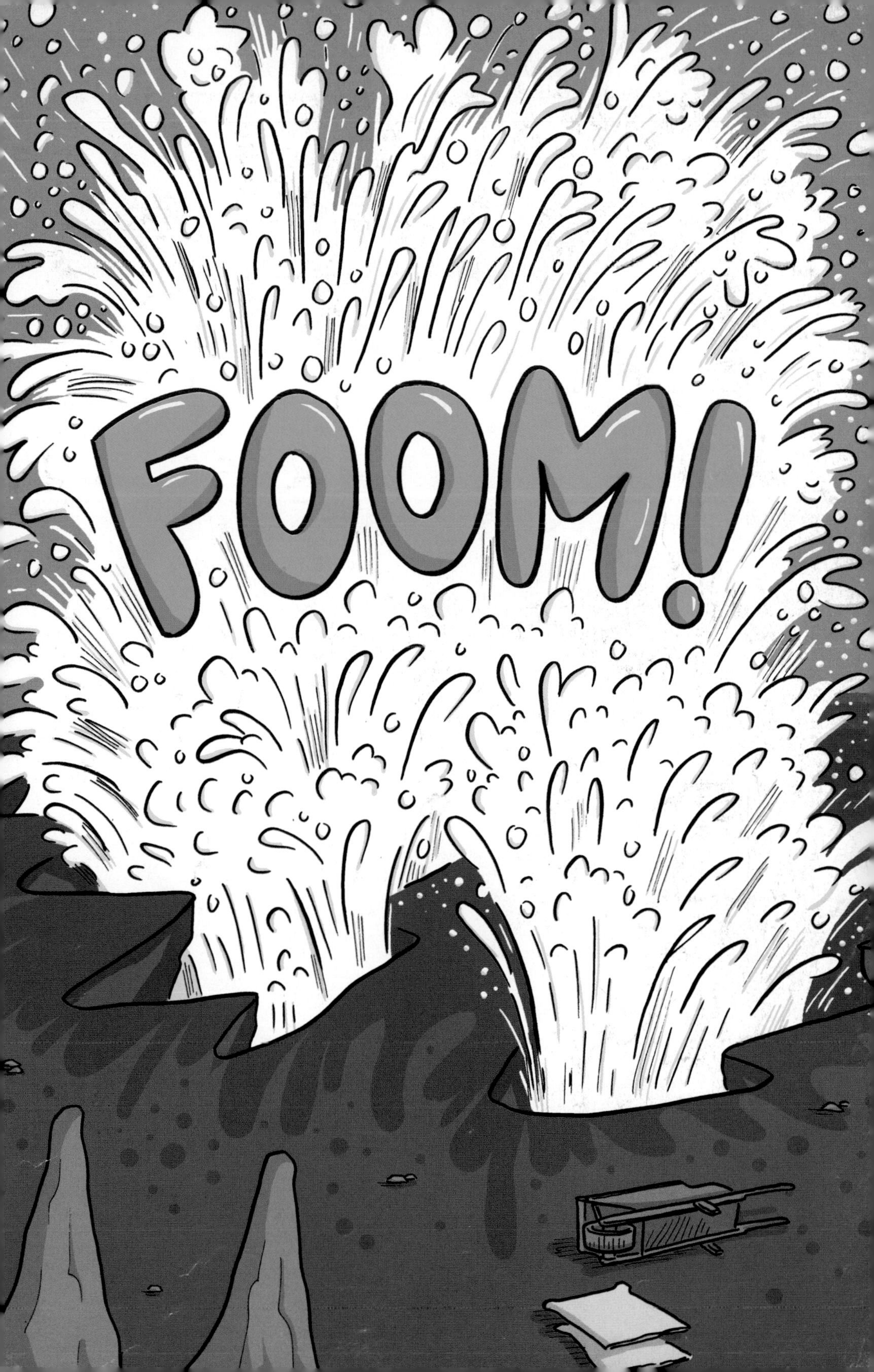
FOOM!

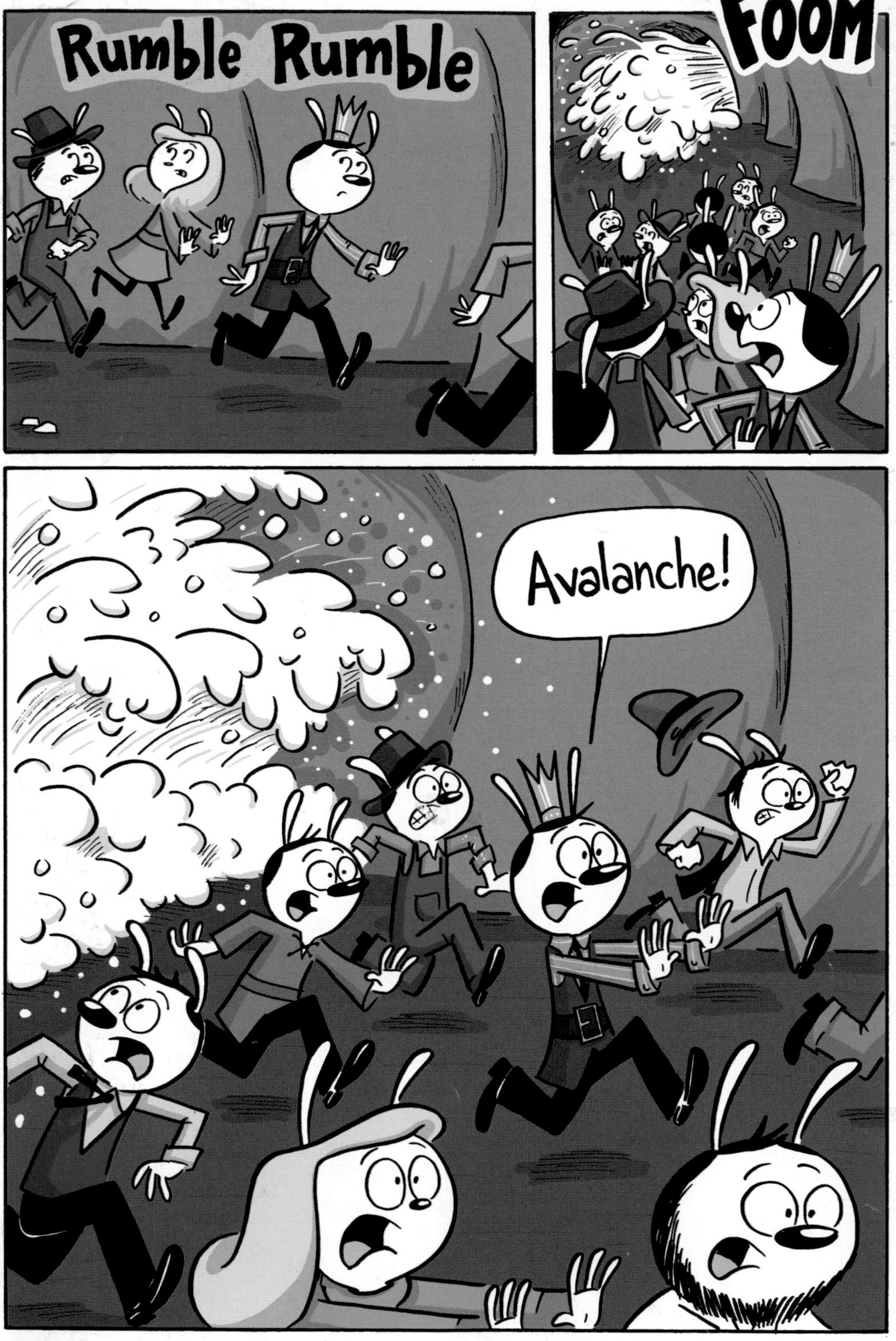
Rumble Rumble
FOOM
Avalanche!

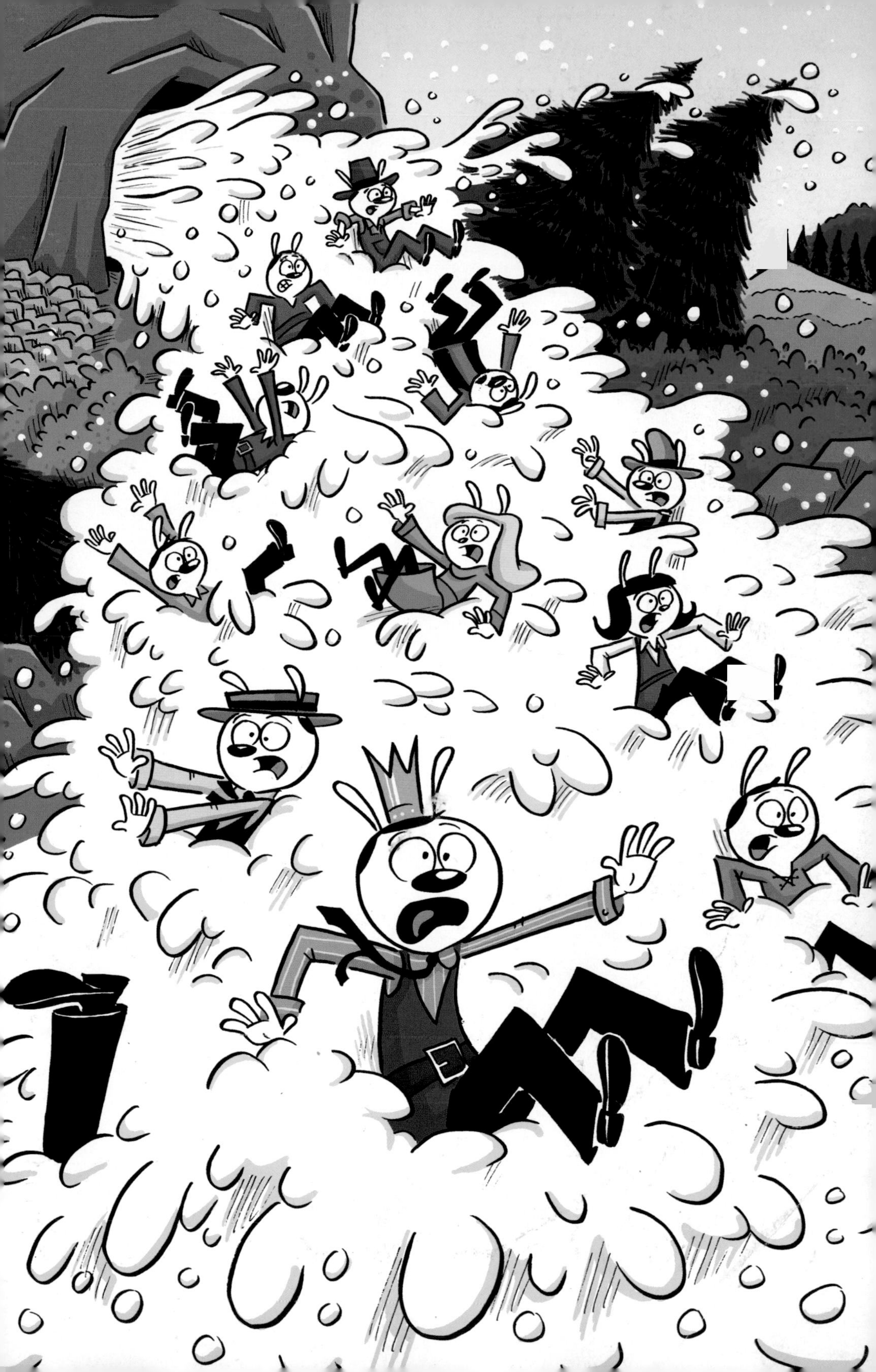

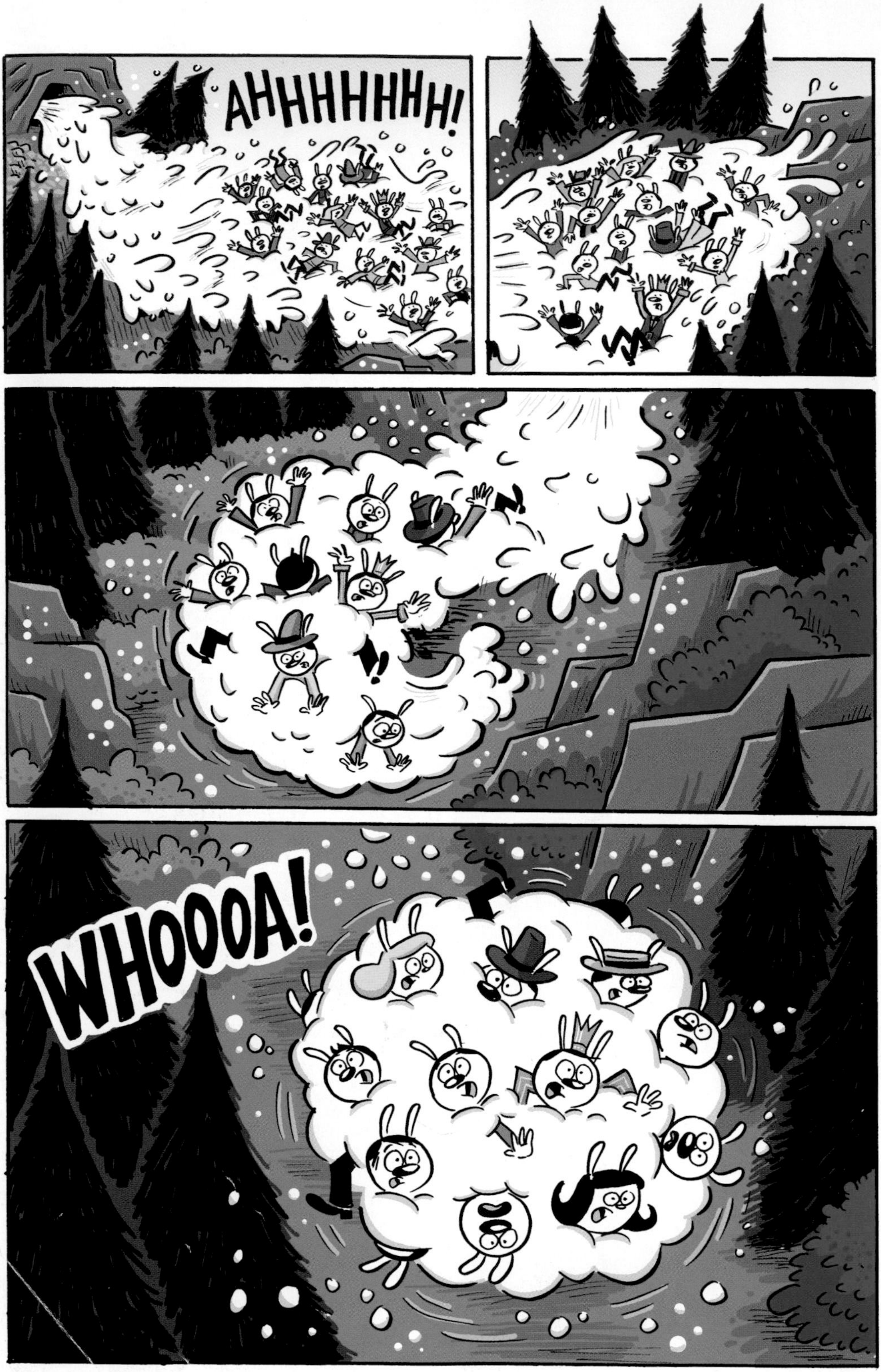
AHHHHHHH!
WHOOOA!

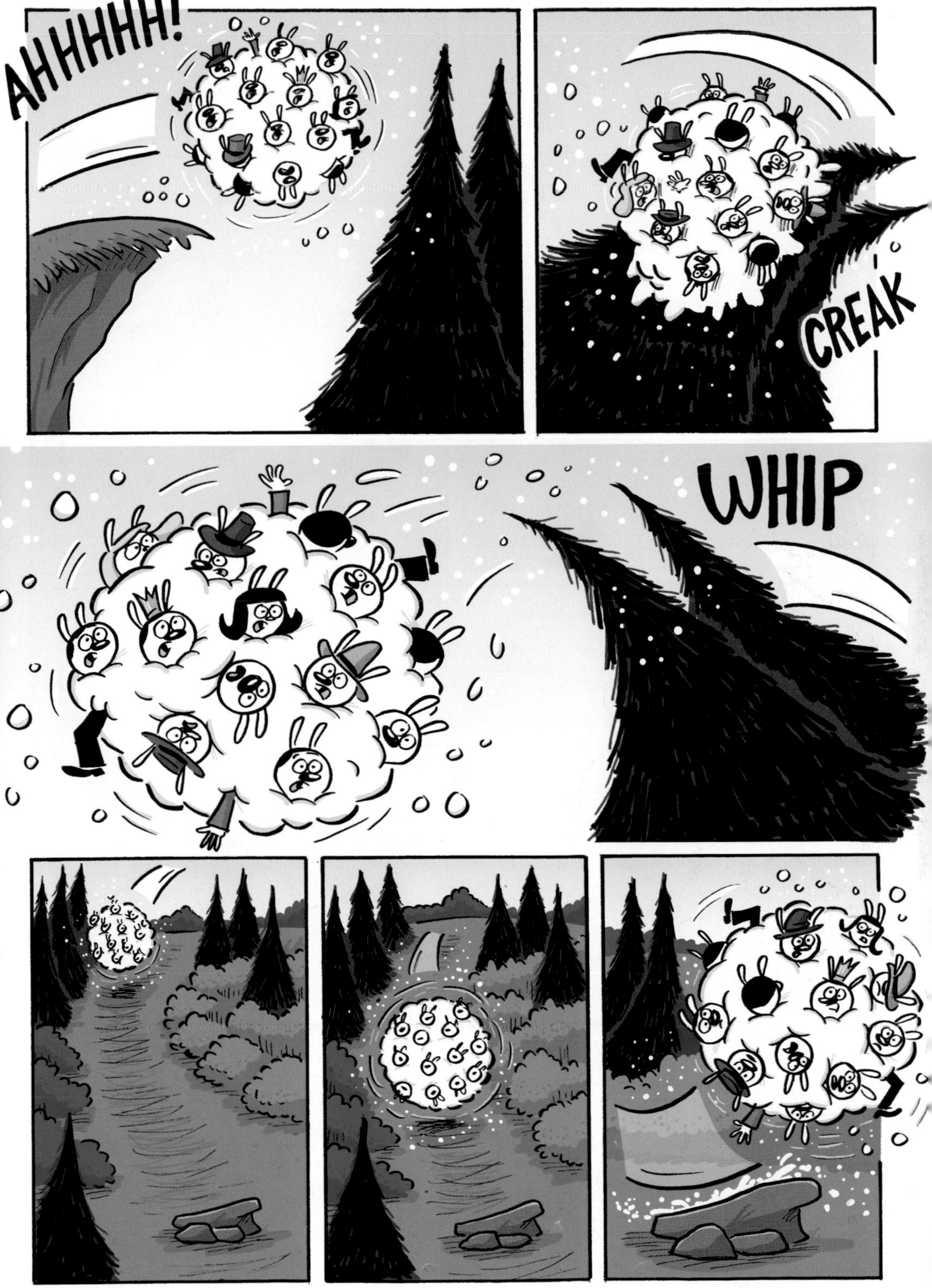
AHHHHH!
CREAK
WHIP

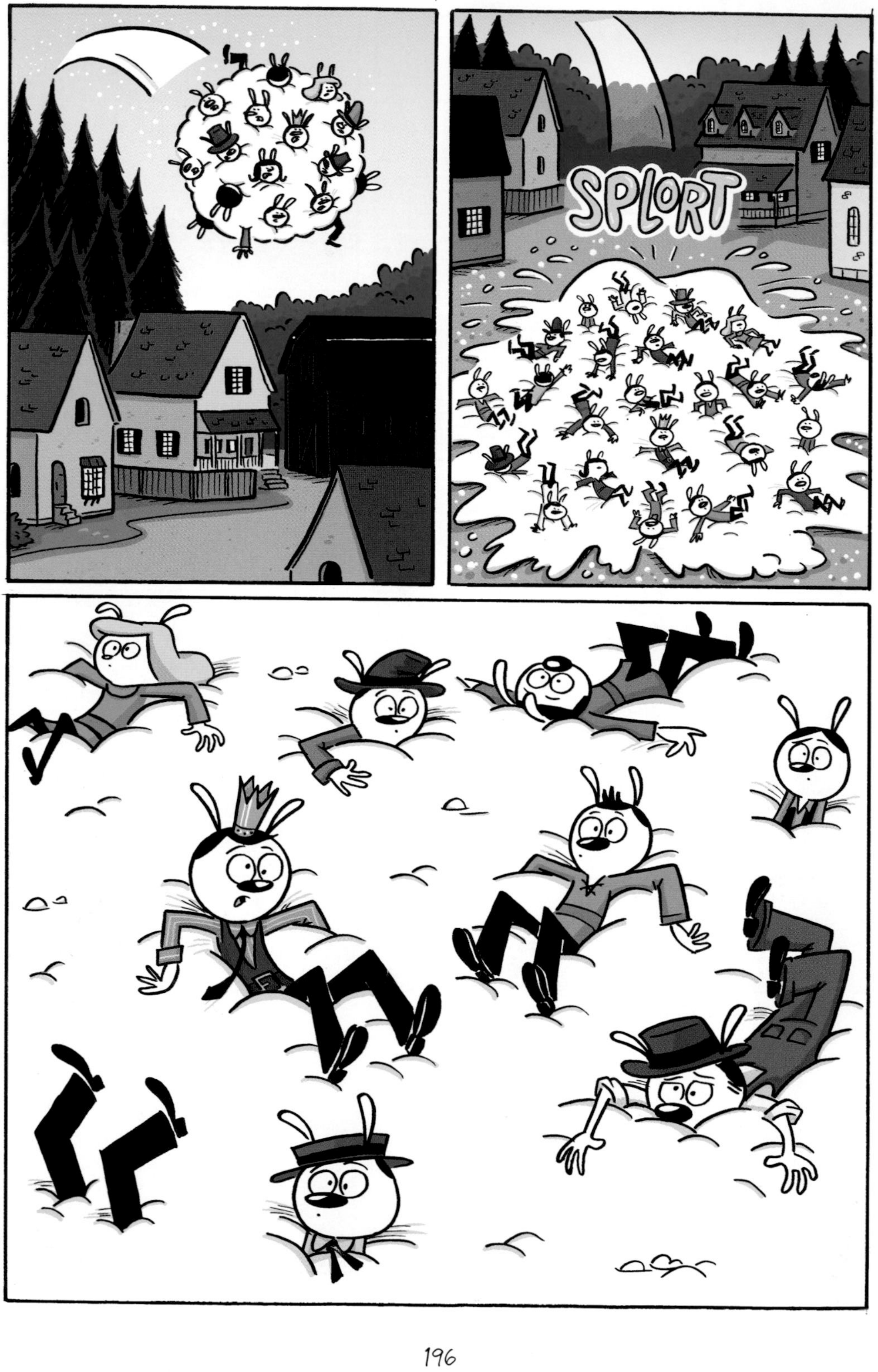
SPLORT

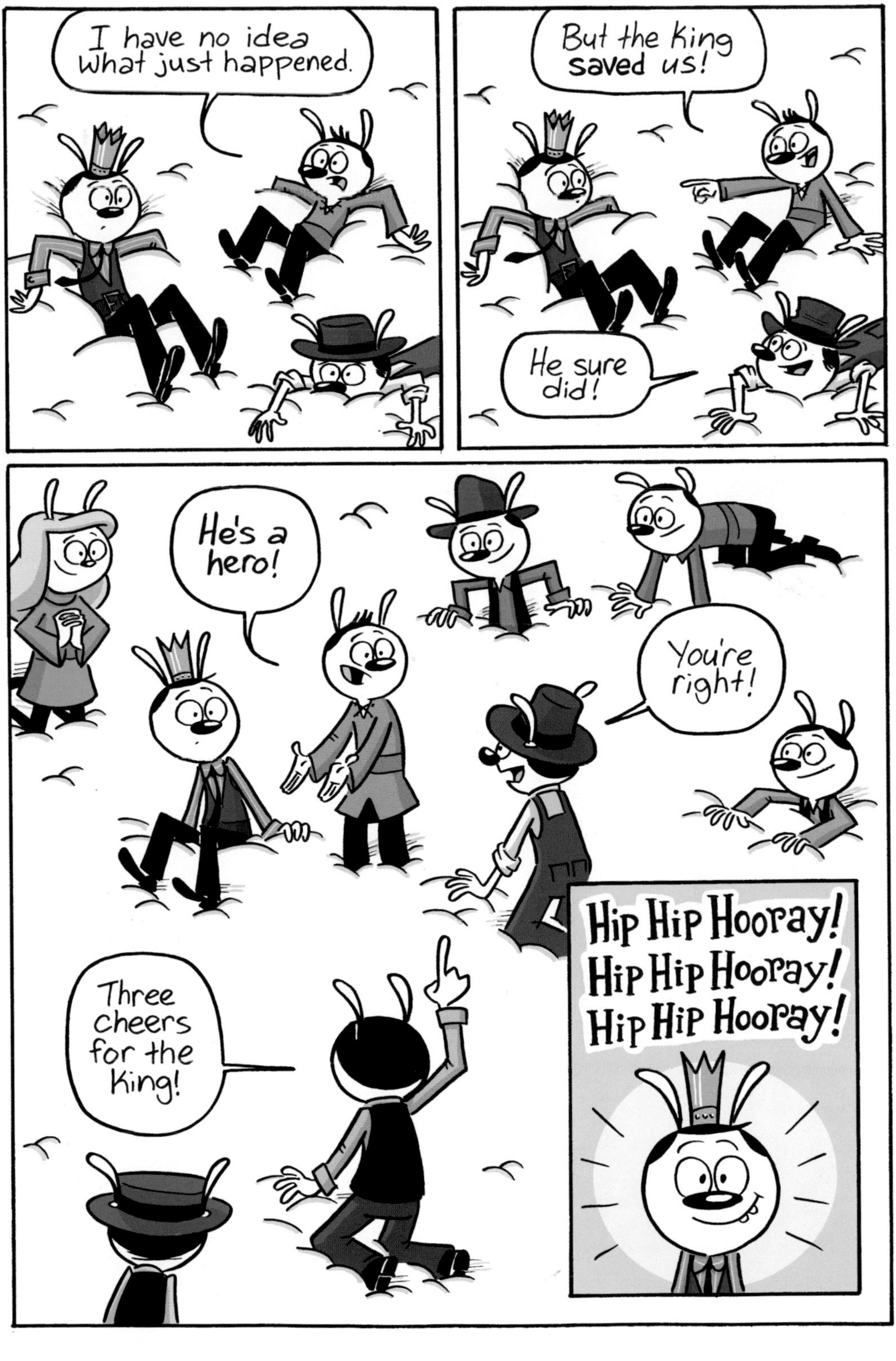
I have no idea what just happened.
But the King saved us!
He sure did!
He's a hero!
You're right!
Three cheers for the King!
Hip Hip Hooray! Hip Hip Hooray! Hip Hip Hooray!

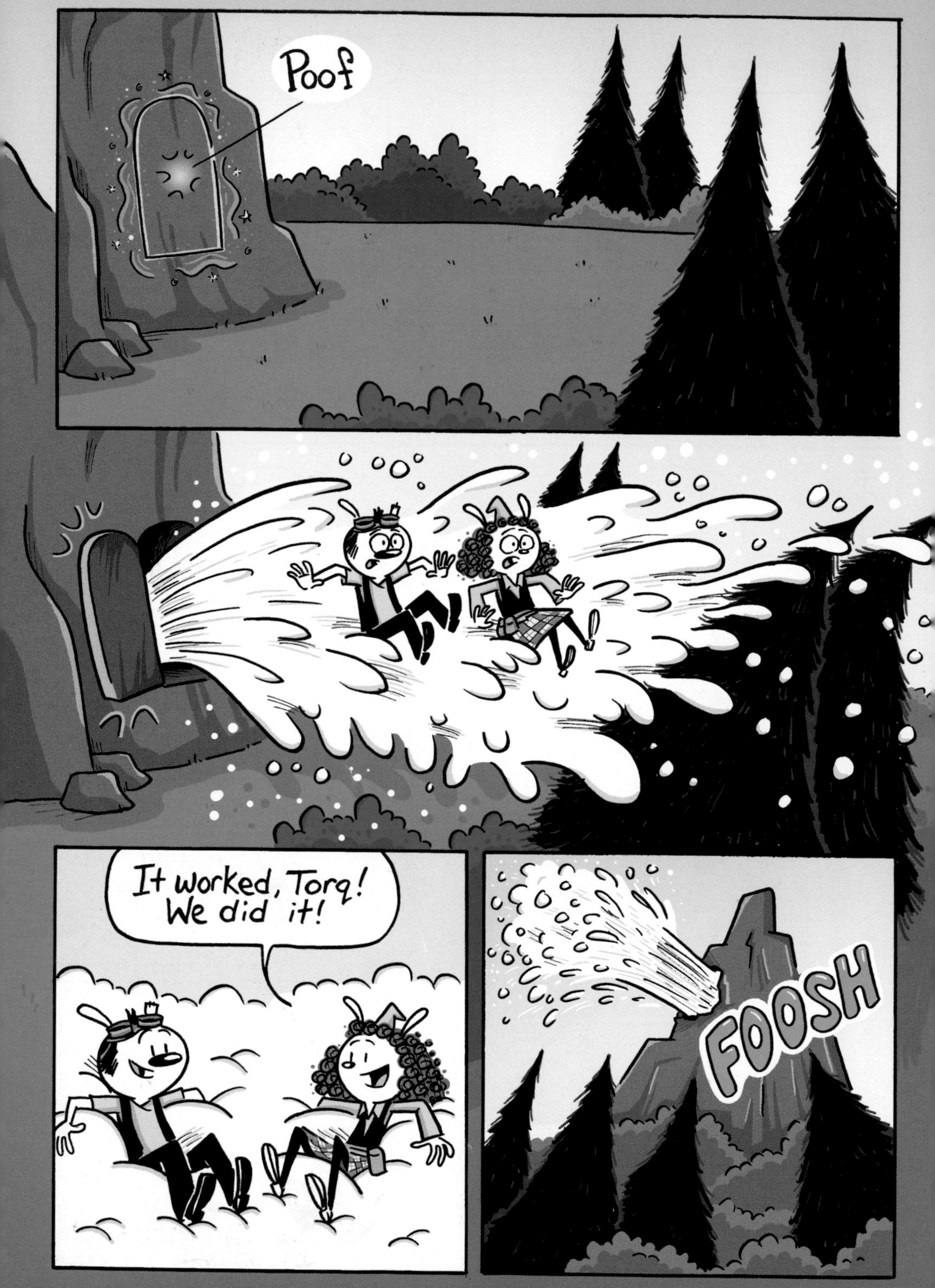
Poof
It worked, Torq! We did it!
FOOSH

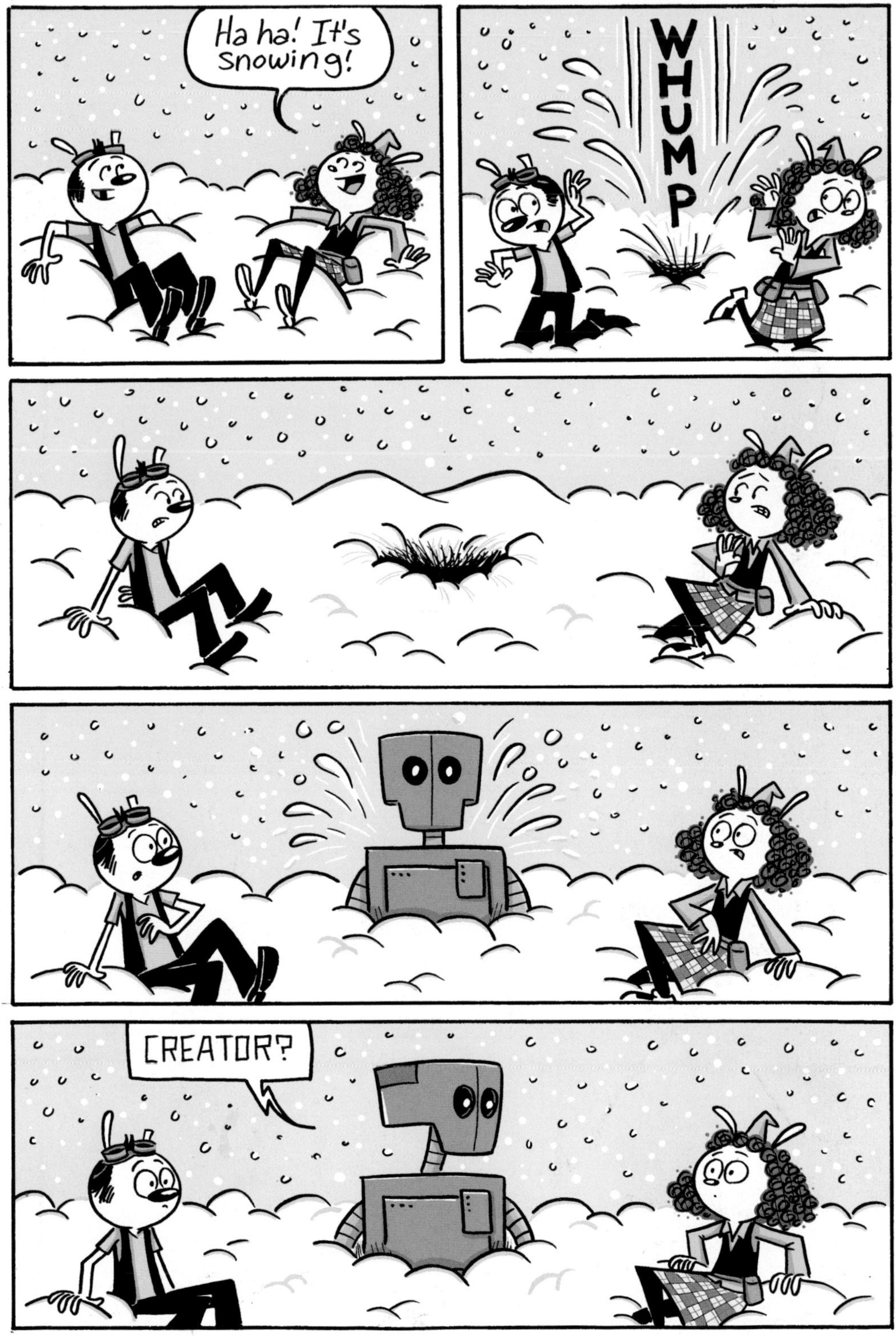
Ha ha! It's snowing!
WHUMP
CREATOR?

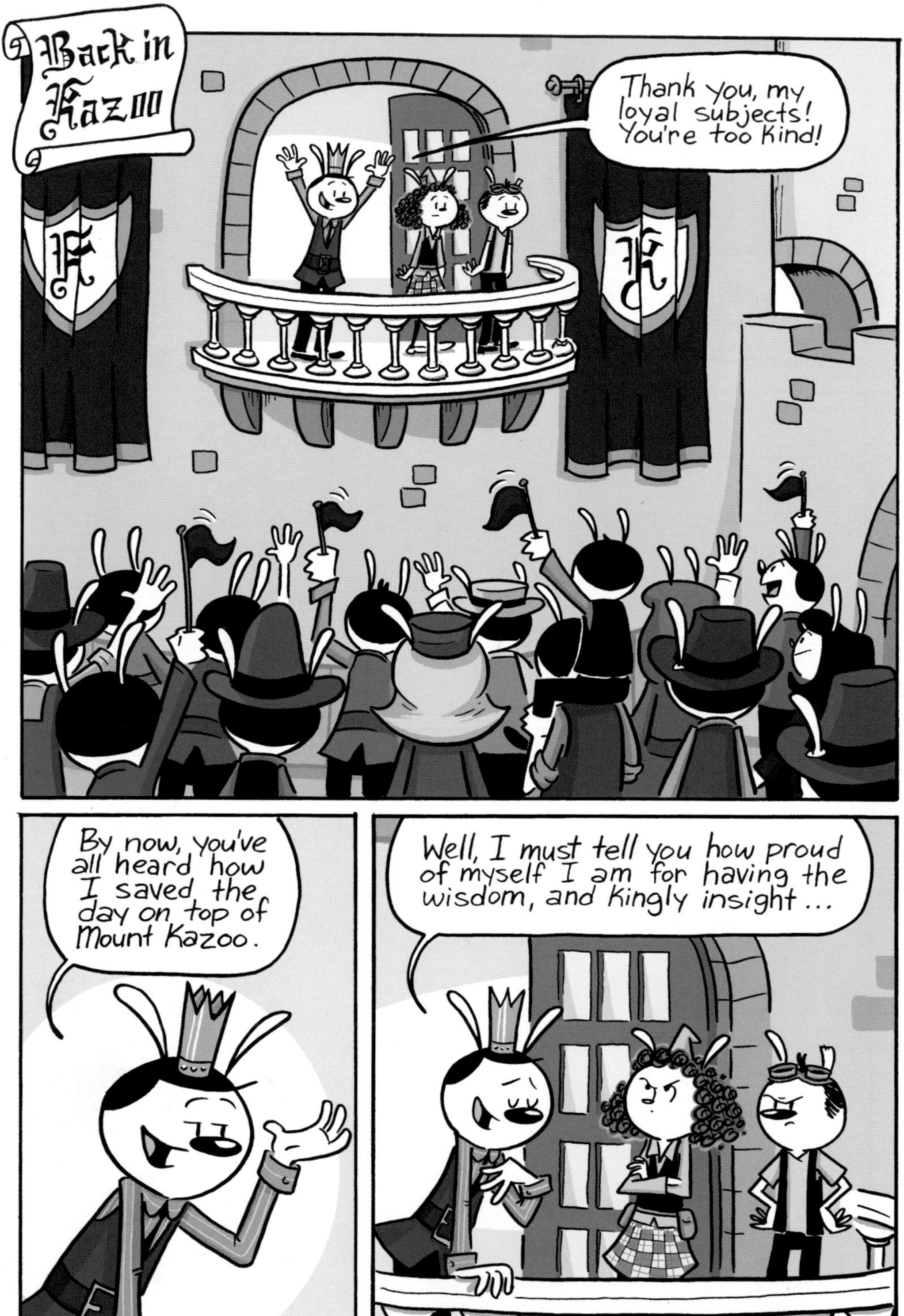
Back in Kazoo
Thank you, my loyal subjects! You're too Kind!
By now, you've all heard how I saved the day on top of Mount Kazoo.
Well, I must tell you how proud of myself I am for having the wisdom, and Kingly insight ...

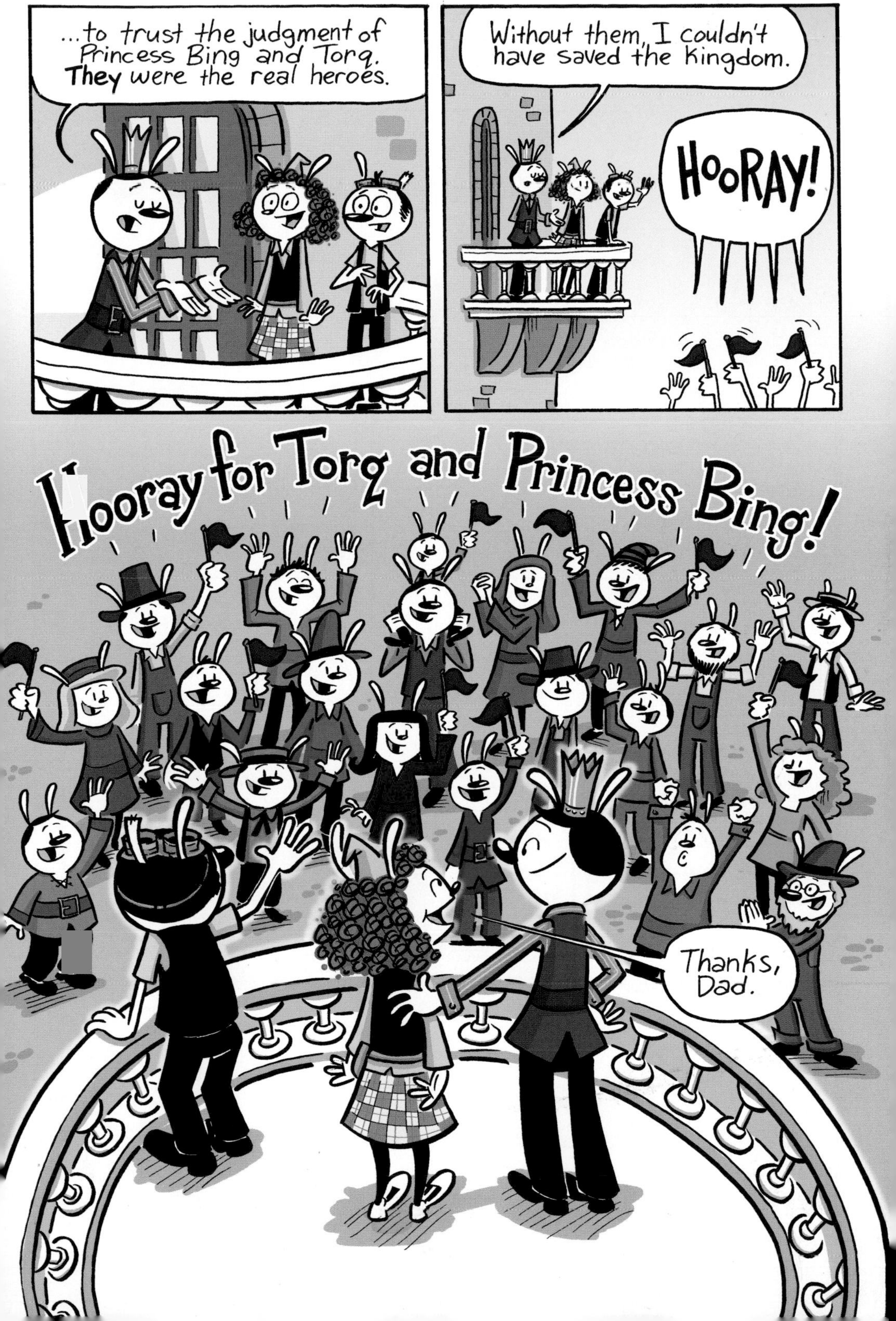
...to trust the judgment of Princess Bing and Torq. They were the real heroes.
Without them, I couldn't have saved the kingdom.
HOORAY!
Hooray for Torq and Princess Bing!
Thanks, Dad.

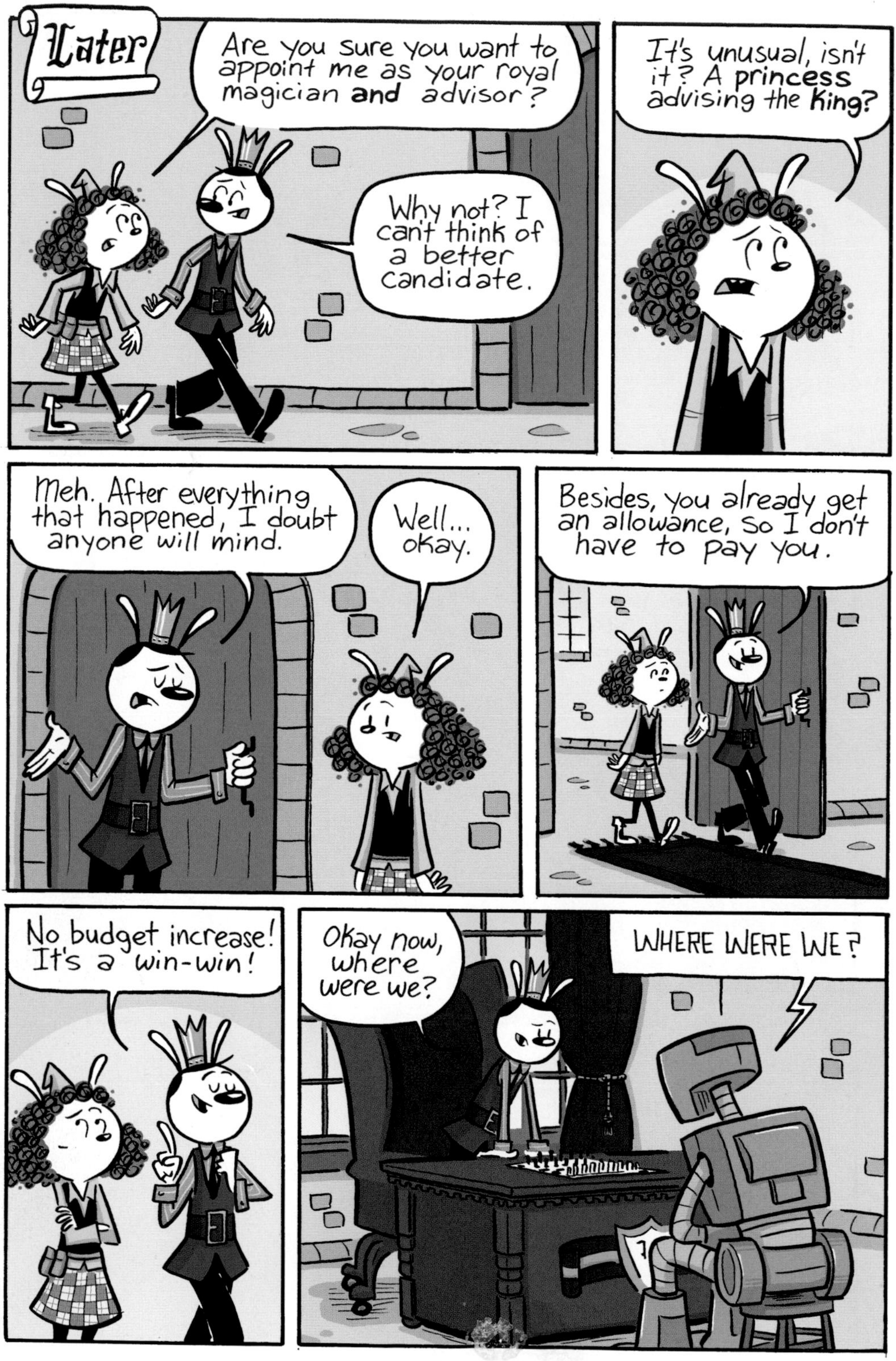
Later
Are you sure you want to appoint me as your royal magician **and** advisor?
Why not? I can't think of a better candidate.
It's unusual, isn't it? A **princess** advising the **King?**
Meh. After everything that happened, I doubt anyone will mind.
Well... okay.
Besides, you already get an allowance, so I don't have to pay you.
No budget increase! It's a win-win!
Okay now, where were we?
WHERE WERE WE?

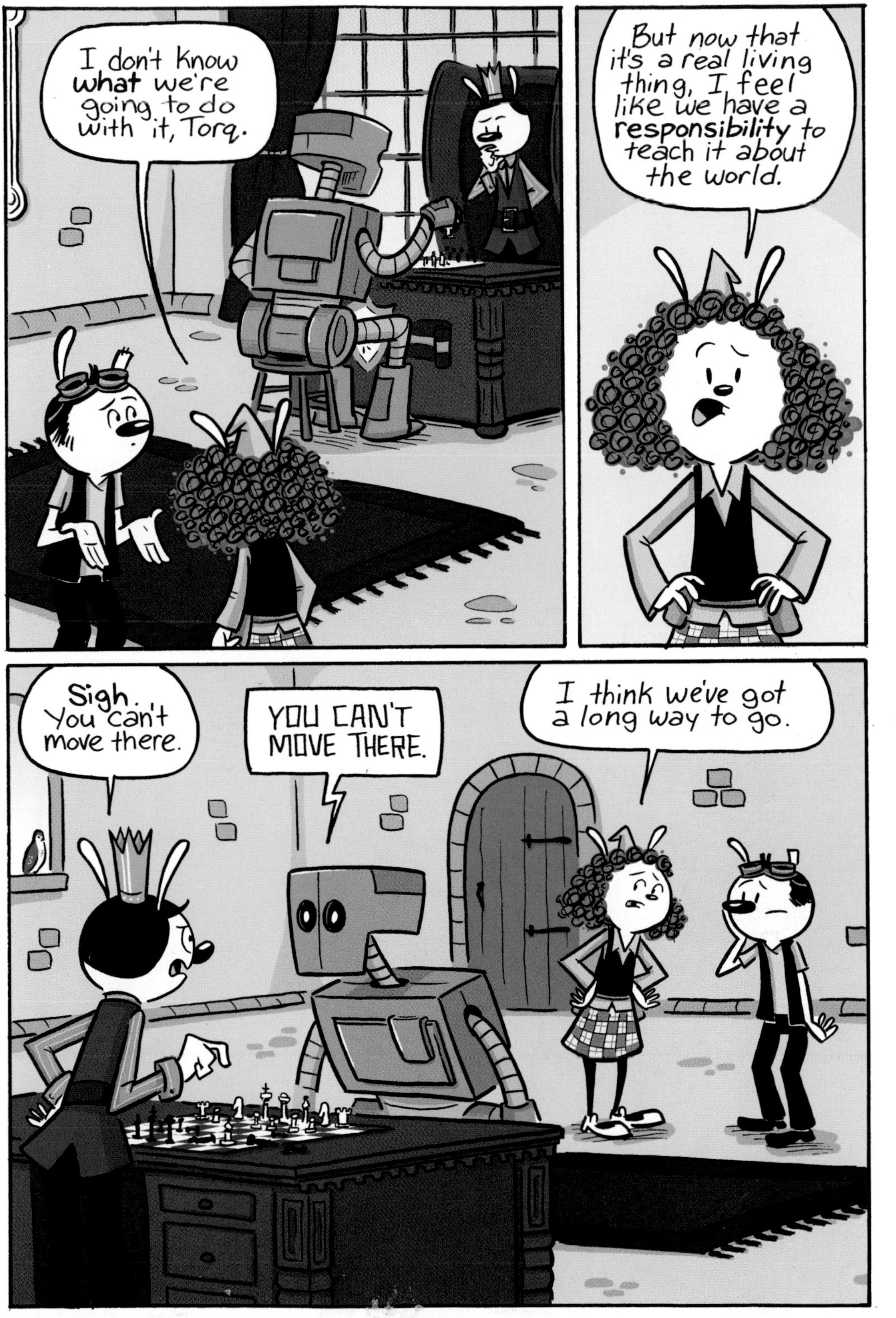
I don't know **what** we're going to do with it, Torq.
But now that it's a real living thing, I feel like we have a **responsibility** to teach it about the world.
Sigh. You can't move there.
YOU CAN'T MOVE THERE.
I think we've got a long way to go.

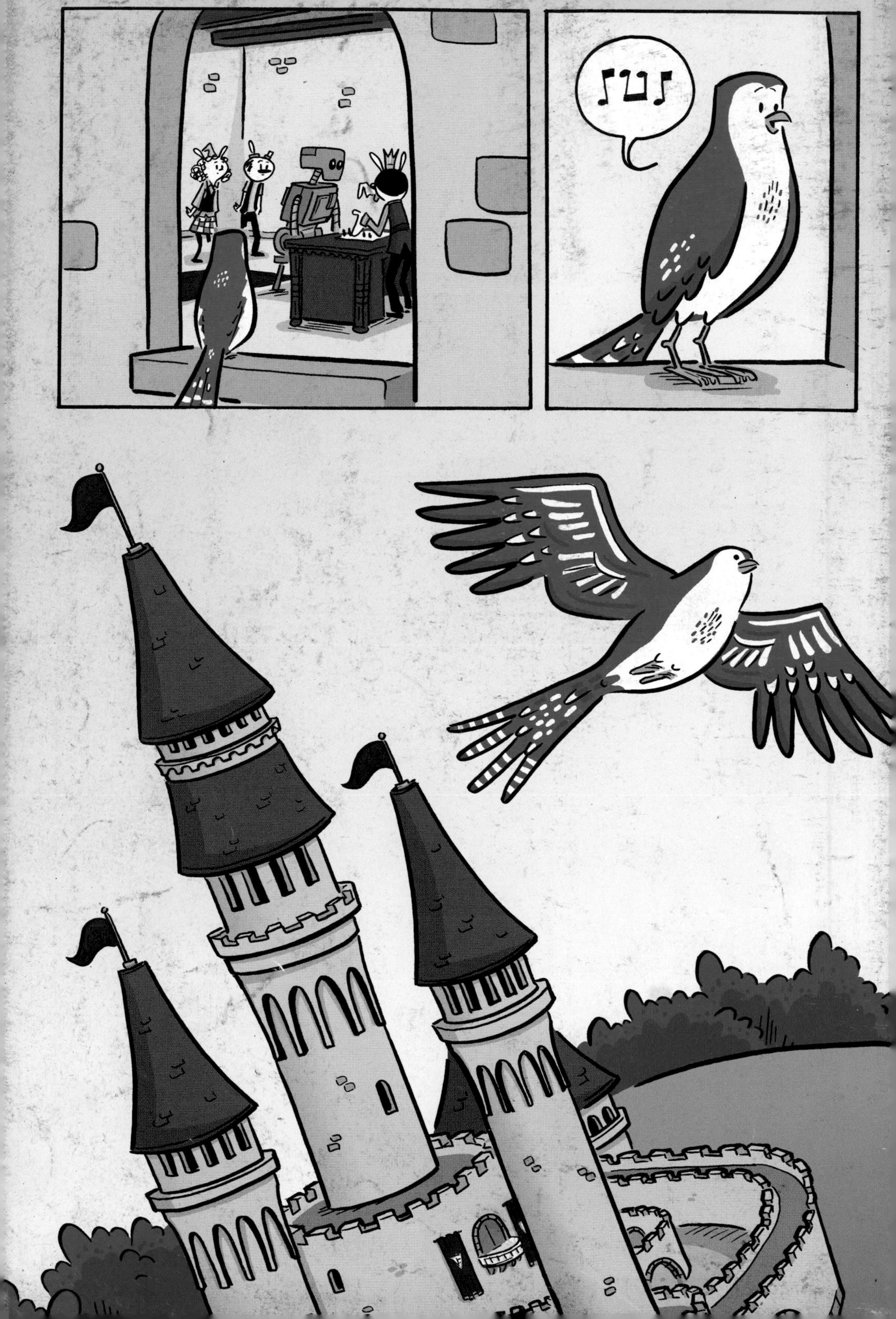

NORM FEUTI was born in Pascoag, Rhode Island. He started reading comics and watching cartoons when he was four, and he hasn't stopped since. His comic strips *Retail* and *Gil* appear in newspapers (the gray things that have tiny comics in the back) throughout the US and Canada. He currently lives in Massachusetts with his wife and two kids.